STAGE BY STAGE

Teaching full time and acquiring all the oddball kids in the new intake are only the first of Beth's challenges when Alan leaves her after twenty-five years of marriage. She also has to turn her untidy Cambridge house into a B & B to make ends meet and then counteract the effect of regular theatrical guests on her impressionable teenage children. Alan doesn't help by making disapproving incursions with his saccharine laden new partner. Beth's real worry though is Owen Pendragon, a touring character actor with wicked hazel eyes, a quirky sense of humour and a tendency to walk around her home in his bathrobe...

STAGE BY STAGE

STAGE BY STAGE

by

Jan Jones

Magna Large Print Books
Long Preston, North Yorkshire,
BD23 4ND, England.

British Library Cataloguing in Publication Data.

Jones, Jan
    Stage by stage.

    A catalogue record of this book is
    available from the British Library

    ISBN   978-0-7505-2735-4

First published in Great Britain 2005 by Transita

Copyright © 2005 Jan Jones

Cover illustration © Melvyn Warren-Smith by arrangement with P.W.A. International

The right of Jan Jones to be identified as the author of this work has been asserted by her in accordance with the Copyright, Designs and Patents Act, 1988

Published in Large Print 2007 by arrangement with
Transita Ltd.

Magna Large Print is an imprint of Library Magna Books Ltd.

Printed and bound in Great Britain by
T.J. (International) Ltd., Cornwall, PL28 8RW

ACKNOWLEDGEMENTS

I would like to thank

Giles, Nikki and Marina at Transita.

all my lovely friends in the RNA for their support and encouragement.

Alison and Kate who read Chapter One first.

my daughter Elisabeth for having the sort of interests (even though I may on occasion grumble about the chauffeuring) which gave rise to the idea for *Stage By Stage*.

my son Dominic for fixing my computer, building my website and for creating Form 7.1, though neither of us dreamed at the time that they would inveigle their way into print.

my husband Brian for never once suggesting that I get a proper job.

CHAPTER 1

'That's it. Enough's enough. I'm leaving.'

Beth's mouth fell open in surprise. The row hadn't *nearly* got to that stage yet. It had only just reached 'The reason I'm marking essays *now* is so I don't have to do them after we get back from the theatre tonight.'

They hadn't even touched on 'Why do you have to drive the kids everywhere? Why can't they go on their bikes?' (Because we're seven miles out of town and who was it wanted to buy a house in Fenbourne anyway?)

And it was unheard of for Alan to skip 'You shouldn't encourage them with this singing and dancing nonsense. It's not going to equip them for life, you know,' or 'Why doesn't anyone put anything away in this house? How am I supposed to bring clients back for a drink when every room looks like a jumble sale in a bomb shelter?' (To which the answer was that Alan had never shown the slightest desire to bring clients back for a drink. He took them to his club or a hotel depending on how much money he thought he was going to make out of them. And the house wasn't untidy *all* the time.)

Alan marched upstairs to fling his golf

things together, his standard response when her 'unhelpful attitude' clashed with his dictums. Angry footsteps dented the floorboards. Beth put her fingers in her ears and tried to concentrate on marking. Such a stupid row – just because Natalie's and Robin's friends were coming back for lunch after the *Stagestruck* class. Why Alan should object to having them in the house now and again (they didn't *live* here by any means) when he'd once stood Robin's entire football team an end-of-season party, she failed to see. Mind, that was before Rob had given up soccer because the practices clashed with dance classes.

The footsteps clumped down the stairs. Alan swore as he struggled with the front door. Beth heard his car unlock with a servile bleep, heard him curse with an uncharacteristic lack of regard for the neighbours. Then he came back, opened the hall cupboard for his golf clubs and went out again. And then he came in again. And went out again. And came in once more.

Unease stippled across Beth's mind. She went into the hall. 'Alan!' she cried, aghast.

He dumped a bag of shoes into the boot of his car.

'Alan, do you want to talk about this?' Beth heard the slight edge of panic in her voice and tried to suppress it.

'No,' said her husband, scooping a rackful

of coats off their hooks. He folded them onto the passenger seat. Through the rear windscreen Beth could see a mountainous bundle wrapped in what looked like the top sheet off their bed. Panic set in with a vengeance, the full ten thousand watt, adrenalin-pumping sort. 'I'll put the kettle on,' she said. 'Let's sit down and–'

'No,' he said again, his face as indifferent as the time he'd told her how he'd severed the Amalgamated Haulage contract because they weren't giving him good enough rates. 'You'll only trot out the same old platitudes. Frankly, Beth, I'm sick of them. To coin a phrase, you should have been paying more attention to the market. Customers vote with their feet. Goodbye.' The echoes of the front door slamming were lost in the roar of his car starting up.

It wasn't possible! Beth skidded into the lounge to glimpse his tailgate already disappearing up the street. Her legs folded under her. She sat down hard on the window seat, her body pulsing with unexpectedness. She looked numbly at the table. Spike Taylor's essay lay open with her red pen on top of it. It was too incredible to take in. Alan couldn't have just left her! He couldn't! Something so life-changing couldn't possibly happen this quickly! Mechanically, she picked up her cup. Even the tea was still warm.

'Sorry,' Beth called through the Galaxy's window as she swerved to a halt in the empty car park.

'S'all right. We've been earwigging under the window. We're going to be in *Wind In The Willows.*' Natalie paused as she opened the car door. 'God, Mum, you look awful.'

Thank you, daughter. Really.

'We're all going to be in it,' said Robin. 'Lisa and Jack too.'

'Mr Edmonds had me sing twice,' boasted Natalie, 'and he said Lisa's dancing was cool.'

'Like you were the only ones he was watching,' said Robin. He and Jack scrambled in and banged the door shut. 'What's for lunch?'

Lunch? Beth's stomach recoiled at the mere thought. 'Pizza and salad. You can put your own toppings on.'

'Decent. Can I have peanut butter and cream cheese?'

'Gross!' squealed the girls.

Beth's mind scrabbled around like an out-of-control spinning top as she pulled away, automatically filtering out the teenage squabbling. Alan. How was she ever going to tell them about Alan?

The air was heavy with thunder. Fat drops of rain squeezed from the sky and fell on the windscreen. She left the kids to turn the freezer upside-down and mounted the stairs with leaden legs. The bedroom looked horrible. Alan's wardrobe hung gapingly open, his drawers pulled out and empty. In the ensuite bathroom, the empty spaces where his razor, toothbrush, flannel and toiletries should have been shrieked at her. Where had he gone? To his club? To the hotel he recommended to business visitors? The mind-boggling thought occurred that maybe he had a lover; Beth pushed it away as an absurdity.

'Oh my stars,' said Sue when she arrived later to pick up Lisa and Jack. She stared at the denuded room. 'What are you going to do?'

'Pass. Wait for him to come back. Wait for him to ring.' It was such an ordinary row – how had it ever blown up into this?

'What about *Oklahoma!*?'

Give me strength, thought Beth. My husband has just left me after twenty-five years of marriage and my best friend asks whether I plan to go to the theatre tonight! Shock touched her again, sending her mind skittering to safe, everyday subjects. 'How did the casting go?'

'Six singing rabbits, eight dancing weasels and stoats, two acting squirrels and a couple of mice. Our four included and we're up for the panto too.'

With an effort, Beth crammed Alan and her cartwheeling thoughts into a space at the back of her mind. 'Terrific.'

'Keep it under your hat. The girls are bumptious enough already. Think they know the lot.'

A trace of Beth's usual humour broke through. 'Naturally. They're fifteen.'

Sue grinned and squeezed her hand. 'Cheer up. Ten to one it's a storm in a tea-cup. He'll be back tomorrow.'

If only. Beth shut the bedroom door, wishing it was as easy to close her clamouring head to Alan's absence.

'Dad's left? Are you serious, Mum?'

'No, I'm just saying it to enliven the afternoon! Of course I'm serious, Nats!'

'But why? What happened?'

'Nothing! Nothing any more than normal. We were having a row and right in the middle he announced he was leaving. I'm not sure we ought to go out tonight.'

Natalie looked incredulous. 'Just because Dad's got the hump? That's not fair!'

'He might meet us there.' Robin offered a sop to his sister's rising temper.

'Yeah, that's right! He wouldn't want to miss it!'

Beth stared. The mind of the average teenager was stunning in its self-absorption. Had they seriously never noticed that Alan only came to musicals on sufferance? That without the threat of 'Everyone else's dad will be there', he'd even have passed up their school shows in favour of making friends and influencing people somewhere more convivial? 'I just don't think it's a very good idea. Suppose he rings?'

'Put the answerphone on!' Natalie's cheeks were scarlet. 'We always go to *FOOTLIGHTS* shows. And we've been looking forward to *Oklahoma!* for weeks!'

'He's probably forgotten,' said Robin. 'What with the row and everything. I'll e-mail him a reminder. He's got his laptop and mobile with him, hasn't he?'

'Yeah, that'll be enough. Why should we suffer just because he's attention-seeking?'

Attention-seeking? Beth had often wondered what her children learned in PSE. Not being a form tutor, she didn't have to know these things. She supposed she must still be in shock That was why she couldn't make the kids see that going out to the theatre the same day the head of the household walked out of the family home wasn't what most people would consider normal behaviour. 'OK, send him a message, Rob.' Even if the world was exploding Armageddon-style around him, Alan would still collect his e-mails.

'You need a nice mug of tea,' said Natalie, solicitous now she'd got her way. 'And I'll choose you something to wear. Are we eating here or when we get there?'

Beth was possibly the only member of the Cambridge Corn Exchange audience not to appreciate the glorious voice of the leading actor that night. The familiar songs might have been being beamed from Mars for all the impact they had on her. Her thoughts were wholly centred on the empty seat at the end of their row. She clutched the programme and stared unseeing at the unfolding drama on stage. Panic threatened to drown her.

'Wasn't he cool, Mum?' enthused Natalie as they hurried under rumbling skies to the car park

Beth returned from the nightmare circle of her thoughts. 'Ellery Valentine? Too sure of himself for my taste. I've said so before.'

'Not *him.*' Natalie was disgusted by her mother's obtuseness. 'The one who played Jud Fry! He can really *act.*' She shivered deliciously.

Understanding briefly broke the surface of Beth's worry. 'Oh, the good-looking one.' Robin grinned at her.

Natalie ignored them. 'His name is Sebastian Merchant. I wonder what he'll be in *Wind In The Willows?*'

Beth's thoughts jolted into a different direction. Firmly tied to a girlfriend, please

God! She knew all about actors' reputations. Almost, she could appreciate Alan's distaste. Except – the kids loved performing. And they were good at it. And Alan didn't object because he was worried for *them*, it was more that Natalie's singing and Rob's dancing weren't the sort of abilities he could make capital out of on the golf course or over a business lunch. God, this whole thing was so *silly!* The kids were who they were. She was who she was. You didn't have to share the same interests to care about someone. There had to be some way they could sort things out.

The house was in darkness when they got back, the answerphone silent. Beth left another message on Alan's mobile, wrapped herself in the duvet and lay sleepless on her side of the bed while outside the sky crashed and the rain ran steadily down the window pane.

'All sorted? How's Alan?' asked Sue breezily in the staffroom on Monday.

Beth shoved exercise books into her pigeon-hole. Her anxiety had now ballooned into full-frontal, gut-clutching fear. This couldn't be happening. Not to her. 'No idea,' she said. 'He hasn't been home. Every time I ring his mobile, I get asked to leave a message. I'm not teaching this afternoon so I'm going over to the office to have it out. Can you give Rob and Nats a lift back?'

With an expression of confidence she was far from feeling, Beth pushed open the swing doors to *Alan Trower Associates.* 'Hi, Judy. Is Alan–?'

'Go straight in, Mrs Trower. He told me you'd be arriving.'

Oh, had he? Despite her mounting fury, Beth paused on the threshold of the inner office to look at him. Well-cut dark hair, nice body... 'I hear you're expecting me.'

Her husband looked up. 'Have a seat.'

She felt her body stiffen at the casual tone. 'I'd rather have a fight.'

His brief smile came nowhere near his eyes. 'Been there. Done that. Too late, Beth. I've left you.'

Oh God, it was true. She sat down in a rush and made herself answer. 'Do I get to hear why?'

Alan leant back in his leather chair. 'Don't you think it ironic that you have to come here to talk to me?'

'I *tried* to talk yesterday. I left enough messages.'

'In between marking books and preparing lessons.'

She gritted her teeth. This was an old tactic. Don't let him do it. Don't let him put you on the defensive. 'It's my job, Alan. I'm an English teacher.'

20

'And a good one. And you enjoy it. Which is fine because you'll almost certainly need to extend your hours.'

Extend her hours? When he'd been on at her for years to cut back? Judy brought in a tray of tea and biscuits. As she left, Beth passed a hand across her forehead. 'What are you talking about?'

'I'm tired of playing second fiddle to the children, Beth. I'm tired of playing second fiddle to your job. So I'm moving out and taking my income with me.'

'Alan, they're *our* children! Yours and mine. You can't just turn them off. They *need* attention. They need transport.'

He smiled in that unnervingly calm way again. 'Which you're happy to provide.'

'It's because they don't do anything you like, isn't it? You didn't complain when Robin was into football. You were the first one on the touchline, running up and down, yelling advice.'

'I'm not arguing with you any more, Beth.'

Dammit, how dared he look so – so distant! And so smug! She returned to the attack. 'And how can I not teach? I'd go mad if I was at home all day.'

He poured out the tea. 'I know. I've faced that. Your commitment was one of the things I fell in love with. But twenty-five years on you're still a teacher, whereas I–'

Alan picked up a digestive and snapped it

21

neatly in half. In the silence, Beth heard the crumbs falling to the plate. 'Whereas you've gone from junior clerk to boss of your own company,' she said slowly. She sat stock-still, her brain functioning for the first time in two days. 'I begin to see.'

'I'm only forty-nine, Beth. Prime of life. I intend to spend the next twenty-five years with someone who is interested in *me*.'

She put a hand on his. He was feeling neglected. Maybe she *had* been concentrating a mite hard on teaching in the run-up to the exams, but she had students she wanted to get the best out of. She had a duty to them. 'It's half-term next week,' she said in a conciliatory tone. 'Why don't you take it as holiday? We can spend it at home, the four of us.'

'Oh, yes, the May half-term. The one where you're constantly nagging at the kids to revise.'

Beth snatched back her outstretched hand as if she'd been stung.

'I've spoken to the solicitor,' Alan continued, as calm as if all this had been decided months ago. 'I'll pay maintenance for Natalie and Robin, of course, and half the mortgage on the house. It comes to term in five years; I imagine you'll be able to take out another mortgage then to buy back my half. I won't press for it until. I don't intend to be unreasonable.'

Beth felt events sliding away from her. 'Alan, this is silly. We can't just throw away all our history. There has to be something we can do. What about marriage guidance? RELATE or whatever it's called these days?'

He looked at her, perfectly good-humoured. 'And waste another year? No. The sooner you face facts the better, the main one being that you aren't going to have nearly as much money as you're used to. You need to see the Head this week. Apply to work full-time.'

A fresh rush of anger beat against Beth's disbelief. 'Sod the Head! What are we going to tell the kids?'

Alan shrugged. 'The truth. I'll tell them after work, if you like. Neither of them have activities tonight, do they? I'll want to see them from time to time anyway.' His massive calm was impenetrable, he was a stranger.

'Fine,' said Beth, the sentiment ash in her throat. She swallowed some tea. 'Where are you staying?' Please not with another woman – spare me that failure at least.

His eyes expressed faint surprise that she had to ask. 'At the club. I've made an offer on one of those flats they're converting in the Maltings.'

All in one day? Oh, come *on!* How the hell long had he been planning this? Waiting for an appropriate row. *Manufacturing* one, even. Nausea filled her. She stumbled to her

23

feet. 'I don't know what to do. Do I kiss you or do we just shake hands?'

He stood too, an executive showing an unsuccessful client out. 'I'm only forty-nine,' he repeated. 'This is my future I'm thinking about.'

A large lump had got lodged in Beth's wind-pipe. It made speaking difficult. 'You'll be over later, then? To – to discuss–'

'Sure. Tagliatelle alla Carbonara would be nice.'

Tagliatelle alla–? She clamped her jaw shut on rising hysteria. She blundered down to the car but it was too big, too spacious. She wanted to be somewhere small and dark and shut away. She pulled up her knees and huddled herself over the steering wheel and let out soundless scream after soundless scream after soundless scream.

The evening passed in a frozen horror. It was as if the four of them were inhabiting an unconvincing soap opera or one of those cruel practical joke scenarios. At the point where Alan said, apparently in all sincerity, that there was no reason they shouldn't remain friends, Beth almost found herself looking for a hidden camera.

Natalie's face changed first to red as Alan talked and then to wax-white, throwing up the dread that she would revert to the teenager-from-hell of a couple of years ago, when a simple enquiry about what she wanted for tea elicited a furious diatribe on how her mother was always hassling her about her diet. But it wasn't until Alan had breezed out, taking with him the decanter and glasses his parents had given them and leaving behind a list of the things he'd be back to collect once he'd moved into the Maltings flat, that the storm broke.

'Nats, please–' Beth said wearily after half an hour of defamatory language that she really hoped Natalie hadn't learnt from her. She supposed she should have expected this kick-back of rejection, should have taken steps yesterday to prepare the kids for it. Was she going to spend the rest of her life feeling guilty? 'We're just going to have to give Dad some space on this. He's–' it sounded lame even to her own ears 'at an awkward period in his life.'

'No he isn't,' said Natalie crudely. 'He wants to trade us in.'

'Actually,' said Robin, eyeing his older sister with a caution which showed that he too remembered the Hades years, 'I'm not that bothered. I mean, it'll be weird not having him around, but at least I won't have to pretend to like squash any more. And I can take that extra modern-dance class without him moaning.'

Rob was so blessedly normal. The heavy fog of oppression lifted a little and Beth smiled for the first time that evening. 'You might have to do a paper round to pay for it, sweetheart.'

Robin shrugged, unbothered. 'Most of the boys in my class do one.'

Natalie poured herself fluidly on to the settee next to her mother. 'What do you mean? Won't there be enough money? What about my singing lessons?'

Beth shut her eyes, drawing strength from the kids' nearness. 'Dad will probably be back by September. We'll manage.'

Famous last words. The bank statement arrived just after half-term. Beth gasped in disbelief. She stared at the alarmingly small sum in the final column and tried to remember when pay-day was.

'I did warn you you'd have to cut back,' said Alan when she rang. 'Did you see the account is just in your name now? Oh, and I've cancelled the joint Visa. The form for your new one is on its way. I shouldn't let it run up too high. Have you seen the Head?'

So much for him being back by next term. At this rate she'd be in a debtor's prison by the first week of the holidays. She tried to concentrate. 'The Head? She was delighted I wanted more hours and she's bumped me up to form-tutor too. But I won't get the extra wages until *September*, Alan.'

She could almost see his pleasant shrug.

'Advertise yourself as a crammer the way you did when we were first married. Turn the box-room into a study and tutor re-sits over the summer. And I've said before that it's high time the children got holiday jobs instead of depending on us for pocket money. Incidentally, I don't want any of the furniture. I've decided to buy new for the flat.'

'He's really not coming back,' said Beth to Sue after school. Robin and Jack were in the lounge. Lisa and Natalie had raced upstairs to finish their History coursework to the supportive accompaniment of *The Darkness*. Beth stared out of the kitchen window. 'I still can't believe it.' Understatement of the year. Her entire life had gone into shock. 'Sue, what am I going to do about money? This house bloody *eats* it!'

'You *could* cram, I suppose...'

'God, yes, I've already put ads in the *Echo* and the *Evening News*. But what about when the exams are over?'

'Lodger in the spare room?'

Beth made a face. 'Suppose we hate them?'

Sue drained her tea. 'B&B then. Cambridge is full of tourists during the summer. Some of them might want to stay out in the sticks.'

'One room's rent is hardly going to make

a difference. I suppose there's the box-room too, if I cleared it. And we could convert the playroom – it's not as if it's been used since Robin discovered the great god, Nintendo.' She winced at triumphant yells from the lounge and hauled open the connecting door. 'I thought you were revising,' she said over the noise.

'We are,' yelled Robin. 'We're playing *Smash Bros* in French.'

'Oh, that's really going to impress Mr Baxter.'

'It should.' Neither boy took their eyes off the screen or their hands from the controllers. '*We've* got all eight of the secret characters and *he's* only got the first two.'

'Ian Baxter is a computer game freak?'

'Yeah. We did a *Legend of Zelda* translation today.'

Beth slumped back into her chair and looked at Sue. 'I give up. In a world where the Modern Languages department has been taken over by Nintendo, me doing B&B when I can't even boil an egg in the morning without intravenous tea sounds almost sane. Where do you suppose I register?'

CHAPTER 2

'I've got to partner Lisa in the show.' Robin's recently-broken voice shot up half-an-octave in outrage.

'Figures,' said Beth, unmoved. 'You're the best.'

'But she's eighteen months older than me!'

'Margot Fonteyn was eighteen *years* older than Rudolf Nureyev.'

'Yuk!'

'B&Bs in tonight,' said Beth, 'so we need to tidy up. I've explained they'll have to be out early on Monday so we can get to school. Oh, and Dad phoned. He's got corporate tickets for you both for Alton Towers.'

'Cool!' said Robin.

Natalie's eyes in the driving mirror were mutinous. 'Do we have to go?'

Beth's gut tightened. 'We've been through this, Nats. He's your father. He still cares for you. If he wants to treat you to a day out, of course you must go.' Natalie looked defiant. Beth resorted to bribery-and-corruption with barely a qualm. 'You can wear that skirt I won't generally let you out of the house in. If Dad complains, tell him you haven't got any money for new clothes.'

Natalie twiddled with her ponytail, assimilating the possibilities, then flicked it free. 'OK.'

'Thank you so much, Mrs Trower, it's been a lovely weekend. We'll recommend you to all our friends.'

Beth summoned up an expression of suitable gratitude and tried not to look at her watch. 'I hope the children didn't disturb you too much.'

The two elderly ladies twittered as Robin carried their cases up the path. 'It's nice to have a bit of life around. We enjoyed that *Eminem* CD. Such inventive lyrics.'

Beth shut the door on them and covered her eyes.

'I told you they were cool,' said Natalie. 'And they paid in cash.'

'They gave me a pound,' said Robin.

'What are you two *like?*' Beth hefted her box of books off the hall floor and felt around for the car keys. Of all the changes since Alan had left, she resented this one most. She *hated* having other people in her house, hated having to clear up constantly, hated the kids having to turn down the TV or the CD player so as not to disturb visitors. *I'm never going to forgive him for this*, she realised in astonishment.

Another thing about doing B&B she

fumed that afternoon stuffing barely-soiled sheets into the machine, was all the washing. People had no idea how much – the phone rang, distracting her.

'Mrs Trower. I'm told you do bed and breakfast.'

For a wild moment Beth thought of denying it, then caught sight of the gas bill wedged in the letter rack. 'Yes, when did you want to come?'

The young woman on the phone sounded as if she had her teeth gritted. 'Fifth of August for a week. Three single rooms.'

'I've got one single and two doubles, but you can use them as singles for a supplement.' She told her the rates, keeping her fingers crossed.

The girl took a clenched breath. 'There's one more thing – we're with *FOOTLIGHTS*, the musical theatre company...'

Beth felt a jolt of surprise. '*Wind In The Willows?* My children are in the chorus for that!'

Relief, pure and unadulterated, gusted down the line. 'Oh, you angel! I've been getting "Sorry, dear, we're booked after all" from everybody else.'

Beth found herself smiling. 'As long as *you* don't mind *REM* and *Evanescence* at five hundred decibels, and not being able to watch TV because James Bond is being stalked over several levels of the Gamecube?'

'I love *Evanescence*. I'll definitely take the single and let you know whether the boys want to share a double or pay the extra for one each. I hadn't realised everywhere would be so busy that week. There's nothing central left at all.'

'Peak tourist season,' said Beth. 'Can I have your name and phone number?' Pity she couldn't ask for a deposit. The kids were getting a tad fed up with pasta and buy-one-get-one-free Supasava sauce every night.

'Cate Edmonds.'

'Edmonds?' said Beth. 'Isn't Ned Edmonds–?'

'The director? He's my uncle. And my aunt's the stage manager, Dad's the producer, Mum does the costumes and *her* brother is set and lighting design. It's what you might call a family business.'

Beth put down the receiver and pencilled the booking in on the calendar. A familiar knot of worry made its appearance in her stomach. Even three rooms for a whole week wouldn't be enough now. Alan had phoned last night. One of the things he'd said was that he wasn't going to pay any more singing, dancing or *Stagestruck* fees. Beth scanned the days: five more weeks until the end of term, then three more until the A-level results were out and she started getting re-sit kids applying. For the first time in her teaching career she hoped the external examiners were real sadists – she needed all the cramming she could get.

'Yes!' Cate put a triumphant tick on her list as she shut off the phone. She caught sight of a blond figure flitting past the open door. 'Seb!'

Seb Merchant winced and reversed direction. 'Hi, how's things?'

'Wicked.' She scribbled Beth Trower's details on a piece of paper. 'One set of rooms outside Cambridge.'

Seb took the address with all the alacrity of a mother rabbit being offered a baby-sitting service by the local boa constrictor. 'You booked them for us?' he said in disbelief. 'What's wrong with them?'

'Nothing. The place is a perfectly good B&B. I'm there too. But you need to phone the woman and tell her whether you and Owen are going to share a double room or have one each.'

'Bed and Breakfast?' Consternation crossed Seb's face. 'Er, Owen really prefers proper theatrical digs–'

'Tough. He should have organised something himself when your landlady retired instead of taking Jasper Annis up on that bet that I wouldn't do it.'

'Oh. You heard about that.'

She looked at him pityingly. 'How long have you known me?'

He reddened. 'Since your first day in college. Point taken.'

'So I should think. I may have only been with the tour two weeks, but I do know what an ASM's job does and doesn't entail.'

'Then why book the rooms for us?'

'Because I want Annis to lose. Owen's just a dyed-in-the-wool comfort merchant with a tongue that could give acid pollution a run for its money. Annis is a thug. Don't forget to ring Beth Trower about the rooms.'

'OK.' Seb hesitated as he left the office. 'It's made it really homely this fortnight, hearing you banging and crashing and shouting at everyone again.'

Cate turned back to the PC. 'There is something seriously wrong with your diet, Sebastian Merchant. Buy some multi-vitamins immediately.' Homely indeed! He'd better not repeat that to anyone else. With abject terror was how she preferred actors to regard her.

Seconds later there was another interruption as Luke Bartholomew materialised in the doorway. Cate suffered a gut-churning, bone-melting moment until she reminded her wayward impulses that she was *never* getting romantically involved with members of her own company *ever* again. Or had they perhaps forgotten what had happened in Swansea?

'I was looking for Stella,' said Luke with a

smile which could charm a Doberman into rolling over to have its tummy tickled.

In Cate's opinion, floppy dark hair and deep green eyes should be surgically removed at birth. She looked pointedly around the empty office. 'She isn't here.'

'No. Sorry, I've forgotten your name.'

'*Oi, you.* Assistant stage managers don't have names.'

He chuckled and came into the room, resting a hand on her shoulder as she typed. 'Can I leave a message?'

Theatre people touch each other all the time. You've been used to it your whole life. It means nothing. 'Depends. How good is your writing?' He laughed. Downstairs the stage door slammed and a flood of raucous language announced the arrival of more of the cast. Cate glanced at her watch. 'Warm-up in ten minutes. I expect you'll find Stella on stage.'

For a moment Luke looked confused.

'Stella,' she repeated. 'My aunt. You were looking for her.'

'Oh. Thanks.' He blew her an airy kiss and left.

Outside her door she glimpsed Seb coming downstairs again. 'Hey, Seb,' she heard Luke say. 'The new ASM – did someone tell me you knew her before?'

'Cate Edmonds? Yes, we went to the same college.'

'Fancy her at all?'

Cate smiled sardonically at Seb's yelp of horror. 'You've got to be kidding! You need a riot shield just to *talk* to her. One guy who messed her about had to be fished out of the canal on Valentine's Day.'

'Really?' said Luke's voice just before it was cut off by the pass door, 'I thought she seemed kind of cute.'

Remember Swansea, Cate reiterated to herself.

Beth staggered into the kitchen. 'Tea,' she said faintly.

Grinning, Rob flicked the kettle on. 'The Year Six Induction Day was that bad, eh?'

'Bad?' Beth's mind grappled with the total inadequacy of the word. It seemed impossible that only this morning she had actually been moderately eager to see what her next-year's class were like.

'There was an ambulance at school today.'

'I know. It was collecting one of the new intake.'

Rob's eyes widened. 'Not yours?'

'He was until I swapped him,' said Beth.

Robin hastily slopped a mug of tea in front of her. 'Mum! Tell!'

'It transpired that two of my future form were sworn enemies and nobody had thought to inform the office. They were at each other's throats before I'd got ten names down the register. I never realised noses held so much blood.'

'And you swapped the one who lost? Mum!'

Beth took a life-reviving gulp. 'To be fair I think Yob got in a lucky punch. Martin looked the dirtier fighter.'

Rob's mouth was hanging open. 'You *kept* the one called *Yob?*'

'It's not his real name,' said Beth.

'Oh, good.'

'But nobody knows what that is. His mum can't find his birth certificate. Felicity thinks they're not trying.'

'Felicity?'

'The girl with the ginger bunches tied up with bows who you and Jack were sniggering at when you just happened to walk past my classroom. Lots of people don't look after hair ribbons properly. Felicity's mother washes hers every day *and* irons them.'

'That lesson of yours – what exactly was going on?'

Beth took another drink of tea. 'Spike Taylor's sister, Star, hijacked my favourite books idea and set everyone to acting out the duelling scene from Harry Potter.'

Comprehension dawned. 'Oh! So the boy lying on your desk yelling "Faster! Faster!" was flying, was he?'

'Yes. I got him and his seasonal-adjust-ment-deficient friend in exchange for Martin Shaw. I wondered why Mr Baxter was being so helpful.'

The phone rang. Robin answered it. Beth wrapped her hands around her mug and wondered how much tranquillisers cost if you bought them in bulk

'It's for you, Mum. Someone about a booking.'

Or sleeping gas, brooded Beth, putting the phone to her ear. Not every lesson, of course, just once a week. On a Friday, perhaps.

'Owen Pendragon,' said a warm baritone. 'Cate Edmonds booked us rooms for the fifth of August week.'

Beth dragged her mind back. 'Oh, yes. She was going to let me know whether it was one double or two with single supplements.' Or *she* could take the tranquillisers. That would be cheaper. Then she wouldn't care what mayhem her class wrought. She could just float on a fluffy pink cloud and watch them.

'Two, please. I understand your children are going to be in the chorus.'

'Yes, they can't wait.' Oh God, she was going to have to take her class for PSE. How on earth was she supposed to instill a modicum of social responsibility in Yob whilst at the same time opening Felicity's eyes to a world beyond hair ribbons? She must have been mad to agree to be a form tutor. There had to be an easier way to make a living!

'It did occur to me,' Owen Pendragon was saying in pensive tones, 'that you might consider the idea of doing full-board. We'd pay the extra, of course.'

Beth's attention suddenly focused on the phone.

'It wouldn't entail anything major. A light meal before the performance. A few sandwiches afterwards. The sort of thing you'd be doing for yourselves.'

'I don't know,' hedged Beth. 'I'm chaperoning the chorus for at least half the performances.'

'Even better. It won't put you out if a show runs late.' The voice became cajoling. 'Do consider it, Mrs Trower. When you're on the road all the time it's so much nicer to eat home-cooked meals than fight your way to a plastic table in a crowded fast-food place.'

'I suppose it must be,' said Beth, weakening. 'You'd pay extra, did you say?'

'Of course.' He named a sum which had her scruples packing suitcases and heading for the nearest airport. 'We get expenses in cash, so there would be no problem about that.'

He really had a very soothing voice. 'OK,' Beth heard herself saying. 'I'll see you on the fifth of August.'

June lengthened into July. The touring company moved into the air-conditioned studio complex in London's Docklands to rehearse *Wind in the Willows*. Cate was so determined to be on top of the job from the word go that she knew the libretto back to front and sideways. She'd chosen not to do vac work with the company on purpose since going to college, deliberately getting her mistakes out of the way at Swansea (hadn't she just!) and Liverpool, so now, apart from her insides turning into a gallon of wet-white whenever Luke smiled, she was every inch a professional. Graham, the wardrobe master, had taken to leaving chamomile sachets next to her cup.

'That man *has* to have been born on a Sunday,' she muttered to her friend Fran who ran the *FOOTLIGHTS* office. 'I don't know how Michael puts up with him. Do you know he told me this morning that a smile uses less muscles than a frown.'

Fran grinned. 'Any forays into the company yourself yet?'

Luke's deep green eyes hung lazily in the back of Cate's head. 'I'd really tell you if there were?'

'I just wondered whose insurance policies to check. I mean, after Swansea...'

She was working too hard, she knew she was. But Exeter went well and Swindon, apart from Ellery Valentine throwing a tantrum when it was billed as a kids' show, even better. Cate drove from there to Cambridge and found Fenbourne without difficulty.

'Hi, I'm Natalie,' said the pretty teenager

who opened the door. 'Come into the kitchen. Mum! One of the *FOOTLIGHTS* people is here.'

'Already?' A dark-haired woman hurried past with a rack of scraped toast.

Natalie pushed open a door at the end of the hall. 'Last night's people are still making pigs of themselves in the dining room,' she explained over her shoulder. 'Would you like some tea? It's fresh.'

Cate felt acutely uncomfortable. 'Yes. No. I'd better come back later.'

'No way! They should have left by now but they came in boozed to the eyeballs and refused to wake up this morning no matter how loudly I played Mum's *Queen* CD.'

Beth – it must be her – returned with a coffee pot. 'I'll give them not strong enough,' she muttered wrathfully.

A slow grin crept up Cate's body as her landlady for the next week shook a quarter of a jar of Supasava Value Coffee into the pot and poured boiling water on top.

Another teenager burst through the door with a rolled-up towel under his arm. 'Jack's here.'

Beth followed him out. 'Remember to *thank* Pete this time...'

'Did they bring Lisa? Lis – you'll never *guess* what the visitors...' The remainder of Natalie's sentence was lost as she dragged her friend upstairs.

Beth returned. 'Any tea left?'

Cate poured her out a cup. 'Are you sure you don't want me to leave? It's get-in in an hour. I could easily go over to the theatre early.'

Her hostess looked alarmed. 'No! You have to tell me a digs landlady's duties.'

An uneasy twinge nibbled at Cate's good feeling. She'd forgotten Owen and Seb. 'Plenty of tea. Feed us constantly or leave sandwiches in the fridge. Get us up on time by any means you like – and don't let Owen run rings around you.'

Beth wrapped her hands around her mug, her face taking on a brooding look. 'He was the one who phoned, wasn't he? Blinded me with tales of fabulous expenses so I'd do full board for you all.'

Cate's twinge grew. 'Yup, that's him. Owen Pendragon.' The one with the comfort fixation. 'Con artist extraordinaire. You won't have any trouble with Seb. Don't worry that he always looks anxious. If Shakespeare himself had asked him to play the third murderer, he'd worry he wasn't good enough.'

'Seb?' yelped Beth, her mug clattering to the table. 'Sebastian Merchant? The one who played Jud Fry in *Oklahoma!*?'

'Wasn't he brilliant? But he *quaked* every night for the whole seven weeks. Sometimes I wonder if I did the right thing tipping the management off about him.'

42

'With the swept-back blond fringe? Every teenage girl's dream come true?'

Cate shrugged, recalling the unlooked-for effect Seb had had on the local girls so far this tour. 'I suppose so, but he's honestly not– Oh, I see! Natalie!'

Across the table, Beth's head was buried in her hands. 'You're paying me masses of money. Which I desperately need. And it's only for a week.' She looked up. 'I suppose it's too much to hope he's a fluffy, un-hip squirrel or something?'

'A weasel,' said Cate weakly. 'Sprayed-on leather and silver chains.'

Beth closed her eyes. 'Natalie's Jill Rabbit.'

Cate tried to recall all the places in the theatre where a lovelorn teenager might attempt suicide. 'Good for her,' she said, falsely cheerful. 'I have to go. Can I leave my bags?'

All the rest of the day, as she and the stage crew beavered to get the set together, she tried not to think about having booked Seb and Owen into Beth's. Not Seb so much, he'd apologise for its being his own fault if he wasn't suited, but Owen was a different matter. He was older and had been touring most of his working life. He was accustomed to *professional* landladies, not B&Bers on the lookout for extra cash. He also had that evil line in repartee which Cate had to counter every day as it was if he wasn't to get the better of her.

The overnight visitors finally departed. Beth spent ten frantic minutes changing bed linen and inventing them a disastrous journey home. She had just bundled the laundry out of sight when the doorbell rang. For a moment, with the afternoon sun in her eyes, she thought the man on the step was Alan. Then he moved and she saw he was younger and more compact and his hair was longer.

'Mrs Trower? Owen Pendragon. You've got rooms for us.'

His eyes were different from Alan's too. They were hazel, and wickedly alive in his mobile face. Her heart gave an odd jump. Behind his shoulder Seb Merchant hovered diffidently, just as good-looking as he had been on stage. 'I'll show you up,' she said with a strong presentiment of disaster.

Natalie's door opened. 'Mum, can Lisa stay for–' Her jaw dropped as she saw Seb. 'Oh my God,' she screamed, and shot back into her room.

Beth cleared her throat. 'That was Natalie,' she said into the silence. 'She's Jill Rabbit. My son, Robin, is a weasel.'

Owen's eyes crinkled in a mildly disturbing fashion. 'I shouldn't let it bother you. Under this nu-skin I'm really a toad.'

The next day dawned belligerently hot. Stuff the visitors' sensibilities, thought Beth, pulling on a pair of shorts. No way could she cook a full English breakfast in jeans. She just hoped they'd be up punctually. It was going to do sod-all for her cash flow if Rob had to eat several lots of spoiling bacon-and-eggs, even *with* the vast sums they were paying for full board. She felt a stab of guilt about that extra money. Comforting as it would be to pay off the outstanding bills, she must have to do more to earn it than simply have tea ready before the theatre and leave them supper after it. Both men had watched TV with them in the lounge last night (though she wasn't convinced Nats had taken in a single word, she'd been so busy *not* looking at Seb). Maybe it was inconvenience pay because they were underfoot all day; no demarcation line like there was with B&Bs.

Beth came out of her bedroom and – oh my Lord! It wasn't only downstairs that guests would be underfoot. Owen was emerging from the bathroom in a waft of Aztec For Men. His dark hair curled damply, his legs were bare and muscled and in his midnight-blue towelling bathrobe he looked the sexiest, most virile pirate ever to have sailed the seven seas. Beth was caught completely by surprise. None of her previous visitors had *ever* looked like this. *Oh hell*, she wailed to herself as a massive pulse of lust pole-axed her.

Wicked hazel eyes skimmed her from head to foot. Aztec For Men swirled in her nostrils. 'Morning, mistress,' he said in an appreciative voice. 'Principal Boy legs before breakfast. Lovely.'

'Breakfast,' repeated Beth inanely. 'I'm – I'm just starting it.' She flew downstairs and thrust sausages under the grill with shaking fingers. She'd have to ask Nats or Rob to set the places in the dining room. She'd probably drop the cutlery drawer if she tried.

But it wasn't Natalie who came pelting into the kitchen next, grabbing a mug from the draining board and filling it with tea, it was Cate. 'I'm late,' she gasped. 'Tech rehearsal in twenty minutes. I should have left a note for you to wake me.'

Beth looked helplessly at bacon only just turning watery white, let alone a nice crisp brown. 'Have you got time for cereal? Or a marmalade sandwich for the car? We eat them all the time.' She reached for the loaf.

'Please.' Cate shook cornflakes into a bowl and splashed in milk. Console-game noises indicated Rob's presence in the lounge. Cate ate at indigestion-inducing speed and grabbed the sandwich. 'You're a life-saver, see you later.' Then, 'Through there, tea on the table,' Beth heard her call.

'Hi, Cate. Bye, Cate,' said Seb's cheerful voice. He came in. 'That smells wonderful!' He too poured himself a mug of tea, then poked his head through the swing door into the lounge. 'Robin! You've got *Pokémon Stadium!* Any chance of a battle if I bring my Gameboy cartridge down?'

Beth felt increasingly out of control. Guests crashing in and out, guests playing video games instead of eating sensibly in the dining room, guests wandering around sexily damp in midnight-blue bathrobes and smelling like the more blatant verses of John Donne. She caught her breath, letting the sausages burn, unable to get the image of Owen, fresh from his shower, out of her mind. It wasn't fair, she'd *always* found clean, wet men arousing (the section of her *Pride and Prejudice* tape where the manservant pours a can of water over Colin Firth's head was practically see-through, she'd watched it so much). It was the reason she'd had to stop taking Rob and Nats swimming. It was the single thing she missed most about Alan being gone: not the sex, but the sight of him in the shower. Dear God, what was she *like?*

Natalie dithered in her bedroom. Did she look cool enough in this for Seb to notice her? And there was the rehearsal this morning and costume fittings and things. Would he be there for that? Her voice! She'd forgotten how to sing! She sang a couple of scales to calm herself. To her surprise a rich baritone joined in from the landing.

'Boring things, aren't they?' said Owen when she yanked open her door. 'You ought to do hum-scales first to warm your voice up.'

'I know,' said Natalie, outraged. 'I did. I have been taught properly!'

'Crime not to be with a voice like that,' agreed Owen. He eyed her strappy white top and hip-hugging jeans. 'Let's see. Stylish, but not obvious. Yup, I reckon that'll do the trick.'

Natalie seethed. 'Are you always this rude?'

Owen grinned. 'Famous for it, sparrow. Where's the nearest pot of tea likely to be?'

As Owen followed Natalie into the kitchen (rather too soon for Beth's comfort after her hastily suppressed fantasies about showers), the superficial resemblance to Alan was so strong she almost expected him to peck her on the cheek and sit down at the table with the paper. The thought did odd things to her diaphragm.

'Visitors usually eat in the dining room,' her daughter was saying pointedly.

'But I can hear Seb in there,' objected Owen, jerking his head at the lounge.

Natalie's head whipped round. 'Has he had tea yet?'

Owen's amused eyes met Beth's as Nats

vanished through the door. 'I didn't *see* the slave chain round her ankle…'

Despite Beth's best endeavours, a chuckle escaped her. 'That's her newest tee shirt and her best jeans. She's going to be sweltering later.'

Owen sat down and hefted the teapot. 'Looks good in them, though. Nice legs obviously run in your family.'

Beth couldn't resist it. 'Only if we're late,' she said with a straight face.

Wicked hazel eyes pinned her. 'Theatrical landladies are not supposed to laugh at their lodgers.'

She dissolved into a swallow of laughter. 'Lodgers who forsake their proper place in the dining room are asking for all they get. This is my kitchen and I can do what I like in it.'

Owen shook out the paper. 'Including fried bread?' Her shoulders quivered. Definitely a con artist. But his v-neck tee shirt revealed a tiny triangle of damp, curly hair and his sense of humour was light years ahead of Alan's and more to the point it had been so bloody *long* since she'd felt like this. 'One slice or two?' she asked.

CHAPTER 3

Natalie stood on the Corn Exchange stage drinking in the screeches of sound from the speakers, the banks of lights going on and off, the hammering of the carpenter fitting sections of orchestra pit together. Beth observed her glowing face with misgiving.

'Got it badly, hasn't she?' said an amused voice.

She jumped. She hadn't realised Owen was standing so close. 'Yes. Robin is far more laid back.'

'Takes all sorts. Were they in last year's?'

Beth snorted. 'Try stopping them! They've been in all the FOOTLIGHTS summer tours since Sue first decided school drama wasn't challenging enough and set up *Stagestruck* to occupy her spare time.'

'She's certainly trained them well. Friend of yours?'

'We've known each other for years. Confession – I'm not a proper landlady.'

'Excellent. Been a long time since I stayed with an improper one.'

Beth's quelling glare was marred by the fact that she was fighting a bubble of laughter. 'In real life I'm an English teacher.'

'Lucky pupils.'

She gave him a sideways glance. He met it blandly. She felt the tiniest wriggle of excitement. Was he flirting with her? It was so long since anyone but Alan had shown an interest that she wasn't sure she'd recognise a chat-up line unless it was accompanied by sirens and a flashing arrow.

Seb crossed the stage. Beth could see why Natalie and Lisa were nudging one another but his conventional lean frame, blond fringe and blue eyes didn't affect her nearly as much as the quirky sexiness emanating from the man beside her. Down girl, she told herself. Alan hadn't been gone three months yet. Have some decency, for goodness sake!

Natalie stood in the costume queue loving the fact that she was back in the theatre, loving the fact that in a few moments she was going to be rehearsing her songs with the musical director, loving the fact that Seb had smiled especially at her. She came out of her dream to see the two smallest rabbits zip up plump brown bunny tummies. 'Oh no!' she wailed. 'I'm not going to look like *that?*'

The wardrobe master tutted. 'Is that any way for a wholesome woodland animal to talk?'

Wholesome! As Natalie started to sing, she

wondered if the English language contained a more loathsome adjective? Seb glanced across and said something to Mum who raised her eyebrows before replying. Owen gave a shout of laughter and clouted Seb on the back. She wished she was dead.

'Well done,' said the musical director, looking relieved. 'We'll call you for the rest later.'

Beth shepherded the choir up the clanging staircase, aching with sympathy at the look of misery on Natalie's face. Worse was to come. The dancers had been costumed in their absence. Beth halted in the dressing room doorway, only now appreciating Owen's murmur of good luck. The wardrobe department had interpreted the weasels' and stoats' baddies image as biker leathers and shades for the boys and brief satin skirts over endless leg for the girls. All of them wore the skimpiest cut-off tee shirts Beth had ever seen. 'Just what Lisa needed,' she said brightly, not daring to look at Natalie's gingham-clad, pear-shaped frame. 'A pair of sleeves and a belt.'

Natalie didn't laugh. Beth hadn't really expected her to.

'Junior stoats and weasels to the stage,' said Cate's voice from the loudspeaker.

Sue winced as Lisa sashayed past her. 'Pete's mum is going to have a fit!'

Pete's mum, thought Beth, seeing the

undiluted jealousy on Natalie's face, wasn't the only one.

'What's the matter with you, sparrow?'

'Nothing,' said Natalie, hunching her shoulders. It was the next day. She was already out of sorts with having to get up early and hold the fort while Mum went shopping. She didn't see why she should make polite conversation too.

Owen dropped down on to the settee next to her. 'Decent first night, so it can't be that,' he said. Natalie saw his eye fall on the local paper. He cocked his head knowingly. 'Review out already, eh? They either haven't printed a picture of you – or they have.'

Natalie's sense of ill-usage boiled over. 'They've printed everyone's picture! Lisa's is way cool and I look about ten!'

'And I'll look a freak,' said Owen. He drank his tea. 'Pity they don't print sound, then *we'd* have the last laugh. Full page spread. Should mean good business for the rest of the week. I'll have to get a copy.'

'That's stupid,' said Natalie. 'No way do you still keep cuttings.'

'Why not?'

'You're grown up!'

He gave the amused look she was coming to hate. 'Which is exactly when you want your cuttings. Bloody insecure bunch, actors. Need constant reminders of past glories. The good thing about *FOOTLIGHTS* is that it's steady work. Uneven, but steady.'

Natalie was torn. She didn't like Owen, but she was thirsty for *anything* to do with the theatre. 'How can it be both?' she said after a short struggle with herself.

'Because touring with four different musicals a year plus a panto would mean financial disaster for a theatrical company if it wasn't for two things. Lottery funding for one, and two – the actors take what parts they're given. No auditions, no arguments, but we *are* still employed and there's no wholesale reshuffling of the troupe every eleven weeks. So last time I was Ali Hakim which is a smallish bit *and* I had to risk life and limb snogging Mel, but at least I looked OK. In this I'm Toad which is a bigger role but my own mother wouldn't recognise me under the green wrinkles.' He shrugged. 'Bad photos happen. Look at April in those big glasses with that duster round her head.'

Natalie frowned, staring at the photo of the leading lady. It hadn't occurred to her that top actors didn't always get things their own way either. 'She was Dorothy last year,' she said. 'And you were the Tin Man. I remember you swearing when you couldn't get out of your costume to go to the loo. At least then Lisa and I were Munchkins together.'

'Christ, sparrow, friendship is a bloody sight more important than clothes! Just because you've got the hots for Seb and you don't think he'll look twice at a cute kid with long ears and a bob-tail is no reason to fall out with your best mate. Your mum's warned him off until you're sixteen anyway. Didn't you hear her when you were singing for Adrian? Agreeing with him that you had a good voice for a *fifteen-year-old?*'

Natalie coloured furiously. He was the rudest man she'd ever met. 'You–'

Mum had come into the kitchen; she could hear her dumping carrier bags.

Owen finished his tea. 'Been called 'em all already,' he said, making for the swing door.

Beth wasn't quite sure how it had come about that she was sitting down in the kitchen discussing teenagers' social problems with Owen when she ought to be making lunch. She'd started efficiently enough, putting the shopping away whilst he rinsed his mug. Then he'd noticed the great wodge of PSE bumph which she was supposed to be doing something meaningful with before term started. The only thing which came to mind at the moment was turning it into briquettes ready to go on the fire once the weather got cold.

'Personal and Social Education,' she'd said in answer to his query. 'Guiding kids through the shark-infested waters of adolescence.'

He'd leafed idly through the index. 'Christ

Almighty. How long do you get?'

She'd grinned. 'Five years. It's an ongoing process. I'm supposed to have a couple of months'-worth of ideas ready to roll by September.'

'In addition to your proper work, presumably. Sorry, I can see now why you weren't keen on doing full-board.'

She'd blinked. For a moment, Owen had sounded as though he'd *meant* it. On the other hand, Cate had several times described him as devious, and having watched from the wings last night, Beth knew at first hand what a superb actor he was. 'I wouldn't have got a lot done this week anyway. And we do need the money. My ex-husband seems to have forgotten how much it costs to keep three people and a sympathetically renovated house alive.'

He'd smiled. Beth was becoming uneasy about that smile. It gave the bed part of bed-and-breakfast undreamt-of connotations.

'So how do you work it all in?' he was saying now, flicking through the section on Bullying and pausing to read the one on Problems with Absentee Parents.

'Videos, worksheets, discussions. Role-playing.'

'Exam Revision Techniques... Drugs Awareness... Don't they already know about drugs?'

Beth chuckled. 'More than we do, probably, but it would be impolitic to admit it. That's the big thing, we're supposed to get them to talk, encourage them to open up. Problems shared and all that.'

Owen's brow creased. 'They'll need to feel safe then. You can't just wade straight in with the heavy stuff and expect them to embrace it. You'll need to build up trust. Work on bonding too. They're never going to open up if one half of the class wants to jump on the heads of the other.'

Beth stared in astonishment. He really wasn't faking the interest. Not unless he was Oscar standard. It came as a bit of a shock after Alan's less than thrilled attitude towards her work. 'That's true. Thank you.'

He met her eyes. His mouth quirked. 'Sorry, am I butting in? We were very hot on trust in The People's Warehouse Experimental Theatre.'

His expression invited her to join in his self-mockery. Instead she grinned. 'I never got further than the Folk Music Appreciation Society and Primal Screams as Learning. How old were you?'

His smile had a trace of bitterness to it. 'Twenty-one. You could have used our angst to power West London. Mind you, in those days we were so broke we'd have bared our soul for a packet of peanuts. Communal hugging was as much for warmth as for solidarity.'

Beth chuckled. She could almost see the young actor he had been – thin, intense, had he always worn his hair slightly long? 'Tread softly because you tread upon my dreams,' she murmured.

His eyes crinkled. For a moment there was a wealth of shared history between them which took her breath away. Beth felt a spark leap from him to her and bury itself under her skin. I know this man, she thought.

Heat hung motionless in the air.

'Lis, sorry if I've been a bit – you know.'

Lisa looked up from her magazine. 'So I should think. I'm not sulking about you singing with Jason, am I?'

Natalie slid a cautious glance down the dressing room to where Jason Peters was obliviously letting *Motorhead* fill his brain. 'I've always sung with Jason. Since when did it matter to you?'

'Since he broke up with Sarah.'

'Seriously?'

Lisa went a little pink. 'He lives in Fenbourne and he'll still be around next week. That'll do me.'

Natalie was appalled at her friend's practicality. 'Yeah, but Seb is–'

'Seb is six or seven years older than we are, drop-dead gorgeous and a professional. No way is he going to be interested.'

'That's why you snuggle up to him in the *Evil Weasel* dance, is it?'

Lisa shrugged. 'Nearest I'm likely to come...'

There was a tap on the open door. Natalie felt herself turn all the colours of a particularly extravagant sunset as Seb himself peered round it. 'Nats, could I have a word?'

She hitched up her shorts and attempted a nonchalant stroll out to the small landing.

'I just wanted your phone number,' said Seb. 'My parents are travelling up from London to watch the show tomorrow night. I thought if I borrowed Owen's spare bed, they could sleep in my room, but I ought to check with Beth that she doesn't mind.'

Natalie tapped the number into his mobile. It was warm from his hand; her heart pounded at her daring behaviour. 'Mum, it's me,' she said to the answerphone message. 'Stop pretending you're out. Seb wants you.'

'Thanks. See you later,' said Seb when he'd finished talking to Beth. He sang a snatch of song as he clattered down the iron staircase. Natalie hung over the rail and watched him disappear out of the stage door.

'What did he want?' said Lisa.

'Phone number of the house. Reception's better on the landing.'

Lisa looked speculative. 'I know we aren't supposed to nag the cast, but d'you think if we gave Seb our programmes he could get everyone's autograph?'

Natalie chewed her lip. 'Owen would be better.'

Lisa shrieked. 'His comments wouldn't be printable!'

Natalie was silent. It was dawning on her that both Owen and Seb were real people, not just actors. 'I'll ask tomorrow,' she said.

'What time is your parents' train, Seb?' asked Beth.

Damn, thought Natalie, handing her mother the last of the lunch plates. She'd been hoping to casually spend time with him herself as there was no matinée.

'Three-fifteen. Oh, and we're having a meal out after the show so don't bother saving me anything.'

'Which reminds me,' said Owen, taking the tea towel fractionally before Natalie could get to it, 'Seb and I want to buy you all supper after the last night.'

Natalie felt her heart skip a beat. Supper with Seb? Cool!

Her mother looked flustered. 'What? Why? Owen, put that down – you're not supposed to be drying up. I *knew* we shouldn't let lodgers into the kitchen.'

'It's nice in here,' protested Seb. 'Homely.'

'Crowded, you mean,' said Beth. 'Alan would never have it that we needed to extend. Said if I only tidied up, we'd have plenty of room.'

A surge of remembered resentment swelled Natalie's breast. 'Dad didn't understand lots of things.'

Her mother flicked her a warning glance. 'Which is why he's now in an upmarket flat by Conran and we're still wedging table legs with offcuts of Robin's resistant-materials project. Owen, will you put that down!'

'Domestic service is good for the soul. Your ex sounds a right prat. When's he coming to watch?'

Beth's and Natalie's eyes collided. 'Alan's, um, very busy this week,' said Beth.

Natalie snatched the tea towel from Owen and started attacking plates. 'If I give you Lisa's and my programmes, can you get everyone to sign them?'

She knew – she just knew – that he was laughing behind her back. 'Put myself out for a couple of kids? You've got to be joking!' He drifted into the lounge after Seb and turned the News on.

Beth pulled the plug out of the sink and fished in the suds for errant spoons. 'Isn't it hot! Are chaperones allowed to wear shorts?'

Natalie scrunched inwardly at the neutral voice. 'You should try being a rabbit!' She dried in silence for a minute. 'I just feel so used,' she wailed.

Her mother hugged her with a soapy arm.

'I know, sweetheart. I suppose the truth is Dad was always on a different plane to us and we never noticed. I'm sure part of him still loves us.'

'Not a very big part. And only when he's being a Family Man to impress someone. Like Alton Towers. He only took us so he could wave an airy hand at the rides and tell that awful organiser woman what a great time his kids were having and what a wonderful idea it was of hers to facilitate family bonding occasions like this.'

On the other side of the door, Owen sang an incredibly rude version of the *Neighbours* theme tune. Beth made a slight choking sound. Natalie heard Seb clear his throat. 'Er, you'll remember Mum and Dad aren't theatre people, won't you, Owen?'

Beth laughed out loud. 'Think positive, sweetheart. We're doing OK. We've got all the lovely *FOOTLIGHTS* money *and* more B&B bookings soon.'

Natalie felt her resentment ease. Who cared if Dad came to see the show?

Heat prickled up her later as she pulled on her rabbit leggings. Despite her resolution to be reasonable, she couldn't help casting a jaundiced eye at her friend's tiny satin skirt. 'I'm getting some air on the landing. Coming?'

Lisa glanced down the room at Jason. 'In a bit.'

Natalie sat on the landing windowsill, fanning herself with her programme. The company were on stage doing warm-up exercises. There was a squirt of sound as Seb raced across to the loo. Her heart gave a quick skip. He was so *gorgeous*. And he would be back in November for the *Tin Pan Ali* tour and again for the panto. She'd be sixteen next month. Lots of girls at school went out with older boys.

Downstairs the crew had propped the stage door open. The smoke from their cigarettes hung on the warm air with her dreams, mixing with the smell of sweat and dust and greasepaint. A faint drift of noise from the market overlaid their murmured conversation. As Seb went back through the pass door, Mum came out dangling a pair of rabbit ears in her hand. Before the door swung shut, she heard wolf-whistles, cat calls and, loud and unmistakable, Owen's voice.

'Sod off, Annis, she's *my* landlady and I get first refusal. Remember it!'

Natalie sat bolt upright, shocked into rigidity. Not at the language, which was no worse than she heard any day at school, but at the sentiment.

'You all right, sweetheart?' said Beth, coming up level with her.

'Hot.' Her mother was *grinning!*

'Poor you. I'll organise some iced drinks.'

63

Natalie stayed where she was. She'd never even considered the possibility that Mum might go out with other men. Nausea and shock fought in her gut.

Warm-up finished. The company surged like surf through a blowhole to their dressing rooms. Seb winked as he bounded past Natalie. Owen, already in costume, held fast against the tide at the bottom of the stairs. He looked up for a speculative moment, then ascended and nudged her until she shifted to make room for him. 'What's up?' he said.

The glow from Seb's wink faded. 'Nothing.'

'Pull the other one.'

'Shouldn't you be turning your face green and wrinkly?' she said disagreeably.

'It can wait. Luke's only just arrived, Ned and Stella are tearing him into bite-sized portions outside my dressing room door and if I have to listen to Monty droning on any more about how different discipline was when he was a young actor, dear boy, this show will be going on without two of its main characters.'

'I like Mr Montague,' said Natalie in a stilted voice. 'He's nice.'

Owen gave her a cynical look. 'He's nice to you because he's wise old Badger and you're frisky, innocent Jill Rabbit. He's a bloody pain to me. I'd rather share a dressing room with that randy lot upstairs.' She stiffened before she could stop herself. He looked at her again with interest. 'Ah, I wondered if that was it. You heard what I said.'

'No.'

Owen shook his head. 'Too quick. Always leave a pause before you answer. But in that case it's Seb's people babbling on about how proud they are of him. Listen, sparrow, your bloody father doesn't know he's born. If I had a kid chirruped as sweetly as you, you'd have to chain me up before I'd miss the show.'

Hot colour flooded most of her body. 'You're only saying that because you fancy Mum. It's horrible.'

'Christ Almighty! A man would have to be in his grave not to fancy Beth in those shorts. The whole chorus has got the hots for her. I was doing her a favour by putting her out of bounds.'

'Oh.' Embarrassment made her uncertain.

'She doesn't need the hassle. That your programme? Give it here. I'll bully the lads into signing while I wait for my room to become habitable.'

'So, where are we eating on Saturday?'

Beth looked up from her book. It was dangerously addictive, this sitting down over a pot of tea with Owen in the mornings. Several times she'd had to remind herself quite strongly that she was *never* going to trust another man *ever* after Alan. Which was difficult when Owen insisted on coming down for breakfast with damply curling hair in a waft of humid, Aztec-For-Men-scented steam. 'You're not serious. I can't believe you make a regular practice of taking landladies out for a meal.'

His eyes danced. 'You're not a regular landlady.'

'Too right. I hate it too much.'

He cocked an eyebrow. 'So why do it?'

'Preferable to starvation, I thought. Mind, I could have been wrong. I mean, the people you're obliged to have in your house–'

'Yeah, I told Seb he was pushing his luck, inviting his parents here.' He stretched his hand across the table and rested it on hers. 'Have we really been such a pain?'

A shockwave the size of the National Grid surged up Beth's arm. Her eyes jerked to Owen's and she knew without a shadow of a doubt that if she'd met him twenty-five years ago, Alan would never have stood a chance. 'I cannot tell a lie,' she said, her voice sounding odd in her ears, 'it hasn't been nearly as bad as I expected.' The current was there all right, strong and steady. It would only take a tweak of the generator... She pulled her hand away and took a gulp of tea.

The phone rang. Natalie answered and

poked her head round the door. 'Sue says can you chaperone this afternoon? She's been let down.'

'Yes, OK.' Beth looked at Owen ruefully. 'For "can I" read "you are" with Sue.'

'You could have said you were busy.'

'Mmm. The trouble is I open my mouth to say no and it comes out y-e-s.'

'I'll have to remember that.' The wicked hazel eyes were gleaming.

Heat mounted in her cheeks. 'Anyway, you don't have to treat us to supper. You'll be shattered.' Although she had to say it would be a wrench. Eating out had been the first thing to go when Alan left. She missed it horribly. The second thing had been Drambuie. She missed that even more.

'Are you kidding? Everyone's on such a high after the last night of a stop that we don't get to sleep until three in the morning anyway.'

'And then it's all over,' said Natalie mournfully.

Owen tweaked her pony-tail. 'Got used to the fluffy bunny image, eh?'

Natalie scowled, then shot over to open the back door for Seb.

'Safely away. Thanks for letting them stay, Beth.'

'They paid my B&B rates. Tea's in the pot.'

'Seems funny, paying to stay in a place which feels so much like home.' He pulled up a chair. Natalie sat casually next to him.

'Seb, sweetheart, having just had the electricity bill, I would be grateful if you *didn't* let feeling at home prevent you from paying.'

'You haven't answered me,' complained Owen. He leaned sideways and pushed open the swing door to the lounge. 'Hey, Rob,' he bellowed, 'where d'you fancy going on Saturday?'

'*Mutant Pizza*,' came back the un-hesitating reply.

Natalie sat up straight. 'Oh, Mum, can we?'

Beth didn't think Nats had consciously brushed Seb's arm, but it would have been obvious to a Venusian swamp monster what she was thinking. *Mutant Pizza* was *the* latest place. She was imagining sitting at a table next to Seb, being seen with him by people from school... She chuckled as she met Owen's inquiring eyes. 'You've done it now. Psychedelic artwork, music off the decibel register, and the most obscene pizza toppings devised by man.' On the other hand, there was zero chance of private conversation which was possibly just as well.

Seb's eyes widened in dismay. 'Er – well, maybe–' He caught sight of Natalie's euphoric face. 'Maybe we can tell them we're allergic to chicken tikka and jam.'

'I think that's probably one of the more

conservative combinations.' Beth glanced at her watch. 'Shit, we've got to be at the theatre at one and I haven't made the sandwiches yet – oh!' She clapped a guilty hand over her mouth as her ears caught up with her lips. 'That's your influence,' she said accusingly to Owen. 'It's a good thing you're leaving Monday.'

Owen's eyes teased her. Across the table, Natalie drooped. An *extremely* good thing they were leaving, Beth told herself firmly.

By some freak of chance (probably connected to the fact that the clutter on the dresser had edged the clock off it that morning, causing a rearrangement in its internal workings) they arrived early at the theatre. Beth left Natalie and Robin to make their way up to the dressing room whilst she dashed in the direction of the market. As she dodged a camera-strung tourist she saw Owen by the Box Office. Except it wasn't Owen, it was–

'Alan!' And he was holding a pair of tickets! 'You changed your mind!' she said, warmth flooding her. 'The kids will be so pleased!'

'The kids?' enquired a predatory voice. A well-groomed woman with unlikely golden hair was curving light fingers round Alan's arm.

'Beth, meet Doone Hennessy,' said Alan, not in the least embarrassed. 'She runs a gift-plan agency.'

'How interesting,' said Beth, not having the faintest idea what a gift-plan agency was and not immediately seeing why she should ever need to.

'If you're Beth, you must be Natalie and Robin's mother. They're great kids, aren't they?'

Beth's hackles rose at the smooth presumption. How dare this stranger talk about her children as if she knew them! 'Yes. Sorry, I must rush. I'm supposed to be chaperoning *Wind In The Willows.*'

'And Nats and Rob are in it? Do wish them luck. It's too bad I've had meetings and dinners all week.'

But surely– Beth's eyes went involuntarily to the tickets in Alan's hand. Doone preened very slightly and patted them. 'Moscow City Ballet. I am *so* into culture.'

Moscow City Ballet? She and the kids had *ached* to see that! 'Aren't we all?' she snapped. 'Robin's school uniform, Alan, a hundred should do. You were right about that growth-spurt; he needs everything.' She stood in a white-hot fury while the tight-fisted bastard she had wasted half her life on wrote a grudging cheque for perhaps double the price of a pair of MCB tickets. 'Nice to have met you,' she said insincerely to Doone, and then hurtled vengefully across the square, praying the bank had a till free.

She placed no reliance at all on Alan not stopping the cheque as soon as he could get to his mobile out of sight of Ms Hennessy, and continued to feel furious and let-down and betrayed and double-crossed all the way through the first half of the matinée.

'So who's handed you a dead ferret after promising you the front runner at White City?' said a voice in the darkness.

Beth was so spooked she nearly fell through the curtain. 'What are you doing here? You're not on yet,' she whispered crossly.

Owen grinned, his Toad make-up hardly visible in the prompt-side shadows. 'Instinct. Going to tell me?'

'I bumped into Alan,' said Beth, her lips barely moving. 'Thought he was buying tickets for the show. They turned out to be for the ballet.'

'Wanker,' said Owen, his attention on the woodland animals. 'There's not even any singing in Swan Lake.'

Beth was surprised into a choke of laughter. The painful band around her heart eased. 'It's not just that he hates ballet and we love it,' she confessed. 'He wasn't busy. He could have come this afternoon to watch Nats and Rob.'

If he'd wanted to. The thought hung un-spoken between them. The singing ap-proached its climax. Natalie's voice led the chorus into a fine, high harmony.

'Beautiful,' breathed Owen in the darkness. He laid his arm around Beth's shoulders and gave her the briefest of squeezes. 'Forget him. It doesn't sound as if he's worth the grief.' Just for a moment, Beth's startled body couldn't think who on earth he was talking about.

CHAPTER 4

During the summer tour the management provided Saturday tea between shows to say thank you to the kids. It was a nice gesture, but in Beth's opinion the free food only marginally compensated for the stress involved in keeping tabs on twenty cocksure youngsters roaming the Corn Exchange stage. She was therefore a trifle distracted when Cate towed her friend Fran over.

'I'd introduce you to Mum and Dad too, but they're busy being gracious and charming to the Ensemble.'

'As long as they're not promising them extra wages or expenses,' said Fran.

'Fran,' explained Cate, 'suffers from the delusion that she, not Dad, holds the *FOOT-LIGHTS* empire together.'

Beth was experiencing mild panic at only being able to count eighteen kids. Then she spotted Lisa and Jason very close together in the wings. Her heart sank. Another complication for Natalie. 'Hi,' she said. She smiled down at Fran's little girl. 'Did you enjoy the show?'

'We loved it, didn't we, Lily?' said Fran. 'It went much better than I expected, having seen the rehearsals. It's amazing how they always pull it off.'

'Duh,' said Cate. 'The only time you ever see the tour is when Dad brings you. Having the Boss out front has the oddest effect on performance levels.'

'Cate!' Luke Bartholomew laid a coaxing hand on her arm. 'Can I use your mobile? I've packed mine.'

To Beth's surprise, Cate glared at the good-looking young actor. 'No. You're not winding *me* round your little finger like you do the rest of my family.'

'Want to bet?' murmured Fran. 'Those eyes...'

He smiled. 'I really have to make this call. Please?'

Cate unclipped her phone, positively seething. 'Don't even *think* about trying this again,' she grated.

'Thanks.' He squeezed her shoulder and walked out of earshot.

'So he's the one,' said Fran in enlightened tones.

'He's the laziest, most unprincipled actor in this company,' said Cate crossly. 'He had Stella frantic this morning sorting out the lack of money in his account when all the time he'd remembered his PIN code wrong. The only reason I'm watching him is because he's quite capable of forgetting that's my Nokia he's using!'

Fran winked at Beth. 'You could almost *eat* him in those Chief Weasel leathers, couldn't you?'

'Is your father here for a reason?' asked Beth.

Cate scowled at Seb and Owen who'd sauntered over from the buffet to join them. Beth was pleased to see Seb had a full plate. He'd need all the sustenance he could get, given the unlikelihood of finding anything edible on the *Mutant Pizza* menu tonight. 'He likes putting the fear of God into the company occasionally,' said Cate. Seb nervously swallowed his mouthful. 'But he's talking to front-of-house about the panto too.'

'If he's decided what it's going to be,' said Fran.

'*Cinderella?*' suggested Owen. 'Can't you see the Voice as Prince Charming and Seb as Buttons?'

'Buttons?' squawked Seb, alarmed.

Beth grinned. She thought a comedy turn would do Seb good. Her heart gave a tiny tremor as Owen winked.

Cate was still watching Luke. 'What does he think I am? *Made* of credit?'

'If Ellery condescends to do panto,' said Fran. 'Him and his kids shows.'

Luke ambled back, handing Cate's phone over with a courtly bow and a breathtakingly beautiful smile. 'There's your answer,' she said acidly. 'Who needs the Voice for Prince Charming when we have Mr Bartholomew?'

Depending on your point of view, it was a good thing they'd booked a table at *Mutant Pizza*. The place was pulsing with light shows, customers and music. A thousand conflicting smells battled for supremacy in the air. Quite a lot of them, thought Beth, downing a glass of wine in an attempt to anaesthetise her tastebuds, were concentrated over their table where Owen, with zero sense of self-preservation, had ordered the Special Medley For Five. She had just bitten into the seriously under-described Chokin' Chili when a shrill shriek exploded in her ear. An eleven-year-old in a fluorescent pink top and an orange mini-skirt trimmed with sequins and fake fur was bobbing up and down next to her.

'You're my new teacher! I'm Chantelle!'

Induction day memories of an asymmetric blonde ponytail and a bouncing dazzle of non-uniform colours assaulted Beth's mind. 'Oh, er, yes.'

'We've been to see *Wind In The Willows.*' She waved the programme she was holding at Robin. 'You were one of the weasels. You're a really good dancer.'

'Hrmph,' muttered Robin into a wedge of We'll Meat Again.

'You were one too,' said Chantelle to Seb. 'My auntie says you're well fit.'

Seb's face had acquired a green tinge which was nothing to do with the lighting. It *could* have been reaction to the excitement of Last Night, but Beth was more inclined to blame the slice of East Meets West pizza which everyone else had avoided. She wasn't sure you *could* blend raw fish and baked beans in the same mouthful. He manfully found his photo in the programme and signed before pushing it across to Robin.

'Ooooh!' screeched Chantelle, hopping from foot to foot. 'I've just realised! You're one of the big boys! You stopped the bus for me when I nearly missed it!' She beamed a look of incipient adoration at him.

While Robin was scrawling his name and looking as though he wished the floor would swallow him up, Chantelle made a further exciting discovery. 'And *you* were the singing rabbit girl!' she screamed at Natalie. 'Can you sign too? You're much thinner in real life!'

Having polished off the decidedly odd Roque Fruit Salad, Owen picked up the last triangle of Chokin' Chilli. 'Ain't it the truth,' he drawled, biting into it.

Natalie took the programme awkwardly. Owen's eyes started watering. Beth passed him what was left of the house white. '*Natalie*

Trower,'he croaked. 'Not much of a ring to it. You'll have to find a better stage name than that.'

'Like Pendragon, I suppose?' muttered Natalie. 'What's your real name? Smith?'

Chantelle gave an agitated squeak and jiggled up and down. 'Are you Owen Pendragon? Mr Toad? Oh, you were my favourite! You were so *funny!* Can you sign too? But you're nothing *like* your photo!'

A faint wash of colour crossed Owen's face. 'It's an old one.' He signed with a theatrical flourish. 'Here you go. Enjoy the rest of your evening.'

Chantelle happily bounced off shouting to her aunt that she *knew* one of the weasels and Mr Toad was there too and she'd got the well fit one's autograph.

'How old?' murmured Beth as the others studied the ice-cream menu. (She hoped Nats and Rob would remember that the word surprise was a euphemism for cayenne or even, so rumour had it, pickle.)

Owen hunched his shoulders. 'Couple of years. OK ten. I was more photogenic at twenty-eight. Actors are vain.'

Beth moistened her lips. 'I'm forty-six.'

There was an infinitesimal silence underneath the thousand-decibel music. Owen looked straight into her eyes. For a moment they were alone in a crazy, psychedelic world. He smiled, not sardonic, not flirting,

78

not even faintly mocking. 'What's eight years?'

Sunday. Beth was alone in the lounge. Cate had already left for Oldham, Rob had gone swimming, Nats had taken a mug of tea upstairs and neither Seb nor Owen had surfaced yet. She sighed, wishing Robin hadn't suggested *Mutant Pizza*. It was a shocking waste of a meal out when they had them so rarely. *And* she'd had to restrict her wine consumption because of driving. Just for a moment she allowed herself a tiny fantasy in which Owen whisked her off in a cab to the Greek restaurant where she and Alan had once been. They'd had beef stew to die for and a glorious dessert wine, but Alan had refused to go again saying the waiters were overly familiar and he didn't approve of all that gloomy singing and the way the chef had burst out of the kitchen to have a shouting match with his brother-in-law half way through the meal. She was still smiling at the memory when the door opened.

'I don't know what you're so pleased about,' Owen grumbled. 'Remind me not to take Rob's advice again.'

He was wearing his towelling bathrobe, his eyes were half closed and his hair looked the way hers generally did first thing in the morning. The urge to run her fingers

79

through it was quite frighteningly over-powering. Beth scrambled to her feet before she forgot herself. 'I'll make a fresh pot of tea. At least you're not as bad as Seb. I assume that was him I heard throwing up in the middle of the night?'

'Certainly wasn't me. I've never been affluent enough to enjoy the luxury of dis-charging what I've paid good money for.'

Beth grinned. 'How about some dry toast? Charcoal is supposed to be good for the digestion.'

He sent her an old-fashioned look. 'Just tea, mistress. I'll let you know when I feel the need to torture myself again.'

When she brought it in, he was stretched out on the sofa with his eyes closed and his robe sliding apart. Beth very nearly dropped the mugs at this first comprehensive look at his chest. He might be ill and unshaven, but he had a wonderfully tough body, was the most fanciable man she'd seen for a long time and he was just *lying* there, all vulnerable and hands-on-ish. She took an extremely shaky breath, counted to three and said, 'I'll put it on the table.'

'Thanks,' he murmured. 'I'd kiss you if I didn't think it would be akin to you being mauled by an emery board.'

For the life of her, Beth couldn't help it. Just for an instant of time she brushed her fingers across his cheek 'Hmm, do you do nail shaping as well?'

His eyes flew open, twin shafts of startled hazel.

Beth retreated to her chair fast. 'Sorry,' she said, 'I shouldn't tease when you're not well.'

He picked up his tea and treated her to another long look. 'It's probably safer than when I *am* well.'

Beth gulped and buried herself back in work.

Seb mopped his plate on Monday morning with a regretful sigh. 'Last decent breakfast until Durham. This time tomorrow I'll be living on Mars Bars again.'

Owen cocked an eyebrow at him. 'I'll see if I can get you in with me next tour.'

'Don't you stay together?' asked Natalie, her chair as close to Seb's as it was possible to get without using mortise and tenon joints.

Seb shrugged. 'Sometimes we're with others in the cast, sometimes not. It's a pity we can't commute from here. It's been really nice this week.'

Natalie blushed. 'Excuse me!' said Beth with more vigour than she intended. 'I've got brand-new courses to prepare in the next three weeks and you lot aren't hugely conducive to work! Plus I need to take a day out to get some more clothes. My teaching ones will fall apart working full-time.'

Owen poured himself another mug of tea. 'Nats has got a nice pair of furry leggings you could borrow.'

Beth waited for the explosion, but all her daughter said was, 'The only good thing about the show being finished is not having to wear them again.'

'I heard Ned wants *Cinderella* to have singing *mice* in the panto...'

'He can't,' said Natalie triumphantly. 'The Corn Exchange put on *Cinderella* last year. They can't have it two years running.'

'Yeah, and the skanky company didn't want us at all!' Robin was still incensed, eight months on. 'Imagine not having a kid's chorus in the Christmas pantomime!'

'Sod it,' muttered Owen.

Beth felt a mild shock. 'That's the first time you've sworn all weekend. I must tell C – oh–'

Seb grinned. 'I miss Cate too. Unbelievable, isn't it? It already feels odd with her having gone off yesterday.'

'Had to,' said Owen. 'She was fitting-up at first light and *we've* got a rehearsal with the Oldham kids at two o'clock. Best get moving.'

A car hooted outside. 'That's Sue,' said Beth, looking at her daughter. 'Ready? You don't want to be late on your first day at Waitrose.'

'Oh God,' said Natalie, flustered.

To Beth's enormous surprise, Owen gave Natalie a hug *and she let him!* 'You'll walk it, sparrow. See you in November.'

Seb stood up too. 'Bye Nats,' he said and kissed her cheek.

Natalie turned bright red and made a strangulated sound. Outside Sue hooted again. 'Go,' said Beth. 'I'll pick you and Lisa up at four.'

'That was cruel,' chuckled Owen, after Seb had disappeared to finish packing. 'Making them say goodbye in front of us.'

'I'm cruel?' Beth picked up the teapot, only to find that it was empty. 'Who was winding her up, may I ask? And that's nothing to what I'll be if he doesn't give *me* a kiss when he goes.'

Owen's wicked hazel eyes met hers. 'What about me? Do I get to kiss you?'

The kitchen lurched around her. Beth felt her heartbeat speed up. 'Maybe in November,' she said, stalling. 'If you say nice things about my cooking for a whole week.'

His smile became downright indecent. 'I'll start composing eulogies now.'

Spurred on by Natalie's cautious phone call about the staff mark-down table, Beth arrived at the supermarket early to pick the girls up. She'd spent the day attempting to organise her ideas on what she'd be teaching this year, but hazel eyes had kept intruding into her thoughts to such an extent that not only had she got very little done, she was also now seeing Owen everywhere. Like over in the dairy aisle for example, where Natalie was rearranging the milk. No, she'd done it again! She ducked rapidly behind the cut-flowers display telling herself she wasn't being cowardly at all. It was simply that it wouldn't be fair to embarrass Nats by having a stand-up row with Alan in front of her daughter's temporary colleagues.

'Natalie! What are you doing here?'

Beth peered furtively between bunches of unseasonable chrysanthemums. Two pints of semi-skimmed had slid out of Natalie's appalled fingers.

'Dad! I'm – um – working this week.'

'Why?'

A familiar, idiotic-question-or-what expression appeared on her daughter's face. 'To earn money!'

'Oh, right.' Her father watched as she clumsily shunted cartons into place. 'Enjoying it?'

'It's OK.' Beth could see Natalie wishing he'd just take the double cream or whatever it was he was there for and go away! She shot a look at the basket on his arm: smoked salmon, baguettes, strawberries, balsamic vinegar, bottle of wine. On a Monday after-noon? He'd never done that for her!

Alan patted his daughter's shoulder. 'Well done, darling.' It was probably, thought Beth bitterly, the proudest he'd ever been of her.

The evening felt remarkably flat. As did the next morning with a steady drizzle, no breakfasts to make, no baritone voice in the shower, no one squeezing the last mug of tea out of the pot before she could get to it and no Aztec For Men drifting about the hallway. Also, everyone had realised the show was over. She had just finished roughing out her Year Seven course when the phone rang for the twelfth time. 'Yes?' she snarled into the receiver, stabbing the page with her pen and thinking it was hardly surprising she'd written *The Irritated Mum* instead of *The Illustrated Mum*.

'Beth? It's Owen.'

'Owen?' Her heart gave a giant leap and the pen went skittering across the table. 'What's the matter? I mean, why are you–? Did you forget something?'

His voice sounded odd. It must be distorted by the phone. 'I'm fine. Not much going on and I wondered whether Waitrose survived yesterday?'

Beth's pulse played leapfrog up and down her veins. '*It* did. The girls spent the evening in front of the TV with their feet on pillows.' She tried desperately to think of something to say. *Had any good showers recently?* came to mind. She suppressed it and settled for a feeble 'How's Oldham?'

'Wet. Not a chaperone in shorts anywhere. Got your lessons sorted yet?'

'I wish! I'm attempting Year Seven. It's *years* since I last taught eleven-year-olds.'

He chuckled. 'Probably like fire-eating, you never really forget how. Oh, Seb's looking hungry already.'

Fire-eating indeed! A smile curved Beth's mouth at Owen's constant unexpectedness. 'He can't be. He ate enough breakfast yesterday for a week.' She recalled with a sudden rush the way Seb had kissed her cheek as he'd left and that Owen too had put his arm round her for a split-second and aimed a kiss somewhere near her ear. Nervousness flooded her. 'You'll never guess – one of my interruptions was Alan demanding to know why I hadn't told him Nats was filling shelves at Waitrose.'

'Nice of him to take an interest.'

'Wasn't it? Pity he wasn't equally concerned about supporting her during the show.' She took a quick breath. 'Owen, I wanted to say – thanks for the other day. For being there I mean. For noticing.'

'No sweat.'

'And I'm sorry *Mutant Pizza* made you ill.'

'My fault. I should have insisted you tell me where *you* wanted to go. I won't make that mistake again.'

Again? There was going to be an again? Beth swallowed, breathless. 'I remembered afterwards there's a little Greek place I've always fancied going back to. We only went there once. Alan hated it.'

'Sounds good to me already.'

And now there really *wasn't* anything to say. She felt like a tongue-tied sixteen-year-old about to have an asthma attack.

'You'll want to get back to your syllabus,' said Owen. 'Have fun.'

She didn't want him to go. The realisation brought her up short. But she felt better than she had all day. 'I might at that,' she said, surprised. 'Thanks for phoning.'

'Beth, you'll have to stop thanking people for doing something they wanted to do anyway. You never know where it might lead.'

She put the phone down slowly. You never knew indeed. Moistening her lips, she dialled 1471 and made a note of his mobile number.

CHAPTER 5

'Luke!' yelled Cate, racing down the stage alley. He couldn't be far. He'd only just gone past the office door when the phone had rung. She saw him and pelted to the end of the street, dodging Bank Holiday shoppers. 'Luke!' she screamed again. He turned in his familiar dreamy fashion just as she tripped on an uneven paving stone. Damn, she thought, arms flailing as the pavement came up to meet her.

But Luke caught her with surprising firmness. 'Everything really does come to those who wait,' he murmured with a smile.

'You may well think so,' she panted. 'Ellery's broken down on the A1 and you're covering.'

Luke's hold tightened. 'I'm playing Rat tonight?'

Jesus, he was unnerving tee shirt to tee shirt. Cate fought for breath and hoped he'd put it down to her being unfit. She pulled away. 'Yes. Ned wants you in rehearsal with April and Owen right now. Come *on!* The mood my uncle's in, he'll give Rat to the front-of-house runner if you're not on stage in ten seconds flat.'

His deep green eyes pulsed excitement as he started to run. Cate could feel the exhilaration coursing through him. When they reached the stage alley, his excitement fizzed out into the open like a live thing. He laughed wildly, caught her waist and swung her up to meet his lips.

Jesus-God, was Cate's last coherent thought as he kissed her, five thousand volts of electricity crackling around them.

'I think I'm going to be sick.'

Owen looked at Seb tolerantly in the mirror. God, it took him back. 'Not in my room, you aren't. Do you want to dress in here tonight?'

Seb swallowed. 'Won't the others think it's odd?'

'Tell 'em you're worried you might break an ankle on the stairs.'

'Don't *say* that! I'll bring my kit down. I wish Mum and Dad weren't away so I could ring them. At least there would be someone rooting for me.'

Owen flicked a glance at the younger man. 'How about Beth?' he said casually. 'Rob and Nats can do some long-distance cheering.'

Seb's face lit up. 'Would she mind? Oh, my phone's on charge at the digs.'

Owen picked up his mobile from the make-up counter and tapped in Beth's number.

'Here. Pass her to me when you've finished.'

Seb wiped his hand on his jeans, fortunately too hyped-up to notice that Owen had the landlady of three weeks ago's code at his fingertips. 'Beth? Hi, it's Seb Merchant. I – I've just heard I'm playing Chief Weasel tonight but Mum and Dad are away and I needed to tell *someone* and Owen suggested... Oh, thanks... Well, I don't suppose I'll be *that* good. No, Luke's not ill, he's playing Rat because Ellery's car broke down on the way from Durham so I've got to play *him*... Thanks. Owen wants a word.' He passed the phone back with a shamefaced grin. 'Better now. I'll get my bag.'

As Seb left the room, Cate skidded into him and demanded that he eat the cheeseburger she'd got him *now* before he did anything else. Owen kicked the door closed. 'Hi, Beth. You didn't mind Seb ringing, did you? It's madness here.'

Her laugh was warm in his ear. 'Of course not. Will he be OK?'

'Yes, he's a bloody natural once he gets on stage but you should have seen him when Cate broke the news. He folded up on a stool and couldn't speak until she jammed a piece of chocolate in his mouth.'

'Poor lad. It's a good thing Nats and Rob are out with Alan or they'd be nagging me to blow next week's housekeeping on an overnight trip to Leicester to watch. I'm sure they think he ought to have been Chief Weasel in the first place.'

Alan. He felt a sharp twinge of jealousy at her ex's name. Which was, of course, ridiculous. 'So did some of us,' he said. 'Where's Alan taken them?'

'*A Trip Round Merrie Englande*. It's a Doone Hennessy Corporate Special. Hampton Court, the Cutty Sark and a rapid burst of *As You Like It* at the Globe.'

'Bloody hell, in this weather? They'll be cross as cats by the time they're back.'

'It could have been worse. She wanted a Genuine Banquet in the schedule, but was frustrated by the medieval attitude of the venues.'

What with the tempestuous voices and racing feet outside his dressing room door, Beth's spontaneous laughter flew across the intervening miles like a breath of fresh air. He could almost see her eyes dancing and her dark hair swinging smoothly back from her shoulders. Without conscious thought, his voice took off without him. 'Beth, I know you go back to school next week, but how do you feel about a paying guest the week after?'

The laughter died quite suddenly. 'A paying guest? You, you mean?'

Jesus, what had got into him? Owen swung to the mirror and stared at his reflection in shock.

'Owen?'

He heard the consternation in her voice and fought to keep his own light. 'I've got some work to do during our rest week but my flat's being redecorated.'

He wasn't convinced she believed him. *He* wouldn't have believed him. A small lifetime later, she spoke. 'So long as you don't burn the place down while I'm out. I'm not sure Alan's paid the insurance premium.'

He put his phone away by rote, trying not to confront what he'd just done. Work, he thought. When you were working, everything else was shut out. He headed up the corridor. And stopped abruptly as Cate's harassed voice issued from the greenroom.

'You want Stella? OK, but we're horribly busy, Beth. We've got a panic rehearsal, I've got to find food and drink for the entire company by five o'clock and it's a flaming Bank Holiday. Here she is.'

Stella's voice. 'Yes, I see, and you're worried about giving a stranger the run of your house. No problem, Beth. He's been with *FOOTLIGHTS* for six years with never a hint of trouble. Trust me, in the theatre world you'd know! And it's perfectly true about the work. Quite smart of him to do it up there.'

Owen stood motionless as a statue. She'd checked up on him! He could hardly believe it. Indignation warred with – with what?

Chagrin? Guilt? Guilt that m
right not to trust him? Chagr
once he really hadn't been pl
Except ... well, yes, he had to
low-down idea for the wee
sneaked into his head...

'MR TOAD!' roared Ned from the wings.
At the same time, Seb hurtled down the
stairs with his bag.

'Sorry, were you waiting for me? Cate
force-fed me a burger, would you believe!
Said she didn't want the responsibility of me
passing out on stage. Honestly! Just because
I knocked myself up a couple of times at
college and she happened to be stage-
managing at the time. She's such a know-
all!'

'I heard that!' yelled Cate.

'ANY TIME YOU'RE READY, MR PEN-
DRAGON!'

Cate slammed out of the greenroom.
There you are! Fancy popping along to the
stage? Only my uncle appears to think the
audio link isn't working and I *really* don't
want the acoustics blown on top of
everything else!'

After some thought, Owen rang Beth next
morning. 'It went well,' he said in the most
cheerful voice in his repertoire. 'The Voice's
car is still in dock, so Luke and Seb are
covering again today. You'd hardly have

ast night they hadn't been playing parts all tour.'

ood. Congratulate Seb for us, won't u.'

'Sure. Beth–' Hell, what was it he wanted to say? Something to banish that trace of reserve from her voice. 'Thanks for letting me stay after the tour. I didn't think until after I'd asked how it might have looked.'

She laughed properly. 'Don't mention it. Sue thinks I'm mad letting a man I only met three weeks ago stay alone in the house while I'm at school.'

A man, what's more, who's been ringing me up every week since on the flimsiest of excuses. She didn't have to say it. The thought was there between them. Owen felt himself grow tense.

'Still,' she continued, 'Stella said *FOOT-LIGHTS* would go bail for you, and I need the cash, so I'm inclined to live dangerously.'

Bloody hell, she'd *told* him she'd checked him out. 'Christ!' he said aloud.

'Yes, pretty flattering, I thought.'

But that wasn't what he'd meant at all.

By Wednesday morning his mind had cleared. He woke to the succulent smell of bacon and mushrooms and reflected that in Fenbourne he'd be lucky to get a bowl of cornflakes before Beth and the kids raced off to school. It wasn't often his mouth bypassed his common sense, but he was beginning to be glad it had. Yes, his flat in London was clean and comfortable. It was also empty. And therein lay the rub and his body knew it. With a sense of near-astonishment, Owen finally admitted that ever since Cambridge he'd been thinking virtually non-stop of smooth dark hair framing a quirky, no-longer-young face with a mouth that flashed into a laugh at the exact moment his own did.

There was a tap on his door. 'Here's your cuppa, Mr Pendragon. There's plenty of hot water and breakfast will be ready when you are.'

Owen drank his tea and vowed never to let Beth know how his regular landladies looked after him. Alan must have been bloody insane to have left her. That very first evening he'd looked across the room to see her face dissolve into a smile and he'd wanted to know her better. The day they'd left, he'd been conscious of a desire to stay. Him who'd been avoiding commitment all his life! He was greedy for the sound of her voice, for information on what she was doing; thirsty for anything which added to his knowledge of her. And his new idea meant he could make the week in Fenbourne really work in that respect. It was so providential he almost had no choice but to go for it.

Ellery Valentine blew into Leicester on

Wednesday. Seb took his demotion back to the Frenchman/weasel philosophically.

'You're crazy,' Cate told him as he stripped off beret, loose trousers and stripy tee shirt in the wings, 'you were so *bad* as Chief Weasel it was scary. How can you possibly be glad to be in the ranks again?'

Seb flushed as she clamped silver bracelets round his wrists and turned him round to check the tape on his body-mike. 'It's just acting, Cate. I don't feel as confident as it comes out.'

'Well you should,' scolded Cate. 'Because it comes out bloody brilliant.'

Seb gave her a harried smile and escaped to the opposite-prompt side. She noticed one of his chains had come adrift and darted after him.

'So the child genius is a common-or-garden weasel once more. I'm surprised that beret still fits, your head must be so big by now.'

Cate froze in the darkness. The speaker was hidden by the flats, but she'd know Annis's voice anywhere.

'Chosen your part in *Tin Pan Ali* yet?' That was Perry at a guess.

Annis gave an unpleasant laugh. 'Nothing less than Ali Baba himself, surely, for our prodigy.'

'Quiet in the wings,' said Cate impersonally. She tugged Seb backwards and fastened the loose end of chain. His face looked white and set. 'Moron,' she whispered, one breath above audibility. 'They're just jealous.' She squeezed his arm and melted back to the prompt exit.

Owen bounded off, pursued by a selection of policemen and a scattering of laughter and applause from the audience. As soon as they were out of sight, the policemen stripped off jackets and trousers and pulled on rabbit heads. On stage April began to sing. 'Christ, it's flat. What's the matter with everyone?'

Cate scooped up abandoned uniforms. 'The Voice is sulking because we didn't miss him enough.'

'Bloody Prima Donna. I'll sort him.'

Cate's eyebrows rose. 'Thanks,' she said.

Owen didn't bother to disguise his disgust. 'Why the hell should the rest of us work our bollocks off just so he can ruin it!'

'Bags? Books? Pencil cases? Lunch money?'

'Yes and we've got *our* stuff too, Mum,' said Robin.

'Cheeky brat,' said Beth. 'God, I'm nervous.'

'They're brand new Seventh Years and it's the first day of term. They're not going to trash the school yet.'

'Thank you, Nats. Sadly, I saw them on induction day; you may be nearer the truth than you know.' But standing in her classroom later, all trace of nerves abruptly left her. *I remember this*, she thought, as she told the new 7.1 to find themselves places. She smiled reassuringly at a stolid child in plaits; memory glowed in her. *This* was what she'd been missing during the past years of teaching rarified top-stream GCSE and A-level courses. Guiding young people, helping them grow. It was why she'd wanted to teach in the first place.

Yob slouched in, his Mohican newly dyed in the school colours. Beth took this as an encouraging omen. The report from his primary school had suggested he might not turn up at all. Her eyes travelled the form, fitting names to faces. She paused in momentary astonishment as a girl with about five feet of loose fair hair got it tangled in the doorway. Ella, she recalled, whose parents ran an Italian trattoria. She'd thought when looking over the records how useful it was going to be having someone with a working knowledge of pizza on the compulsory Charity Food Stall day. The cheerful redhead last seen hijacking Beth's English lesson helped Ella get free. Lord, you'd think with modern hygiene regulations it would be inbuilt in the girl to keep her hair tidy! Maybe she was rebelling. Beth revised her thoughts on asking about discounted takeaways.

A studious-looking boy sidled in, followed by a girl with self-important ginger bunches tied up with large green bows. She and her friend took the central desks in the front row. Beth's heart sank a little. Felicity May Rose Goodchild. There were already four messages in Beth's pigeon hole from Mrs Goodchild regarding her unique and precious daughter.

'Settle down,' she said. 'Yes, thank you Felicity, I can see Ella's hair is caught in Star's watch.' She hid her mouth, almost laughing aloud as she remembered Owen's words last night when he'd rung to wish her luck.

'They won't all be little sods,' he'd said.

Strangely enough, just at this moment she didn't care if they were. She *wanted* to know them; she *wanted* to set their eleven-year-old feet pointing in the direction of adulthood. For the first time she even felt charitable towards Alan for having made it necessary for her to be a form-tutor because of the extra money.

As she opened the register and smiled at her class, she reflected that though she'd known him such a short time, Owen with his wicked eyes and sideways smile was far more vivid in her mind than her ex-husband. Whatever his motives were, her own doubts were fading. It would be good to have him in the house again. He made her laugh.

There was a party on Saturday night to celebrate the end of the run. Cate and the crew entered the function room of the pub after get-out, considerably later than the performing contingent of the company.

'If there's one thing I hate,' commented Graham, 'it's being sober when everyone else is high as a bloody kite.'

Luke came up with a tray. 'I persuaded the barmaid to keep you a bottle of wine.'

Everyone took a drink and drifted off. 'Why?' said Cate.

His deep green eyes laughed into hers. 'So I wouldn't have to fight to be allowed to buy you one.'

Cate regarded him. Last week, when she'd told him he was playing Rat, he'd been so exultant he'd kissed her. The memory did disturbing things to her diaphragm. 'You've never fought for anything in your life.'

'Waste of energy,' agreed Luke. He gestured to the minuscule dance floor. 'Shall we?'

But Mel shimmered sinuously over and took his arm. She was wearing something tiny in black satin which clung where it touched and it touched everywhere. Cate, whose end-of-run party outfit consisted of taking off the sweatshirt she'd done get-out in, hated her. 'You carry on,' she said. 'I've got drinking to catch up on.'

'Hi, Cate,' said Seb. 'You look nice.'

Cate flicked a disbelieving glance at her dusty jeans.

'Normal, I mean,' said Seb. He swayed; it occurred to Cate that he was drunk. 'I never know what to do at end-of-run parties. I must have been away the week we covered them at college.'

'Ask Owen,' said Cate.

Seb smiled in an ingenuous, boy-next-door-growing-up sort of way. 'He's got me into some of his digs next tour. He thinks I need taking in hand.'

'You jammy sod! His digs are the cushiest on the circuit.'

Seb hiccuped. 'I hardly even notice his swearing now. Do you remember Beth saying "shit" and clapping her hand over her mouth?'

'I must have been at the theatre. I'm glad we're doing the panto there.'

He steadied himself against her arm. 'I wish we knew what it was going to be. It was *Robinson Crusoe* last year at Swindon. Adrian writes the music.'

'I heard. Who does the book?'

'Friend of his, I suppose. Ellery says he's not doing panto whatever it is. Isn't that weird? Do you want to dance?'

'No.' She studied him with foreboding. 'Do you?'

'It'd be nice to be like the others,' said Seb wistfully.

'Jesus,' muttered Cate. She flushed as Luke's lazy eyes met hers across Mel's languid body and in a moment of inattention let Seb tug her towards the dance floor. She swallowed the last of the wine. 'I hope you appreciate how much damage this is going to do my reputation!'

Owen felt as if high octane fuel rather than blood was zinging around his veins at Mrs Harris's breakfast table on Sunday morning. Cate eyed him suspiciously. Owen thought he knew why. 'Hangover, poppet?' he asked, by way of leading her on.

'Don't get them. Besides, after drinking with the crew for the past five months, half-a-dozen glasses of wine are a drop in the ocean.'

He moved in for the kill. 'Enough for you to sink your principles and dance with our Seb, though. Not to mention a certain green-eyed charmer–'

'But not you, so I couldn't have been that drunk,' she shot back.

'I was going to ask towards the end of the evening, but you were otherwise engaged.' He smirked as a tide of red suffused her face. 'Fear not, sweeting, even if the rest of the cast saw you in that taxi with Luke, they'll assume they were hallucinating.'

'Sometimes I really hate you.'

He hefted the pot. 'Tea? Or are you on

black coffee?'

She aimed a snake-venom look at him. 'You have no idea how much of a misery I am going to make your life over the next tour.'

'Can't touch me until tomorrow week.'

'Jesus, you really are in a good mood. How foul.'

Some five hours later, however, Owen was feeling more than a little jittery. First night nerves were one thing, they vanished as soon as you set foot on stage; how the hell was he going to manage at Beth's for a week without blowing any chance he might have with her sky high? He pulled up outside the house and took a deep breath before hauling his bag out of the boot.

'Hi, sparrow, how's school?' Damn, too loud.

'Horrible,' said Natalie, opening the door wide. 'They've made me a bloody prefect.'

'Hi, Owen,' called Robin from the dining room. He had books all over the table and wore the deeply injured countenance of a person whose own mother didn't trust him to do homework unless it was where she could see him. 'What do you know about algebra?'

Owen blenched. 'Enough to stay well away from it!'

'Me too. Bummer, isn't it?'

Beth came into the hall, back-lit from the

kitchen, her dark hair swinging smooth and free. As their eyes met, Owen caught an echo of his own nervousness, an answering pulse. His tension evaporated a little. 'It's been a bastard of a journey,' he said, smiling. 'Any tea in the pot?'

Over supper, eaten in a kitchen even more untidy than he remembered, he filled them in on the rest of the tour and the *Tin Pan Ali* casting, making them giggle helplessly as he mimicked Monty's offended tones and Mel's displeased strut.

Natalie retaliated with her Waitrose fortnight, and Robin turned the tennis course Alan had sent him on into a week of laughs instead of the solid boredom which Owen suspected it had actually been.

'And how about you?' he asked Beth, finally allowing himself to look at her properly. 'What's it like teaching full-time again?'

'It's only been a week,' Beth demurred.

'She's a wreck,' crowed Natalie. 'Revenge is ours.'

'And you should see her class!' Robin went off into whoops.

Owen cleared his throat. 'Actually, I was wondering if I might.'

'Are you interested in alien life forms then?'

'No, I – er – really would like to come into school for a morning.'

Beth looked at him with astonishment, the other two with disbelief. 'Why ever?' they said in unison.

'To observe,' said Owen in an off-hand voice. His eyes slid away from their sceptical looks. 'Find out the latest buzz-words, the newest jokes.' It sounded a little flimsy now he said it aloud.

'You won't get them from Mum's form,' said Natalie. 'Most of them live on another planet.'

'And you really don't want to go there,' added Robin. 'Remember Chantelle from *Mutant Pizza?* The others are worse.'

'The thing is, Owen,' said Beth, ignoring her children, 'you need permission from the Head and she'll want to know why.'

A wave of embarrassment surged through Owen. He hadn't felt like this for years. 'I'm writing the Christmas Panto,' he mumbled. 'It helps if it's topical.'

'Wicked,' said Robin.

'Why didn't you say so straight off?' chided Beth. 'I'll ask tomorrow.'

For once Owen was at a loss for words. A mad mixture of exhilaration and shame bubbled inside him. He'd got away with using the panto as an excuse to watch her at work. But there was something else – he struggled to place it. She hadn't made any derisory comments; she'd accepted it as a perfectly normal thing for him to be doing.

Ever since he and Adrian had first collaborated on the annual pantomime four years ago he'd hidden his authorship from the cast, knowing full well what the sniping and sarcasm was likely to be, but it dawned on him now that Beth didn't doubt the script would be anything but good. She had perfect faith in him. He stared at her, his world at a standstill.

Natalie was talking. 'What's it going to be?'

He reassembled his wits. *'Jack And The Beanstalk.'*

'And what are we?' demanded Robin.

'Kids from the Old-Woman-Who-Lived-In-A-Shoe Children's Home.' He grinned at Natalie, stinging with relief. 'Not a bob-tail in sight, although I can't make any promises about gingham.'

She stuck her tongue out at him. 'What's Seb? What are you?'

'Trade secret.'

Beth's head throbbed with the aftermath of too much wine as she dried up bedtime mugs and put everything ready for the morning. After all her soul-searching, Owen was here and nothing had changed. He'd fitted in as if he'd never been away, laughing with the kids, telling them about the tour, giving her his sideways teasing glances.

Upstairs the spare room door closed

softly. Beth's head jerked up, her heart jumping, but there was no further noise. She set her jaw and forced herself to drink two glasses of water. Enforced temperance obviously wasn't good for a person. It made their body forget how to cope with alcohol, made them unrealistically optimistic. Owen was here to work. He'd said so. And now that he'd told them what he was working on, it made a depressing amount of sense. And yet something *was* different. Beth couldn't escape the feeling that his whole performance this evening had been very nearly an act. There was something else, something she'd almost glimpsed when he'd mentioned the pantomime. It worried at her in much the same way that next door's terrier nipped the postman's ankles all the way up the path.

Turning off the lights, she went upstairs. Doubts pressed in on her along with the darkness. Perhaps she'd been kidding herself all along, imagining nuances because she *expected* them given Owen's teasing comments last time and his phone calls and the fact that he was here at all. She shifted in the bed with a sense of desolation. It hadn't felt so empty since Alan had first left. She thought of Owen, lying just across the hallway, and was crippled by a stab of loneliness. What would he do if she went in to him now? Run a mile, probably. Pack his bag and hightail it to London, decorators or no decorators. She was too old for him anyway. (But 'What's eight years?' he'd said in *Mutant Pizza*.) And her body was saggy and tired compared to the supple, stretchy chorus girls he was used to. (He likes your legs. He said so. And he also said it wouldn't be safe for you to tease him if he was well.) Beth stared up at the dark ceiling, not knowing what to think, not knowing what to do, not even knowing how she'd act if he *did* make a move. Dear God, why did life have to be so complicated?

CHAPTER 6

'You can come in on Wednesday,' said Beth. 'My lot have got English with me followed by Drama with Sue. I'm hoping it's just because they're still shell-shocked by the move from small, cuddly primary school, but I've got the nastiest suspicion that 7.1 is the Head's revenge on me for resisting turning full-time for so long.'

'The weirder they are the better,' said Owen easily. He poured out two mugs of tea and leant against the dresser to drink his. He'd been writing up a storm all day and her coming back like this at the end of it was the icing on the cake. The whole pantomime was mapped out in his head now, he'd had a long phone call with Adrian about the musical numbers and felt tremendous. If it wasn't for the pull of watching Beth at work, he could almost resent taking half a day off. 'Cate doesn't think actors would recognise the real world unless it grabbed them by the throat and tore their larynxes out,' he added.

Beth laughed. 'From what I've seen backstage she's absolutely right.' She took a swallow of the tea he'd made. His heart flipped oddly as she closed her eyes with a sigh of appreciation. 'Oh, and I don't know whether you were planning on writing in the evenings as well, but Sue wondered if you'd like to go over to hers with us tomorrow? She generally feeds us once a week. Says it stops me getting paranoid about counting the cost of every swirl of cream and clove of garlic. No obligation if you'd rather not, but she *is* a far better cook than me.' She smiled at him. 'And you'll like Pete. It'll be fun.'

As it happened, Owen would much rather not. This week was intended to get to know *her.* But she was smiling in a casual, friendly fashion and he was seduced by the tug of acceptance. He shrugged. 'Why not?'

Now this, thought Owen the next night, was seriously weird. He was a self-confessed hedonist, right? Yet even with two of Pete's generous scotches cauterising his nerve endings and a smell way better than anything Beth produced wafting from the kitchen, he *still* wanted to be at Beth's, telling her how the day's writing had gone while Rob killed off a galaxy-load of aliens and Natalie ran up the phone bill in the background. She came in carrying plates, dark hair swinging, laughing at something Sue had said, and he felt his heart lift to meet her.

'What's this?' she teased, looking at his brimming glass. 'Is Pete bribing you to write Lisa and Jack good parts in the panto?'

He switched easily to dinner-guest mode. 'You know how it is. I've told him I'm incorruptible, but hell, if it makes him happy...' He shrugged mock-helplessly.

'What will you, have, Beth?' Pete waved a hospitable hand at the drinks.

'You only offer because you know I'm driving. I'll have wine with the meal.'

Natalie was sitting stony-faced in a corner of the settee (due to Lisa and Jason acting as if they hadn't eaten for a week on the doorstep). 'Pretty soon you won't need to worry,' said Owen. 'Nats can drive.' She looked up, ponytail flying. Loss jabbed him unexpectedly. How long since *he'd* felt so bad about something as daft as a mate pulling and him not? 'Yes, just over a year and the road will belong to her.' He was rewarded by a faint smile at the allusion to *Wind In The Willows*.

'Ahem,' called a plaintive voice from the kitchen. 'I don't like to bother anyone when you're all having a good time, but I've run out of gin in here...'

'That's my wife,' said Pete fondly, and strolled out with the bottle.

Beth grinned. 'I'll warn you now she's going to invite you to *Stagestruck* on Saturday to see what the kids are capable of. I did tell her you probably already knew, but there's no arguing with a juniper-soaked drama teacher.'

Bloody hell, not *more* time away from Beth! But he kept his expression under control. 'I suppose it's fair exchange for a good meal.' He cocked his head as the front door clicked. 'Love's young dreamers have finally managed to say goodbye.'

In a flash, Natalie shot over to the music centre as if she'd been immersed in the CD collection all along. Owen winked at her. She was learning.

Beth lay in bed full of good food and good wine and good company and more laughter than she'd had in weeks – and wide bloody awake again. For all she'd tried to kid herself that Owen was simply another guest at Sue's table, it hadn't worked. She'd felt in her bones that they were very nearly a couple. She'd watched him laughing uproariously at Pete's earthy jokes (in the way that Alan never had, Pete being only a plumber who still got his hands dirty), she'd listened to his anecdotes of theatrical life, she'd thanked him silently for not downplaying the frequently grotty bits. She'd seen Sue nod approval, seen Natalie's eyes widen as she'd made the connection that not everything stage-related was glamorous. But most scarily of all, she'd seen the way he'd looked when she came in after helping Sue clear away. She'd seen the tiny 'Good, you're back, it hasn't been the same without you,' smile in his eyes. And God help her, she'd smiled back.

And yet after a last cup of tea, he'd said thanks for taking him and good-night-sleep-well and now she was in here and he was in the spare room and all she could think about was how nice his chest had looked that time his bathrobe had slid open when he was ill and how she'd quite like to explore it with her fingers.

The real problem was that forty-six years of middle-class conditioning had not equipped Beth for one-night stands. Or even one-week stands. In her world it was commitment or nothing and she'd already decided she was *never* going down that road again, not after Alan.

'Nice room,' said Owen next morning, strolling over to Beth's classroom window. Maybe his vision was still impaired from the scotch and wine consumption of the previous evening, but the modern-art statue (a misguided governor's gift to the school) looked even odder from this angle. There was writing on what might have been the statue's head. 'Hey, do you know this says–'

'Yes,' said Beth hastily. 'Given the spelling, we suspect Yob's arch-enemy. The janitor's advertising for a sand-blaster.' She moved a chair to the side of the room. 'Will this do? Do you want to take notes?'

'I'm an actor,' Owen reminded her. 'Remembering stuff comes with the job.' Not that there would be much. You could get all the latest language off the TV. But he hungered to watch Beth teaching. It was the reason he was here. It was almost becoming obsessional.

'This *is* 7.1.' She rummaged for a pen and notepad. 'Bet you a bottle of Supasava Bulgarian you'll need this.'

Owen watched the first kids straggle through the door. Beth turned to greet them and was his no longer. It was worse than last night at dinner. He felt a pain as sharp as bereavement.

'Right,' said Beth as she closed the register. 'The more observant amongst you will have noticed that we have a visitor.'

Owen felt his lips twitch. The kid by the window wouldn't; he was already dozing off. How come Beth hadn't spotted him and said something?

'His name is Mr Pendragon and he will be with us for English and Drama. He is a writer observing life in a large school.'

A girl Owen associated with acute indigestion bounced in her chair. 'No, he isn't! He's an actor! He was Mr Toad in *Wind in the Willows!* You are, aren't you? You signed my programme in *Mutant Pizza*.'

'Hey! I saw that! Wow, was that you? You were really good!'

'*Mutant Pizza?* Blimey, it's well expensive there.'

'I went once and I was sick. They do horrible things to the ice cream.'

'Coo, are you famous?' asked a shock-headed boy next to the dozing one.

They could almost have modelled for Wee Willie Winkie and Little Boy Blue, thought Owen, amused. 'No, not really,' he said. 'I'm–'

'Mrs Trower,' interrupted a carroty-haired girl with bunches and large bows.

'Yes, Felicity?'

'I've got a letter for you from my Mummy.'

'Another one? Thank you. I'll read it–'

'It's to say we're getting too much homework. My Mummy says too much homework is bad for people.'

Owen had had years of practice in keeping a straight face. He gave Beth eight out of ten as she said, 'I'll make an appointment for your mother to talk to the Year Tutor. Homework develops and extends the work you do in lessons. It's important.'

A boy with a rainbow Mohican had glazed over. A lad with glasses was telling the world his dad had bought him a PC to do *his* homework on. Owen turned to survey the rest of the class and found that now he'd started to think in terms of nursery rhymes, lots more characters were clamouring for recognition in his head.

Chantelle was leaping up and down (Jack-Be-Nimble, perhaps?). Another girl was disentangling her friend's long hair from her own crammed-full PE bag. Owen stared at the long-haired one in fascination. None of the awful Felicity's (Little Bo Peep? Mary Mary?) oversized bows here for decoration. Instead there were beads, tiny pasta stars, a sprinkling of bronze chrysanthemum petals, a cobweb or two and even a biro tangled in her hair. Sally-Go-Round-The-Moon to the life. His admiration of Beth exploded to fill the room; how ever did she teach this collection of oddballs and remain sane?

A buzzer sounded. 'Registration is now officially English,' said Beth over 7.1's increasingly noisy observations regarding homework. 'Books out please.'

Owen's eyes slewed to Dozy. The shock-headed boy had nudged him awake and was getting books out for him. His fingers groped for the notepad.

The Mohican's hand grazed the air. 'I ain't got no book. Me bruvver sold it down the market.'

7.1 swivelled to look at him, mouths agape. 'Then tell your brother he had better get me another copy of *The Illustrated Mum*, or send in £3.99 to pay for a new one,' said Beth with unimpaired calm.

'Mrs Trower,' said Felicity importantly. 'At our *old* school, Yob wasn't *ever* allowed to

116

take things home because his brother *always* sold them.'

By the end of the hour Owen had filled ten pages with notes and sketches, was incredulous that Beth had not so far been tempted to strangle Felicity with her own ribbons, and was determined never, ever to visit the estate where Yob (and presumably his brother) lived.

'Drama,' mused Beth. Owen tore his eyes away from where the girl with the long hair had just swept up someone's pencil case and where the dozing child was being fitted into his backpack by his obliging friend, to see her skimming the class with a faint frown. Her expression cleared. 'Star, would you see Mr Pendragon doesn't get lost on the way to the Drama Studio?'

A red-haired girl with the personality of an unharnessed sun beamed at him. 'OK, and if we do, Spike will find us.'

Beth turned to Owen with a smile which squeezed his heart. 'Star's brother has built-in radar. He must have been late to three-quarters of his lessons last week because he was directing 7.1 around the building. Enjoy the rest of your morning.' And in a much lower voice she added, 'I'll see you at home.' His last sight of her before the irrepressible Star towed him from the room was of her rubbing her forehead before putting away one set of books and getting out another.

Beth dropped her box of books, shut the front door and leant back against it. God, what a day. Having Owen distractingly on the edge of her vision and playing merry hell with her concentration for the first hour had only been the start. It was just as well her straitened circumstances restricted the buying of alcohol to one bottle of cheap red every other Saturday night or she'd be a dipso by the end of term.

Mind, a lot of today's angst could be blamed fairly and squarely on the Music department. It should have been obvious two minutes into 7.1's initial lesson last week that Chantelle in particular oughtn't to be sat anywhere *near* the expensive new keyboards Music were so proud of, let alone actually allowed to use them. And certainly not paired up with hyperactive, I-wonder-what-happens-if-you-plug-this-lead-in-here Shock. Most of Beth's lunch hour had been spent in phone calls to Chantelle's mother and Shock's, first of all explaining why their children were being given detentions and secondly reassuring them that it had actually been a very small explosion and no one had been hurt. And *then* Ursula Goodchild had rung to see why there hadn't been any feedback yet from the note she'd sent only that morning with Felicity. It had taken all

Beth's self-control not to bite the woman's head off. Tea, she thought, straightening up. And noticed the answerphone flashing.

'Beth, I'm back from Quito do Lago. Useful contacts. Splendid golf. I've got a window in my schedule on Thursday so I'll be over about six-thirty. Nothing too heavy to eat. Don't want to spoil the flavour of the Portuguese white I brought back.'

Jesus, that was all she needed! Alan *always* did this – invited himself over at a moment's notice as if they had nothing better to do with their evenings than wait for him to turn up. 'Dad's back from the Algarve,' she said noncommittally as she entered the kitchen. 'He's coming for a meal tomorrow.'

Robin made a face. 'He's going to want to know about the tennis course.' He went into the lounge and switched on the television.

'Shit,' said Natalie from the depths of the fridge. 'What are you going to do about Owen?'

Something Beth didn't want to analyse quivered in her breast. She shrugged. 'Dad was the one who made it necessary for us to take in paying guests. He might as well meet one of them. Why are you eating chocolate when you're about to go to your singing lesson?' Time was when she wouldn't have dared say that to her daughter. She wondered whether her relationship with Nats would have matured this quickly if Alan hadn't left.

'Because I've just had science followed by maths. I *need* chocolate.'

'Does your complexion need chocolate?'

'Mum, hormones give you spots, not chocolate. Everyone knows that. OK, I'm gone. Where's my music bag?'

A few moments later Owen came downstairs. 'Thanks for this morning. I got enough material to fill a dozen Shoe Orphanages.'

Beth put the kettle on, her tension unknotting. 'I did warn you. By the way, Alan's coming over tomorrow.'

'I heard. What the hell sort of man "finds a window in his schedule" for dinner with his own kids?'

Beth's head snapped round. 'Have you been listening to my messages?'

'The phone was ringing when I got in. I couldn't *not* hear it.'

'Sorry.' She swilled out the teapot, trying to calm down. 'I wasn't exactly enamoured of his phrasing myself.'

'Will you stop apologising? I might be lying. I might be a serial snooper. I'll eat upstairs tomorrow, OK?'

Beth's temper shot back up to the boil again. 'You will not! You're *paying* for your meal which is more than bloody Alan is. I just hope he doesn't put you off it.'

'You've changed the lock!' said Alan, standing outraged on the doorstep with a useless key in his hand.

'Yes, I mislaid a key, so I thought it was the most sensible thing to do.' She hadn't, of course. She'd woken in a cold sweat one night dreaming that he'd walked back into their lives as precipitously as he'd walked out. She was in the d-i-y store the moment it opened next morning.

'I always said having lodgers wasn't one of your brightest ideas.'

'They aren't lodgers, they're visitors. And I don't know who you said it to, but it certainly wasn't to me.' Her irritable reply was interrupted by the sound of Owen's rich, baritone laugh in the lounge.

'Who's that?' demanded Alan. 'Has Natalie got a boyfriend? Why didn't you tell me? What do his parents do? Why is he here when this is a family dinner?'

Resisting the really quite strong urge to invent Nats a biker lover called Big Dave with a cross-dressing greengrocer for a father, Beth compressed her lips and said, 'Mr Pendragon is one of our visitors. He's paying me for bed, breakfast and an evening meal all week so I'll thank you to be pleasant to him. Customers vote with their feet, remember?'

'Really, Beth, anyone would think I'm insensitive.' Alan stalked past her to the kitchen, made the standard comment about her not having got any tidier recently and proceeded to rearrange the contents of the fridge in order to fit the wine in. 'I hope this avocado isn't for today,' he said. 'They're full of cholesterol.'

'Fine. I'll clingfilm yours and have it for lunch tomorrow. It'll save making a sandwich,' snapped Beth.

'I don't know why you don't ever do a simple pasta salad as an appetiser.'

'Because that's what we're having for the main course!'

Things went from bad to worse. The moment Alan discovered Owen was an actor, he dropped all pretence of politeness. Instead he extracted a ball-by-ball account of the tennis week from Rob, then gave Natalie several possibilities for part-time employment. After which he reminisced on his own first Saturday job and ran them through a particularly crucial game of squash he'd played with a client of (surprise, surprise) Doone Hennessy's which he'd had to lose without it looking as if he was throwing it. He also told them in exhaustive detail about his golfing break. 'The chaps at the club have been recommending the Algarve for years because of the superb facilities and I must say they were right. If you'd ever taken to golf, we could have gone before, Beth. But you need a professional outlook on life to appreciate the game properly, which you haven't really got, have you?' He turned urbanely to Owen. 'Do you play at all?' Clearly he didn't expect an answer in the affirmative.

Owen gave a dangerous smile. 'Never saw the point.'

'No, I dare say there isn't much call for doing deals on the course in your line of work. Although golf isn't all business, you know. It keeps you fit too.' He patted his stomach complacently.

'So does dancing.' Owen speared a pasta spiral, apparently oblivious to Alan's change of colour. 'I reckon half an hour with a good dance captain is easily as knackering as strolling around taking a swing at a ball now and again. They did a survey recently which showed dancers were fitter than football players.'

Beth had to bend her head to hide the laughter in her eyes.

'This pasta is a touch soggy, Beth. Dried, I suppose. I've told you before – you get far better results if you buy fresh.'

'But you don't get nearly so much for the money.'

'Quality over quantity always pays. Talking of which, the mushrooms au gratin would have been more successful with organic field ones.'

As opposed to the marked-down-but-you-need-to-use-them-this-minute sort she'd picked up from Supasava on her way home along with the avocados.

Natalie, who so far hadn't contributed at all to the conversation, finished her plate with a flourish. 'That was nice, Mum,' she said. 'Is there any more?'

Beth bit the insides of her cheeks.

It was sadly against what Alan perceived as Family Time ethics for him to go as soon as the meal was over. Instead he drank a cup of coffee in the lounge ('Still using instant, I see,') whilst Beth crashed dirty crockery around in the sink. Owen winked at her and took his coffee upstairs.

'Well, goodbye,' said Alan at last.

Thank you, Lord. 'Bye.'

'Yeah, bye Dad,' said Robin.

Natalie barely waited for the door to close before racing to her bedroom and playing *The Darkness* very loudly indeed. Robin disappeared to vent his feelings on his Gameboy. Beth slammed books into her box for the morning. She heard the lounge door click and the clink of a glass and knew that Owen had come in to get the malt he'd brought with him. 'Sorry,' she muttered. 'You'd have done better eating upstairs after all.'

'Forget it. Here, I think you might need this.' He put a glass in her hand.

'Thanks.' The wine had been another irritation. Alan had been so insistent on 'No,

I'm driving, but don't let me stop you', that Beth had found herself totally unable to get more than off-sober.

'It was interesting. I'm glad I met him,' said Owen. He half closed his eyes and rolled the whisky round his mouth with sensual enjoyment.

Beth stared disbelievingly. Glad? When he'd been insulted in so many ways she'd been within an ace of throwing Alan out, bills to pay or no bills to pay? God, he meant it! He looked bloody ecstatic! 'Why ever?' she asked before she could stop herself.

He gave a slow, provocative grin. 'Because now I know for sure that you go for dark-haired men of average height.'

Agitation grabbed Beth's diaphragm. *Oh no! Not tonight!* She really *couldn't* cope with any sort of declaration when she felt all sand-papery and scoured and bad-tempered because of Alan. She sat abruptly and took too large a gulp from her glass. The whisky exploded in her mouth with a kick of raw power. 'Is your flat really being redecorated?' she heard herself gasp.

His eyes met hers: limpid eyes, actor's eyes. 'Can't afford it with the rates you charge.'

Damn and blast! She simply wasn't ready. 'Not tonight, Owen,' she said, too rattled to be anything but direct. Also mortified because it had been a foul evening (and the pasta *had* been soggy) and she quite desperately didn't want him to think she'd married the person Alan had turned into over the last twenty-five years. 'I know there's no sense in it, but each time I caught your eye, I felt as if I was cheating.' And that even with Doone Hennessy's name cropping up every third sentence. 'I don't want to feel that way.'

He eyed her neutrally. For a truly ghastly moment she thought she might have read him wrong. What if he'd had nothing more in mind than an idle flirtation to pass the time? 'I can't believe you still love him,' he said.

Relief. Huge relief. 'God, no.'

He gave his sidelong grin. 'Has he ever understood the kids?'

She sipped the malt. Straight whisky was too sour. She felt stressed and irrational and her taste buds craved the Drambuie she hadn't been able to afford since May. 'It was different when they were little,' she said. 'I wouldn't say he ever *enjoyed* them the same way I did, but he didn't used to be like he is now.' She got up. 'Do you mind if I put ginger wine with this?' Last weekend's B&Bs had left the end of a bottle behind. She'd tidied it into the hall cupboard and forgotten about it until just now, which was why there was still some left.

'As long as *I* don't have to drink it.' He sipped his whisky reflectively. 'Nats really hates him, doesn't she?'

'It's the desertion aspect.' Beth tasted the augmented drink. Her eyes watered. Did the percentage proof of one part of a mixture soak up the other? Or were you supposed to add all the bits together to work out how legless you were getting? 'She's at the age where she takes everything personally. Don't tell her you noticed, she's trying not to let it show.'

'Christ, I spent years doing that with the result that I never see my family at all! Sod being civilised, she wants a good slanging match with him to clear the air!'

Beth felt herself bristle. 'Are you telling me how to manage my own children?'

'Jesus! Of course not! I'm–' Owen took a deep breath. 'I'm simply suggesting you don't make my mistakes.' He made a wry face at the amber liquid in his glass and stood up. 'I'd best get back to work.'

Oh, God, this was all going wrong. What must he *think* of her? Bruised ex-wife to spitting mother cat in two seconds flat. She'd definitely blown whatever might have been building between them. 'Owen–'

He turned.

'I'm sorry.'

'Forget it.' He went quietly out of the door.

Beth took a long swallow of her drink and put her head in her hands. The silence of the room settled round her. *It's too soon anyway,* she told herself feebly. And then, quite a lot later, *damn*.

Two more days, thought Owen watching the Galaxy drive to school. Two sodding days to retrieve something from yesterday's disaster. As soon as the words had left his mouth last night, he'd realised he'd read Beth's mood all wrong. He'd been so cock-a-hoop at discovering she really did detest her ex that he'd assumed she would be as relieved as him once Alan had gone – and had let the chain off his mouth accordingly.

He could have kicked himself for being so stupid. So insensitive. The whole object of this week had been to get to know Beth and to see if he couldn't persuade her that it might be rather nice if she got to know him too. He hadn't rushed things. It had damn near killed him to hold back, but she was so different to the women he usually met that he had actually enjoyed the old-fashioned sense of courtship. He wanted to make her laugh. He wanted to see her smile just for him. He wanted to soothe her with cups of tea.

He also wanted, quite desperately, to make love to her. He kicked the skirting board to relieve his feelings, then went upstairs to fetch the panto script. On the way back, he passed her closed bedroom door. He rested his hand against the painted wood. It was like a mantra. He wouldn't go in there until she invited him. This once in his life he was going to do something properly.

'Why did you marry him?'

It was Friday night. Owen had eaten with them and then disappeared upstairs. Now Beth looked up from her marking, startled. 'I beg your pardon?'

Owen crossed the room to pour himself out a whisky. Beth was beginning to think his excuse for not keeping the bottle upstairs because if he did he'd drink too much of it was just that – an excuse. 'Why did you marry Alan?' he repeated.

Because I fancied the pants off him and was too nicely brought up to live in sin. 'I told you yesterday, he was different when we first met. Less didactic. More open.' She paused. 'Nicer.'

Owen sat down opposite her. 'When did he change?'

She rubbed her forehead. 'I don't know exactly. When we were first married we both worked long hours so there wasn't a huge amount of time for conversation. I'd just started teaching and was determined to do it properly. Alan was ambitious and wanted to impress contacts with his ability and staying power – his goal was always to be his own boss. I suppose I only really noticed when I was cut dead in the supermarket by the wife of an old friend of his.'

'I don't follow you,' said Owen.

'I'm not telling it very well.' Beth fiddled with her pen, ashamed all over again at having ever married Alan. 'When Alan first set up on his own, he rented office space from this friend. Tony gave him a really good deal and put clients his way to start him off. In return, Alan used Tony's haulage company for all his trading. They both benefited.' Beth looked up and met Owen's eyes. 'Time went on. Alan got bigger and more successful. Much bigger. Moved into his own place. Companies courted him. It was Tony's wife who cut me. It turned out Alan had dumped Amalgamated Haulage because Tony couldn't compete on rates.'

'Bastard.'

'We had a *huge* row about it. He genuinely couldn't see he'd done anything underhand. It was around then he started nagging at me to apply for a job in a private school because the pay and prestige would be better. We had another row about that.' And had continued ever since, really.

'So why didn't you leave him?'

Beth looked at Owen in surprise. 'Well, because we were *married*, of course! For better for worse. And I had Nats and Rob to think of by then. You don't walk out on your children's father simply because his ethics have taken a bit of a downturn. And it

130

wasn't all bad. Yes, there were rows, but Alan would just storm off to play golf, sleep in the spare room, and it would all be forgotten in the morning.'

Owen got up. 'Seems an odd sort of relationship.'

Thank God, an opening. Beth so needed to say this before what had happened yesterday soured things. 'Your way of life seems odd to me. It doesn't mean there's no common ground between us.'

He paused, his hand on the door handle. His eyes met hers. 'I'd like to think not.'

She stood up too. 'Owen, I haven't been myself the last few days what with re-starting school and having a classful of new kids and Alan coming over.' And not knowing what your intentions are. And not knowing whether I want to encourage you or if I'm too much of a wimp to let my life get messed up all over again. And wishing I was the sort of person who could invite you upstairs for a shower without it meaning anything.

He smiled, almost as if he could read her subtext anyway. 'We all have baggage, Beth.'

'But my cupboards are so full, mine keeps spilling all over the floor.'

He laughed and with the sound, the world miraculously righted itself. 'At least no one can accuse you of being less than honest.'

She raised her eyebrows. 'That's a good thing, is it?'

He grinned wickedly as he left the room. 'It's refreshing.'

Refreshing. What an epithet. 'Do you want a cup of tea?' she called after him.

His voice drifted down the stairs, laden with overtones. 'Never been known to refuse an offer yet.'

CHAPTER 7

Cate was in the workshops mastering the magic door-cum-stairs to Sesame's warehouse. Having set up a haphazard pile of large cardboard boxes with careful reference to the plans and clipped in an invisible fishing line, she pulled the cord to make them tumble down and the glitter-encrusted doorway appear.

'Very pretty,' said Luke from behind her.

She almost jumped out of her skin. 'What are *you* doing here? It's rest week.'

'I wondered if you'd like lunch.'

Cate's eyebrows snapped together. 'Why? Have you been banned from somewhere and want me to talk you back in?'

He gave his infectious laugh and captured her hand. She knew he had to be up to something but Last-Night-Party recollections seemed to have temporarily disconnected her reasoning. 'Where are we going?' she muttered.

'Greenwich. My mother's giving the grandchildren a day out.'

'And I'm an excuse for you to leave early?' His palm felt strong and capable and all sorts of other things that she suspected he wasn't. She couldn't believe she was going with him like this. *Remember Swansea*, said a despairing voice in the back of her mind.

'You'll enjoy it. You like children. We've never been through a summer tour without a single juvenile disaster before.'

'I keep your nieces and nephews occupied while you put some sort of squeeze on your mum, is that it? I'm hardly dressed for lunch.'

'You look good to me. Why don't you wear colours more often?'

'Duh! Because I work in the wings seven weeks out of eleven and if I don't wear black the audience might possibly spot me!'

'You wear black at rehearsal too.'

'That's an image thing.'

He grinned and set himself to draw her out. By the time they were crossing Greenwich Park in fitful autumn sunshine, his arm was round her shoulders and her guard was right down. Especially when he gazed into her eyes with deep green tenderness, stroked her cheek with the back of his hand and covered her mouth with his. The taxi hadn't been a one-off! He meant it! Cate's heart gave an enormous leap! Any number of bedazzled phrases surged to her lips just as she heard an imperious 'Yoohoo!' from a WI matron towing four bored, brushed-smooth infants in her wake.

'Luke, darling, how lovely. And you must

be Cate. He's told us all about you.'

'And then,' ground Cate, shredding old contracts into satisfyingly illegible ribbons, 'the cheeky sod had the nerve to link his arm in his mother's and leave me to entertain the Midwich bloody Cuckoos for the next twenty minutes!'

'Shows initiative though,' said Fran. 'You'd never think he was sneaky just by eyeballing him. Was it a good lunch? What explanation did he give on the way back?'

'Didn't get a chance. As soon as I'd choked down the last chocolate profiterole, I said I was sorry but I had to get back to work and left.'

Fran chuckled. 'Hunky though, isn't he? Shame there's nothing inside. Or not, depending what you want from a bloke. He'll tell you what it was about soon.'

Cate tore another strip with savage intentness. 'Get bloody real. I know what it was about! He wanted to prove a girlfriend's existence so his mother would stop match-making for him. He'd probably have taken you if I hadn't been here. If we see him again before Monday's read-through, I'm a docker's floozie.'

But it was only Friday when Cate looked up to see Luke leaning against the doorway of the large rehearsal studio she was marking out. 'Mad at me?' he said.

135

He could have been posing for an acting manual. *Fig 16: Boyish Apology*.

'Should I be?' she grated.

'I thought if I told you, you might not come.' *Fig 18: Ingenuous Explanation*.

'Dead right. Whereas now you know for certain that I'll never go with you anywhere again.' She registered with fury that his smile still did treacherous things to her. Sweet Jesus, hormones had a lot to answer for.

'It makes Mother happy to think I've got a girlfriend.'

Cate walked backwards with the last length of tape and stuck it down. 'Keeps her off your case you mean. Why pick on *me* for your mythical lover, anyway?'

'You're so in control,' he said obliquely. 'Every bit of you is alive.'

'I work hard. I plan. I like thinking of all the things that are needed, anticipating what might go wrong.'

'I like creating magic,' said Luke. 'Walking out on stage and convincing the audience they're in a different world. Suspending reality.'

Fig 24: Sincerity, thought Cate without rancour.

'Sorry about Tuesday, it was a shifty thing to do.'

'See me arguing?'

'Forget my sister's thirtieth, you're probably busy tomorrow. Can I buy you a pizza now to make up?'

Ye gods, thought Cate, I must be bloody certifiable.

'Tea! Now!'

Beth hit her head on the cupboard as she straightened up. 'What happened to *you?*' She'd never seen Owen this ruffled. No one could be less like the resigned actor she'd waved off to *Stagestruck* a scant four hours ago.

'I got more bloody ideas, that's what! Rob, that slap-stick routine you and Jack did. Was that impromptu?'

Robin was peering at the shepherd's pie in the oven. 'Our baking-a-wedding-cake is better.'

'Certainly better than *Cinderella*'s last year,' said Beth.

'Mind, we're prejudiced.'

Owen balled up his notes and hurled them at the wall. 'How does Sue work the panto? Two teams?'

'Lay the table, Robin. Yes, because it's two shows a day for three or four weeks.'

'So if I have Rob and Jack, I'd need another pair for Team B. Who?'

'Kirsty and Lauren?' said Robin.

Natalie nodded.

'Sod it. No boys?'

Beth retrieved his mangled notes. 'Don't

be sexist.'

'It's a question of *names,*' said Owen. 'You can't have girls called Jack-Be-Nimble and Jack-Be-Quick.'

'The audience wouldn't mind,' said Natalie, doling out plates. 'They'd think it was funny. Will we sing?'

Owen fixed her with a basilisk eye. 'That,' he said, 'depends on Adrian.'

Better. Whatever it was, he'd accepted it. Beth spared a moment from scraping stuck runner beans off the bottom of the saucepan to grin at him.

He went upstairs to work after lunch. Robin cycled round to Jack's; Natalie disappeared into her bedroom. Beth jettisoned the washing up to mark 7.1's first attempt at creative writing. She was on the nineteenth 'Why my Mum/Dad/Primary Carer is Special', and making a note for the Special Needs co-ordinator that the literacy hour with its attention to spelling and grammar had bypassed Yob, when Owen flung himself into the kitchen.

'I'm a good listener,' ventured Beth.

'I was doing all right until I met your bloody class and then went into sodding *Stagestruck!* Perfectly good panto with cute kids to sing and dance. Now I've got Wee Willie Winkle and Little Boy Blue fighting for equal rights in my head and if I don't have Rob and Jack doing a decorating scene alongside the Dame, I'll never be able to look myself in the face again.'

'Who else have you got?'

'You bloody name it! Bo-Peep with masses of bows. Little Johnny Green as a punk.'

Beth grinned, catching his drift. 'Except he wouldn't have drowned the cat, his brother would have sold it.'

'Sally-Go-Round-The-Sun.'

'Oh, Star of course.'

'Because then I can work that other child's hair into Sally-Go-Round-The-Moon. I've got to have Lisa for her. The list's endless!' He smote the table. 'But where the *hell* am I going to use Natalie?'

An astonishing gamut of emotions flooded Beth. 'How do you mean?'

'Christ Almighty! I mean if I make her Mary-Had-A-Little-Lamb or Polly-Put-The-Kettle-On, I'll wake up one morning with my throat slit!'

It mattered to him! Her daughter really mattered. Beth couldn't speak for a good ten seconds. 'Margery Daw,' she dredged up. 'I've always been convinced she was the bolshy type.'

Owen stared for a moment, then kissed her full on the mouth. 'Orphanage foreman! Beth, you're a star. Paper, quick, I need to write this down!' Warmth teetered dizzily through her as she watched his sloping italics dash across a page of her pad. He unclipped his phone. 'Ned'll need to see them. Stella can work out a schedule that leaves us both a Saturday morning free.'

Beth couldn't have eavesdropped if she'd tried. His fingers were burnt into her shoulders, his lips seared onto hers. The kiss, nothing more than an impulsive guerdon saluting her idea, had shaken her to the core. What sort of relationship could she have with someone who kissed so easily, so impersonally? It was beyond her experience.

'Fortnight today,' he said, breaking in on her reflections. 'Sue's number?'

'That was wonderful,' said Owen. 'I can't remember the last time I had Sunday lunch.'

'Nor me,' said Robin cheerfully. 'Mum doesn't do it usually. Jack and I go swimming Sunday mornings and get chips at the pool.'

'Rob, I'm touched. You gave up chlorine and junk food to say goodbye to me?'

'Nah. Jack's got to go to his Gran's.'

Beth laughed at Owen's look. 'No egos pandered to in this house.'

'It's why Dad left,' said Natalie.

Beth could wish Nats *hadn't* mentioned Alan. He'd phoned last night to check she'd remembered his father's birthday. By the time she'd assured him the card was in the post, he'd mentioned it on Thursday and when had she ever forgotten anyway, Owen had taken his drink upstairs to wrestle with his script some more and there was the last evening gone.

'Wouldn't have it any other way,' Owen was saying with an assumption of bravery. He made a face. 'I'd best be off. It's read-through first thing in the morning.'

He was going already? Panic pricked needles of fire over Beth's body. Would he say anything? Do anything? She levered herself up from the table, steeling herself to be casual. 'Good luck with the writing. And have fun with *Tin Pan Ali*. Where do you open?'

His eyes were friendly and uncomplicated. 'Canterbury. We rotate a week backwards each tour so the last stop of one is always the first of the next. Stops the venues thinking they're being discriminated against.'

'And it'll be half-term when you come to us, so we can watch the show every night without Mum nagging about school next day,' said Robin with satisfaction.

Owen picked up his bag from the hall. 'Christ Almighty, a fan club! Practise that decorating idea, Rob. It needs to be good for Ned.' He paused. 'Bye, Beth. Thanks for this week. Take care.'

He was going and there wasn't a blind thing she could do about it. Beth was conscious of immense, irrational annoyance that the kids were milling between them so he couldn't even give her a hug like last time. 'You too,' she said. She wavered for a split-second. 'We'll miss you.' There, she'd said it and he could make of it what he wanted. 'Keep in touch.'

His eyes met hers and for that brief instant they weren't uncomplicated at all. 'Count on it,' he said.

Sunday morning. Cate came awake slowly, her head hazy with thirtieth birthday champagne cocktails and dancing all night in an improbable marquee. The problem with possessing the sort of metabolism which protected you from hangovers was that you didn't have the normal incentives to stop drinking. People failed to appreciate this. They probably hadn't woken up with total recall of doing as many staggeringly stupid things whilst under the influence as she had.

She stretched gingerly. Her heart stuttered as her skin told her this wasn't her bed. *Bugger*, she thought, opening her eyes on an airy attic with stars scattered across the ceiling and billows of Arabian Nights gauze falling from the frame of a modern four-poster. Memory hit like a sledgehammer. *Had they been careful*, was her automatic reaction, followed almost instantly by *Was he likely to tell the rest of the company?*

Yes to the first question and probably no to the second, thank the Lord. The Luke

Bartholomews of this world were easy-come-easy-go, so secure in their own persona they didn't need to inflate their egos by puffing off sexual prowess.

Did she want to do it again? That was her final thought. It coincided with Luke opening his wonderful deep-green eyes behind a tumble of floppy brown hair. The answer was as inevitable as the way his slow smile filled her with honey. Her common sense retreated to a despairing rumble as his hand, warm with sleep, stretched out to caress her from breast to thigh...

'We've *had* all this,' said Adrian Chambers as Cate entered the rehearsal room. 'First the Heavies sing a line, then Seb and the Tinies sing it slightly twisted. If you don't sing yours right, the audience aren't going to get the neat twist in Seb's and the whole song falls apart.'

Owen was watching from the side.

'Annis being a pain? How novel,' breathed Cate.

'Jealous,' he murmured back. 'Trying to mess up Seb.' He was sardonically amused. 'Watch though. Watch what the lad's doing.'

After a couple of seconds, an astonished pride filled her. 'He's doing the steps as a parody! And everyone's following him.' Her eyes went to the dance captain. 'How come Red isn't saying anything?'

'Annis cut him out with that new bint in the chorus last night. Better get lover-boy in here, sweeting. We're on next.'

Damn him, how did he know? Even *she* wasn't sure they had anything going. 'I can easily change your triple-strength tea bags for Earl Grey,' she warned. But Luke was already moving into position. As Cate watched, he became Sesame the warehouse janitor, half-flash-half-foolish, waiting for his cue. She irritably blinked away an eyelash and bent over the script ready to prompt.

The rehearsal finished. Luke brushed her with the slenderest of mischievous glances before laying a detaining hand on Adrian's arm. Cate tidied up, listening with half an ear to Owen and Seb at the noticeboard.

'Blast. I'm not called until late tomorrow.'

'Nice lie in with a mug of tea and Saturday morning telly. I don't remember you complaining at Beth's.'

'Home *isn't* Beth's,' said Seb with feeling. 'Mum and Dad are always so *considerate*. They make more noise tiptoing past my door than Nats does playing *The Darkness* at full volume.'

'So find yourself a house-share. Cut loose.'

Luke and Adrian were winding up their conversation. Cate lost the thread of what Owen was saying. '–if you fancy a trip out?

You'll have to stay at mine tonight.'

Seb looked as if Christmas had come early. 'I'll shoot home and grab a bag!'

Luke sauntered casually across. 'Going anywhere near my place?' he murmured. 'There's a bottle of wine in the fridge needs drinking...'

'Hi, Rob. Sue about?'

Natalie, her attention caught by Owen's voice, turned reluctantly from where she was changing into jazz shoes ready for the *Stagestruck* session. Every time she saw him she missed Seb not being there too. She ached for Seb so much it hurt. Even when Richard Manning had made tentative advances during study period, she'd been unable to summon up more than a weak smile and an acceptance of help with her science homework. She braced herself, looked, and saw Seb himself with Owen and Ned, his blond fringe falling over his eyes. Her heart banged. Immense, unexpected delight filled her. 'Seb!' she cried on a half-laugh and flew across the room without realising what she was doing.

Afterwards, Seb tried to work out what had come over him. The truth was that after three weeks of being Mum and Dad's dear Sebastian overlaid with two weeks of Annis's derogatory remarks, it was such a massive ego boost to have someone young and pretty and bursting with joy running to-wards him, that he simply caught her in his arms and kissed her.

Oh my God. Stars exploded through Natalie as her lips met his and her feet left the ground.

Oh my God, thought Seb as he let her go.

'Put him down, sparrow.' Owen's amused voice broke through her rose-coloured haze. 'It's me and Ned you're supposed to be making up to. The lad's only here for the ride.' He tweaked her ponytail. 'Find Sue, there's a good kid.'

'Right,' she said in a strangulated voice, and sped as if live snakes were at her heels to the side office where Sue briefed her staff.

'Why didn't you *tell* me?' hissed Lisa.

For a moment, Natalie felt equally aggrieved. Even if there *had* been anything, Lisa had been welded to Jason every spare moment since the beginning of term. They'd really squeezed her out. The moment passed. She and Lisa had been friends since they'd filtered staff-room tea side by side through their mothers' placentas. 'Nothing to tell,' she muttered. 'I had no idea that was going to happen.' She couldn't help turning her eyes towards Seb. He smiled at her. She smiled back, dizzy with relief.

'Something seems to be happening now,' said Lisa enviously. 'God, you're a lucky cow! Good thing you're sixteen in a fortnight.'

'Lis!'

Beth pulled into the car park ready for the end of the session and nearly ran into the wall as she saw Owen's Megane. She'd forgotten he and Ned were checking out the kids today. She locked the Galaxy with fingers that shook a little and went inside.

Owen was in the main hall with Sue, watching the Seniors dance. Ned and Seb were there too. Beth looked at the back of Owen's head through the grid of orange wires in the safety-glassed window and struggled to untangle the welter of emotions inside her. She'd known him precisely eight weeks, and for half-a-dozen of those he'd been somewhere else in the country entirely. Yet seeing him unexpectedly like this, what she most wanted was to run her fingers through his too-long hair, have him laugh at her with his wicked hazel eyes, and feel his tough, dancer's body hard against hers. It didn't even shame her that there were probably six other women scattered along the *FOOTLIGHTS* tour route and another one in London who felt exactly the same way.

Out of the corner of her eye, she saw Sue slip into the corridor to pump the klaxon. Owen stretched in his chair. As if he'd sensed her scrutiny, he turned his head and met Beth's eyes through the squared glass. Her insides melted into a pool of lust as he gave a wide, wonderful smile and jerked his head for her to come in.

But when she'd fought to reach him against the tide of kids streaming out, there was the table between them, Ned to be polite to, and Seb looking powerfully nervous about something. Owen's fingers just had time to give hers the briefest of squeezes before Natalie hurried up and plunged into disjointed speech.

'We're ready, Mum.' Robin and Jack raced up. She was supposed to be delivering them to a paint-balling party in Bury St. Edmunds.

'Get in, I'll be there in a minute. What *is* this, Nats?'

Natalie gulped and became coherent. 'Seb wondered if we could have a burger while the others talk about casting and then you pick me up later?'

Owen's eyes were pulling her. She had to exert considerable control to concentrate on Natalie. 'But I'm taking Rob and Jack to their party!'

Natalie jiggled anxiously. Seb looked as if he'd rather wrestle tigers than offer an explanation. Owen gave a wry smile. 'No sweat, Beth. We've got to be back in London by four. I'll drop Nats off as we come through.'

'*Please*, Mum?'

She didn't have time to understand. 'Was that my car horn? Oh, OK.'

Natalie gave a squeak and flew away to change her shoes. Seb followed. Owen came out from behind the table, smiled deep, deep, deep into her eyes and clasped her hand again. 'I'll ring you later.'

It sounded like a promise. Beth cast a distracted glance at her daughter, wanting to know what was going on, wanting to remember this feeling of Owen's fingers hard around hers, hating everyone else for being in the way. 'I'm trusting you,' she muttered.

'Novel,' he said with a chuckle. 'But nice.'

Natalie's whole body was singing and dancing and jigging up and down with delight. She listened while Seb gave the lunch order, not taking her eyes off his face.

They found a space at the end of a bench and sat down. 'It's good to be back,' said Seb. 'Sorry I kissed you like that in front of all your friends, but I was so pleased to have escaped from home for a morning, and so pleased to see you and Rob again that when you raced towards me, I got carried away.'

Natalie's heart gave an erratic wobble in its orbit round Venus. 'That's all right,' she said. 'I really liked it.'

'Yeah, but it'll have given completely the

wrong impression. You'll be hassled for days.'

'I – I can cope.'

'I was dead impressed by the session,' he continued. 'When Sue told you to line everyone up and pretend you were a ballet-sergeant-major I nearly died.'

He didn't love her! It hadn't meant anything. What had Cate said? An actor's kiss is worth less than a politician's promise? 'That was Owen's idea,' she said, her fizz of euphoria flattening faster than her coke. 'He wants the Shoe Orphans to have a bolshy leader. Seb, did you only kiss me because–'

'Owen?' Seb looked genuinely puzzled. 'What's it got to do with him?'

'Because it's his script, of course. Did you really kiss me just because–'

'*Owen* is writing the panto? Bloody hell!'

'Didn't you know? Wasn't I supposed to tell you? Oh, God.' Natalie's voice shook. She felt a tear drip down her nose. She looked miserably at the rest of her burger and thought she probably wouldn't ever eat again.

'Oh, Nats.' Seb tipped up her chin, his blue eyes packed with remorse. He kissed her very gently on the lips. 'I loved you running towards me like that. It gave me a high like you wouldn't believe. But I'm not vain enough to think it was anything more than a spur-of-the-moment impulse. We've only known each other a week. You're not in love with me any more than I am with you. Can't we just be friends?'

Not in love. But he was so gorgeous. Natalie's burger tasted like cardboard. She looked up to find his eyes behind the blond fringe anxious and caring. *Friends.* She took another bite. The burger tasted better. 'OK,' she said and clicked her coke cup uncertainly against his.

Seb's grin was part relief, part accolade. 'Good girl. Now, tell me about *Jack And The Beanstalk*. Owen said he was just giving Ned a second opinion on the kids.'

'Can you talk?' said Owen's voice over the phone.

'Easily,' replied Beth drily. 'Robin's still out and Natalie is upstairs playing the saddest CD tracks she can find at roughly twice the safe decibel level. I'm expecting a joint visit from the Noise Abatement Society and the NSPCC any minute.'

Owen's rich chuckle sounded in her ear. 'Christ, I wouldn't be that age again.'

Beth's stomach clenched. Had he always sounded this sexy? 'Nor me. Any reason in particular?'

'Seb's been having problems. When Nats ran across the room with this wonderful smile on her face, it was such a shot in the arm he forgot other people might not under-

151

stand our extrovert profession and kissed her. *That's* why he needed to talk to her. To explain.'

'Oh, lord.'

He laughed, sounding inappropriately joyous. 'Beth – at the risk of sounding extrovert myself, I wish we'd been able to stay longer today.'

Her heart thumped. 'Me too. I – I suppose you're not free tomorrow?'

'You jest, mistress. Unbroken rehearsals from now until we open.'

So that made it four long stretched-out weeks before she saw him again. 'Just a thought,' she said. 'Stay in touch, won't you? And tell Seb not to worry.'

'Impossible. He was *born* uptight. Nats has got Margery Daw, by the way. Ned loved the idea. And it's yes to the boys, too.'

'Thank God for that. Have you finished writing?'

'Yes. That's why I haven't rung. Too busy, what with that and rehearsals too. Bugger, I'm being called. Bye, Beth.'

'Bye,' echoed Beth. The phone went dead. 'I miss you,' she whispered.

Upstairs Natalie's door was pulled open. 'Mum,' came a tearful voice. 'Have we got any hot chocolate?'

Ten pm. Seb stood outside the *FOOT-LIGHTS* complex and inhaled the damp air.

Across the road the Jolly Bargee was belting out Saturday night karaoke.

'Not gone home yet?' said Cate coming down the steps behind him. 'What dedication.'

'You're a fine one to talk!'

'Necessity. If you go wrong on stage, you can improvise. If my props aren't ready, everybody in the company will have my guts for garters.'

'Owen says guts are out this year. And have you *heard* Ned on the subject of improvisation?'

He felt her studying him and tensed himself for the third degree. But, 'Fancy a drink?' she asked.

Seb glanced at the pub. 'Not if Annis is in there.'

'Stand up to him,' said Cate, exasperated. 'You're ten years younger than he is with more talent in one toe than he's ever had in his life. He only bugs you because you let him.'

'Tell me about it,' said Seb glumly.

She cuffed his ear. 'You need food. How about the set-meal-for-two in The Golden Dragon?'

'Can we make it the set-meal-for-three? I only had a burger at lunchtime.'

They walked briskly to the Chinese. 'So, what else is up apart from Annis being an arsehole? You've looked like a streak of misery all afternoon.'

He should have remembered she never missed a trick. 'What do you know about girls, Cate?'

'Considering that I am one, you mean?'

He looked at her with a grin. 'Girls like Natalie.'

She frowned. 'We haven't got a Natalie.'

'In Cambridge. Beth's Natalie. Ned and Owen were vetting the *Stagestruck* kids for the panto today. The thing is, when we got there, Nats ran across the hall looking, oh really pretty, you know, and pleased to see me and uncomplicated–' He took an unhappy breath. 'And I kissed her. Like Cathy and Heathcliff. I couldn't not have done. Nobody could.'

'So?'

Seb stared. 'So I *kissed* her. And she thought it meant something. And I had to tell her it didn't. And she cried and I kissed her again and it still didn't mean anything and now I feel like a real shit.'

The waiter put a platter of spare ribs and two glasses of coke in front of them. Cate picked up a rib and eyed Seb over the steaming sweet-and-sour sauce in the way he and the rest of the college had learnt to distrust within three minutes of first meeting her. 'You could do worse.'

'What?' Seb was so startled he swallowed his coke the wrong way.

She thumped his back. 'She's pretty and talented and she's got a crush on you. Just what you need to keep your end up with Annis. A lovely innocent affair to boost your confidence and make you feel ten feet tall.'

'Cate, I can't *use* Nats like that!'

'No?'

'No!'

'Good,' she said, dropping the spent rib on to the plate and choosing another. 'I was going to poke your eyes out with this if you'd said yes.'

Seb grabbed a rib too, and tore at the meat feelingly. 'Now I remember why I was so shit-scared of you at college!'

'Really?' she asked, interested.

'We all were. What am I going to do about Natalie?'

'That's between you and her,' she answered. 'But I know what you're going to do about Annis. You're going to stand up to him like you did just now to me. Think of all the puerile things he says and have answers ready for them. But don't be conciliatory – the aggro between you works really well on stage.'

Seb stared at her. 'You're all heart, Cate.'

'*Much* better.' She grinned. 'Whose is the last rib?'

'Mine,' said Seb, taking it.

CHAPTER 8

Cate stared at Luke in disbelief. 'No, of course we can't have dinner with your mother in Canterbury on Monday night! It's the final dress rehearsal! We probably won't get out of the place until two in the morning!'

Luke blew her a kiss and spoke into the phone. 'Did you hear that, Mother? OK. Bye.' He watched as Cate furiously pulled her clothes on. 'Are you leaving?'

'I don't like being used.'

'But she never believes *me* when I tell her I can't go over.' He stretched beneath his Arabian Nights canopy like a particularly at-one-with-himself cat.

'I can't imagine why.' *Call me back*, she willed as she ran down the four flights of stairs from his attic. *Apologise. Don't let me go like this.* But he did.

It was obvious from the beginning of the rehearsal next morning that she wasn't the only one nursing a smouldering temper. Annis was taking his hangover out on Seb. Ellery was boasting of a magazine feature being done on him over Christmas and saying it might mean he couldn't go to the

Bahamas. Owen was in such a blind rage about something unspecified he was ripping shreds off anyone foolhardy enough to stray within range. At the break, Cate went up to the office and found Fran with her ear glued to the inner door.

'–grace us with his sodding presence for *Jack And The Beanstalk* after all!'

That was Owen's voice. What the–? The noise of chairs scraping caused them to make a hasty dash for the other side of the room.

Owen paused at the office door. There was a trace of reserve in his voice as he said, 'Posters for *Jack*, Stella, when are they likely to go up?'

'Hopefully, the week we're there with *Tin Pan Ali*.'

'Not before?'

'I doubt it.'

Luke was waiting downstairs, his soft hair falling back from his face. He pulled Cate into the kitchen. 'I'm sorry for using you last night. And I'm sorry you didn't stay.' The embrace was balm to her wounded feelings. Not only had he apologised without expecting anything in return, he was kissing her on *FOOTLIGHTS* property where anyone might come in as if he didn't care even if they did. 'Come back with me later?' he murmured.

This was ridiculous. How hard could making the first move be? Beth tipped the last of the Supasava Bulgarian into her glass for courage and made another attempt at dialling Owen's mobile number.

'Sorry I can't take your call,' said his recorded voice, 'but if you leave a message I'll get back to you.'

Even his disembodied voice did disastrous things to her self-control. 'Hi, it's Beth,' she said in a rush. 'I just wanted to wish you luck for Monday. Nats and Rob do too. God, I hate talking to answering machines. Bye.' She replaced the phone with shaking fingers. Done. And the good luck card would be waiting for him. She felt as nervous as a Regency debutante waiting for her come-out ball. She could still feel the pressure of Owen's hand squeezing hers. She could feel his warm, firm mouth on her lips. She could see his chest with its enticing covering of springy dark hair. In three weeks' time he'd be back here. It would be up to him then. And if a person couldn't fly in the face of their upbringing at forty-six years of age, when the hell could they?

'Mum!' Natalie's screech brought Beth out of the kitchen at panic speed. Her daughter was gazing in stupefaction at the present she'd just unwrapped. 'Dad's given me a mobile for my birthday!'

'*What?*'

Robin shot into the room. 'Cool!' He held

out his hand for the manual.

Fury raged in Beth's breast. Alan hadn't even told her! She struggled for control. 'My present's just money, sweetheart. I thought you could buy yourself clothes.'

Natalie looked up, her eyes brilliant. 'Thanks, Mum! How do I register, Rob? I have just *got* to ring Lisa!'

Beth went back into the kitchen. She reckoned she had about half-an-hour until Lisa and possibly Sue as well arrived hotfoot on the doorstep. She was right, but since Sue brought with her three trays of party nibbles plus a bottle of Drambuie which was a present to *her* for having a daughter achieve the astonishing age of sixteen, she generously forgave her.

Through the swing door they heard Lisa's voice. 'What about *him?* Did he send anything?'

'I got a card from all of them,' said Natalie off-handedly. 'Seb, Owen and Cate. Seb's signature's got four kisses after it.'

'Pity it didn't have his phone number. You could ring to say thank you.'

Beth suspected her daughter already had Seb's number engraved on her heart. But, 'We'd better help get the party ready,' said Nats. 'The way Mum's been acting this week, I'll be grounded for the next hundred years otherwise.'

'Probably the menopause,' replied Lisa as

they started pushing furniture towards the walls.

'Menopause indeed,' muttered Beth wrathfully, thumping the kettle on.

Sue grinned. 'It's our own fault for being so up front about the pitfalls of being a woman.'

Did they really seem that old to their children, Beth wondered hours later. She and Sue had retreated to her bedroom while the party shrieked and flowed beneath them. Sue was peering at the bottle of Gordon's. 'Damn, I've drunk it all. *And* we've run out of pizza. Whose turn is it to brave the descent to the kitchen?'

'Yours,' said Beth. 'Is that the phone? I didn't think there was anyone left to complain about the noise.' She scrambled across the bed to answer it as Sue left.

'Hi, reached the throat-slitting stage yet?'

'Owen!' Irrational gladness filled her, mingling with Drambuie fumes. It was a potent mixture.

'How's it going?'

Beth laughed. 'Noisy. I'm surprised you can't hear it from there. Rob's staying at Jack's and Sue and I are camped upstairs with nice Mr Gin and lovely Mr Drambuie so I might not make much sense quite soon.'

He chuckled. 'You've been holding out on me. You never said anything about seeing other men.'

Beth fizzed with intoxicated happiness. 'It was a blind date. I knew nothing about it. Sue brought Dram round for me so she could keep Gordon all to herself.'

'And you took the poor sap to bed straight away. Shame on you! Is it going to last?'

She giggled, looking at the nearly empty bottle. 'I doubt it. He's got no staying power.'

'Sucked him dry, eh? Serve you right for using him so cavalierly when all he had in mind was a spiritual relationship.'

'Stop,' said Beth, helpless with laughter. 'I give up. Thanks for Natalie's card. It was very diplomatic.'

'Thank *you* for the good luck message. And the card. I particularly liked the black cat on crutches.'

Beth found she was grinning foolishly into the phone. 'I thought you might. How was the opening night?'

'Great, except the moving stairs got stuck in Act One and the Voice only just didn't launch himself into the void, more's the pity. Apart from that, everyone is still pissed off with him, Seb hasn't had a show-down with Annis, and I haven't throttled Mel yet. How about you? How's your class?'

He cares, she thought mistily. 'Yob's dyed his head yellow and green as a tribute to Norwich Football Club. *Ella*'s hair got caught in several people's science experiments on Monday and now has blue and purple crystals scattered through it. Felicity has new bows. They're so large she needs Air Traffic Control's permission to do PE. Teaching this week has been like time-warping to the Seventies.'

Owen's chuckle was warm and wicked in her ear. 'I remember it well.'

'You're not old enough.' Through the noise, Beth heard Sue's tread on the stairs. She gulped the rest of the Drambuie to give herself courage. 'I miss you, Owen.'

There was a small pause. Then, 'Not long now,' he said, a ripple she'd never heard before in his voice. 'Exeter and Swindon, that's all.'

Two weeks, thought Beth, aiming the phone at its holder to a blast of *Electric Avenue* as Sue negotiated the door. And it'll be half-term too, so no dashing off to school in the morning without seeing him. With luck and a following wind, she'd catch another glimpse of that bathrobe. And that chest. And those legs. Maybe even all of them at once. As she rolled off the bed to help Sue, her own legs didn't feel as if they belonged to her. Especially when she found her eyes being drawn quite irresistibly to her en-suite shower...

An hour or so later, she surveyed the shambles in the lounge with floating Drambuie detachment. Lisa was outside saying a protracted goodnight to Jason. Natalie, rather surprisingly, was doing the same with Richard Manning.

'I'll just bet you want to clear up now,' said Sue.

Beth made an apologetic face. 'Better than coming down to it in the morning.'

Sue looked resigned. 'It's a point of view. Hand me a bin bag and tell me who it was on the phone earlier that made you go all liquid and giggly.'

Beth felt her colour rise. 'Owen. He – um – thinks we'll enjoy *Tin Pan Ali*.'

Her friend raised a disbelieving eyebrow. 'He rang you after the show just to tell you that?'

Beth sat on the floor with a rush and sorted scattered CDs into cases. 'I like him, Sue. I think I might like him a lot. Don't spoil it.'

Sue chuckled. 'Wouldn't dream of it.'

The lounge door opened. Natalie peered in looking, to Beth's fond eyes, impossibly pretty even in a tousled, five-hours-later sort of way. 'Lisa and I are going to crash. Thanks for the party, Mum, it was cool.'

'Wicked,' said Lisa. 'Night, Mum.'

'Don't bother helping,' said Sue to the closing door. She looked at Beth. 'Were we ever that young?'

Beth slotted the last CD into place. A

memory of Owen flicking through making scurrilous jokes about the names came to her. She grinned. *He* could make her feel sixteen again, no problem.

Exeter, then Swindon. *Tin Pan Ali* was getting rave reviews. Owen revelled in the applause and cut out the local photo spreads, but one corner of his mind remained unswervingly fixed on Cambridge. 'Beth,' he said when he phoned during the Swindon week (he hadn't bothered with excuses since Natalie's party), 'what time do you go to bed on Saturdays?'

Her laugh wound through his veins. 'Depends how much marking I've got to do, whether either of the kids needs fetching from a party, what the late film is and if the B&Bs have given me anything alcoholic.'

'This Saturday?'

He heard her flick through the diary by the phone. 'Lisa's sixteenth. Nats is sleeping-over and I'm having Robin and Jack. No B&Bs. I don't know what the film is, but I promise I'll be up by the time you get here Sunday.'

Adrenalin kicked in without warning. Owen called on reserves of technique to keep it out of his voice. 'I was thinking I might leave right after the show,' he said. 'You know what we're all like, high as a kite, especially in a good stop like Swindon, no chance of sleeping anyway. I could be with you by one o'clock. Two at the latest.'

He heard her indrawn breath, counted the heartbeats in her pause. Her voice came back, as carefully neutral as his but with an undercurrent of suppressed excitement which made his pulse race. 'I'll put *Pride and Prejudice* on and amuse myself with the ironing. Give me a ring as you go past Royston. I'll have the tea and digestives ready.'

Owen looked at himself in the mirror and almost didn't recognise the blazing exhilaration on his face. 'Chocolate ones?'

Midnight. First St Albans, then Hatfield disappeared in a blur of speed. Just two hours ago Owen had been taking curtain call. He still had a buzz from it. Stevenage. The A505. Royston. The needle was flickering at ninety mph as he punched the speed-dial button for Beth. 'Still up?'

'Elizabeth is only just reading Mr Darcy's letter,' she said, a wobble of laughter in her voice. 'How did it go?'

Owen eased off the accelerator. 'I think they liked us. What's for supper?'

'Crust of dry bread? Morsel of cheese?'

He eased off some more. 'Hell. No tea?'

She laughed properly. 'Owen, I'm a teacher. I've *always* got tea!'

The doorbell chimed just as Darcy dived into the lake at Pemberley. Prophetic or what, thought Beth as she went into the hall with wildly banging heart.

He stood on the doorstep like, but so unlike, that first time. 'Hi,' he said.

'Hi,' said Beth.

They went through to the lounge, neither of them knowing quite what to say. Elizabeth Bennet and Darcy were having much the same problem.

'The tea's ready,' said Beth.

'You need a new tape,' said Owen. 'The quality of that one's crap.'

Beth hastily turned it off. 'Only in a couple of spots. How are plans for *Jack?*'

'The books arrived this week. The Voice is furious.'

'He doesn't want to do it after all, does he? He's too sophisticated for panto.' She sat on the sofa, about as relaxed as a coiled spring.

After an infinitesimal pause, Owen sat next to her, wrapping his hands around his mug. 'My views exactly.' A dull flush coloured his cheeks. 'I was in such a temper when I thought he might. Bloody near lost control.' He gave her a shamed, sideways look. 'Writing *Jack* was *hard!* I was buggered if I'd let anyone wreck it.'

'Would it have been easier if you'd told them you were the author?'

'Compared to what? No matter, he's out

of it. And Ned pulled a fast one on Annis. Let him think Seb is Tom-Tom-the-Piper's-Son on the grounds that the part would have been Luke's if the Voice had been Jack. Annis is Baron Hardup's sidekick. He can be booed to his heart's content alongside Monty.'

His nearness and openness were doing such strange things to her senses that it was a couple of seconds before Beth caught up with what he was saying. 'But if Luke is the lead and Seb is the juvenile and Monty is the villain, where does that leave you?'

For the first time since she'd known him, Owen's hazel eyes failed to meet hers. Instead he stood up and looked at himself in the mirror over the mantelpiece. With a hand that wasn't quite as assured as usual he made a bouffant gesture to his hair, then batted his eyelashes at his reflection. 'It costs such a lot to make a girl look cheap these days, doesn't it?'

Beth stared at him, her mind seething with unvoicable contradictions.

'I mean,' continued Owen, flicking his lashes with a careful fingertip, 'never mind Hardup's bloody mansion, it's *me* Llewellyn-Bowen ought to be making over.'

'Dame Trot? You?' Her voice was a thread.

He met her eyes in the mirror. 'Made my debut as Mrs Crusoe last year. The advantage of being the writer is that you get all the best lines.'

She swallowed. Whatever she said now would be crucial. 'Was it fun?'

He turned, picked up his tea again and moved edgily over to her A-level group's *Arms And The Man* essays. 'Wonderful,' he said, leafing through the top one, 'except I didn't pull. Let's face it, who's going to look twice at a bloke in false eyelashes who dresses up in women's clothes for a living?'

This was it. Make or break time. Beth's heart was beating so hard she thought it might batter its way out of her chest. 'Me?' she said.

Everything about Owen stilled.

She walked carefully across and removed both mug and essay from his hands. 'Providing you don't wear curlers in bed. Or borrow my tights. I have enough trouble with Natalie.' She met his incredulous stare and licked dry lips. 'You'll have to help me here, Owen. I'm out of practice at this.'

His mobile face erupted into a dazzling smile. *'Yes!'* he yelled, and wrapped her in his arms. 'Oh, Beth, I've wanted to do this for so long.' He bent his head and kissed her long and hard. Very long. And very hard.

Bliss. More than bliss. Sensations she hadn't realised she'd missed flooded back into her body. After an aeon of ecstasy that might have equally lasted five minutes or five hours, she threaded her fingers through his hair. 'Me too,' she said. 'You may have guessed.'

He kissed her again. He ran his hands around her denim-clad hips, let them linger on her inner thighs. 'So have you got something upstairs,' he murmured, 'or shall we use one of your Marigolds down here?'

'Owen!' Beth was shocked and laughing and wildly aroused all at the same time.

His wicked hazel eyes held hers. 'Only kidding. I've got the conventional fancy dress in my bag. Beth – this *is* all right, isn't it?'

He was holding her so close it felt as if he was inside her already. Her hands quivered on his back. 'It feels so right I'm getting seriously worried about midnight.'

His teeth grazed her throat; his hand felt for her breast. 'Midnight's long gone, mistress.'

Beth gasped and arched against him, desperate to go further but unwilling to surrender this present glory. 'Be gentle with me,' she said on a half-laugh.

They climbed the stairs in the muted glow from the landing. He dropped his bag inside her door and as it closed behind them spun her jubilantly to the bed.

Beth's last thought before he drove everything else from her head was to pray that Rob and Jack wouldn't be up too early in the morning.

'Luke! What time is it? I'm supposed to be in Cambridge!'

'Mmm?' As always, he was sleepily and sexily aware of her.

Cate pushed him away. 'I've got to be in Cambridge by lunchtime! Jesus, remind me never to sleep with you on a Saturday night again.'

He rolled into the warm hollow she'd left. 'OK. See you tomorrow.'

She pulled her clothes on, ran her fingers through her hair and pelted out of the house. Shit, where was the car? Cate put a brake on her panic and forced herself to take deep, calming breaths. Last night – last night she and the crew had gone to the pub after get-out. Most of the cast had still been there. That was why she'd stayed. Because Annis had been ugly drunk and needling Seb. Cate had instinctively looked for Owen. For all his caustic tongue, he could defuse situations like this without even raising a sweat. But he wasn't there.

Maybe Seb had noticed her glancing round, maybe it had stiffened him. As she'd headed for the bar, he'd said loudly, 'I really don't think my sexual proclivities are anything to do with you or *FOOTLIGHTS*. Dancing, singing and saying the right words at the right time – that's what counts.'

'And having the right props,' Cate had

interrupted. 'Which you didn't tonight, Mr Annis. That's the third time since we began the run that you've had to come to me for a spare bow-tie.'

Annis had swigged his pint, laddishly offensive. 'Give it a rest. Pretty boy over there has already slapped my hand.'

Cate had felt steel snapping into place in all her muscles. 'Can you possibly be referring to the Wardrobe Master?'

'Going to make something of it?'

'Too bloody right I am. Out!'

He'd sat on his bar stool and laughed in her face. 'I haven't finished my drink, little girl.'

'Want to bet?' She'd squeezed the pressure point just above his knee, kneed him hard as he'd automatically shot forward, then jammed her arm underneath his elbow as he'd doubled-up in astounded rage. Seb had grabbed his other side to help her run him through the door. Annis had swung a punch at him and missed, before staggering towards the taxi rank bellowing revenge.

'Shit, Cate, that was impressive.' Seb had high-fived her enthusiastically before heading back into the pub.

'Luck. He was concentrating on you. He's such an MCP that he didn't expect *me* to do anything. Element of surprise.'

'It was still impressive,' Seb had said. 'Almost as good as when you pushed Stuart

Melville into the canal after you found out he'd been two-timing you. Another drink?'

But the barman was before him. 'On the house,' he'd said, sliding a lager towards her. 'Lovely manoeuvre.'

And then Luke had drifted up and Seb had demonstrated what she'd done all over again and others had crowded round and one drink had led to another and here she was, outside Luke's digs, when she was supposed to be on the A4.

Her digs! That's where her car was! She'd known she might need a taxi after get-out, so she'd walked in yesterday morning. She set off for them at a jog.

All the time she was helping Lisa and Sue clear up on Sunday, Natalie was in a fever of impatience to get back home. She'd looked up Swindon to Cambridge on the Internet and discovered the best journey time was 2 hours 47 minutes. So if Seb left his digs at ten, say, he could be in Fenbourne as early as one. And as midday approached and Lisa *still* showed no signs of wanting to dispense with her company and go round to Jason's, Natalie grew frantic.

'What shall we listen to next?' said Lisa, her fingers trailing lovingly over her brand-new CD music centre.

'Anything,' said Natalie, trying to sound relaxed. 'Is that the phone?'

'Hey, guess what! I got enough birthday money to buy a mobile of my own!'

'Wicked.'

'Lisa! Jason's on the phone,' called Sue from below.

At last! Natalie shot off the bed and followed her friend down the stairs.

Lisa leant against the wall with the receiver to her ear. 'Hiya. Mmm? Oh, nothing much.' She winked at Natalie. 'Tidying up. Listening to CDs... A walk?' She raised her brows at Natalie who nodded encouragingly and made signs to indicate that she'd leave. 'OK, Nats was just going anyway. See you in a bit.' She put the phone back. 'Come too, if you like,' she offered. 'Or ring Richard. Pity he lives in Ashwell.'

No, thought Natalie fervently, *it wasn't*. 'Can't,' she said. 'Cate and Owen and Seb are coming this afternoon. Mum will need a hand.'

'Seb, eh?' Lisa smirked. 'Poor Richard.'

'I told you. There's nothing in it. Give me a ring tomorrow – we can go shopping for your mobile.'

As soon as she was out of sight she broke into a run. 'Please don't be there yet. Please,' she whispered. And he wasn't. Owen's Megane was outside but there was no sign of Cate's Fiesta or Seb's Golf. Owen was drinking tea in the kitchen as she opened the back door. Mum was getting out cheese and biscuits. He'd obviously just cracked a joke because she was laughing.

'Hi, sweetheart, how was the party?'

'Cool. Nearly as good as mine. Hi, Owen.' She scanned the kitchen. Only two mugs. 'First one here?'

Her mother was slightly flushed. 'Cate went straight to the Corn Exchange. She said she was running late. Do you want lunch?'

So Seb definitely hadn't arrived yet. Natalie edged towards the door. 'I'll have a shower first. OK if I use your hair-dryer?'

Beth paused fractionally. 'Fine. It's in my wardrobe.'

'Thanks.' Quick, say something normal. 'Don't eat all the Brie, will you? I love it when it's all runny and sell-by-date-ish like that.'

Owen winked, lazily good-humoured. 'Fear not, sparrow. No need to rush the transformation scene.'

'Owen!' said Beth, half-laughing.

Natalie didn't care. She raced up the stairs and had the fastest shower and hair-wash on record, not even giving a thought to how unusually tidy Mum's room was as she fished the dryer down. She changed, changed again, and finally settled for jeans and a skinny top. Then she fetched a plate of cheese and biscuits, put the radio on and wedged herself into her windowsill to watch for Seb. Another hour ticked by, during which she convinced herself that she'd embarrassed him so much he'd decided not to stay with them after all. When at last his Cabriolet slid to a stop, she flew down the hall and out of the front door as if her heels had wings.

'Seb!'

'Hi, Nats.' He turned from getting his bags out of the back seat and flicked back his fringe. He met her eyes carefully, didn't avoid her.

In a single, astonishingly long moment, Natalie felt herself grow up. Seb didn't have to kiss her, didn't have to touch her. He was there. There was something between them. It was enough.

'Where have you been?' she teased. 'Owen arrived ages ago and Cate's already doing get-in.'

He winced. 'Why doesn't she get hang-overs like normal people? She drank just as much as me last night. At least, I think she did. Am I allowed in?'

She laughed happily. 'I'll make some tea.'

Supper was wicked. Having spent the afternoon in low-voiced conversation with Owen, followed by a couple of computer games with Robin, Seb was finally sitting beside her, telling her all about *Tin Pan Ali*.

'Don't listen to him, sparrow. It's all lies,' said Owen, liberally refilling glasses. He seemed different today, supercharged with energy and hardly swearing at all. Natalie felt rather that way herself.

'We're coming to see it tomorrow,' she said. 'Sue got party-rates. And again on Saturday. In the decent seats, what's more!'

'You'll like it,' said Cate, who had arrived half-way through the meal and was now eating rapidly to catch up. 'Owen hams like no one's business, but everyone else is really good.'

'Thank you, sweeting. I'll remember you in my memoirs.'

'Yes, but Cate, Ned *told* him to go over-the-top-Italian when Carooni is pretending to be the Major Domo in Act Two–' Seb broke off, taking in Cate's dead-pan expression. 'Oh, sorry.'

Cate finished her wine. 'Better,' she said. 'That didn't take you nearly as long to catch on to. Before I forget, Beth, can I have breakfast at seven?'

'Sure,' said Beth. 'I'll be up about half-six, anyway.'

'Half-six?' spluttered Owen.

Natalie's brow creased. There had been the tiniest laugh in the back of Mum's voice. And she was humming the Eurythmics *'Seventeen Again'* as she cleared up.

Robin looked at the clock. 'Hey, *The Man With One Red Shoe* is about to start.'

Seb pushed his chair back. 'Great. I *love* that film.'

'*I* love Tom Hanks,' murmured Cate to

176

Natalie. 'Owen, you didn't hear that.'

Natalie hesitated, wanting to watch the film, wanting to sit next to Seb if at all possible, but knowing she ought to help with the washing up.

Owen winked at her. *'I'll* keep your mum company while she toils.'

Natalie looked at Beth. 'Really?'

Beth grinned. 'I'll let you off this once.' She threw a tea towel at Owen. 'Domestic service,' she quoted, 'is good for the soul.'

Natalie grinned too, and went through the swing door. Robin was draped across the two-seater, Seb was in one corner of the big settee, and Cate just settling herself into the other. Perfect, thought Natalie, plumping herself down between them. Seb smiled at her from behind his fall of blond fringe. Double perfect, she thought happily.

The swing door closed behind Natalie. A second later they heard the film start. Owen stood up and Beth moved with beating heart into his arms. As his lips covered hers and his tongue swept sensually across the roof of her mouth, she melted against his vibrant, compact body and wondered how she could bear waiting until everybody had gone to bed before making love to him again. She slid her hand down to pummel his gorgeously neat backside and felt him swell against her.

'Playing with fire, mistress,' murmured

Owen. 'I've seduced women in kitchens before.'

She threaded her other hand through his hair. 'Not kitchens with swing doors leading to lounges where your colleagues and landlady's kids are watching TV.'

He hooked his leg round her ankles and threatened to unbalance her. 'Always a first time.'

They kissed again, their bodies closer than Beth had believed it was possible to get with four layers of clothing between them. She wriggled her hand until she could feel the crisp springiness of his chest hair through his tee shirt. Lust swept through her. 'I suppose there's no chance you'd like a shower tonight?'

'Going to share it with me?'

'You never know.'

He held her tightly. 'Christ, Beth, I wish–'

'I'll see if there was any left.' Cate's clear voice came from the other side of the door. Beth instantly spun away from Owen and turned on the taps in a frantic rush of soapsuds. 'Wine, Beth. Did we finish it all?'

Beth dumped glasses in the rapidly filling sink. 'Yes. Do you want to open another bottle? Or there's beer.'

'Beer do, Seb?'

'Fine.'

'Being barmaid, sweeting?' Beth heard Owen say. 'I'll have a Scotch.'

'In your dreams! Besides, it's impossible to dry up while drinking. You end up tipping it all over the tea towel. Isn't that right, Beth?'

Beth turned her head. 'Famous government slogan – Don't Drink And Dry.'

Owen's wicked hazel eyes caught and held hers. She heard Cate complain, 'You're worse than *he* is,' as she carried the beers into the lounge.

'We're going to have to tell them,' said Owen, reaching for a glass to dry. 'Because I tell you straight, woman, I can hardly keep my hands off you.'

Beth plunged dessert bowls into the suds at random. 'I know we'll have to,' she said breathlessly. 'I'm just not sure how.'

'Can I have a coke, Mum?' called Robin.

'Get it yourself,' she shouted back. Owen's arm deliberately brushed hers as he dried another glass.

Rob darted in, propping the door open with his foot so he could still watch the film. 'Hurry up,' he said to them. 'You'll miss the good bit.'

This time it was their thighs which briefly touched. A tremor ran through Beth. 'Oh, I don't think so.'

'No danger of that at all,' agreed Owen.

They watched the last hour of the film from separate armchairs, Owen nursing his favourite malt, Beth letting the fiery sweetness of the Drambuie he'd brought her trickle along her veins.

'What's this?' she'd murmured when he'd produced it. 'Bribery in case I failed to fall for your charms?'

'Self defence. I couldn't face you desecrating my whisky again.'

The late night hot-chocolate-or-milky-tea ritual seemed to stretch to infinity.

'At last,' said Owen, ghosting into her room wearing nothing but his midnight-blue bathrobe and linking his hands in a wonderfully possessive fashion around her hips. 'Sod the shower, Beth, I want you like there's no tomorrow.'

Beth wound her arms fiercely round his neck. She felt herself tremble, felt her breasts peak and strain towards him. 'Then get on and bloody take me.'

His eyes gleamed. 'Just like that? No foreplay?'

'Give me strength, Owen!' She was damn near hyperventilating with frustration. 'What the hell have we been doing all evening if it wasn't foreplay?'

He slipped her dressing gown off her shoulders, then wrapped his around them both. Beth gasped in surprise. 'Actors should never neglect the basics,' he said.

He was so, so close. She was drowning in the smell of Aztec For Men and the touch of his terry-towelling. 'Just get *on* with it,' she begged.

'Final answer?' he teased, holding her tighter.

'Owen!'

'Don't say you weren't warned. I hope these double-strength chappies live up to their name. Oh Christ, Beth.'

Yesterday she'd been nervous. Today she was so ready it wasn't true. As soon as he entered her, she took off like a rocket.

'God, I'm sorry,' he said a few moments later. 'I haven't done that since I was a teenager.'

She lay under him, tangled in bathrobe, glowing and euphoric. 'You can't be sorry,' she said with conviction. 'Not if that was as good for you as it was for me.' She pulled his head down to let her tongue twine gloriously with his. Inside her, he stiffened and twitched. She let out an involuntary gasp as a further shiver of delight rippled through her.

Owen was startled but approving. 'It hasn't done *that* since I was a teenager either. Let me out, woman, I may need a change of costume.'

Much, much later Beth said, 'I'm not that good a bet, you know. The kids have always come first, my body's shot, I spend ages on schoolwork and my cooking's quite a long way from Cordon Bleu.'

Owen laid a trail of tiny kisses from one

breast to the other. 'A man could betray his country for one of your breakfasts – and I don't give a bee's fart about the rest. I just want to lie with you like this, always and forever.'

Happiness, painful in its intensity, gushed her upwards by several feet. His busy, flickering tongue kept her there. 'What,' she said, *'exactly* like this?'

He shifted slightly. 'Mmm, no, maybe like this. Or like this. Or this is good...'

'Admit it, you don't know what you want from one moment to the next.'

She felt his mouth curve into a smile against her skin. 'Now that's where you're wrong, mistress. I know precisely what I want in say the next five minutes. Slither down here and I'll whisper it to you.'

Beth slithered.

CHAPTER 9

Watching the show on Monday night was a very curious experience. As soon as Owen appeared, the rest of the cast faded away for Beth. She followed his flamboyant progress from one side of the stage to the other, her ears filtering out everyone but him. When he made his exit she snapped back to reality with something of a shock.

'What did you think? Magnificent or what?' said Owen cheerfully as the cast emerged from the stage door to be pounced on for autographs.

'Decent!' said Robin and Jack, doing a passable rendition of the thieves' dustcart dance.

Sue grinned. 'They've been trying to convince me there's still time to change the school production to *Tin Pan Ali* even though they know perfectly well we're making the casting decisions for *Grease* tomorrow.'

Owen looked at Beth closely. 'What's up?'

How could he know? 'Nothing,' she said, 'except I haven't the faintest idea what happened in your scenes.'

Owen's eyes held hers. The others in the alley might not have existed. 'Then you'll have to come again,' he said, a deep joy in his voice. 'But not tomorrow.'

Her hand strayed towards his. She pulled it back. 'Why not tomorrow?'

He'd noticed the movement. His mouth quirked. 'You'll laugh.'

'I've been laughing since Saturday night.'

His eyes crinkled. 'Me too. But I'd rather you didn't. Not this time.'

She wanted to touch him, hold him. 'Then I won't. Tell me.'

'I want to come back from the show and find you at home. I want you to look up from marking and smile at me. I want to make us a cup of tea and wind down just by talking to you. Stupid, right?'

Beth's heart was beating uncomfortably fast. 'You realise you'll have Rob with you? He and Jack nipped out at the interval to buy themselves limited-view tickets.'

Owen smiled in a way which melted her bones. 'Makes no difference.'

'Owen!' Natalie brandished her programme at him.

Beth drew away, unsure what was happening to her.

Tuesday morning. Cate heard Beth singing in the kitchen. As she pushed open the door Beth's head whipped round. 'Oh,' she said after an infinitesimal hesitation, 'I didn't realise you were going in early today.'

Cate helped herself to a mug of tea. 'The moving staircase stuck again so I need to check it out. Didn't you hear the unmagical thud as we forced it forward by hand just after Luke said "Open Sesame" and it didn't?'

'Never noticed a thing. Is it going to be tricky?'

'Just a thorough grease job.' She felt Beth's eyes on her and squirmed. 'I've been having lowering thoughts about Luke.'

'If he ever wants to stay...'

Cate drank her tea. 'That was my lowering thought. He's taken such good care no one knows about us, that if he *was* here he'd be indistinguishable from Owen and Seb. Except he'd doubtless sneak into my room under cover of darkness. But even then only because I was handy. Bloody actors. You can't trust them further than you can throw them.'

Beth's back was towards her. 'There has to be more to it than sex, surely,' she said, her voice a little stiff.

'Only when he *wants* something more than sex. Sunday morning he didn't give a toss that I was going to be late. The only time he's ever been voluntarily sensitive was when I ripped up about using *me* to make excuses to *his* mother!'

Beth smiled, almost with relief. 'There you are then. He listened and it made a difference.'

'Pity it didn't last.' She finished her tea, remembering how he'd ambushed her coming down from the office that time there was all the fuss about the Voice possibly doing the panto, how sweet he'd been. 'The bastard!' she yelled. She met Beth's startled eyes. 'He did it so I'd back *his* claim against Ellery's if Ned put *Jack* to a vote. As soon as he knew he'd got the role it was business as bloody usual!' She simmered, furious with herself for being so taken in.

Beth put toast and marmalade in front of her. 'Pile it as high as you like. I got it dirt cheap because it's got a sell-by date of next week. Think of it as medicinal.' Her voice grew carefully non-committal. 'You could always turn the tables and use *him* just for sex. I'm told it's very therapeutic.'

Cate was nicely greasy, and the moving stairs behaving as if they'd never given trouble, when she became aware of muffled voices from the stage door. She sat back on her haunches, her muscles tense. There was no matinée today, no reason for anyone to be here this early. She strained to catch the whispers.

'Sure there's no one in?'

'Why would there be?'

'Piss off if you're chicken,' said a third voice. 'This won't take long.'

There was a creak as the greenroom door

186

opened. Cate let Annis, Perry and Matthews get half-way across the stage before she straightened up and said, 'Morning, boys,' in a voice like a whiplash.

They spun in an explosion of foul language. She faced them down, blazingly furious at whatever they were pulling, knowing only that *FOOTLIGHTS* was *her* company and she'd defend it against meddling toerags like these while there was still breath in her body.

'Forgot my mobile,' said Annis in a surly voice, daring her to contradict him.

'It's not in the wings. I check them every night.' She watched until he 'found' it behind a rack of costumes in the dressing room, then ushered them out into the alley and locked the door. Then she rang Stella.

From her bedroom window, Natalie watched Sue reverse into the drive. 'Cheryl Foster will have got Sandy,' she said to Lisa with dismal certainty.

'And boring Paul will be Danny,' said Lisa. 'It's well unfair. We're better than Cheryl's crowd but they always win the parts because they're older.'

'At least you're bound to be Cha-Cha.'

'Yes, but if I was Rizzo and Jason was Kenickie, we could dance together.'

Privately Natalie thought there was more chance of Robin swapping his Gameboy for a graphics calculator. They crossed fingers

187

at each other and sauntered down to the kitchen.

'Good meeting?' asked Lisa.

Sue eyed them with amusement. 'Lovely, thank you. Natalie, you're Sandy.'

A huge grin split Natalie's face. Triumphal cheering sounded in her ears. Her chest felt as if it would burst.

'What about me?' said Lisa.

'Cha-Cha. Sorry, pet, but you're the best dancer we have. Leonie's going to choreograph the Competition Dance especially for you.'

Lisa didn't even try to hide her disappointment. 'And I'll have to do it with Paul Bowman and he can't dance for toffee.'

Sue and Beth exchanged glances. 'Paul isn't Danny,' said Sue, her words dropping like small stones. 'Jason is.'

Natalie came out of her dizzy delight and stared.

So did Lisa. 'But Mum, Paul's got the best voice in the school. Everyone *knows* he'll be Danny.'

'Then everyone is wrong. Danny has to be an all-rounder, which is what Jason is. All the staff agreed.'

'No!' yelled Lisa, her face turning bright red. 'No!'

Natalie stiffened. 'I've sung with Jason before, Lis.'

'In concerts! And when you were both

188

rabbits! And I wasn't going out with him then, was I?'

'What's that got to do with anything?'

Lisa stamped her foot in frustration. 'You're Sandy, he's Danny! *He's going to have to kiss you!*'

'It won't bloody mean anything!' Natalie shouted back. 'You ought to be *pleased* for him.'

'*It isn't fair!*' screamed Lisa.

'What the hell is all the racket?' yelled Owen, pushing open the door with his hair tousled and his dressing gown on. Even Lisa faltered before the picture of an angry man, woken up against his will.

'Lisa is being stupid!' spat Natalie. 'Just because I'm Sandy in the school play and Jason is Danny.'

Owen looked at Lisa. 'What are you? Cha-Cha?'

Natalie's voice was tight with rage. 'Yes, and she's jealous because Jason and I might have to kiss and she doesn't trust me! It's bloody *acting*, Lisa!'

'So? Going to pretend you won't enjoy it? I've seen you watching us!'

'You're hardly discreet! What am I supposed to do, stare at the wall?'

Owen slammed an exasperated hand down on the table before they could spring at each other. 'Christ! Nats, how many boys have you kissed?'

'I–' Natalie couldn't concentrate with the anger boiling inside her. 'Seven?'

'Remember what it felt like?'

She glanced at him contemptuously. 'No!'

'Good. Lips together, eyes closed.' Owen took a stride across to her, gripped her shoulders and put his mouth over hers. Her eyes opened wide in shock; a chair scraped as her mother scrambled up. 'There,' he said, stepping back, 'what did that look like, Lisa?'

Lisa's mouth worked. 'Pretty hot,' she managed.

'It was supposed to. Nats, how did it feel?'

She scrubbed her mouth vigorously. 'Disgusting! Like the time I had my tooth out and the dentist gave me gas.'

'Nothing like a kiss then?'

'No way!'

Owen smiled sardonically and turned to Lisa. 'How many boys have *you* kissed?'

'Nine,' muttered Lisa, backing away from him.

Natalie could hardly bear to look. He'd done that to her? Gross! She felt sick!

'One stage kiss. *You* teach it to your boyfriend. *He* can use it on Natalie. Now will someone please get me some tea!'

Mum's hands were gripping the table. She jerked her head at the girls. Natalie couldn't get out into the hall fast enough. Lisa shot out too and stood with her back pressed flat against the closed door. They stood there, chests heaving, half raw, half defensive.

'Seven?' said Lisa at last. 'I thought it was only six.'

'I thought yours was only six too,' said Natalie. 'Who were seven, eight and nine?'

'Thank you, Owen,' said Sue. 'From the bottom of my heart.' She stood up. 'I've got to go into Cambridge. I'll take the girls for retail therapy.'

Beth hoped her smile looked normal. 'Never failed yet.' There was silence in the kitchen after she left. Beth cleared her throat. 'Pretty good acting.'

'Outraged artiste. One of my best impressions.' His eyes met hers. 'Shit, it bothered you, didn't it?'

Her temper exploded. 'My brand-new lover making a heavy pass at my daughter? Of course it bloody bothered me! Did you think it might not?'

He caught her hand. In spite of her cocktail of feelings, the pressure of his fingers sent ripples along each and every nerve. 'I didn't think full stop,' he said quietly. 'I'm sorry, Beth. I realised how it must look as soon as I saw your face.'

'It was horrible.' More than horrible. Devastating. Her legs were still in shock and try as she might, she couldn't help hearing Cate's bitter animadversions on actors dinning in her head.

He let her hand go and drank his tea, then cocked his head at the silent lounge. 'Where is everyone?'

This was what Alan did, pretended everything was all right when it wasn't. She rubbed her forehead fiercely.

Owen stood and gathered her into his arms. 'I really am sorry, Beth. Believe it or not, I was trying to help. Instead I hurt you. I'll try thinking next time.'

Not like Alan, she thought as every separate part of her dissolved into his embrace. Not like Cate's Luke either, her brain insisted. 'And *I'll* try to remember actors have a different outlook on life,' she said.

He held her close. 'So where *are* the others?'

'Seb's taken Rob and Jack to the Leisure Centre. Nats was horribly torn. She desperately wanted Seb to see her in a swimsuit, but she also wanted to be here when Sue got back from the casting meeting.'

'And professionalism won. Good for her. At that age, I'd have opted for the pool every time. The hours I used to spend posing on the diving board, or thrashing up and down, sizing up who to accidentally swim into next.'

Given the shaky state of her feelings, Beth thought she did well only to give an involuntary gasp at the image of Owen hoisting himself athletically out of the water and climbing, dripping and glistening, to the diving board.

'*Now* what have I said?' Damn him, he'd spotted her weakness. His eyes were warming, turning mischievous.

'Nothing.'

'Hmm.' His fingers walked up her spine. 'Fancy checking out your shower?'

He *had* picked up on it! Helpless lust gripped her. 'It's the middle of the day,' she said weakly.

'But we're alone in the house, mistress.' Now his eyes were definitely wicked. 'And an actor's landlady has to be flexible.'

It was lust, decided Beth that night as she briskly marked creative poetry exercises (very creative in Star's case, less so in Felicity's, non-existent in Yob's). Pure, unadulterated lust fed by freedom from responsibility. Nothing else could explain the totally wanton way she had behaved in the shower with Owen. Really appallingly wanton, she recollected, blushing hotly. She hadn't known you *could* do all those things in a space three foot square. It was sex, that was all, after five months of abstinence, and when *FOOTLIGHTS* moved to Oldham at the end of the week that would be an end to it. It might flare up again at Christmas and if it did, well, that would be nice. *Nice?*

screamed her libido in disbelief. Of *course* it would be nice. It would be bloody *wonderful!* But Beth had chaperoned in the wings too often and listened to too many of Cate's stories about actors changing partners as frequently as they changed scripts, to let her sex drive or imagination take her any further.

There was the sound of a key in the front door. Rob burst in, telling her the show had been even better than the night before and *please* could she advance him the week after next's pocket money so he could go again tomorrow? Seb followed, strung up and tense-but-happy, and then Owen. As he came through the doorway, she turned her head towards him and surprised such a look of astonished joy on his face that her heart leapt up and battered to be recognised. 'You're marking,' he said as if they were alone in a marble hall with crystal fountains playing softly in the distance. 'Tea?'

'Please,' she replied.

He walked across the room towards the kitchen, resting his hand briefly on her shoulder as he passed.

Oh dear God, realised Beth, staring at a page of Chantelle's multi-coloured loops and curls unseeingly. *I'm in love with Owen.*

'Hi,' said Seb, bounding into the kitchen next morning. 'I smell bacon.'

'Sorry it's so early,' Beth apologised, 'but Nats has got a singing lesson to make a start on the *Grease* songs and if I don't get into the market today we're going to have no vegetables for the rest of the week.'

Seb sat down next to Cate and helped himself to cereal. 'When is the show?'

Natalie was simultaneously eating her own bacon sandwich and cutting bread for Robin's. 'Six weeks' time. The week before the end of term. Sue doesn't believe in letting people get stale.'

Seb's spoon paused briefly. 'Middle of December. We're in rehearsal. We could come up and see it.'

Beth's head whipped round to see Nats narrowly miss severing her index finger with the bread knife.

'Good idea,' said Owen, sauntering in. 'You watch us all the time. Why shouldn't we watch you?' He leaned over Beth's shoulder. 'Mmm, poetry in a pan.'

'What has got *into* you this week?' said Cate in disgust. 'I can't take much more niceness.'

'You didn't see him yesterday,' said Natalie with feeling.

He was wearing Aztec For Men again. Oh God, and his hair was damp. Beth felt her bones liquefy. She prayed no one else would notice the effect he was having on her. 'Is that bread ready, Nats?' she said.

Natalie hastily spread margarine and ketchup and passed the plate across. 'Did you mean it?' she asked Seb shyly. 'About coming to see *Grease?*'

Seb chased a spoonful of cornflakes around the bowl. 'If we can get away.' He eyed Rob's plate in a way Moses would definitely have disapproved of. 'Could I have my bacon in a sandwich too? They're so Sunday-morning-at-college-ish.'

Owen was flicking through the paper. Beth was aware of his every move. 'More bread, Nats, and then you'd better go. Rob, yours is ready!'

Cate went upstairs. Natalie departed for her singing lesson. Seb took his bacon sandwiches into the lounge to watch cartoons with Robin.

Owen moved behind Beth and blew down her ear. '*I'd* like eggs and fried bread and tomatoes with mine,' he said. 'Mushrooms too if you've got them.'

She twisted in his arms, absurdly happy. 'Cate warned me you were a con artist. All this sex is a ruse to get extra breakfast, isn't it?'

'You guessed,' said Owen, gathering her into a good-morning kiss just as Cate remembered she hadn't picked up her tea, Seb pushed open the door to ask for ketchup, and Natalie came flying back down the side path.

196

'Forgot the music,' Natalie panted. 'I – oh, *shit!*' She stood frozen, staring in total shock at her mother.

No! No, not like this! Beth's joy fled. She pulled away from Owen and crossed the room, appalled. 'I was going to tell you, sweetheart.'

Natalie jerked into motion. 'I'll be late.' She snatched up the score, whirled round and seconds later they heard her feet thudding up the path.

'I knew it,' said Cate with immense satisfaction. 'I *knew* it wasn't just winding Monty up every night which was putting you in such a sickeningly good mood.'

'Lay off,' said Seb. He grinned at Owen and Beth. 'Congratulations. I think it's really nice.' He peeled open his sandwich and added liberal quantities of ketchup to it. 'Poor Nats, though. The least you can do, Cate, is to ring Stella and ask if she and Rob and Beth can watch from the company box tonight.'

'Sebastian Merchant! Are you being assertive?'

Seb retreated behind his fringe. 'I might be.'

Beth felt flustered and pressured. 'There's no need.'

Cate unclipped her mobile. 'What's the point having power and influence if you don't abuse it?'

'Well, thanks, but – oh God, Owen, your breakfast!'

Owen turned from the frying pan, spatula in hand, smirking. 'It's a good thing some of us keep our heads in a domestic crisis.'

It was the last straw. Beth was no longer in control of her life. She untied her apron and passed it over his head. 'Keep it some more and finish off then,' she said. 'If I go shopping now, I should be home before Natalie has time to work herself into too much of a state.'

She got back with very little idea of what she'd bought and no idea at all of what she was going to say to her daughter. She found Nats sitting stonily on her bedroom windowsill. 'I'm sorry, sweetheart. I really *was* going to tell you.'

Natalie didn't look at her. 'Are you *in love?*' she said, spitting the words out.

'It only happened on Sunday,' said Beth. 'Neither of us has any idea *what* we are yet.'

Natalie stared resolutely at the house-over-the-road's roof. 'Are you sleeping together?'

Beth took a deep breath. 'Yes,' she said. 'I've been chucking him out at dawn into his own bed.' There was what might have been a glimmer of a smile on her daughter's face. 'I'm still charging him rent too.' The smile grew even though Natalie swung her hair down to hide it. 'And Cate's got us into the company box for free tonight as a what-a-relief-it's-all-out-in-the-open gesture.'

'Did she know then?'

'Nobody did. I told you, it only happened Sunday. Rob still hasn't got a clue unless Seb or Owen have filled him in. I like Owen a lot, Nats.'

Natalie almost looked at her mother properly. 'OK. I don't think *I* like it, but I'll be OK as long as I don't have to be nice to him.'

Beth sat down on the bed with a rush. 'Thanks. Although I'd rather you weren't actively unpleasant. God, I *so* need a cup of tea. How about you?'

Natalie nodded and slithered off her window sill. 'No one's done the washing up yet.'

'You amaze me.'

They went down to the kitchen nearly in accord. 'Shit, Mum! What's in all these carrier bags?'

Beth focused on the shopping with misgivings. 'No idea. We may have to be inventive with the menus.'

Her daughter pulled a large pineapple out of a bag, followed by six dressed crabs and a heterogenous collection of bones. 'And then some,' she said.

Natalie sat on the other side of the room from Owen as they watched the lunchtime news, not sure she ever wanted to speak to him again. All this time, he'd been worming his way into Mum's bed. God, she felt sick.

'—organisers are red-faced as Digby Sellwick, the local entrepreneur who was to have opened this week's Fireworks Display, was arrested last night for fraud. They are now hoping to attract someone from the world of entertainment. Mr Sellwick, whose meteoric career...'

'We went to that last year,' said Robin. 'It was well cool.'

'*Well cool,*' muttered Beth. 'No one would believe you had an English teacher for a parent.'

Cate's mobile erupted into life. 'Hi, Stella!' Natalie saw an unholy gleam appear in her eyes. 'Isn't it obvious? Owen, of course. He'd be *delighted.* His Dame Trot costume arrives tomorrow for the photoshoot.' She passed the phone across, making a Strike One gesture in the air.

Natalie exchanged a puzzled look with Rob as Owen, with every appearance of amiability, agreed to open Cambridge's Bonfire Night Display in full Pantomime Dame regalia.

'Nicely done, sweeting,' he drawled, throwing the mobile back.

'That was really underhand,' said Seb hotly. 'Spoiling Owen and Beth's last evening.'

Natalie was startled by his vehemence. So was Cate, to judge by her expression. 'Crap. Actors love showing off and it'll be great publicity for *Jack And The Beanstalk*, especially if you go too.' Her eyes went thoughtfully to Natalie and Robin. 'I don't suppose Lisa and Jack would like to be up on the platform as well?'

Robin did a standing back-flip in his excitement. 'Of *course* they would! It means we get to watch the display from the Stand! Cool or what!'

Cate was already on the phone back to Stella.

'Tell her I'll need somewhere to change,' called Owen. 'I'm buggered if I'm standing round in petticoats and a purple wig all night.' He looked across at Beth, an odd expression on his face. 'Do *you* mind?'

Natalie felt a sharp pain under her ribs as her mother smiled at him. 'It's your job.' She gathered up the lunch plates and took them into the kitchen. Natalie made to follow, but stopped when she realised Owen was going through. God, this was horrible! She felt like a spare part in her own house.

'Sorted,' said Cate. 'Have you got dungarees, Nats?'

Natalie nodded. Beside her, she sensed Seb steeling himself. 'It was still dirty,' he said doggedly. 'I agree it's good publicity, but you suggested it mainly to annoy Owen.

Why do you always have to be one-up?'

Cate shrugged. 'It's more comfortable.'

Robin started up the Gamecube, handing a controller to Seb. Natalie felt scratchy and unwanted. She followed Cate upstairs.

'Does it really upset you?' said Cate. 'Owen and your mum getting together?'

'Of course it does. They're – well, they're old!'

'But your dad's going out with that gruesome gift-plan woman and you aren't wound up about her.'

'That's different. I hate him.'

'And it doesn't bother Rob.'

'Power cuts and battery failures are the only things that do. He's so unstressed I could strangle him.'

'You should meet *my* brother. Lands on his feet every time. I like your mum, Nats. And if she likes Owen, incomprehensible as it seems...'

'Oh God, I know. I know what I must look like to everybody. It's just – they're sleeping together...'

Cate raked her hair. 'I can't pass judgement on that. Bloody Luke only has to look at me and I'm falling into bed with him. The only way not to is to shut my eyes every time we have a conversation. It's a natural attraction thing. Different for different people. Addictive too, which you'll find out for yourself one of these days.' She changed tack abruptly. 'D'you want to come in with me this afternoon? Potter around backstage?'

Natalie bit her lip. 'You don't have to,' she said.

Cate grinned. 'I need you as protection from Luke's "It's been four days, aren't you missing me yet?" eyes.'

'Yeah, right.'

'True. If I can hold out a whole week, I can go to bed with him in Oldham knowing I'm not a total pushover.'

'I won't be in the way?'

'Straight up.'

As soon as she stepped through the stage door, Natalie felt her scratchiness fall away. The actors might grope each other as a matter of course in the wings, but sex had no part in this busy backstage world. Away from Lisa and Jason's constant kissing, away from Mum and Owen, away from Seb and the uncomfortable, longing way he made her feel, she felt as if this dusty, creaking, greasepaint-scented otherworld might really be for her. When the cast trickled in as if this was any old job and started on their dance and vocal warm-ups, she ached to take part.

Owen's eyes had been on her from the moment he'd arrived. After a series of cross-stage leaps, he challenged her. 'Join in if you want.'

'Shut up,' she said. 'I hate you.'

He shrugged. 'Suit yourself.' But when the cast dispersed, he jerked his head. 'Let's have it out in private, sparrow.'

She followed him. 'I don't have to.'

'Then we do it in the corridor.' He opened the door to his and Luke's room. 'Mr Bartholomew, you are officially deaf for the next five minutes.'

Luke smiled at Natalie and switched his personal CD player on while he set out greasepaint tubes and powder. A jolt ran through her; he was nowhere near as good-looking as Seb, but she rather thought she saw what Cate might mean.

'So,' said Owen, sitting on his chair and gesturing for her to take the spare one in the corner, 'do you really hate me?'

'Of course I do, you're being disgusting with Mum.'

'It's not disgusting at all,' retorted Owen. 'It's remarkably pleasant. Of course it's not the same when you have to keep checking your pacemaker...'

'Shut up,' said Natalie. There was a small silence while she stared fixedly at his make-up case. He was setting out his things too, not quite in the same order as Luke, but as if it really mattered where each stick went on the bench. Natalie dragged her attention back to what she wanted to say. 'The thing is, I almost liked you. But now I know you were only being nice to me to get on the right side of Mum. I *hate* being used like that.'

Owen slipped on a wide band to keep the hair off his face. 'Christ, how self-centred can you get!'

Natalie blinked in shock. Owen continued to talk while he applied a swarthy base. 'Teenagers. You think you're the centre of the sodding universe. I fell for Beth as soon as I saw her. Neither you, your dad nor Rob came into the picture at all. I couldn't believe my luck when she seemed to like me too. If I've put *you* right a couple of times, it's because it irritates me beyond belief to see you getting the wrong end of the stick so often.'

'You mean – you *do* like me?'

Owen cast up his eyes in exasperation. 'You have the makings of a good kid. Let's not put it any higher than that, shall we?'

CHAPTER 10

Early rising, thought Beth on Thursday morning, clearly wasn't Owen's best thing.

'Whose stupid idea,' he growled as Cate jogged his elbow pouring out her second cup of tea, 'was it to have the panto photo-shoot on a matinée day?'

'The publicity people. If you *knew* all the things I've got to do today as well as getting two shows ready!'

Natalie came pelting downstairs in the year-before-last's dungarees. 'They're too short!' she wailed.

'Wouldn't be bad on stage,' said Cate. 'See what Graham thinks.'

'You're certainly not going to the Firework Opening in them,' Beth said firmly. 'You'll freeze to death.'

'Occupational hazard,' said Owen. 'On the *Joseph* tour we were forever doing publicity stuff wearing nothing but bloody dung-arees.'

'When was that?' asked Seb.

Owen caught Beth's eye. '*Several* years ago. I was the fire-eating brother with the range of useful voices. I was never more pleased in my life than when my contract was up.'

Natalie's eyes were enormous. 'But it's a wicked show!'

'I saw it at college,' said Seb over more marmalade than even Rob could fit onto one piece of toast. 'I *yearned* to play Benjamin. Did you go, Cate?'

'Who d'you think organised the trip? It looked like bloody hard work. Probably why Owen didn't like it.'

Owen poured himself another mug of tea. 'Excuse me, sweeting, I loved the show, it was the *schedule* I hated. Matinées two days out of three and the only time off is spent driving from one venue to the next. And it gets so sodding tedious doing the same routines day in day out for over a year!'

Beth frowned as she flipped another lot of toast into the rack. 'West End shows run longer than that.'

'The actors live at home. And some folk don't mind doing the same things over and over. I get bored.'

'That's because you're a miserable sod and have zero life,' said Cate. 'It's only the challenge of learning a new show every eleven weeks and sneering at everyone in sight which keeps you going. That and being cosseted by your handpicked landladies. You should *see* the way Mrs Harris in Canterbury treats him, Beth. Cream teas as soon as he sets foot in the door. Electric blankets at night. Morning tea in bed. Seb thought he'd been warped to a parallel universe this tour.'

'Shut it,' said Owen, his hazel eyes flashing dangerously.

Cate raised her eyebrows. 'I was only–'

'I said shut it! I know things about you too. For instance that you haven't been laid this week–'

'Owen, that's a bit–'

'Butt out, Seb, this is *my* quarrel! My love life is nothing to do with you, Owen!'

'Then don't make *my* life a subject for *your* inconsequential anecdotes!'

'Inconsequential–' Cate spluttered with rage.

'Are you bringing Nats and Rob in for their costumes, Beth,' said Seb desperately, 'or would they like to come with me?'

Beth raised her voice. 'Thanks, but I'm picking up Jack and Lisa and staying to chaperone. You could all come with us, except we'll be gone by the matinée so you'd have to get a taxi home.'

Attracted by the acrimonious exchanges Rob was standing open-mouthed by the swing door. Seb gave him an awkward grin. 'Not watching again, then?'

'No money.'

'You were the one who wanted the extra dance lessons,' Beth pointed out.

'I could–' began Seb. 'I mean, there might be enough of the expenses money left to–'

'No way!' said Robin, colouring. Beth saw

208

an idea stray across his face. 'Unless you want to pay me for cleaning your car?'

'Done,' said Seb promptly. 'What are the limited-view seats? A fiver?' He got his wallet out.

'Cool! Mum, can I give Jack a ring?' He dashed into the hall without waiting for an answer.

Beth glanced cautiously at Owen and Cate, but the spat had disintegrated and Owen was gazing after Rob.

'He can go too,' called Rob. 'Sue says she'll take us if Seb can bring us home.' He bounced back, dropping the *Fenbourne Echo* and *The Stage* on the worktop.

'Seb's car will be here being cleaned,' Owen reminded him. 'I'll do it.'

'Wicked,' said Robin.

Beth handed Owen *The Stage*. 'You can read it first. As compensation for not being cosseted.' She was surprised not to receive a jokey reply. Instead he buried himself in the theatre reviews. In anyone else, she'd have said the barricades had just gone up.

'Decent! Look at these!' The kids rummaged enthusiastically through the bag of costumes on the stage.

'Old stock,' said Graham indulgently, rescuing a swirling rainbow skirt in blues and pinks and purples. 'Except this which Cate's mama made as soon as Sally-Go-Round-

The-Moon was described to her. And a most *edible* wig to go with it, full of stardust and comets.'

'Wicked!' gasped Lisa.

From the dressing rooms came a barrage of un-Dame-like oaths. Graham tutted. The kids giggled.

'What do we do with the costumes after the fireworks?' said Beth.

'Fran's organising a courier, but could you *please* make sure Owen packs Dame Trot's stuff up carefully? He's inclined to be a little careless when rushed.'

'He's inclined to be a pain in the arse,' said Cate coming on stage. 'He says Mum hasn't taken into account the fact he has to breathe, plus he's not mad about the orange pigtails.'

'What about Luke?' said Beth, sotto voce as Cate prepared to follow Graham off.

Cate glowered. 'Luke is looking imposs-ibly bloody handsome as Mum knew he would when she designed Jack's tunic and tights to match his eyes! It's Seb she's skimped on.'

Ned appeared. He drew Beth aside. 'Young Natalie,' he said without preamble. 'Sitting GCSEs in June, Cate tells me. What's she doing after that?'

Beth looked at him warily. 'A-levels. Music, Drama, English and Psychology.'

'Stunning voice for her age. Cate says

210

she's Sandy at school this Christmas. Mind if Adrian and I watch?'

'Why?' said Beth, too astonished to be polite.

'We're thinking of *The Lion, The Witch and The Wardrobe* for the summer tour. If April plays the oldest girl, I want someone Natalie's age for the younger one and I *don't* want to break in a new kid every week.'

Beth drew a quick breath, her head whirling. 'Please don't think I'm not grateful, or sensible of what a tremendous opportunity it would be, but ten weeks on tour when you're only sixteen is a long time.'

'That's why I'm asking *you*, not her. Think it over. I'll speak to you in the New Year.'

Beth watched him go, deeply perturbed. It was one thing to talk about her daughter being born for the stage. It was quite another to wave her off into a hotbed of sex and gossip for two-and-a-half months before she was even seventeen.

'Well, beloved, how do I look?'

Owen stood before her in Lily Savage make-up, orange pigtails, voluminous purple skirts and climbing boots.

'Oh my Lord,' said Beth involuntarily, clapping a hand to her mouth.

'I wish you meant that,' said Owen, his hazel eyes wry. He turned and surveyed the kids. 'Fall in!'

They looked up, startled, then scrambled

into line.

'Names?' barked Owen.

'Jack-Be-Nimble and Jack-Be-Quick,' recited Robin and Jack in unison.

'Have to be nimbler and quicker than that, lads,' said Owen. He produced a wooden spoon from his pocket and pointed it at Lisa. 'You?'

'Sally-Go-Round-The-Moon, sir,' said Lisa, trying not to laugh.

He rapped her knuckles.

'Margery Daw, *ma'am*,' said Natalie, saluting.

'Take a medal that girl,' said Owen. 'Dismissed.' He turned back to Beth. 'Revolted, mistress?'

Beth chuckled. 'Never. But I do think you need some really *large* purple bows on those plaits. At least two each side, one at the top and one at the end.'

Delight skimmed across Owen's mobile face. 'A la Felicity! I'll tell Graham. What did the Guvnor want?'

Beth rubbed her forehead. 'Later. Go and sort out your ribbons.'

Seb appeared. Beth couldn't see what had offended Cate about his costume, except that it was maybe a bit plain and ragged. 'Seb, how old were you when you had your first long engagement?'

'I spent eight weeks playing Mustard Seed and understudying Puck in Regent's Park the summer after my GCSEs, if that's what you mean.' His eyes lit up in remembrance. 'It rained the whole time and Bottom's head smelt *dreadful* and we all got colds, but I thought I'd died and gone to heaven. Being paid to do something I loved instead of stacking shelves in Tesco. I thought I'd really arrived!'

Beth smiled bleakly. 'Thanks.'

Owen and Beth sat downstairs quite late after the show. 'So what was Ned after?' asked Owen.

'He might want Nats to be Lucy in *The Lion, The Witch and The Wardrobe* all next summer.'

Owen's mouth twitched. 'That'll bugger up Alan's plans to get her a holiday job. More Drambuie?'

Beth's mood lifted fractionally. 'Yes, please. And I'd thought of that too.'

'Monty will be bloody Aslan, I can see it now. Bets I get landed with the Beaver.'

'Or the nice fawn who's turned to stone halfway through.'

'Thank you, beloved.'

'I'm just worried, Owen. Over-protective, probably. I can't possibly say no because Nats would kill me, but...'

He handed her the drink and shunted a slithering pile of books out of the way to sit next to her. 'Best thing that could happen, if you ask me.' His mouth twisted wryly as she looked at him, startled. 'Look, Beth, granted this is a sodding awful business to be in. Granted there are ten jobs going for every five hundred people to fill them. Granted the saddest, most screwed-up people on this planet are out-of-work actors. But she's a clever kid, she's stage mad, and if it's what she wants, you won't be able to stop her. A summer tour when you're sixteen doesn't enrol you for life but it *will* strip away the stardust. And if she does decide to make a career out of it, a summer tour with *FOOTLIGHTS* is a bloody great entry on your CV. Ned's fair. Stella will keep an eye on her.' He paused. 'I'll be there too.'

'I know.' She leaned into him and felt him stiffen. 'What's wrong?'

'Tired. Too long a day.'

Ice showered into her stomach. 'Owen, I've been a teacher longer than you've been an actor, and if there's one thing I recognise it's evasiveness. Is it us? Because if it is, I'd so much rather know about it now.'

'No!' He put his free hand to her cheek, forcing her to look at him. 'No, it's not us, except maybe in a way I don't quite believe yet.'

Hope seared her veins. She suppressed it. 'Then what?'

He hunched up again. 'Going to Oldham next week, messing around with the kids this morning, Rob washing Seb's car.'

'I'm sure he'll do yours if you pay him.'

There was a closed expression in his eyes. 'I've got a son, Beth.'

She was still for a moment. What was she supposed to say? He wasn't giving anything away. 'It figures. Nobody as appallingly sexy as you could get to thirty-eight without at least one reasonably serious relationship along the way.'

Owen drank again. 'Thank you, beloved. It's really not that big a deal. It's just – he's around Rob's age. It occurred to me this morning he might be washing cars for extra money too. And I don't have any idea what he'd spend his fiver on. I don't see him. I don't know him.'

'Want to talk about it?'

'Not much.'

'It might help.'

He shifted irritably. 'It was just an ordinary, messy, juvenile disaster, OK? We were both with the RSC being paid peanuts because we were just out of RADA. You know what kids are like at that age. Far too intense, everyone sleeping with everyone else, you don't know what day it is half the time, let alone whether you took precautions.' He paused. 'And we made a child.'

There was nothing she could say, nothing that wasn't trite or clichéd. She lifted her head and kissed his cheek. 'Oh, Owen,' she breathed.

'What could I do? I clung on to the RSC, doing Shakespeare after bloody Shakespeare, working part-time to pay the rent on a crappy bedsit, not realising how frustrated I was getting. Soon after Davy was born, the RSC offered me a tour. It was so much extra money that I took it and – oh, Beth, I swear to you I came alive again. I was free! Free, free, free! I sent Michelle all my pay out of sheer guilt and lived on whatever I could bum off the others in the cast. There was colour in the world again! There were snatches of song on the wind! When the tour ended I stuck it out for a week at home then signed on to do panto in Hartlepool. On the strength of that and the Shakespeare, I got a place in a *Return To The Forbidden Planet* tour. I don't remember how far we were into the run when Michelle wrote that she was getting married to the decorator who'd been doing up the boarding house, but I do remember the relief.'

The last drops of Drambuie lingered on Beth's tongue. Owen's malt was long gone. 'Did she stay with him?' she asked.

'Yes. But neither of them wanted me to have anything to do with Davy. They were going to have more children and they didn't want Davy feeling different. I said to hell with that, I'd send money each week through the bank, and if they didn't use it for his keep they could put it in the Post

Office for him. I said I'd always send cards at birthday and Christmas with my current address and they'd better bloody see he got them.'

There was a stretched-tight pause. Beth could feel Owen's pain. The pain of knowing himself a coward. The pain of having opened up his soul, only to find it shallow and illusory. 'And then I ran. There was a *Guys And Dolls* tour wanting cannon fodder, a season at Liverpool Rep, pantomimes, *Joseph*, a couple of bit parts in the West End, another tour. Anything and everything. I never looked back. Never even wanted to.'

They were silent for a long moment. She took his lesions and made them her own, knew she loved him, knew she couldn't ever tell him now in case he ran from her too. She rubbed her cheek on his hand and kissed it. 'We grow from our mistakes as well as our successes,' she said. 'Coming to bed?'

He met her eyes. 'I don't know. Evidence of things done and all that. Can I just hold you until I fall asleep?'

She smiled and pulled him to his feet. 'Not down here, lover. You'll get a crick in your neck.'

At around four in the morning Beth awoke. Owen's arm was flung across her. Carefully she eased it off. *You can't trust me,* that was what he'd been saying. *As soon as I feel trapped, I'll run.* But wasn't that exactly what she'd been thinking not long ago? That she'd never risk another permanent relationship? Certainly not with one who could rouse her so easily to desire because of all its attendant emotions like shame and despair. Beside her, Owen murmured in his sleep; his arm quested for her. She slipped her hand into his, waiting until his breathing lengthened before turning with her back to him. Alan had resented that, as if in trying to be comfortable, she'd been rejecting him. It had astonished her the first night with Owen how he'd tucked himself companionably against her like a pair of serving spoons in a velvet box. She smiled in the darkness. Perhaps she should think of being with Owen as like getting out Granny's best cutlery to set the table on special occasions. Not to be used every day in case it got spoiled and the joy of using it wore off. A rush of knowledge swept up to her shoulders, then trickled back like the tide gathering. Maybe love *didn't* mean having to be with someone all your life. Maybe it meant letting them live the way they wanted. Trusting them to love you. Enjoying togetherness as it happened. Another wave came in and went out, reinforcing the impression. Beth's last thought before drifting back to sleep was that loving Owen would mean redefining a lot of things she'd thought were written in stone.

Towards dawn she woke again, this time

because Owen was kissing a lovely swirly pattern across her back. 'Feeling better?' she murmured.

He moved closer. 'Does that answer your question?'

She smiled and twisted in his arms. 'Mmm, so you are. What a nice way to wake up.'

'It seemed a shame to waste it.'

'You're so right.'

A distinctly congenial interval later he said, 'How did you and Alan meet?'

'Owen!'

'What? What have I said?'

'I *refuse* to talk about Alan in bed with you!'

'I only wanted to know. I told you about Michelle.'

'Downstairs. Fully clothed. When we hadn't just been wishing each other good morning in the nicest way possible.'

'I aim to please.' His fingers played idly over her skin. 'It obviously wasn't at work. And he doesn't look the type to strike up a conversation at the check-out counter of the supermarket. Mutual friends? Party?'

Beth felt her face heat. 'I'm not telling you.'

He looked at her more closely in the gathering light. 'You're blushing! Don't tell me you used to earn money on the side by leaping out of birthday cakes?'

'Certainly not.'

'Then what?' He propped himself up on one elbow, his fingers becoming more concentrated. 'You don't play golf. I can't see you on the squash court. No dogs, so you couldn't have been walking them... Swimming! You met him at the swimming pool!' Beth buried her face in his chest. 'Beth! You married him for his body! Into the shower – exorcise those memories once and for all.'

'Oh no, Owen,' protested Beth, giggling helplessly as he hauled her out from under the sheets. 'Owen, I can't. Not again...'

It was always a mistake to congratulate yourself prematurely. Over breakfast Cate had boasted to Beth that as far as performances were concerned, this had been the best week of the tour so far. Huh! After the worst Saturday matinée in the history of popular entertainment, she stormed down to the dressing room Luke shared with Owen with all guns blazing.

'What the hell were you playing at this afternoon?' she yelled. 'You'd have been off five sodding times if I hadn't been on your tail!'

He sat at the mirror, cleansing pad in hand. 'Oh, yeah. Thanks.'

'Wrong answer, old son,' murmured Owen, which did nothing to pacify her.

'What do you mean, *thanks?*' she bellowed.

'Shh. Something wonderful has happened.'

'Dead right. I haven't turned you inside out and used your guts to sew the tabs together!'

'My father rang. I haven't seen him for years. He's only in Lincoln – I can call in on my way up to Oldham.' He reached backwards and took her hand, not noticing that it was shaking with rage.

'Tremendous. That's why I had to prise you and Mel apart with a crowbar at one point was it?' Bugger, she hadn't meant to mention that; now he'd put her rage down to her being a jealous, unstable cow when it was nothing of the kind.

'I was happy. It didn't *mean* anything. I was all right on stage.'

'I certainly couldn't fault you,' contributed Owen.

Cate whirled round, wrenching her hand free. 'Butt out, before I turn you into pulp too!' When she turned back to Luke, his expression was dreamlike once more. She grabbed his shoulder to make him look at her, then slapped his face so hard that her hand was still stinging from the impact an hour later. 'In six weeks' time, you are going to be playing the lead in the panto. I swear to God, if you pull this afternoon's stunt again at *any* point up until opening night, you won't get to say word one of your first line! I'm serious, Luke. *FOOTLIGHTS* means vastly more to me than you do!'

She made herself furiously busy between the matinée and the evening performance. Even Annis, who appeared in the wings *before* cast-call for once, veered off without needling her. Owen and Seb had booked a table at some Greek restaurant tonight to treat Beth and the kids. Seb had said to join them when she'd finished get-out. She bloody would, too. Just to prove she didn't need Luke flaming Bartholomew to have a good time. She was so cross in fact, that when Natalie came to find Stella during the evening interval, she didn't pay the incident nearly enough attention.

'Mum told me to tell you,' Nats began. 'There are two men sitting behind us. We noticed them because they were being irritating. Whispering all the way through. Things like *oh yes, very nice* and *useful range* and *plenty of stamina.* When that last song was on, one of them said, *exactly what we're looking for.*'

Stella exchanged a look with Ned. 'Which seat number are you?'

Natalie told her. 'And just before the interval, the other man tapped his programme and said, *worth keeping an eye on this one too.*'

'Thanks. It's probably nothing, but... Take her back, Cate. I'll check with the ushers.

Oh, Nats, don't show any particular interest in them, OK?'

Seb was clattering down the stairs for the second half as they threaded their way through the rank of thieves' dustcarts. Too early again, thought Cate in exasperation.

'Making out, Seb?' drawled a voice above them. 'Nice choice. What's your name, baby?'

Cate's fists balled. 'My guest, Mr Annis.'

To her amazement Seb slipped his arm protectively around Natalie's waist. 'And she's just leaving. See you later, Nats.' He gently propelled her through the door.

Annis leered. 'Tonight's the night, eh? Like you'd *so* know what to do.'

Cate's temper snapped. 'Piss off, Annis! Seb, find Graham. That sleeve needs a stitch in it!' She stormed on stage to check the transformation from alley to grand garden, too rattled to examine exactly why it was that she was so irritated.

'–delighted to welcome Dame Trot and cast from the forthcoming Corn Exchange pantomime, *Jack And The Beanstalk!*'

Owen stepped forward, primped his outrageous hair and beamed at the crowd. 'Evening, Cambridge!'

'Hello, Dame Trot,' called a scattering of voices.

No one would believe, thought Beth as

Owen looked the crowd over, that his entire persona wasn't submerged in Dame Trot. Performing was in his blood, he could no more not do it than he could fly. He raised exaggerated eyebrows at Seb. 'Did he say we were coming back here at Christmas?' he said loudly.

'That's right, Dame Trot,' said Seb, playing up.

Owen put his hands on his hips. 'We'll have to do something about this audience before then! Evening, Cambridge!' he bellowed.

'Evening, Dame Trot,' hollered back the crowd.

'Better. Now, my son Jack can't be here tonight, he said something about a *giant* excuse,' he paused and the crowd laughed, 'but I've brought Tom-Tom-the-Piper's-Son with me. He's in love with my daughter Mary-Mary-Quite-Contrary. We call her that because she says "yes" every time she means "no". Popular girl...'

The crowd laughed again. 'Bit of a rabble,' Owen said in a loud aside to Seb.

'They want you to finish so they can get to the food.'

More laughter. He was doing this so *well*. Beth understood all over again that acting was an integral part of Owen, that without it he'd only be half alive. A memory of him selling trinkets in the background of an

Oklahoma! scene as if it was the only job worth doing in the world slid into her mind. Owen waved his hand at the kids. 'And this scruffy lot are from the Old Woman's Shoe Children's Home. Jack-Be-Nimble and Jack-Be-Quick.' Robin and Jack bowed. 'Sally-Go-Round-The-Moon.' Lisa did a twirl, her sparkling wig and rainbow skirt flying. 'And their foreman, Margery Daw.' Natalie came to attention and saluted smartly.

'Shouldn't there be more of you, Ms Daw?'

'Lost 'em, ma'am. Eating hot dogs, ma'am,' said Natalie, saluting again.

'Well,' said Owen over the crowd's laughter, 'you don't want to listen to me all night...' He paused. Seb and the others shook their heads enthusiastically. The crowd laughed again. 'So I now declare this Christmas Shopping Evening open!'

'Oh, no, it isn't,' chorused Seb and the kids.

'Oh, yes, it is,' said Owen.

'Oh, no, it isn't,' roared the crowd, catching on.

'Oh, yes, it – what am I doing here then?' said Owen.

'Look behind you!' yelled the others.

Owen cupped his ear. 'I beg your pardon?'

'Look behind you,' roared the crowd delightedly.

Owen turned to study the banner on top

of the stand. 'Cambridge City Council Bonfire Night and Grand Firework Display,' he read aloud. He scratched his wig. 'So I'll have to get the Christmas presents elsewhere?'

The crowd laughed. 'I'm afraid so,' said Seb.

Owen turned back and cleared his throat. 'I shall be going shortly,' he said. 'But I'll leave Tom-Tom and the kids to enjoy themselves and I hope you'll all come and see us at the Corn Exchange over Christmas and New Year.' The crowd cheered. 'And now it is my very great pleasure to declare Cambridge City Council's Bonfire Night and Grand Firework Display officially open!'

At his words a large starburst appeared in the sky, followed by a fair of soaring rockets. Owen applauded as if opening a provincial fireworks display was the highlight of his life, then moved to the back of the stand where the organiser wrung his hand. 'Marvellous, Mr Pendragon. If you'd like to change in the storage area below, there'll be refreshments when you get back.'

In the makeshift dressing room, Beth helped Owen out of the costume and, mindful of Graham's instructions, packed the voluminous skirts away with meticulous care. 'You were terrific,' she said and meant it. 'I'm glad you're a man again though. I didn't fancy a photograph of "Teacher In Clinch With Dame" in tomorrow's *Cambridge Evening News*.'

Owen gave her a travelling mirror to hold while he removed false eyelashes, beauty spots and the rest of Dame Trot's make-up. 'I'll remember that. No cross-dressing sex on the menu at Christmas.'

'Well, not out in the open,' said Beth. 'Governors have such old-fashioned attitudes and I really can't afford to lose my job.' She grinned at him. 'Also your lipstick looks totally wrong on me.'

Owen took the mirror back His hand lay on hers for an ocean of time, gone in the blink of an eye. 'I am going to miss you so bloody much next week.'

Oh, God, he'd said it! The pit of Beth's stomach contracted. She stared at him, naked and unprepared. 'I'm going to miss you too.'

They embraced wordlessly, desperately. Intermittent coloured light from the display filtered through the cracks in the plywood. Staccato bangs echoed like gunfire in the distance.

'This is daft,' whispered Beth, scrubbing at her eyes. 'We're adults. We can cope with this.'

CHAPTER 11

'It's really odd living in proper lodgings again after Beth's,' said Seb as they perched on uncomfortable, tilted seats to munch quarterpounders and watch the Oldham rain trickle down the window. 'I miss the kids, don't you?'

'I miss Beth more,' said Cate. 'How's Owen bearing up?'

'They phone.'

'See how the mighty are fallen. Will it last?'

Seb flushed. 'I'd like to think so. People don't care enough in this business.'

Cate snorted but forbore to tease him. 'So how did the firework opening go? Did the local TV team cover it?'

His eyes lit up. 'And radio. It was great, you should have been there. We did the dialogue we'd rehearsed and the kids were spot on. As for Owen...' He unfocused for a second. 'He really *was* Dame Trot. Better even than Mrs Crusoe last year. Don't laugh, but I learnt more in that half-hour than the whole term's character course at college. And all it was was a firework display.'

She crumpled her burger wrapper into a

ball. 'I might have known. That man wrong-foots me every time.'

'Cate, he's got sixteen years more experience in the business than we have. What does it matter?'

She shrugged. 'He just winds me up.'

'He winds everybody up,' said Seb. 'That's no reason to take it personally. I honestly think he cares for *FOOTLIGHTS* as much as you do. Ice cream?'

'You know your trouble, you're too bloody nice.'

'It's the genes. I gave up fighting them years ago.'

She never could decide whether he deliberately refused to rise to the bait, or simply didn't see it coming. 'Don't you ever get hurt?' she said when he came back.

He pocketed the money she pushed across the table. 'All the time. It's better than not feeling anything at all. At least you know you're alive. And if you don't, it's a bonus.'

'There is so much wrong with that philosophy, I don't know where to start! Bloody unreal, that's what you are.'

He dug his spoon into the tub. 'A lot of people seem to think so.'

'Like Annis?'

Seb's mouth twisted. 'Sticks and stones. I can take it.'

'Why don't you have a word with the management? Ask if there are any openings coming up in the small-cast plays?'

He flicked his hair back and looked her straight in the eyes. 'Because running away doesn't solve anything.'

'It's not running away. It's a change of scene.'

She needn't have bothered. 'I'm not ready,' he said stubbornly. 'I haven't finished learning. Besides, most of the time it's fun.'

The next day Luke sought her out as she was checking the Tinies' dustcarts. 'I thought I'd see if we were speaking yet. And if so, whether you fancy a drink after the show?'

One of Seb's wheel nuts was loose. Cate pushed the cart on to the stage to test it. She started the Tinies' dance. After a few steps, the cart jammed. A few steps more and it jammed again.

'I didn't realise you knew the moves,' said Luke.

She looked at him in disbelief. 'I'm the ASM! I know everybody's moves. You want to open your eyes sometime.' She frowned as she checked the axles. There was grit or something in the bearings. She moved back to the other carts.

Where Seb's had stood overnight, the floor was clean but a hand's sweep behind was a thin line of fine sand. 'Get Stella,' she said, and when her aunt appeared, 'Sabotage. Someone wants to make Seb look bad on stage.'

'That's insane,' said Luke.

But the image of three men creeping around an empty theatre was blazing in Cate's mind. 'How the hell do we prove it?'

'We can't,' said Stella, watching grimly as her niece dismantled the jamming wheel. 'Fix it and I'll log it in the book. Send Seb to me when he arrives, no point keeping it from him.'

'Is my magic doorway OK?'

Cate snorted. Egotistical or what? 'I check it before every performance, Luke, but I'll go over it again after I've examined the other carts. Sorry, no drink. I'd rather be here until lock-up from now on.'

'I'll see you for supper back at the lodgings, then.' Which he did. And at which he produced a bottle of wine. And after which they gravitated naturally to her bed.

He was still there in the morning: flushed with sleep, amoral as a child and undeniably beautiful. She slid out of the covers without waking him. 'Sex isn't a pill, you know,' she told his sleeping form. 'Take one at bedtime and it'll be all better in the morning.' But he didn't hear her, and in any case, she'd take bets he wouldn't agree.

'What do you mean, there's dirty work going on?'

Owen sighed down the phone line. 'Cate discovered sand in Seb's dustcart bearings.

It's not making for a terrific atmosphere. And having got Seb into my lodgings, I'm now hearing his angst day and night.'

'Penalties of being a father-figure.' Beth winced as she heard the words leave her mouth. 'Happens to me all the time at school. One of the kids wants a word – and suddenly break's gone and I haven't had a cup of tea.'

'I wish I was there. We could have one together.'

'I wish you were too.'

If Owen being in Oldham was bad, Durham was even worse. Something to do with it being three hundred and fifty miles away instead of a scant hundred and sixty. After missing two calls because she was in after-school meetings, Beth jumped every time the phone rang and took to moving it with her from room to room.

'I want you like there's no tomorrow,' said his voice fiercely into her ear after one evening show.

Passion boiled around her. Astonishment and loss dead-heated in her heart. 'Half-way there, lover. Ten more days and then we've got all Sunday together.'

'But I *miss* you. It's never happened before.'

'I miss you too.' It was true. There was an ache in the empty side of the bed, a space where he wasn't. 'More than I ever missed Alan. He's here for dinner tomorrow. They discussed the possibility of Doone coming too but she insisted it was *his* quality time with *his* children and she'd never forgive herself if she infringed on it and gave them complexes.'

'Christ Almighty! Is that woman for real?'

'It didn't occur to either of them that I might have a say in the matter.'

'What are you going to cook? Wild mushrooms a la Provençal?'

'Shepherds pie. Cheap, filling and one of his all-time unfavourites. And when he moans I'll say he should have given me more than twenty-four hours' notice.'

'Ring me after he's gone.'

'Will do. God, just the thought of him is making me tired. Sleep well.'

'Goodnight, mistress.'

Pause. 'I can't put down the phone.'

'Both do it together then. One, two...'

Beth cradled the phone like a bereft teenager. It rang again, startling her.

'Tell me about something else. How are the *Grease* rehearsals?'

Her heart liquefied. 'Exhibition dance is sensational. Rest isn't gelling. Sue's tearing her hair out.' Beth was only tenuously holding on to what she was saying. How *could* she want him this much? How could he want her?

'Nats and Lisa still speaking?'

'As far as I know. They haven't been spending much time together what with rehearsals on top of everything else.' Suddenly even talking to him was too much. 'I'd better go, Owen. I've still got half a pile of books to mark *and* I've got to prepare tomorrow's PSE lesson.'

'What's it on?'

'Working out problems. Everything from admitting you have one to deciding what to do about it.'

'Sod that. Tell them to grow up and sort things out for themselves like the rest of us have to. How about *this* Sunday? We could rent a room at the Travelodge in Leicester and play dirty weekends.'

'I can't. I'm helping Sue supervise her rehearsal.'

'Jesus! Meetings with parents, meetings with kids, favours to friends. I'm not surprised Alan left you.'

It was like a sword thrust, worse because his words were so unexpected. Beth felt numb with misery.

There was a stricken pause. 'Shit. I didn't mean that.'

Tears welled up in Beth's eyes. 'And *you* aren't busy in rehearsal or on stage every time I want to talk to you? Owen, I can't tell the kids it's OK to trust me in the classroom if I let them down outside it.'

'I know. It's your job. I'm sorry. I'm *sorry*. My mother should have cut my tongue out at birth. Put it down to rampant jealousy.'

'That's stupid. Who are you jealous of?'

'Christ, just name it. Alan for one.'

'*Alan?* I don't believe it. Why?'

'Because he's coming for dinner tomorrow night and he's going to be sitting at the same table as you and he used to be *your husband!*'

'That's crazy.'

'Crazy. Desperate. What's the difference? Who was your meeting with this afternoon?'

'Yob. To find out why he was bunking off art, when painting is one of the few things he told me he enjoyed.'

'So why was he?'

To give him his due, Owen was *trying* to sound interested. Warmth crept back into Beth's body. 'You'll like this. Because the pieces of paper they use in the art block are too small.'

'So you've asked the teacher to give him a bigger sheet, right?'

'Close. It turns out Yob really prefers to paint on something the size of a bus shelter. Or that nice bit of end wall down by the shops. Or the loos in the Rec. Those are especially good because the council white-wash them now and again so he can start over.'

Owen's laughter roared out of the phone, banishing the lost feeling and making her toasty and safe and warm once more. 'I can just see him doing it too,' he chuckled. 'An aerosol in each hand. I have got to hear how you solved this.'

'Oh, come on. And you a theatre man.'

'Beth! I've said I'm sorry.'

'Why is it we can't play Mr and Mrs Smith this weekend?'

'*Grease!* You've got him painting the backdrop!'

'During lessons, so he can listen to what the teacher's telling the rest of the class about the Impressionist movement at the same time. Owen, I'm counting the days just as much as you are.'

'I know. I'm a selfish git who's taking a hell of a long time to adjust. Ring me tomorrow night, OK?'

'You know I will.'

'OK then. One, two...'

Three. This time the phone stayed silent.

Natalie stared at the history books spread out on her desk. The phone downstairs chirped. She looked at her watch. Ten-fifteen. The show must be over. Her mobile gleamed at the corner of her vision. Dare she? Memories of the lunchtime rehearsal mocked her. Without giving herself time to think, she punched Seb's number.

There was an endless moment while it rang. Natalie imagined the whole Ensemble patting pockets and rummaging in bags to see whose mobile was going off. Then,

'Hello?' said Seb's voice.

'It's me, Natalie.' God, how naive did that sound?

'Nats?' Seb's voice lost its wariness, became warm and concerned.

'Um, look, just say if this isn't a convenient time, but I so need to talk to someone about the *Grease* rehearsals.'

'I was only taking my make-up off. What's up? It can't be the songs.'

The implied praise hung in the air, glowing. 'No, it's – it's Lisa.' There! She'd said it. She was talking about her best friend behind her back. Disloyalty as sharp as stomach ache writhed in her.

'Still hassling you about acting with Jason?'

She felt a surge of gratitude towards him for putting it so matter-of-factly. 'She *watches* us every rehearsal. It's horrible. But I can't say anything to Sue because she's Lisa's mum. And I can't say anything to Mum, because I don't want her to fall out with Sue. And I can't say anything to Lis, because–'

'That's the problem with having a best mate,' said Seb. 'They know so much better than anybody else how to hurt you.'

'But I haven't *done* anything,' she wailed.

'You don't have to. I had the same problem. I was just that bit brighter, that bit more popular. He couldn't hack it.'

She scrubbed at her eyes with her free

hand. 'But why should Lis be jealous of me? We get the same marks in class. I might sing better, but she's *way* smarter at dance. How did you deal with it?'

'Left school and went to college. No use, I'm afraid. I can tell you what I do *now* at rehearsals if it helps?'

'*Anything* would help.'

'Well, I–' He faltered; she imagined him blushing. When he spoke again his voice was lower and more intense. 'I concentrate on me, the other actors and the director. I ignore the onlookers, the crew, everyone. I just build the scene in my mind and live it.'

His sincerity burned through the ether. Another of those life-changing moments exploded her in consciousness. *Take yourself seriously! Be an actor!* 'Thanks, Seb,' she said, meaning it.

'Ring again if you want,' he said. 'Otherwise I'll see you next month.'

'Right.' Natalie hardly heard him. She felt all loose and stretched, as if she'd been playing a part and was only now back in her own body. 'Goodnight.'

'Much better, folks,' said Sue approvingly.

'That was good,' said Lisa in an off-hand voice as Natalie bent to scoop her bag and coat from the pile on the hall floor.

'Thanks. It's still not a patch on your dance scene.' She was careful to keep her delivery exactly the same as her friend's.

Lisa hoisted her own bag. 'What are you doing after school? Want to come over?'

There was a bottleneck at the door as everyone tried to get out for afternoon registration. 'Can't,' said Natalie. 'Singing lesson. Then all that science homework. And I've still got to finish the history.'

'Did mine last night,' said Lisa smugly.

For the life of her, she couldn't help it. 'I meant to but I was on the phone to Seb. Did I say he's coming to watch *Grease?*' She moved smoothly towards the door, leaving Lisa to stare with a most satisfactory stupefaction in her wake.

'So, how was dinner?'

'Dire.' Beth curled up on the sofa, tucked the phone under her ear and sipped her carefully hoarded Drambuie. 'Alan's still on his healthy eating kick. He brought organic kiwi-fruit juice with him instead of wine, for God's sake, and then spent half an hour enumerating the dangers of including too much red meat and saturated fat in one's diet. I was very tempted to tell him that the mince was so cheap, I'd be surprised if it contained any recognisable cuts of meat at all.'

Owen laughed. 'What stopped you?'

'Little things. Christmas. Car insurance. How are things there?'

'Same old, same old. Cate's prowling the

wings like someone demented. How was your PSE lesson?'

Beth felt herself blush. 'I, um, took your advice.'

'Good God, you don't want to do that. What advice?'

Beth grinned. Despite the protest, he sounded quite flattered. 'Leaving it to them to think of solutions. They were more inventive than I expected. And they decided all by themselves that it all had to be fair.'

'In what way?'

'Well, Clifford is going to teach Yob how to use the computers in the IT room, and in return Yob stops Cliff being thrown off them by tough kids who want to play games every lunchtime.'

He chuckled. 'I thought you didn't condone violence. What else?'

'Chantelle's taking Veronica home for a dance-mat session once a week to help her lose weight and get fit, and Veronica is going to make a colour-coded chart so Chantelle knows which stuff to bring in for lessons each day. Felicity is being particularly generous. She's letting Karen help groom her pony because Karen's family can't afford one. In return, Karen tells Felicity as soon as anyone tweaks her ribbons undone.'

She could feel his smile. 'All a matter of scale, eh?'

'I enjoyed it. Listening to them putting

forward suggestions. Taking each other seriously. Being mutually supportive.'

'Building trust, in fact.'

'Which is what you said last summer, if I recall.'

'If you're going to remember all the half-baked philosophy I come out with, I'm ringing off. I shouldn't have knocked your job, Beth. It's who you are.'

Warmth wreathed around her. 'It's more that if I'm going to do something, I won't do it half-heartedly. Like you and performing. You wouldn't skip a show just to see me, would you? We both have ideals.'

He heaved a sigh in her ear. 'Yeah, it's a right bugger. So – nine days and counting then.'

She blew him a kiss down the line. 'Nine days and counting,' she echoed.

Get-out at Leicester. The end of the tour. The first person Cate set eyes on at the party was Seb. 'Look at him!' she said. 'Chatting easy as you please to Adrian, April and Red. MD, leading lady and dance captain! Why not just tattoo 'Teachers' Pet' on his forehead?'

'You need a double tequila,' said Graham. He slanted a disparaging look at her black sweatshirt. 'You will try to make an effort for the panto party, won't you, dear?'

The music finished as, head spinning

pleasantly, Cate slammed down her second drink. Luke had already given her a lazy wink over Mel's draped shoulder. She thought she might attempt a spot of public claiming. But when she looked again, Mel's tongue appeared to be most of the way down his throat and he wasn't trying any too hard to fight her off. Sod you then, she thought, perturbed by the strength of her reaction. She ordered half a bitter, slid off the bar stool, and headed for the food.

'Hi,' said Seb happily. (What was it about end-of-run parties that made him drink too much?) 'I've just been talking to Adrian.'

'I saw. Make yourself conspicuous, why don't you?'

'I was telling him about *HMS Pinafore* at college. Remember?'

'It's the sort of thing which sears itself on the brain – putting on Gilbert and Sullivan with no costumes, no props and an all-black set.'

'We had a piano.' He folded two pieces of disparate pizza together and bit into them with infectious enjoyment. 'I *so* don't want to go home tomorrow.'

'I thought you were looking forward to the panto?'

'Panto, yes. Parents, no. Routines. Questions to show how interested they are. Sensible food. Schedules pinned to the memo board...'

She grinned and helped herself to two slices of garlic bread and the last wedge of caramelised onion tart. If Luke wasn't interested tonight, there was no point worrying about pristine breath.

'It's all very well you laughing,' continued Seb. His eyes followed the onion tart. 'But I'm twenty-two, Cate, not twelve. And some time I've got to tell them I'll be looking for a place of my own in the New Year. Are you going to eat all of that?'

'Yes. Anyway, they'll probably be expecting it. You'll get back in January to find your mum's already ringed the flatshares in the local paper.' She glanced around. 'I knew someone was missing. Where's Owen?'

'At Beth's but I'm not supposed to tell anyone.'

'Bloody hell! Fidelity strikes!' She reached for her beer to discover Seb absent-mindedly sipping it. 'Oi! Buy your own!'

'Sorry.' He handed it back. 'Have you ever felt like that? Wanting to be with someone every minute?'

'No,' she said shortly. 'Well, almost. At Swansea last summer. He turned out to be married.'

His eyes met hers, shocked. 'Shit, Cate, I'm sorry. What happened?'

'He left. I'm only telling you this because you've drunk so much you'll have forgotten by tomorrow.'

'Walked out of the play? That's awful!' Seb finished the beer in consternation.

She shrugged. 'Couldn't act with his arm in plaster.'

There was a tiny silence while she tore off a chunk of garlic bread. 'Remind me,' said Seb, *'never* to get on the wrong side of you.'

'Better replace that drink then.'

'OK.' His alcohol meter must have reached full. A succession of sneezes caught him by surprise. She fished a tissue out of her jeans pocket. 'Thanks,' he said, and stooped unsteadily to pick up something she'd dropped. 'Why have you got a bag of sand, Cate?'

Shit! She'd found it in the ensemble room during clear-up and had brought it with her for safe-keeping. She stuffed it back in her pocket. 'Are you going to get me that beer or not?'

'Was it the same sort as in my cart in Oldham?'

Jesus, he was quick. Unless it was telepathy. 'How should I know? One grain of sand looks much the same as another.'

He finished his food in a brooding silence. 'Annis.'

'We can't prove that.'

'Don't have to. Where is he?'

'Drinking at the bar. Think, Seb! He's stronger than you and twice as dirty in a fight. Also you're drunk and *we can't prove anything!'*

'I'm not that drunk.'

'Yes, you bloody are.' She looked over to the dance floor. Neither Luke nor Mel were anywhere to be seen. *Sod* him. 'Let's get out of here.'

Outside, Seb slung his bag over his shoulder and strode away from the town centre, heedless of the cold. Cate had to jog to keep up. 'Good thing my lodgings are in the same road as yours.'

His hair streamed back from the angry lines of his face. 'You didn't have to come.'

'And have everyone on my back when you walk out in front of a car because you're too riled to pay attention? No, thank you!'

'It's not as if it's my fault,' he burst out. 'I didn't *ask* to be Jud Fry. It wasn't *me* who gave me Luke's understudy. And we were *both* thieves' leaders in this!'

'But *you* are a hundred times better than he is and everybody knows it. Slow down, I'm getting a stitch. There's no point denying it, Seb.'

'What's he going to come up with next? It's not fair if he ruins Owen's panto because of me.'

Cate stopped dead. '*Whose* panto?'

They'd reached their street. Seb came to an abrupt halt outside his lodgings. 'Oops,' he said guiltily.

Huge numbers of disconnected incidents lined up and joined hands in Cate's head.

How could she not have seen it before?

'Cate,' he pleaded. 'I wasn't supposed to tell.'

His fringe had flopped back down. She smiled into the dismayed blue eyes behind it and patted his arm. 'It's all right. You won't remember you have.'

The alcohol seemed to have caught up with him again. She had to support him up the path. 'At least I won't have to worry about the panto props falling apart,' he mumbled as she opened the door. 'You'll bring them back to Beth's and sleep with them.'

'I do hope that wasn't a compliment. Can you get up to your room OK?'

'Aren't you coming in?'

What?

But then, 'I forgot,' he said. 'You don't live here, do you?' He ruffled her hair. 'Night, Cate. Sleep well.'

Sleep well, indeed! 'I'm sure I shall,' she said to his departing back 'Nothing more guaranteed to induce it than doing the last get-out of the tour followed by a brisk chase in sub-zero temperatures through the suburbs of Leicester.'

She was wasting her breath. He'd gone in. 'What the hell,' she muttered. 'Sleep well, Seb.'

CHAPTER 12

At ten o'clock on Saturday night by Beth's reckoning, Owen had been taking his final bows in the Haymarket, Leicester. At not quite midnight he was in her hallway, she was in his arms, and the door still stood open. 'I thought you had an end-of-run party to go to?' she said after a deep, deep kiss that made her wild for more.

He kicked the door shut. 'First time I've missed.' He smoothed her hair away from her face, his eyes stripped of their wickedness. 'Anything pressing to do down here, mistress, or can we adjourn to your bedchamber?'

'Adjourn away, minstrel.'

He raised an eyebrow. 'Minstrel? It's got a ring to it.'

Her fingers rippled his hair. 'Snappier than strolling player. Although I did consider vagabond.'

He kissed her again. 'Jester? Fool? Clown?'

She moved her body against his. 'Lover?'

He looked into her eyes, a smile curving his lips. 'I can't believe how much I've missed you.'

'I can't believe how much I've missed *you*.'

The night dissolved into a segue of love and sleep. Beth woke on Sunday morning to find his thigh hard against hers and almost groaned aloud at the knot of lust and desire still within her. They made love, showered slowly, made love again. Underneath the euphoria, Beth knew it was too good to last. No one as wickedly sexy, and virile, and just plain *accomplished* as Owen could possibly be satisfied with her for the rest of his life. But in the meantime ... she sang as she cut the bread for toast.

Natalie was telling Owen about the Shoe Orphan routines over a pot of tea, and Robin was making an extremely messy fried egg sandwich he'd invented himself, when the doorbell rang. Beth tugged her Haymarket sweatshirt down over her hips (they were selling them to raise money for the fight against closure, Owen had explained, to which she'd replied that if he wanted to buy her something, he really didn't have to spoil it with reasons) and opened it.

Alan and Doone stood on the doorstep looking like a country-weekend photo from the more-money-than-sense mail-order catalogues which erroneously fell through the letterbox from time to time. 'We're here,' said Alan unnecessarily.

Beth gaped, horribly conscious of her mussed hair, her glow of repletion and the aroma of Aztec For Men drenching the air.

'So I see,' she managed to say.

'The last Sunday in November. The Club Car Rally. You can't have forgotten.'

Try me. And that air of faint surprise had always irritated her. 'Alan, it's been six months since you left.' She heard the kitchen door creak and knew the others had their eyes and ears glued to the gap. She just hoped Rob had turned off the gas under the frying pan.

Alan gave a hearty laugh. 'We have to defend our title. Doone's packed a marvellous hamper for lunch.'

Fury dripped into Beth's soul, releasing her paralysis. 'Then I hope eating it will make up for the disappointment of us not being with you. It's out of the question, Alan. Natalie and Robin have got a rehearsal, and I've got a B&B visitor. If you'd thought to mention it the other day, I could have saved you the journey.'

Alan shot a look at the closed dining room door and lowered his voice reprovingly. 'Really, Beth, you've got no business sense. You might have *told* us you had a guest. Naturally you can't come if that's the case, but the kids can miss a footling rehearsal, surely?'

'Alan says Rob's a real whizz at those cryptic clues,' added Doone.

Enlightenment at last. This was an image issue. The rally was a *family* thing. Plus, Alan wanted to win. 'It is *not* a footling rehearsal, it is the school production of *Grease* which Natalie is starring in!' Beth's anger was alive, pulsating in the hallway and reverberating around the walls. 'For which you still haven't told me whether you want Tuesday, Wednesday or Thursday tickets!'

Alan took a step backwards. 'I – er–'

'We'll check our diaries,' said Doone soothingly. 'Honey, I don't want to rush you, but...'

'Nice one, Mum,' said Robin, deeply impressed.

'Tea?' said Owen.

'Please. Can you believe the nerve of that man?'

'Shame, though,' said Natalie wistfully. 'It would have been really cool to have beaten him...'

'Hi, Beth. Leonie's not outside, is she?'

Beth frowned, about to leave now she and Owen had dropped the kids off. 'Is she supposed to be? I didn't think the competition dance needed any more work.'

Sue jabbed at her mobile. 'She's my second adult. Damn, *still* off! What the hell am I going to do?'

Underneath the worry there was a flash of calculation in Sue's face. 'No,' said Beth. 'I've got one solitary afternoon before Owen goes back to London for three weeks. Don't

250

do this to me, Sue.'

'Problems?' said Owen wandering up with Robin and Jack in tow.

Beth couldn't speak. Any other time she'd have kept an eye on the more exuberant element of the chorus while Sue directed. But the last three empty weeks were pounding in her head and she could feel Owen at her shoulder wanting to be alone with her as urgently as she wanted to be with him. More kids arrived. The outside world was full of the sound of their parents driving off.

'Shall we start warming up?' called Lisa. A ring of faces looked across inquiringly.

'Leonie hasn't shown,' said Sue to Owen. 'I'm not legal with this many children without another qualified teacher here.'

The ring of faces shifted to look at Beth. She seethed impotently. How was Sue making this seem *her* fault?

In the accusing silence, Owen's fingers gripped hers. 'No sweat. What would we do otherwise? Cup of tea and the Sunday papers, that's all.'

'Bless you. You're both life savers.' Sue clapped her hands. 'OK, kids, spread out.'

Beth gazed wrathfully after her. 'You notice she didn't once look at me directly! Sometimes it's a real sod having Sue for a friend.'

'That's why I gave up mates years ago.' He

moved closer. Her body cried out for his. 'Read-through is at ten. If I stay tonight, will you feed me breakfast at five?'

Her ears drummed. The intensity in his eyes dried her throat. 'You need to ask?' She tried to find more words and failed.

Sue put a tape on. Owen glanced at the kids. 'Jesus wept, does she call that a warm-up?' He strode across the hall, full of irritable energy.

When Owen arrived, Cate was putting the first week's rehearsal calls on a circle of chairs.

'Busy yesterday, sweeting?' he asked, skimming his eyes over the marked-out floor.

She aimed one of her spiky looks at him. 'A week's work in one day? Piece of cake. What were you doing? Lotus-eating at Beth's?'

'Something of the sort.' He helped himself to tea. His mind went back to last night.

'Why did you stay?' Beth had asked in one of the intervals between love and sleep. 'Alan would have run a mile.'

'That was one reason,' he'd replied.

She'd laughed, running her hand over his chest, not taking him seriously. 'And once there, you couldn't resist taking over,' she'd teased.

Except that hadn't been it at all. He'd seen Natalie's face. She'd been expecting him to say no as her father would have done. He'd seen Rob's face too, sunnily confident that of course he'd help out. And he'd been furious. Furious at Sue's manipulating of Beth. Furious at his own need to vindicate himself in Rob and Natalie's eyes. Furious at the discovery that he possessed a latent better nature after all these years considering no one but himself. And as always, his fury had found outlet in work.

Seb arrived, libretto and score in hand. Owen laid a bet with himself that he'd be off the book by Wednesday. 'Hi,' said Seb. 'I hear you were a hit yesterday.'

Owen slowly swivelled his head. 'Say that again?'

'I spoke to Nats last night. She said school's never seen a rehearsal like it.'

'You spoke to Natalie?'

'She wanted to know when we were coming to *Grease* so she could order tickets for us.'

Owen regarded him for a long moment. 'Possibly asking me while I was actually there slipped her mind.'

Letting himself into the flat that evening felt odd. Normally it welcomed him after a tour. He took pleasure in its comfortable chairs, its clean lines, its peace. Tonight it felt empty. A mocking symbol of his life. There was a pile of post, messages on the answerphone, invitations to dinner from friends and sometime colleagues, exactly as there had been for years. For a moment, everything inverted and he saw the last few months as a mad aberration of his normal life.

Aberration? Or salvation?

He poured himself a whisky, realising with unpleasant clarity that he had a choice. He could go back four months, back to being the self-sufficient hedonist who'd lived here before. Or he could throw a few clothes about, tumble a cushion or two, and let Beth fully, completely and without reserve into his life. His mouth quirked at the thought of her in this flat. She wouldn't fit! She trailed clutter like other women spent money. And look at all the things she'd bring with her – her children, her friends, *their* friends, her form, her problems, *their* problems, her commitment, her integrity, her honesty... She was a window on to a whole slice of world he'd forgotten. He found himself checking the time: Monday evening, she'd have done the shopping by now, fetched Rob from his tap class, have the kettle on. Choice? He kicked a cushion off the sofa and reached for the phone.

'Minstrel?' Her low laugh undulated along his veins. He'd have to be raving to go back to sterility.

'Ned's scheduled Seb and me a rehearsal at *Stagestruck* on Saturday. OK if we come

Friday night? No expenses money.'

'Idiot.'

'Beth – when I come up for the panto – can we talk?'

He heard her let her breath out, knew the corners of her mouth were lifting. Her voice sang through his bloodstream like the very best malt, kept under lock and key in a Scottish cellar for the Laird himself. 'Yes, please.'

'Good.' It seemed to him that they could spend their whole life on an open phone line and not need to speak.

'I was thinking of you this morning,' she said. 'Were you nervous? How did the read-through go?'

She'd remembered. Warmth filled him. 'Not quite as toe-curlingly awful as I expected. Some of the jokes even sounded vaguely amusing. They still don't know I wrote it. Listen, Seb and I can come to *Grease* on the Tuesday. It'll be easy because we're in the Corn Exchange for the whole production week instead of making do in the warehouse.'

'You mean you'll be here earlier than you thought?'

Desire rose in him at her eager tone. He couldn't keep the grin off his face. 'Yes, Tuesday's a rest day while the crew do get-in, but I thought I might drive up Monday night.'

She chuckled. 'Seb and Cate won't be able to get in themselves if you don't! I'll be at school, remember?'

It was a measure of how far he'd travelled that he felt nothing but a vast content. 'It's your job.'

'Mother's invited us to dinner next week. She's coming to Town shopping.'

Cate continued to stack chairs. 'That's nice.'

'She wondered if we could bring a list of performance times with us.'

'By the coffee urn.'

'Cate–' He came up behind her with soft laughter in his voice. 'You told me yourself never to sleep with you on a Saturday night again.'

She stood still. 'I'm not sure I meant you could sleep with someone else.'

His hands slid around her. 'Silly. It didn't mean anything.'

It never did. Did it mean anything when he slept with her?

There was the sound of running feet in the passage. 'Cate, I forgot to ask – oh, sorry.'

Luke let her go. 'You can ask, but I warn you, she's not in a giving mood.'

Seb's eyes darted between them uncertainly.

'Panto tickets for his family,' said Cate. 'He'll have to book them properly like everyone else.' It was a good thing Seb had interrupted them. She stacked the last chair, conscious that she was breathing unevenly. This was ridiculous. Yes, Luke was on a buzz from playing the lead. Yes, he was playing it wonderfully (and knew it). He was still so amoral it wasn't true. What in the world was wrong with her?

She was still wondering as she drove up to Cambridge a fortnight later. She drew up behind Seb's Cabriolet outside Beth's house and grinned to see a *Jack* poster in the window. Although she'd have slit her wrists rather than admit it in front of Owen, the script was screamingly funny and Adrian's songs very easy on the ear. Cambridge was in for a treat.

Owen himself opened the door. 'Morning, sweeting. The mistress of the house is filling tomorrow's dole queue with knowledge, but there's tea in the pot.'

'I can't get used to you being this domesticated. Is it for real?'

He gave her a sardonic look. 'Do you seriously expect me to answer that?'

'You don't generally have problems with brutal frankness. Hi, Seb. What are you doing here so early?'

'If you'd been living with my parents for the last three weeks, you wouldn't need to ask.'

'So you lied about when you had to be

here? I'm impressed.'

'Being around you must be rubbing off on me. Who knows, by the end of the run I might even be able to stand up to Annis without backup.'

'Seb?' Cate was confounded. She'd never heard him do bitter before. She glanced at Owen. 'Out with it. What have you done with the real Mr Merchant?'

Owen spread his hands. 'He was like it when he arrived. Probably nothing a cup of tea and a flapjack won't fix.'

Cate brightened. 'Beth left us flapjacks?'

'Mum sent a tin with me,' said Seb. 'She lured me inside to pick it up it while Dad hid my Christmas presents in the boot of the car.'

Cate cuffed him round the ear. 'And where did you leave theirs? In the middle of your bed with a large 'Do Not Open Until Xmas' notice on them, I'll bet. They love you. Stop being such a misery guts.'

Seb gave a reluctant grin. 'Smart arse.'

In the kitchen, Owen flipped them newly-cut door keys with 'CATE' and 'SEB' on the tags. 'Beth left these so you can come and go as you please.'

'That's nice of her,' said Cate. 'She *is* nice.' She looked at him meaningfully.

He chuckled. 'Teach your grandmother, sweeting.'

'Cate hasn't got a grandmother,' said Seb.

'She sprang fully formed from a trigger-happy giant cactus.'

Cafe narrowed her eyes. 'It isn't me he's spending too much time around. It's you.'

'What's the time, Mum?'

Beth sighed. 'Three minutes later than when you last asked. There's no point getting there too early, sweetheart.'

'I hope you're going to be this eager to do the panto,' said Owen.

Beth grinned at him, still elated at the thought of his being here for a whole month, then hastily wiped her face as she saw Natalie's lowering look

'Vocal warm-up,' ordered Seb. He sang a scale. Rob joined in. Natalie followed. With a wink at Owen, Seb slipped into *Summer Nights*. Natalie blushed and sang Sandy's lines, even when Owen took it upon himself to ad-lib the Pink Ladies chorus in an excruciating falsetto.

'Bravo,' applauded Beth. 'Been mugging up, Seb?'

'I was Danny myself at school. It came back to me as I sang.'

'Branded on your brain at an impressionable age,' said Owen. 'I could still recite *The Lady Of Shalott* given half a chance.'

'One of my Year Nines turned that into a rap last term,' said Beth. 'It worked surprisingly well.'

'You were supposed to ask for a demonstration.'

She laughed. 'I'm an English teacher, minstrel. I'm not obliged to listen to Tennyson outside the classroom.'

Settled into the front row, with Owen at her side and Seb next to him, she felt achingly happy. She waved to Pete a few seats away and prayed that the kids would give a good show and that nothing would go wrong.

'Nice drama studio,' said Seb. He'd seemed a bit quiet when they'd first got home from school, but jollying Nats out of her nerves had got him back to normal. 'We did all our plays on a stage the size of a postage stamp to a lingering odour of lunchtime's pizza and chips.'

'Pizza and chips?' Owen's voice was rich with derision. 'In my day it was boiled cabbage and lumpy custard.'

'Lumpy custard doesn't smell,' Beth protested.

'It does if it's burnt!'

His hazel eyes laughed into hers. Her muscles clenched without warning. Her ears thrummed and her heart turned to lava and boiled in her chest. She groped for his hand with a sense of impending glory.

His fingers clasped hers. The laughter in his eyes became something so much warmer it stopped her breath. His lips parted. 'I lo–'

'Beth! There you are,' came a peremptory voice from the aisle. 'Have you saved our seats?'

Alan! Just as Owen was about to– She surged upright and turned around in fury. Only the pressure of Owen's knee against her calf kept her voice level. 'I told you when I sent the tickets it was first come, first served. You should have got here earlier.'

His expression tightened. 'I didn't realise there would be so many people.'

'You've been coming to school shows for over ten years! There are *always* people!' Out of the corner of her eye, she could see Owen pretending he wasn't with her. Good. Because if Alan recognised him and said just one disparaging word about actors she'd probably thump him in front of half a school of parents.

'My fault,' said Doone with the sort of tinkling, fairy-light laugh which just knew everything would be forgiven her. She laid a three-quarter length, red satin sleeve on Alan's arm. 'I couldn't decide what to wear, could I? What's going to be best, honey? End seats down here or those central ones a few rows back?'

'Central,' said Alan curtly. 'It isn't as if we'll need to nip out for drinks during the interval.'

Doone gave another delighted laugh. 'Bad boy! Just think of the example you'd set the students! Don't you worry, I'll mix us up something special later...'

Beth sat down, simmering with rage. She looked sideways at Owen. He and Seb were enumerating the positive points of the drama studio to each other in the effortless way only actors can carry off successfully. 'Sorry about that.'

Owen's eyes met hers. 'I bet she fakes a wonderful orgasm.'

She clapped a hasty hand over her shriek of laughter. 'You are appalling!'

'You should hear the innuendos he worked into Dame Trot,' said Seb. 'Stella banned half of them.'

'Oh, thank goodness,' said Beth at the interval. 'As long as it goes this well for the next two nights, we should make it to the end of term without mass suicides. You couldn't ease round a fraction and tell me if Alan's headed this way, I suppose?'

'Safe for the moment, beloved. He and Ms-Most-Likely-To are operating on a prosperous-looking couple sitting next to them.'

'He'll be selling them something. With any luck, he'll forget I'm even here.'

But she'd reckoned without the conscientious Ms Hennessy. As they waited for the performers at the end of the show, she was accosted once more.

'That was a bonus,' said Alan rubbing his hands. 'I made a couple of useful contacts and one chap was very interested in Doone's Company Gift Plan.'

With a strong effort, Beth bit back a comment on it not being a total waste of an evening then.

'Now, now, we shouldn't be talking business, we should be saying what a great job the kids did. Natalie has such a pretty voice, Beth. As for Robin – how his legs didn't tie themselves into knots during that dance I will never know!'

Beth forced her face into a smile. 'Thank you. It was good of you to come.'

'Oh, no,' said Doone earnestly. 'I believe parents *should* support their children. This may be only a school show to us, but in years to come it's going to give these young people a significant measure of inner confidence knowing their role models thought enough of them to come and watch it.'

My God, thought Beth, did I really spend twenty-five years with a man who is actually *choosing* to go out with this woman?

'Now,' continued Doone as if she was conferring a favour, 'we've got a pretty tight schedule over Christmas what with client parties and dinners and so on, but we'd *really* like to fit in some quality time with you guys.'

Behind her, Owen was telling Pete an extremely dirty joke. Beth had no doubt that he was also listening with huge amusement to her conversation. It almost made it bearable. 'What a shame,' she said. 'Natalie and Robin are going to be tied up with the panto every day, and I'll have a houseful of theatrical lodgers to look after.'

'That's too bad,' said Doone comfortably. She linked her arm in Alan's and gave him a roguish glance. 'Well, I've got a breakfast meeting tomorrow, so I'd better get some beauty sleep in.'

'As if you need it!' There was a cocky triumph in Alan's look as they left.

Beth swallowed an instant's bile before realising Owen was back at her side, steady and watchful. 'One of these days,' she vowed. 'I am going to kiss you long and slow and passionate right under their smug, self-satisfied noses.'

He rested a hand on her hip. 'Sounds good to me.'

He meant it. It wasn't all show, all external like Alan and Doone. He really meant it. A quiver ran through her. 'I wish we were at home right now,' she breathed. Her voice had gone suddenly husky.

His eyes were brown-green promises of forever. 'Me too. I lo–'

'Hi, Mum! Were we good?'

Beth made an exasperated sound in her throat. 'Terrific,' she said, giving her son a hug. 'You too, Jason. You played Danny beautifully.'

'Did you see Cheryl and Paul go wrong in the dance? They had to be made out before us!'

'Not that wrong,' snapped Cheryl Foster, coming through the door. She saw Seb. 'Oh wow! Tell me you're somebody's brother I haven't met until now.'

Lisa pushed past. 'Seb Merchant,' she said carelessly. 'We're acting with him in the panto.' A look of pure power crossed her face as she slid her arm around Jason's waist. 'He's waiting for Nats.'

'Teacher's pet and this hunk? That is just so-o likely.'

Beth stiffened. Natalie herself came through the door, still Sandy in her head, blissfully unaware. Cheryl and her clique watched with the eyes of bunched jackals. 'Two to one he pulls it off,' said Owen in Beth's ear.

Seb, with beautiful timing, looked up, put his arm casually around Natalie's shoulders and kissed her cheek. 'You were amazing,' he said.

Unselfconsciously she smiled into his face. Happiness radiated from her.

Beth swallowed her shock. 'It was great, sweetheart. You must be shattered.'

As they left she felt eyes on their backs, heard Lisa's malicious 'Told you!' and pictured her snuggling into Jason's arm. But there *couldn't* be anything between Seb and Nats. 'Do you know something I don't?' she said to Owen, her lips barely moving.

'Seb mentioned they speak on the phone.'

'And you didn't tell me?'

There was a tiny hesitation. 'It didn't occur to me that it was my business.'

Not his business? Hurt lanced through her. Feelings she'd thought were becoming clear were twisted awry. He'd sided with Seb. All men together. She drove home with panic invading her lungs.

'Beth–' He caught her in the kitchen while she was failing to make a tray of tea. 'Beth, stop this. She's sixteen.'

She blinked tears away. 'It's not that.' How could she say she'd had expectations, made assumptions.

He took the kettle out of her hands and put in on the worktop. 'It's what?'

'If you don't know I can't tell you.'

'If you don't tell me, I'm not likely to find out, am I?'

He was getting angry. Any moment now he was going to storm out. Sleep in his old room. She caught her breath on a sob.

'Christ, Beth, this is ridiculous!' He pulled her to him and kissed her.

Fire sizzled back into her breast, sheets of it, amber and scarlet and cinnabar and tangerine. An inferno blazed around them as her eyes were locked in his arrow-straight hazel gaze. A second shock ran through her: this was the first time in her entire life she'd maintained eye contact whilst kissing. It made the act so immediate, so instantly arousing. His jeans tightened at the exact moment her crotch twitched towards him.

He released her lips slowly but kept their lower bodies touching, teetering on orgasm. 'I've been trying to tell you all night, Beth. I love you.'

Oh God! She jerked against him and climaxed uncontrollably, half her heart spiralling up to the heavens. 'I love you too,' she gasped. 'I've known for ages.'

He dropped his head and covered her throat with nipping, loving kisses, each one a pinprick of desire, a promise of elation. 'I wish you'd told me.'

She was on fire. She fought her fingers past his shirt to clutch a handful of crisp, curling chest hair. 'You're joking. Tell a sexy, promiscuous, itinerant actor that I've fallen in love with him? What do you think I am, crazy?'

He buried his face in her neck for a long, shuddering, intensely erotic moment, then lifted it, his eyes full of wickedness and love. 'Not promiscuous, mistress. Not since I've known you. But now you mention it, do you fancy a quick screw while the kettle's boiling?'

'You mean we just haven't?' asked Beth. 'Fully clothed, too.' She rubbed his groin softly. 'Do you suppose the Department of Health knows about this? It would solve the problem of unwanted pregnancies at a stroke.'

Cate drove Rob and Nats to *Grease* on Thursday. The house lights were just dimming when instinct made her turn. 'Bloody hell!' she ejaculated, and as soon as the interval released her, moved purposefully through the audience.

'Hello, Cate,' said her uncle affably.

She looked from him to Adrian. 'Wasn't *The Lion, The Witch and The Wardrobe* one of the possibilities for this summer? Is it just Natalie you're interested in?'

'That's my girl,' said Ned. 'What do you think?'

'She's got a crush on Seb.'

'Noted. Don't say anything. I need to have another word with her mother first.'

Cate returned not at all easy in her mind. It was all very well for Ned to be blasé about first love, but he'd forgotten what it was like to be sixteen. When the kids came in for a technical rehearsal on Saturday, a second potential problem arose. Cate saw Annis and friends lingering in the wings as Natalie went past.

'Phwoar, I fancy that.'

'Boy Wonder's bit of stuff,' said Annis. 'How long do you give me to pull her?'

'No chance. Ugly bugger like you?'

'Going to put your money where your mouth is?'

As soon as they broke for coffee, Cate grabbed Seb. 'There's a problem with your tickets,' she said loudly, and hustled him out of earshot.

'What do you mean? No one's coming up until after Christmas.' Seb's mouth tightened. 'I had a letter from Mum this morning reminding me to ask about staying at Beth's again.'

'Annis is laying bets that he can get off with Nats.'

Anger flickered into life at the back of Seb's blue eyes. 'She'll never fall for it.'

'I know *that*. Nobody in their right mind would. I'm telling you because–' Suddenly, with him looking less compliant than usual, it was difficult to say what was in her mind. 'He's under the impression that you and she– Look, he might needle you, that's all.'

Seb smiled humourlessly. 'So what's new?'

'I'm just warning you, all right?' She was so rattled that she went on, 'There's something else. Don't tell her, but Ned's considering Nats for Lucy in *The Lion, The Witch and The Wardrobe*. The whole ten week tour.'

Again there was the flicker of a boundary in his face. 'She'll be good.'

'Of course she will. That's not what I meant.'

He compressed his lips. 'Then what?'

God, did she have to spell it out? 'I just don't want an act of kindness to rebound on you, OK?'

In the Arctic blast which followed, she wondered how she could ever have thought of him as amenable. 'Currently,' he said, icicles in every syllable, 'Natalie is the one person *not* trying to run my life. Believe me, it makes a pleasant change.'

CHAPTER 13

By morning, Cate had worked herself into her blackest mood ever. 'Bloody rest day,' she said, scowling across the breakfast table. 'You ought to all be in working.'

Owen raised sardonic eyebrows. 'Never heard of over-preparation?'

'You can't tell me *you* think we'll be ready to open Tuesday?'

'Nothing rehearsing until midnight Monday won't fix, sweeting.'

She pushed her chair back. 'I'm going in. It won't be *us* that aren't ready!' She felt better to find the crew hard at work too but it was a different story when Luke drifted in in a state of otherworldliness just as they were wrapping up.

'Hi, Cate. Father just rang me on his elf's mobile.'

There was a choking sound from one of the technicians.

'He's coming over after Christmas. Can we get him into the company box?'

'The father of the lead part? You do ask some daft questions, Luke. Did you really say his *elf's* mobile?'

'Yes. He's Santa at a department store in

Lincoln. He says it would be a great job if it wasn't for all the children.'

More howls from the crew. Cate glared at them.

'By the way,' Luke continued, 'Mother wants to know what time we'll be arriving Christmas Eve. She's got people coming for drinks.'

'What time *you'll* be arriving,' Cate corrected him. 'I'm at Beth's for Christmas. She's invited Ned and Stella too.'

'Really? That's nice of her. She's always struck me as the hospitable sort.'

'She is,' said Cate. 'Did you notice whether any shops were still open? I must buy some presents.'

Luke put an arm around her shoulders. 'I've got a better idea,' he said.

Cate slid in early next morning to find Beth already up. 'What's the matter?'

Beth rubbed her forehead. 'I remembered I promised my form a treat when we first discussed building the class into a team. How do I confess I can't even afford a packet of crisps?'

A wicked, bubbling, gem of an idea seeped into Cate's mind. She leaned sideways and whispered in Beth's ear. 'You're not to tell Owen.'

Beth shrieked with laughter. 'Deal! Definitely a deal! I'll set it up with the Head this morning.' She glanced at the clock and yelled up the stairs for Natalie and Robin to hurry up. 'Yesterday therapeutic, was it?'

Cate felt herself reddening. 'Not bad, for someone from another planet. What did you do?'

There was the tiniest pause. 'Went swimming.'

'This time of year? Wasn't it cold?'

Beth's voice was muffled as she shoved packed lunches in bags. 'Not so as you'd notice.'

'Maybe I should have come with you. The trouble is, I always forget how unfit I am and do too much.'

'Yes,' said Beth. 'I was pretty wrecked by the time we got back.'

Upstairs they heard Seb calling something to Rob.

'Shit,' said Cate, feeling herself flush. 'I'd better go. I've managed to quarrel with him.'

Beth stared. 'With *Seb?* Good God, how?'

'Opening my mouth once too often.' She scuffed her trainer against the table leg. 'I saw Ned at *Grease*.'

'Oh. That.'

Now Cate felt guilty because of only having looked at the summer tour from Seb's angle. 'I'll keep an eye on Nats,' she said gruffly. 'If you trust me after my abysmal record with Luke.'

'Of course. And I know I have to let her do it if it's offered. I just–'

Cate got up to go. 'She'll be all right. No one will try *anything* once they know Owen is involved with you.'

A couple of hours later she was busying herself with props and keeping one eye on the stage door so she'd see Seb arrive. As soon as he did, she took a deep breath and cornered him. 'I'm apologising. Make the most of it.'

'Bloody hell!' said Seb.

She glowered. 'It's your own fault. You shouldn't make it so easy for folk to take advantage of you. It gives other people this insane desire to stop them.'

He ducked, his hair falling forward. 'It was just too much, you as well. Straight after that letter from Mum saying she'd found me a nice flat-share with the son of one of Dad's colleagues and perhaps if I popped back at Christmas...'

'Told you so. But you're staying with Beth and the rest of us, aren't you?'

'Absolutely! Oh, and you were right about Annis. He was humming *Three Little Maids From School* in the dressing room yesterday.'

That did it. She was watching him hawk-fashion from now until get-out.

First Night. By late afternoon, Beth was almost as sick with nerves as Owen. She slipped into the auditorium to watch the final rehearsal before taking over on official chaperone duty. Owen was on stage. Even through her collywobbles, his script made her laugh.

'Jack's father was called Jack too. Jack-of-all-trades. Jack of all the maids more like! As soon as the seven-year-itch struck he started scratching all over the village. You wouldn't believe how many Jacks there are at the Orphanage. *My* Jack's quite different, devoted to Baron Hardup's daughter, Jill. Many's the time he's gone up that hill with her, fingering her pail and working her well. I've never known such a household for getting through water! Here's his friend, Tom-Tom-the-Piper's-Son. *His* mother developed a passion for music one pantomime season...' Beth grinned as Owen glanced archly into the orchestra pit and there was a flute-type squeak.

Seb ambled in from the wings and waved cheerfully to the pit. 'Hi, Dad!' The flautist blew a guilty 'Hello'.

'Well?' said Owen. 'Found any apprentices for our decorating business? If you mean to marry Mary-Mary, you need to deliver me some dosh for her dowry.'

'They're here for an interview now, Dame Trot!'

'And none of them want paying?'

'I told them it was Community Service, just like you told me.'

Maternal pride swelled Beth's chest as she heard Natalie shout 'Fall *in!'* and then the Orphans marched, danced or just plain shambled down the aisle. Owen watched them climb on to the stage and assemble themselves. 'And where are the apprentices?' he said.

Seb gave a beaming smile. 'This is them.'

'Shoe Orphans all present and correct, ma'am!' said Natalie, saluting.

Owen looked at Lisa and the girl who played Sally-Go-Round-The-Sun dancing, Little Johnny Green spray-painting the scenery, Robin fighting Jack, and Wee Willie Winkie covering Little Boy Blue with a rug. 'They're present,' he agreed. He pointed to the end of the line. 'Except that one.'

'Little Boy Blue, ma'am. Never run out on a job yet.'

As they swung into *Fit to Work, Fit to Play* with many bends, stretches and narrow misses, Beth stifled her giggles and headed for the dressing room.

'They're just doing this song and the one from the top of Act Two, then they're having tea,' said Sue. 'I must get these licences down to Stella.'

'Fine,' said Beth. She listened to the relay through the room's loudspeaker. Even with the distortion, Natalie's voice was clear. Owen's too. She felt a hand squeeze her heart. In three weeks' time the panto would be over and the cast would have a fortnight off. Would he stay with them? And what about afterwards? She still wasn't sure that an actor's 'forever' meant the same as hers. Losing Alan had been traumatic, but shamefully painless as far as her heart was concerned. She didn't want to think how devastating losing Owen would be. She heard clattering on the metal stairs.

'When? Tonight?' said a voice she didn't recognise.

The other voice was unpleasantly derisive. 'Nothing like a pratfall on the first night to cheer a bloke up.'

It could easily mean nothing, but nobody could walk school corridors and not recognise a veiled threat when it was waved under their nose. Beth wrote a rapid note and hurried down to lay it on Owen's make-up bench. He'd fixed most of his good luck cards around his mirror but hers was propped up in front of it, and next to it was the one she'd sent for *Tin Pan Ali*, the one with the black cat on crutches. He'd kept it. For a moment, she felt so absurdly happy it was as if Christmas lights were flashing on and off all round her heart.

That evening she was on greenroom duty, ready to rush kids off stage if necessary. Most of the time her eyes were glued to the monitor. She had an ache in her side from laughing. Owen followed the Orphans off at one point, leaving Luke, April and the pantomime cow on stage. 'A-plus,' she said, holding the door open for the kids to go through. 'I want to be out there watching.'

'You like it?'

Jason and Lisa were the tail enders. Beth jerked her head at them to hurry. 'I love it. Owen! Is that any way for a respectable widow to behave?'

'Where does it say I'm respectable?'

On stage, Baron Hardup had discovered the lovers. 'Unhand my daughter!' ranted Monty.

'But he was only teaching me how to milk Daisy.'

'Nice one, Jack,' called Georgy Porgy.

'If there's any milking to be done, I'll teach you myself!' roared Monty.

'No one better,' said Luke in an aside to the audience.

Beth clutched Owen's arm. 'That's him. That's the man on the stairs!'

Owen looked at her, astounded. 'Luke?'

'No, Georgy Porgy.' She twisted to look at the monitor but the stage staff were in the way.

'Ah. In that case–' There was a flurry of activity as stagehands got squirt bottles into position for *There's An-udder Thing You Should Know*. 'I'll sort it after this. See you later.'

Lisa and Jason were kissing on the stairs.

'Let's have a slightly more professional attitude, shall we?' said Beth briskly. She chivvied them in front of her, surreptitiously scrubbing carmine-red lip paint off her neck.

'Mum, do we really have to go to school this morning?'

'Yes, Robin, otherwise the Head will think better of letting you perform during term-time.' Beth crammed lids on lunch boxes. 'Find Sue in the drama studio as soon as morning lessons are over, OK? I'll bring you all home after the matinée.' She thrust a third ham-and-cheese doorstep in a bag and passed it over Natalie's head.

Cate took it and gave a surreptitious wink. 'Think of it as training for when you're in the last rep in Britain, Rob, rehearsing one play all day and playing four separate bit parts in another one at night.'

'At least I won't still be doing a paper round.'

'Don't be too sure,' said Cate. 'You'd earn more.'

So why do it? But Beth already knew. She'd seen it in Seb's face when he talked about the roles he'd played, read it in Owen's body language as soon as they got within a hundred yards of the theatre. *I love him – and half the time he belongs to another mistress entirely.*

She thought of him again as she shepherded her giggling, awed and excited class into the Corn Exchange for the matinée that afternoon. 7.1 had been *highly* impressed with her notion of an end-of-term treat. Their parents had been impressed with it being free (courtesy of slow ticket sales for the first matinée and a desperate need on the part of the management to dress the house so the cast didn't get dispirited right at the beginning of the run). The house lights went down, the orchestra faded, 7.1 stopped prodding each other with rolled-up programmes and watched as Luke came on stage.

'Hello! My name's Jack. What's yours?'

'Star!' yelled Star, a seasoned pantomime-goer.

'Chantelle!'

'Oo wants ter know?' shouted Yob belligerently.

'My mummy says you shouldn't tell strangers your name,' said Felicity in a carrying voice.

Luke put his hands over his ears. 'I'll just call you *everyone*. Here comes Dame Trot. She's my mum. Don't tell her I've been with my girlfriend, Jill, all morning, will you?'

'JACK!' screeched a voice from off-stage. 'Where are you, you good-for-nothing lay-about?'

Yob nodded. 'That's 'is Mam,' he said confidently.

Owen bustled on. 'I like her ribbons,' said Felicity.

'Have you found us any work?' said Owen. 'Baron Hardup will throw us out if we can't pay the rent.'

Luke shook his head sorrowfully. 'Sorry, Mum, I've asked everyone.'

Owen noticed the audience. 'Who are this lot?'

'Everyone!' The audience roared with laughter.

Owen faced them. 'Has he been with you all day?'

Behind his back, Luke nodded vigorously.

'Yes,' lied the audience in delight.

'Go on! You've been up that hill with Jill. I bet you can't give me the name of a single person here!'

'Oh, yes, I can.'

'Oh, no, you can't.'

'Oh, yes, I can. They're–' A piece of paper on the end of a violin bow was passed up from the pit. 'They're on this list.'

Owen snatched it. 'Merivale Infants School?'

A small forest of hands waved from the front stalls.

'Hello, there,' said Owen. 'We'll try not to keep you up too late. Wildwind Over 60s Club? I don't believe that! You must have made it up!' A chorus of ribald shouts from the tiered seating disabused him. He made an archly bouffant gesture to his hair. 'I know your sort. We'll try not to keep *you* up too late either. Rawlinson Community College.' His voice faltered. 'Form 7.1.'

All around Beth, her class went crazy, jumping up and down shouting 'Here we are!' 'Over here! Over here!'

'My word,' said Owen, regaining his Dame Trot persona, 'Whatever are they putting in school dinners these days? Haven't you got a teacher with you?'

'It's Mrs T!' 'Mrs Trower!' 'She's here! Look!' Beth was pulled to her feet by excited hands as the spotlight found her.

Owen looked at her. 'You, on the other hand,' he said, 'can stay as long as you like.' The Wildwind Over 60s hooted with appreciation.

His speech merged into the pantomime proper. Beth's form screamed with delight at the antics of him, Seb and the Shoe Orphans, booed Baron Hardup and Georgy Porgy, and sighed gustily over the lovelorn Jack and Jill. A grinning Cate slipped out at the interval to give Beth a note. 'I haven't enjoyed myself so much for ages,' she said. 'He was *so* cross with me.'

The note read, 'You are a terrible woman and I adore you. I'll meet you in the lobby.'

7.1 didn't even notice the average-height, dark-haired man who sat next to their teacher on the bus back to school. They were too busy talking about the pantomime and asking Robin, Jack, Natalie and Lisa for autographs. 'I have never,' said Owen, 'corpsed in my life until that moment! First bloody matinée too! You had remembered who I'd based the Shoe Orphans on, I suppose?'

'They loved it,' laughed Beth. 'And so did I. Are you expecting me to drive you back after I've handed these kids to their parents and dropped ours at home?'

'Of course. I suppose it was the demon-spawn ASM's idea, was it?'

'Well, we didn't exactly pay for the tickets.'

Natalie barely noticed the end of term come. She loved being in the theatre, even just for three speaking scenes and half-a-dozen songs at the back of the chorus. And the feeling she got leading the Shoe Orphans down the aisle on their first entrance and then taking her very own bow at the end – she doubted there was a word for it in the English language

There was also Seb. She was seeing him every day, *working* with him even. At home though, things were as they always had been, much as she longed for more. Christmas Eve came. *The Sound Of Music* was on TV. Rob was at Jack's, Owen in the kitchen with Mum. She shifted uncomfortably. She was used to the idea of them being together now but it still embarrassed her when they touched each other or kissed. She turned her head to look at Seb, stretched out on the big settee re-reading her GCSE copy of *Twelfth Night*. Happiness stole over her. Without thinking she began to hum the refrain from *You Are Sixteen*.

He eyed her from behind his fringe. 'Know the rest of it?'

'Jason and I did it at the Easter concert.'

He scissored fluidly off the settee. She blushed and felt a tiny thrill as he started the song. He held out his hand and she realised he was expecting her to dance around the furniture as Liesl had done with Rolf. With his fingers firm under hers, she forgot her mother and Owen on the other side of the swing door, she forgot Seb was six years older than her and vastly more experienced. She only knew their voices might have been made for each other and she loved him more than she'd loved anything in her whole life. It was totally and utterly inevitable that the song would end with a kiss.

'Nice,' he said, keeping his arms around her.

'Very,' she said breathlessly, almost unable to speak for the stars and Catherine wheels that were exploding all around her. He bent his head and kissed her again. The world stopped. Nothing else existed for her but him.

'Nearly time for the matinée,' he said.

'I suppose so.' Random sentences formed in her head and disintegrated when she tried to voice them.

'Half an hour, Nats,' called Beth from the kitchen.

'OK,' her tongue replied.

They were early, almost the first ones there. Beth left them at the stage door and disappeared in the direction of the market to get tomorrow's vegetables. Owen gave a casual grunt and ducked into his dressing room. Natalie and Seb climbed the stairs to the half-landing where the *Stagestruck* room was. Their hands touched.

'Love's young dream,' drawled an unpleasant voice above them. 'But which of you is baby-snatching, eh?'

'Keep your mouth shut, please, Annis,' said Seb, standing, it seemed to Natalie, a thrilling amount taller all of a sudden.

'Keep your mouth shut please,' mimicked Annis, coming down the stairs. 'Blimey, you're so nice it's a wonder the pansy brigade haven't banged you senseless by now. I'll show you what a real man tastes like–' He reached past Seb and gripped Natalie's wrist.

'Get your hands *off* her,' snarled Seb, his fist making contact with the man's chin.

The resultant crash on the iron stairs brought both Cate and Stella out of the

285

office. 'Mr Merchant!' bellowed Stella.

'Good for you, Seb,' said Cate, giving him a gleeful hug. 'I *knew* you could do it!' She took Natalie's hands. 'Are you all right, Nats? What happened?'

Natalie discovered she was shaking. 'He said foul things about Seb and then grabbed me. So Seb hit him.'

Stella sniffed the air grimly. 'Drinking before a performance. Who's the under-study?'

A burst of chatter announced the arrival of Sue and the others. Cate squeezed Natalie's hands. 'If you want to talk later, come and find me. Right now I need to check whether Mr Annis had a particular reason for being in early.'

Natalie felt the others' attention shift abruptly away from her. Stella regarded her niece with narrowed eyes. Seb was looking as grim and determined as Cate.

'Nats? What's the matter?' Sue ran up the last few steps.

'I'll see you on stage,' said Seb gently. He kissed her cheek and took the stairs two at a time after Cate.

'Ripped stitches in the gusset of Seb's tights and a pair of perfectly legitimate scissors in Annis's kit,' said Stella. 'We'd be laughed out of court.'

Cate glowered. 'Ripped stitches designed

to cause maximum audience amusement the first time Seb touches his toes in the *Fit To Work* routine!'

Her aunt shrugged. 'We can't prove anything.'

'You could sack him for harassing Nats!'

'Not on one incident.'

'Drinking backstage makes two.'

'He's had a warning and won't be on tonight. How's Natalie?'

Cate scrubbed crossly at her hair. 'Head over heels in love.'

Stella chuckled. 'Sexy young men flattening bullies tend to have that effect.'

'But she's making him feel like a knight errant!'

'So?'

'She's bright, she's clever, but she sees him as a hero. And all he wants to do is protect her. Neither of them are letting the other be themselves.'

Stella levered herself to her feet. 'Not our problem. Is Beth in? I ought to ask about tomorrow.'

'She said turn up as soon as you like after breakfast.'

Counting squirt bottles in the wings while Ned rehearsed an unprepared Matthews against the clock, Cate smirked at her uncle's steady stream of profanity. 'Thanks,' he said as she handed him a tongue-stripping coffee. 'Remind me never to skimp on understudy rehearsals again.'

'If you'd listened to me in the first place, you'd have been ready for Annis pulling a stunt like that.'

'If I listened to you, there'd be no one left in the company by now.'

But contrary to her uncle's prognostications, the matinée went splendidly. Eventually Luke held both hands aloft and stepped forward. 'Thank you, everyone!' He grinned, boyishly delighted at the ripple of amusement the word 'everyone' produced. 'You have been a wonderful audience, but I'm afraid we're going to have to let you go!' Laughter. 'The *FOOTLIGHTS* Musical Theatre Company wish you all a very merry Christmas – and if you'd like to see the show again in the New Year, we're here until the twelfth! God bless.'

'Nice speech,' said Cate drily. 'Think of it yourself?'

'I shall miss this when Ellery comes back.'

'Look on the bright side, he might get eaten by a barracuda.'

The stage door was already banging as sketchily cleaned actors dashed out. 'If we could hurry just a trifle, Mr Bartholomew,' suggested Graham, edging him in the most deferential manner possible towards his dressing room, 'only we've got a crew Christmas party waiting for us to grace it.'

'Sounds good. Can I come?' said Luke,

pausing at the door to let Monty out and then standing obediently still while Graham extricated him from his costume.

Graham looked at Cate. She shrugged. 'I doubt we'll know he's there.'

The party included presents. Cate gasped for breath when she saw the totally outrageous dress composed of scarlet feathers and satin which Graham and Michael had given her. 'For the Last Night party,' ordered Graham.

'Yum,' said Luke. He gathered up the glasses. 'Same again?'

'I suppose it *is* just the sex is it?' enquired Graham.

'I'm afraid so,' sighed Cate.

'Thank goodness for that. Lord knows he's a lovely player, but it would be a terrible blow to your parents if the heir to the Edmonds empire turned out to have *completely* lost her discriminative faculties.'

CHAPTER 14

Beth awoke on Christmas morning to the lovely festive sensation of Owen kissing her neck. She slid her hand across his chest. 'Morning, minstrel. Happy Christmas.'

He smiled at her, wickedness and promise in his eyes. 'Happy Christmas, mistress. Would this be a good time to tell you I love you?'

She adjusted her body to fit his, skin against skin. 'Probably the only time. As soon as my feet hit the carpet I'm going to be running.'

'Then I love you.'

'I love you too.'

He bent his lips to hers, his fingers sliding sensuously around her breast.

'But,' she murmured, doing a small exploration of her own under the bedclothes, *'until* my feet hit the carpet, there's no reason I can think of to rush.'

Afterwards, knowing she should get up, knowing there were a thousand and one things she should be doing (foremost of which concerned an extremely large turkey which arrived annually from one of Alan's clients and which she wanted to get in the oven before anyone realised she had no right to it this year), she twiddled her fingers in his chest hair and said, 'I've got a confession to make.'

'As long as it's not that Alan and Doone are coming to lunch, I can take it.'

'God, no!' Beth felt ill at the very idea. 'I haven't got you a very original present.'

'It's not a bottle of Scotch, is it?'

'As if!'

'Or the same as you gave Alan last Christmas?'

'Why would you want monogrammed golf balls?'

'And has it kept you awake nights worrying?'

'Absolutely not.'

He kissed her. 'Then I'll love it.' He wriggled down to nuzzle her neck. 'Yours isn't very original either,' he said in a muffled voice. 'It's the sort of thing anyone might give anybody. But it's how I feel.'

Robin was already up, playing *Donkey Kong* with Christmas presents on the screen instead of bananas. 'Thanks for the stocking, Mum.'

'Sorry it wasn't more interesting.' Both stockings this year had been short on gifts and heavily bulked out with things like toothbrushes and flannels (and in Rob's case, batteries) that the kids actually needed.

'It was cool,' said Robin. 'And I'm wearing the Nintendo socks, see?'

Natalie's extravagant item had been golden-glitter nail varnish. She came downstairs blowing on her fingernails to dry them. 'Happy Christmas, Mum.'

'Happy Christmas, sweetheart.' She didn't miss her daughter's swift reccy as she dropped a present on her brother's lap. 'It's not new,' Beth heard her warn him. 'I got it from that game-exchange place.'

'*Castlevania!* Wicked!'

'And only a one-player game,' remarked Natalie with satisfaction.

Seb clattered down the stairs at the same time as Cate. Beth muttered a small, unseasonable curse as both he and her daughter changed colour. She saw her irritation reflected in Cate's face. 'You too?'

Cate grimaced. 'I just don't think they're right for each other.'

Everybody helped to peel vegetables, lay tables, juggle saucepans and pour drinks. The house filled with the aroma of illicit turkey. Even better, Ned and Stella had brought enough wine that Beth's conscience gave up in a very short space of time with only a token kick.

More presents appeared. 'You don't mind if I open my family ones down here, do you?' said Seb. 'I was going to do them upstairs, but it didn't feel right.'

'I should think not,' said Beth. 'How am I supposed to face your mother next week when she asks whether you liked her – what *is* that?'

'A calendar,' said Seb with a sigh. 'With everybody's birthdays filled in.'

'This is from me and Seb,' said Cate, handing Beth a bottle of Drambuie, 'for putting up with us.' Her eyes slewed to Owen, negligently tossing a small wrapped box in one hand. 'That had better not be for me.'

'Just a small thing I felt expressed your personality, sweeting.'

'Owen, really!' scolded Beth as Cate unwrapped a pair of jet-black earrings in the shape of sculls. Her detachment vanished as he handed *her* a small wrapped box as well. 'Oh,' she said, flustered. That size, it *had* to be jewellery. Please don't let it be the sort of modern brooch with an offset diamond which Alan had customarily given her. 'Yours is in the cupboard.'

'It was worrying you that much?' he teased.

She pulled a soft parcel from the hall cupboard and put the Drambuie distractedly in its place. She really, really didn't want to open his present. His eyes burnt into her averted head, forcing her fingers into movement. The paper revealed a Past Times box. With the sort of deep breath she last remembered using at the exhortation of a born-again midwife, she gingerly lifted the lid.

A round silver locket engraved with an intricate Celtic knot met her eyes. She recognised it at once. How could she not when she'd yearned for it ever since its first appearance in the Past Times window? She lifted it out with shaking hands, knowing how the inscription on the reverse ran.

May the road rise to greet you
May the wind be always at your back
May the sun shine warm upon your face
The rain fall soft upon your fields
And until we meet again
May God hold you in the hollow of His hand.
Traditional Irish Blessing

Tears blurred her vision as her fingers fumbled with the chain. 'Oh God, Owen. And all I gave you was a jumper.'

He'd pulled it on, the intense brown-green of its Aran pattern highlighting his eyes the way she'd known it would. 'Would you believe no one ever did before?' He circled her waist with Aran arms and kissed her wet lashes before moving down to her lips. 'Sometimes the way I feel about you scares me.'

The locket warmed against her breasts. It might have been there for ever. *Until we meet again...* As his hold tightened and his kiss deepened, she knew she wanted to live with Owen every day of her life. But in four weeks he'd be in London rehearsing for the next tour. Then Leicester, Canterbury, Exeter and Swindon before another week here. Two months of fleeting, overnight visits. Would his love last until March? How could she bear it if it didn't?

The doorbell rang. Beth pulled herself back from somewhere so far away it hurt.

'Hi, everyone,' said Luke Bartholomew. 'This is my father.'

Owen told her later a professional actor couldn't have handled the situation better, especially the way she'd clapped frozen peas over Luke's eye and thrust Cate's knuckles under the cold tap. She herself felt as divorced from reality as when she'd set fire to her hair with the cake candles during Natalie's third birthday party and had absently beaten the flames out whilst singing *Happy Birthday*. At the time it had seemed perfectly normal.

Luke's father ('Willoughby Bartholomew. Merry Christmas. Pleased to meet you.'), by the simple expedient of simultaneously discussing game releases with Robin and the state of provincial theatre with Ned, appeared blithely unaware of any ructions. As Owen drily commented, whatever his deficiencies on stage, he played the perfect-guest role to perfection, even offering to help with the washing up. 'Done it no end of times to keep body and soul together.' He glanced roguishly at Ned. 'Although I wouldn't say no if you've got a chorus part going.' He beamed genially round the table and transferred the largest slice of steaming turkey to an already piled plate.

'I am just so sorry,' said Cate later as she helped carry out empty plates. 'I could *kill* Luke for taking advantage of your better nature like this. He *knew* you wouldn't turn him and his blasted father away.'

'Forget it.' Beth poured them both refills from a bottle she'd stashed next to the sink. 'Quite honestly, by this stage of the proceedings, two extra is neither here nor there. Besides, Willoughby's providing so many one-liners I'd slip Owen a notebook if I thought he could still focus to write.'

'I swear if Ned gives the wretched man a job I'll make him coffee with curry powder in for the rest of my life!'

After lunch, for reasons not unconnected with copious quantities of alcohol, Seb and Luke made the discovery that Christmas wasn't Christmas without a game of Twister. Rob dashed upstairs to unearth it.

'Twister!' enthused Willoughby. 'Such innocent fun.'

'Your grandchildren are probably having innocent fun with your old set right now,' said Cate. She winked at Beth who immediately dissolved into giggles. 'You'll be able to meet them when they come to watch the panto.'

'I don't think so,' said Luke, oblivious to his father's choking on a mouthful of wine. 'They're horrible kids.'

'Didn't stop you introducing me to them.'

'But you are strong,' said Willoughby. 'I, alas, find young children sadly wearing. And Margot and I were never really suited, you know. It's probably kinder if I don't raise her expectations by meeting her again.'

Robin bounced back into the room with the Twister set. Beth, nearly weeping with laughter, was unprepared for Owen pulling her to her feet to join in. 'Nine people can't possibly play Twister on the same mat,' she said.

'Nine sober people can't,' agreed Owen, his hand lingering on her hip, 'but it's a well-known fact that the more drunk you are, the bendier you become.'

'*I'm* not drunk,' said Natalie.

'No need. Teenagers are naturally supple.'

'Left foot blue,' said Stella, who'd bagged the spinner before anyone else thought of it. 'Two appendages per circle, not necessarily your own.'

Maybe Owen was right, thought Beth with a heady sense of unreality as people wove legs and arms over and under everyone else's. It did seem easier with a bottle of wine inside her. But then, 'Oh, no!' she wailed as the phone rang.

'One move and you're out,' said Owen.

'If Beth makes a move, we're *all* going to be out,' pointed out Cate.

Stella passed the phone under the knot of bodies.

'Hello?' said Beth, laughing.

'Merry Christmas, Beth.'

Oh God, it was Alan. She bit the inside of her cheek in an effort to stop giggling. At least it was too late for him to demand the turkey back. 'Merry Christmas, Alan.'

'No!' growled Natalie.

'Who is Alan?' enquired Luke's father from the far side of the grid.

'Beth's ex,' hissed Cate.

'Tell him we've eaten it, thank you, and very nice it was too.' Owen dropped his head to nibble her ankle. The Twister framework creaked. It was a good thing Alan hadn't yet succumbed to the lure of a videophone. She had another fit of the giggles just imagining it, and tried to concentrate on what he was saying.

'–pop in tomorrow.'

What? Him here, or her and the kids there? She screwed up her brain to think through alcohol fumes. 'Um, we're a bit busy with *Back and the Jeanstalk – Jack and the Teenbaulk* – the pantomime.'

Robin burst out laughing, setting everyone else off. The tangle of bodies teetered. Someone proffered a glass to her lips. It seemed to help.

'Beth, have you been drinking? What on earth are you doing?'

Her sides ached with trying to keep a straight voice. 'I'm doing Christmas, Alan. Look, I'll have to go – I'm holding everybody else up.'

He must have heard the shrieks of mirth as the others realised what she'd said. 'Perhaps I could speak to the kids?' he said testily.

Beth peered under her left arm, tears streaming down her face. 'OK, here's Robin. He doesn't seem too tied up.' She pushed the phone towards him amidst a fresh gust of laughter.

'Happy Christmas, Dad,' shouted Rob into the receiver. 'Thanks for the present. Pardon? We're playing Twister. Nats, Dad wants you.'

'I can't,' said Natalie.

There was a split-second of silence. 'You can get that arm free, sweetheart,' said Beth.

A mutinous look settled on what she could see of her daughter's face. A sinewy hand abruptly shot out and scooped up the phone for her. The framework lurched, but held. 'And I thought you could act,' Owen taunted.

Furious, Natalie wriggled her hand loose. 'Happy Christmas, Dad. Thanks for the top-up voucher. No, we're both in the matinée tomorrow. OK, bye.'

'Attagirl,' said Owen.

'Whose turn is it?' asked Natalie, ignoring him.

'Oh dear,' said Beth. 'I must have gone sober. My bones have set.'

'Dad's enough to turn anyone sober. He didn't mention the turkey, did he?'

'Fortunately not. Or the Christmas cake.'

'Christmas cake? Great!'

'Seb! You *can't* be hungry already!'

'He's been hungry ever since I've known him. Shit, I'm falling...'

As Cate's arm gave way and they all collapsed, Willoughby Bartholomew emerged unscathed and settled next to Stella. 'Splendid fun. And Christmas cake *does* sound rather appealing, don't you think?'

Long after everybody slept, Cate lay awake. Just after interrupting Beth and Owen in an advanced clinch in the kitchen before coming up to bed, she'd run into Seb and Nats on the landing. Seb's arms had been around her, strong and protective, her head raised to his in innocent confidence. Cate had swerved blindly into the bathroom and very nearly brought up the entire day's food and alcohol. Now, every time she closed her eyes the scene was replayed on her eyelids.

Jealous, her inner self taunted? *He's a friend*, she snapped. Wish Luke was more like him? *Get real!* Her mouth felt horrible.

She thrust herself out of bed and went downstairs for a gallon or so of water.

She'd only been back in her room two minutes when there was a soft knock on her door. She opened it with a sense of inevitability. Willoughby had unblushingly wangled an invitation, so he and Luke were in Owen's unused room. Sure enough, Luke, in boxers and floppy Renaissance hair, was leaning against the doorframe. 'Still mad at me?'

'Yes. You had no right to trade on Beth's good will like that.' But all the same, she didn't turn him away. She studied his eye. 'That won't show tomorrow, not with make-up on.'

His arms came round her. Familiar desires stirred. Cate hated herself for letting them comfort her. She opened her mouth to protest. It came out as, 'We'll have to be quiet.'

He smiled his lazy, gut-dissolving smile. 'Any way you like,' he said. He planted a line of kisses along her throat, his hands already arousing her beyond the point where she could have sent him away.

She made one last attempt. 'Why do you do this?'

His fingers teased off her night-clothes under the cool sheet. His own followed. He pulled her to him, warm and confident and easy. 'Because it's nice. Because it's Christmas. Because you like it too. Because I'm happy.' He kissed her serenely, joyously, and her spark of resistance died.

When she awoke, he was still there. Her heart contracted at how his hair fell softly over his face, at the way his arm lay across her. 'I wish you were different,' she whispered. Tears pricked her eyes because she knew he never would be. Meeting Willoughby had shown her that. Like father, like son. She kissed his forehead for the last time. 'Wake up,' she said, a catch in her voice. 'Back to your own pallet.'

He stretched sleepily, rolled with drowsy grace out of the bed and padded down the hallway. Cate scrubbed her eyes. Just once he might have argued.

It was between Christmas and New Year that the letter came. Owen read it through with a sense of mounting disturbance. He checked the signature with disbelief. 'Jesus wept. It's from Davy.'

Rob looked up from the Nintendo magazine he'd borrowed from Jack. 'Who?'

Beyond them, framed in the doorway, Beth had her hand to her mouth. Owen cleared his throat. 'My son.'

'I didn't know you had one.'

'Fathers,' commented Natalie, 'are the pits.'

Usually the remark would have amused him; today it grated. Beth spoke quickly. 'It's very nice of Dad and Doone to take you out after the matinée.'

Natalie flashed a look at her mother. 'No, it isn't. Either he wants to show us off or it's Doone Taking An Interest.'

'So suggest she takes an interest in the state of yours and Rob's winter coats.' Her eyes were still on him. 'Is Davy well?'

His throat felt swollen. 'He wants to meet me.' Thoughts leapt and jumped in his head. 'Why?'

Beth moved to sit on the arm of his chair. Her hand rested on his shoulder. 'How old did you say he was? Fifteen? I'd say he wants to find himself. Wants to know whether the parts of him that don't fit his family come from you.'

Something very like panic crept along his veins. 'What do I do?'

Her arm fed him comfort. 'You mean he hasn't given you his phone number?'

This was such a mistake, thought Owen, watching the doors of the London train open. He knew him instantly: thin, dark, intense. A reflection of the boy he had once been. For a moment he wanted to run away, turn round, go home. It was like confronting his own mortality.

'Davy–' His voice came out as a croak. Nerves jangling, he called on his stage persona. 'Davy!'

The boy came over, hitching up his Nike

backpack warily. Owen recalled that his stepfather was tall, heavy-set and blond. Judging by Davy's expression, he was laying the blame for his own lack of inches well and truly where it belonged.

'Hi,' he said, far too heartily. 'This is weird, isn't it?'

'A bit.'

Around them, passengers seeped off the platform. Owen turned towards the exit, talking too fast. 'Like I said on the phone, I've got to be at the theatre by one. I thought perhaps we could go to McDonald's for a bite to eat first.'

'Cool.'

'So,' said Owen once they'd parked the car. 'What do you want to know about me?'

Davy missed his footing on the kerb. He half-smiled, quick and uncertain. 'Everything, really.'

Owen felt a snap of tension ease. How difficult could this be? 'There's a coincidence,' he said drily.

Another nearly-smile. 'What – what do I call you?'

Not Dad or Pa obviously. Such a little thing, a word. 'Try Owen. I'm sorry – this really *is* weird. The number of times I've wondered about you...' They ducked around a weave of cyclists. Owen pointed across the market square. 'The theatre is just up there.'

Davy's head lifted. He moistened his lips.

'Can I go backstage?'

'Sure. I hope it won't put you off, seeing me in my Dame make-up.'

'No.'

The answer came out a shade quick. Owen waited until they were sitting at a crowded slice of table before trying again. 'Tell me about you. What do you like?'

Natalie would have given him a look and muttered 'music'. Rob would have launched into a panegyric on Nintendo. 'English,' said Davy. 'And drama.'

Whoa – defensive or what! 'Your mother will approve,' he said, hoping he'd struck the right casual note. 'Doing drama for GCSE?'

Davy's eyes lifted to meet his. They were blue-grey like Michelle's. Christ, he'd completely forgotten. 'Yes. Dad thinks it's a waste of a subject. Doesn't bother him that all Shane wants to do next year is sport.'

'Shane?' In his mind, Owen heard Beth say in her please-don't-let-this-sound-like-advice voice, 'He's probably fighting everything at home and wants to know whether life with you would have been different.'

'My brother. Then there's Tyrone, Austen, Anne-Marie and Cara.'

Jesus! Owen sent a horrified and fervent prayer of thanks to whichever god had organised Barry to decorate that long-ago boarding house, thus delivering him from a lifetime of fatherhood.

'Do you live here now?' Davy was asking. 'Only always before, the cards said 'Care of *FOOTLIGHTS*' and before that it was a place in Fulham.'

It had been a moment of pure indulgence that, putting Beth's address on Davy's card. 'Because we were fixed here for Christmas. Most of the time we're on tour so it's easier for the office to forward my post.'

'Oh.' There was a tiny silence, as if Davy was digesting the information. 'Do you do pantomimes often?'

'Once a year.' The glib retort was out before he could call it back. 'Been to one yourself yet?'

Davy sounded evasive. 'No. Mum and I went to see *An Inspector Calls* by the Colindale Players.'

'Any good?'

'Yeah. I wanted to do their summer school, but it was the same week we were going to Pontins.'

Owen repeated his thanks to the gods.

'It rained.'

Owen looked at him blankly. 'I'm sorry?'

'At Pontins. It rained.'

'Probably the same week we were in Oldham. It rained there too.' And I realised I was in love with Beth. Rainbows and jagged sun amongst the clouds. For a moment he revelled in the astonished glory of that knowledge. His eyes flicked to Davy; how in

306

Christ's name was he supposed to make conversation with a son he'd barely thought about for fourteen years? A son who lived in Colindale and went to Pontins for his holidays?

The people whose table they'd shared left. Another tray was dumped in the empty space. 'These seats taken?' said Seb.

Owen's head jerked up. 'What the hell are you two doing here?'

'Hi, you must be Davy. I'm Natalie.' She glanced at Owen. 'January sales,' she said in an voice of exaggerated patience. 'We talked about it at breakfast.'

'Strangely enough, I had other things on my mind. Davy, meet Seb Merchant. He's an actor too. Nats is Beth's daughter. You'll see her later playing a bolshy foreman, a role she is particularly comfortable with.'

'Hi.' Seb grinned across the table. 'Looking forward to the show?'

'Um, yeah.' Davy stared at Natalie. 'You're in the company?'

'Only for the panto.'

'That's cool, though.'

She grinned. 'Yeah.'

A thoroughly unworthy idea crawled into Owen's brain. He caught Natalie's eye. 'Davy's doing GCSE Drama like you.'

She gave him a look which said quite clearly that he now owed her. 'Which module are you on? We're finishing *King*

Lear. I *hate* the eyeball scene, don't you?'

Owen sat back with guilty relief. 'Buy anything?' he asked Seb.

Seb was watching Nats with an odd look on his face. 'Not much. We ran into Lisa and Jason, so I chatted to him while the girls vanished into changing rooms. Nice lad. Wanted to know which stage college I went to and what had made me pick it.'

He glanced at Natalie and Davy again. Owen recalled Beth's reservations about the age gap. Shit, he thought, if I encourage Seb I betray Beth, but if I do what she wants I mess up as likely a lad as I've worked with in years. 'Finished?' he said to Davy, copping out. 'My make-up takes a while to get on.'

And now what do we talk about, he wondered, applying the Dame's base colour as Davy sat, a silent, intense shadow in a corner of his room. 'It sounded as if you were interested in the theatre, from what you were saying to Nats.'

The thin face lit up, taking him uncomfortably back to Michelle's less than balanced enthusiasm for anything she admired. 'Yeah! We did *The Merchant of Venice* last year at school. I was Shylock.'

'Excellent,' said Owen.

'Mum said I reminded her of you. She said when you acted you really turned into that person. I want to go to RADA after A-levels. Mum says I'll love it.'

His eyes shone with fervour. Owen felt even more uneasy. He'd never looked back on those idealistic days filled with an unreality of pot and politically-correct coffee with affection. 'Plenty of places to choose from. There's pages of adverts in *The Stage*.'

'But you and Mum went to RADA.'

Owen beat down a flicker of irritation. The repetition was pure Michelle, adhering obstinately to an idea no matter how many counter arguments were put her way. 'That's not to say we wouldn't either of us have done better at East15 or Central or Italia Conti.'

'Italia Conti?' said Davy. 'But that's for–'

The door opened. 'Time for Davy to go up to the box,' said Cate.

Thank Christ for that. 'Enjoy the show. Beth or Nats will come and get you when it's over.'

Five blessedly quiet minutes later, Beth herself slipped in.

'OK?'

He applied a cupid's bow to his mouth. 'Barely.'

'I've been thinking of you. I almost came in, but it occurred to me I might be infringing on your personal space and giving him complexes.'

'I wish you had.'

She massaged his shoulders. 'The first meeting is bound to be tricky. But we do have a problem, minstrel. Rob and Jack are on again tonight because Kirsty's sick. Bang goes the Rob-entertaining-Davy plan.'

Owen leaned back against her and rotated his neck. 'Wouldn't have worked anyway. He is scarily like Michelle. Almost certainly regards computer games as overwhelmingly frivolous. Sit him down and give him a *Hamlet* tutorial instead. He'll lap it up.'

She dropped a kiss on his head. 'We'll work something out over tea. Break a leg, lover.'

She was so close, yet so detached. 'Beth–?'

She turned.

'I wish I'd met you years ago.'

'Years ago I was married. And you were even more all over the country than you are now.'

'Years before that then.'

She looked at him. He couldn't even begin to guess what was going on in her mind. 'Me too,' she said.

They ended up watching the second house: her, Natalie and Davy. Beth hadn't the heart to say no when Nats suggested it (because *she* hadn't seen the panto from the front yet) and Davy had looked up, eyes huge at the thought of going to the theatre twice in one day.

Ned slipped into the company box during the second half. 'What do you think?' he

310

asked Natalie.

She grinned, thoroughly at ease with him now. 'Not as good as we are.'

Davy frowned. 'This bit's OK.' He nodded to the stage where Robin and Jack were causing chaos by copying the Dame and Tom-Tom's decorating. 'But the acting is too artificial.'

'It's a *pantomime*,' said Natalie. 'It's *supposed* to be done like that. The trick is to get the audience involved with the characters even though they know it's not real. Just because something isn't Ibsen, it doesn't mean it's not an art form in its own right.'

Beside her, Beth felt Ned shake with laughter. 'Well said!' And to Beth he murmured, 'Are you at home tomorrow morning? Both of you?'

Pellets of ice dropped through Beth's body. The summer job. He was going to offer it to her. 'We are.'

He got up. 'I'll drop by.'

She leant back, hardly seeing the antics on stage.

He was earlier than she expected next day. The air was still sticky with marmalade toast when he rang the doorbell.

'Guvnor,' said Owen. 'What a pleasant surprise.'

Cate peered backwards through the propped-open swing door from where she and Natalie were doing a Win-A-Hundred-Pounds-Celebrity-Crossword. 'Did you want me? Why didn't you phone?'

'I've come to offer Natalie the part of Lucy in *The Lion, The Witch and The Wardrobe* for the summer tour.'

Beth groped for Owen's hand. Knowing hadn't helped at all. She was too agitated even to feel amused at the astonishment on her daughter's face.

Natalie gasped. 'For the week you're in Cambridge? You're offering it to me already? I'd love to!'

Ned smiled. 'The whole tour.'

'The whole–' She looked incredulously at Beth. 'What about my GCSEs?'

'We've double-checked the dates. Exams will be over before rehearsals start,' said Beth. Years of sounding calm while her insides were in turmoil stood her in good stead. 'It's entirely your decision.'

'It's not full time,' said Ned. 'You'll be back for A-levels.'

Natalie's eyes shone brilliantly. 'Yes!' she said. 'Yes!'

Only a miserable, child-hating killjoy couldn't have been pleased for her. Beth gripped Owen's hand hard. 'Well done, sweetheart,' she said.

Owen returned the pressure before hugging Natalie in a comradely fashion. 'Good on you, sparrow. I couldn't ask to be turned to stone for anyone nicer.'

'Who says you're not going to be the evil dwarf?' ribbed Cate. She too hugged Natalie.

After Ned left, Natalie pirouetted wildly around the room. 'The company. I'm going to be in the company. Oh my God, Lisa will kill me.'

Davy's thin face was sharp with jealousy. 'I read *The Lion, The Witch and The Wardrobe* to Anne-Marie and Cara last year. I didn't realise it was a play.'

'A musical,' corrected Natalie. She looked at the others. 'Does Lucy sing a lot? How come I didn't audition? What's everybody else?'

'Ned and Adrian saw you in *Grease*,' said Cate. 'I wouldn't have known myself if I hadn't spotted them there. The actual cast list won't be decided for months yet. *Hot Mikado* is only being put up next week.'

Owen had his winding-up face on. 'Late casting is deliberate policy so that by the time we know we've got a bum part, it's too late to look for something else.'

'It's a wonderful system,' protested Seb. 'You don't have too long to worry about what might go wrong before you're in the thick of rehearsals. Then you're too busy learning the songs and too tired from practising Ned's choreography to care.'

Beth's eye fell on Davy. He'd turned white.

'Musicals?' he said jerkily to Owen. 'I

313

thought you were a *real* actor.'

'They all act!' said Natalie. 'You've obviously never seen *Oklahoma!* I was on the edge of my seat watching Seb as Jud Fry.'

'*Oklahoma!*' The scorn was unmistakable, as was the shake in his voice. 'That's not *serious* acting!'

Owen was very nearly as white as his son. 'What the sodding hell did you expect? It's in the name: *FOOTLIGHTS Musical Theatre Company!*'

'You just haven't watched enough shows, Davy,' said Robin cheerfully. 'Can I get your cuttings book to show him, Owen?'

'I'd like to see it,' said Seb. He reddened. 'I could bring mine down too, if you want?'

My son, the peace-maker, thought Beth. She wrapped her hand firmly around Owen's clenched fist. 'Help me make a fresh pot of tea.'

As the door swung to, she heard Cate say astringently, 'It'd be smarter not to knock things until you know a little more about them. Try *Blood Brothers* or *Miss Saigon* if you think musicals can't be serious. And look in Seb's book for the review of him playing *The Thing* at college in his second year – shivers down the spine weren't in it. He should have been snapped up on the spot by a West End scout.'

As soon as the door shut, Beth pinned Owen's rigid frame with her body and

314

kissed him.

'Don't do this,' he ground out, refusing to unbend. 'Don't cheapen yourself to make *me* feel better.'

'I'm not. I'm buying your gratitude so you'll look after Nats over the summer.'

His hazel eyes held hers for an eternity of fury and shame. With a sudden movement, he buried his head in her neck. 'Beloved, I want you so much at this moment that I could do it right here up against the wall.'

'Me too. Except we aren't up against the wall, we're up against the door. Mind, the sight of us propelled through the opening as one would probably ensure Davy never wanting to set eyes on you again...'

He gave a reluctant laugh. 'I love you, Beth. Never leave me?'

For a moment she'd forgotten. Pain ate into her bones. I, lover, am not the one who's going to be doing the leaving.

CHAPTER 15

The last Monday of the run. Seb hung back on stage as the shout went up that the cast for *Hot Mikado* had been posted.

'Not interested?' Cate was half-way up a ladder greasing a revolving flat.

He shrugged. 'Not going to run away, is it?'

She sent a sharp look at him. 'Read it in the office if you like.'

He flushed. 'Stop babying me.'

'Stop pretending there's nothing wrong.'

'It's a jam by the board, that's all.'

'Yeah, right.'

He turned, goaded, to catch up with the throng. Annis was looking triumphant. Sweat from warm-up gleamed on his bare arms. 'Covering Ko-Ko!' he said. 'Covering the Lord High Executioner! Beat that, pretty boy!'

Seb pushed past him and stared at the list. He noticed that *his* name was higher up the Ensemble. He also noticed it was Monty who was Ko-Ko. Monty had never missed a performance in his life.

'Back to the ranks,' murmured Luke. 'It was nice while it lasted.'

316

'Crap,' said Cate, overhearing. She gave the flat an experimental twirl. 'Pish-Tush is hardly the ranks. You knew the Voice would be back this tour.' She flicked a dagger-glance of sarcasm at Seb. 'OK now?'

He seriously considered hooking his foot round her ladder. 'Fine.' But he wasn't. Sue's New Year's Eve party, lively with Lisa and Natalie's friends, weighed on his memory like an undigested meal. He honestly hadn't considered the age difference until that evening. Standing arms-round-waist with Nats, he'd caught himself casting rueful glances to where Owen and Pete were roaring with laughter. The trouble was, he remembered being sixteen as if it was yesterday, every topic the crowd had brought up he'd empathised with; it had brought home to him big time that the best thing about being twenty-two was leaving all those problems behind.

Also there was Nats herself. She was so *innocent*. Her kisses were sweet and wholesome and awoke violently grown-up, un-boy-next-door urges in him. Seb slammed his fist against the wall. He couldn't be the one to do it. *Because* she was so trusting. *Because* she was so open. *Because* she was so headily in love with him. God forgive him, he'd got so that he was relieved the nights she wasn't on, nights when he could be himself. The truth was he'd used her to make himself feel better, the one thing he'd sworn months ago he'd never do. He couldn't even confess to Cate and endure a well-deserved tongue lashing, she was the most evil-tempered he'd seen her, the slightest thing was apt to set her off.

On Friday it did. Owen filched the toast she'd made from under her fingers and within seconds all three of them were yelling blue murder at each other. It was surprisingly cathartic.

'End-of-run stress,' mumbled Seb, ashamed. 'I don't really think you're a psychotic, bloody-minded control freak, Cate.'

She shot him a beetling look from under lowered brows. 'And I probably shouldn't have said you were a gilded, goody-two-shoes Sir Galahad. I'm sure you could be just as nasty as the rest of the human race if you overcame years of conditioning and put your mind to it.'

'I'm not apologising,' growled Owen.

'Nor am I! I'm just saying I shouldn't have said it.'

Seb chafed. 'I wish we were rehearsing again. Everything's more focused.'

They got to the theatre early. As Seb went into the empty ensemble room he saw his tap shoes half out of his bag. He reached down.

Cate came in. 'Seb, I – Jesus!' She snatched them out of his hand. 'Murdering bastard! These are greased!'

'Annis worked it out at last, has he?' said Owen, following her.

Seb's brain had slowed to jelly. 'Worked out what?'

Cate answered, shaking with rage. 'That with you covering Luke and Luke covering the Voice, you're a lot more likely to see centre stage next tour than he is. How dare he pull something like this in *my* company. I'm going to bloody kill him!'

Seb sat down numbly, refusing to admit it could be true. Annis hated him that much? That much?

Friday afternoon. Natalie came out of the stage door after the matinée with Seb and stopped. There seemed to be an entire primary school in the alley waiting for them.

'Look, it's Tom-Tom! Oh, please, can you sign my programme?'

'And mine?'

'And mine? Ple-e-ase?'

She stepped back as he laughingly signed autographs. His mobile went off. He hooked it under his chin and continued to sign as he talked. 'Hi Mum. No, we're all going out for Sunday lunch so I'm not travelling back until Monday. I *can* make appointments for myself, you know. Oh, OK, Tuesday will be fine.'

Natalie looked away hurriedly. He'd

sounded different talking to his mother. Purposeful. *Older.* The thought squatted in her head, daring her to face it.

The house seemed really quiet that evening. Natalie dried up in a silence fully as abstracted as Mum's. 'Are you going to miss Owen?' she asked. It wasn't what she'd been going to say. She wished she hadn't when she saw quick pain lash across her mother's eyes.

'Yes.'

'Seb ... doesn't seem that bothered.' The fleeting sympathy in Beth's face should have warned her. 'He's been different the last few days ... older...'

'Sweetheart, he *is* older.'

Tears welled up behind Natalie's eyes. 'I love him so much, Mum.'

'Of course you do. I don't see how anybody couldn't. And if *you* were twenty-two as well, you'd have as good a chance of happiness as anyone on the planet. Whatever happens, it'll be a wonderful first love to remember.'

Mum had put the horrible, squatting, nebulous thoughts into words! It was too sudden. Natalie's world spun out-of-control-sideways. Grief, unanticipated and shocking, tore at her ribs. 'No-o-o!'

Beth hugged her. 'It's not over yet.'

Colour drained out of the kitchen. A barren landscape filled her mind. She wrenched away. 'You think it will be?'

'Love, you're going to be apart for such long periods.'

Pain made her unreasonable, made her lash out. 'So will you and Owen. And he's *way* less patient than Seb.'

Her mother's face was a mask of winter. 'I know.'

Sunday night. Rob had gone to bed. Mum and Owen were tactfully in the kitchen. Cate had left early that morning. Natalie sat on the settee tucked into Seb's side and watched the end of the film. There were tears in her eyes. They'd been there on and off all day. 'I wish you weren't going,' she said.

He turned his head and squeezed her shoulders. 'I need to find a flat before rehearsals start. I won't get a chance after.'

'I suppose.'

'And you've got Mocks, you don't need distractions.'

Her voice wobbled. 'Don't you sometimes really hate life? Don't you sometimes wish it could be one never-ending show?'

He shifted. 'I used to.' His words seemed reluctant. 'But life doesn't go away. There comes a time when you've got to head-butt it into submission.'

'That sounds like something Cate would say.'

He was silent for a moment then kissed

her, long and lovely and achingly tender, as if he knew it might be the last time. 'I'll ring you tomorrow after school. We'll survive.'

Survive. Who wanted to just *survive* when they'd thought they were on the brink of heaven? Her tears mingled with the taste of his kiss.

Last week Owen had done nothing but sleep. This week he was starting to brood. Beth watched him rove the room as she marked. 'Want to read some essays on why well-meaning friends should have kept their noses out of Romeo and Juliet's business? Tell me what you think.'

'Romeo and Juliet?' he echoed bitterly. 'Bit up-market for me.'

Thought so. It was high time this was nipped in the bud. Beth straightened her spine and prepared for battle. 'We've already watched the *Romeo and Juliet* film, but Cate's sending me your in-house video of *West Side Story* too. I know which version my class will prefer.'

'Pap for the masses. Easy-to-digest culture.'

'More people have got pleasure from *West Side Story* than have even heard of Gielgud or Olivier. A company like FOOTLIGHTS draws them into the theatre, gives them a taste of magic that lasts a lifetime.'

Owen stared into the mirror over the

mantelpiece. 'But I'd be doing it even if they were a two-bit, head-up-their-arse bunch of amateurs,' he ground out. 'Davy was right. I've sold out to the song-and-dance men.'

She gave Star an absent B-plus (fired with enthusiasm after the panto, the child had enrolled at *Stagestruck* this term and was engaged in a one-girl crusade to get the rest of the class to join too). 'It's easy staying physically fit, is it? Keeping your voice in shape? Acting, singing and dancing all at the same time?'

'Christ, Beth, you're an English teacher! You're not supposed to agree with the bastardisation of literature!'

She brandished a graffiti-covered exercise book. 'Lover, it would take your friend Yob an entire academic year to wade through *Pygmalion*, but *My Fair Lady* is his mother's favourite film. You wouldn't believe the difference in his attitude when it dawned on him that he could not only contribute to the class discussion on popular versus classical entertainment but that the other kids would listen to what he had to say.'

'So?'

'So he's swum a stroke towards a society which might otherwise let him drown. So blockbuster musicals gross vastly more than other West End plays and an English teacher who ignores them has just lost sight of the world. So you love what you do and you're terrific at it. Michelle falling pregnant with Davy simply forced you into your vocation earlier than most people. There's no need to feel guilty.' She bent her head to decipher Yob's thoughts which were, as always, strikingly different from the rest of 7.1's. (*Best fing to do in a nife fite is to scarper. Then Romeo woodn't of got nicked. An' he shoodn't of gone to that church. Everyone nose vicars is dodgy.*)

Owen came to stand behind her, resting his hands on her shoulders. She held Yob's book up so he could read it and was rewarded by a reluctant chuckle. Then, 'Should I ring Davy when I'm back for rehearsals?'

Beth's heart contracted at the thought of the coming tour. She cleared her face and looked up with a wry smile. 'He'll read an insult into it if you don't.'

Cate stared at the drawings for *Hot Mikado* unseeingly. Her mind, as it had been for days, was replaying the end-of-panto party. Graham hadn't let her not wear the scarlet dress and she had to admit, it had given her an astonishingly glamorous feeling to wriggle into it after the stress of get-out, and let him brush up her hair, gel it, glitter it and add a sprinkling of body stars. It had also given her quite enormous pleasure to turn down Annis's lecherous advances the moment she'd shimmied up to the bar. That split-second when his alcohol-soaked brain had tumbled to the fact that it was the ASM-from-hell he was propositioning had been satisfying beyond belief. And she'd danced with Seb, who was gently drunk as usual, and the music had changed and they'd stayed on the floor. Big mistake. Big, big mistake. Possibly the biggest mistake of her life so far. She'd never danced with him slowly before. And never in an outrageous dress made of satin and feathers and with a distinct lack of anything which might in its wildest dreams be described as a shoulder strap. And certainly never so close that she could identify which shower gel he used and accurately estimate his chest size.

'That was lovely,' he'd said in her ear as the song drew to a close. His hands had stroked the satin round her hips. 'Un-expected.'

Unexpected? He didn't know the half of it. It had come crashing down on her in one fell, bolt-out-of-the-blue swoop exactly why she'd been ratty ever since he'd been going out with Natalie. Jesus, she was so *stupid*.

The phone rang. Fran answered it with a repressed snarl. Footsteps pounded up the staircase. Cate looked up as the office door burst open and experienced a jolt which sent every nerve in her body diving for cover. 'I need to see the Guvnor,' said Seb, breathing hard.

Fran threw him a sour look. Cate drew its fire without even thinking. 'Join the club. Fran's typed her resignation three times already in between fielding phone calls and rescheduling meetings. We don't know where *anyone* is. Dad got a call at breakfast that sent him into the stratosphere and he seems to have taken Stella and Ned with him.'

'Shit.'

'Anything I can help with?'

'No.' His eyes were warily apprehensive. 'So don't try.'

It was like a slap in the face. 'Dream on!'

He flapped his hand at her curt tone. 'I didn't mean – shit, Cate.'

She stood up. He'd been plastered. Why should she have thought he'd remember? It wasn't as if they'd done anything. There was obviously no need for her to have left Beth's in a blind panic so early on the Sunday morning. 'Cup of tea?'

'Cate, I'm not telling you.'

She clipped him round the ear exactly as she would have done three weeks ago, only having a marginal tussle with herself as to whether or not she was ever going to wash that hand again. 'Found a flat yet?'

'A flat share.' He gave her the address.

'Too close to here. Every time there's a late call you'll wake up with half the cast on your floor.' Whoa – stop it, girl, don't go there.

326

Seb gave her his familiar grin, the one acknowledging her as a friend. 'Don't spoil it. Can you give me a ring when the Guvnor gets back?'

'Hi Beth.'

The pseudo-warm vowels were unmistakable. Beth shifted her grip on the phone. 'Doone. Hi.'

'It's about Saturday.'

'Saturday?' Owen's last evening. On cue, he materialised in the doorway.

'Alan's fiftieth birthday.'

'I know. We've sent a card.'

'I'm throwing him a surprise party. I really want you guys to be there.'

Beth backpedalled fast. 'That's very kind of you, Doone, but I don't think–'

'I'm hiring a suite at the University Arms with a buffet and disco. There'll be friends, my clients, Alan's clients, and people from the old days. I'm sure you can see how it would look if Alan's own family couldn't be there.'

'But Natalie's got mock GCSEs next week. And I've got a paying guest until Sunday.'

'The actor, right?'

Beth's eyes met Owen's, alarmed. 'As it happens.'

'Honey, the male ego is a fragile and wondrous thing.'

'It's *what?*'

'So we are celebrating a pinnacle. Maturity plus vitality. Mind and body in peak condition. I will add Mr Pendragon to the guest list.'

'Doone, it's really not–'

'I know I don't have to remind you that Alan still owns half your house.'

Already icy at the mention of Owen, Beth froze completely. 'No, of course not. I only thought that inviting the birthday boy's ex-wife might look a bit odd.'

Doone's laugh rolled confidently down the line. '7.30 for 8. Be there.'

'If we don't find a parking space soon, we're going to run out of petrol.'

'It's bluffing,' said Robin, peering over her shoulder at the gauge with the assurance of a veteran video-games player. 'Ignore it.'

'We could tell them Cambridge was full and go home instead?'

'Thank you, Natalie. We'll stop off at the all-night estate agents on the way for particulars of really cheap houses, shall we?'

'Look! There's Dad and Doone in a taxi!'

'Oh God!' Beth's gaze whipped frantically from left to right as she U-turned into a gap in the oncoming traffic. 'OK, back to the hotel, Natalie gets out, says she's Alan's daughter and asks if there are any spaces.'

'Bound to be an improvement on me.

Especially if she rolls her skirt up.'

'But I don't want to go to Dad's evil party!'

'None of us want to go!' screamed Beth, slamming her indicator on and causing a gaggle of cyclists to make graphic gestures at the car. 'Nor do we want to find ourselves sleeping in the street!'

Ten minutes later they belted out of the stairwell and into the rear of the function room a fraction of a second before Alan (in black tie) and Doone (in an astonishing confection of tulle and spangles) were conducted through the main door. 'Surprise!' yelled the rest of the room.

A look of shiny pleasure settled on Alan's face. He planted a huge kiss on Doone's lips.

'Yuk,' said Robin. 'Look, Nats, that creep who asked you out at the last car rally has seen us.'

'Shit, that's all I need.'

'So get to the food,' said Owen. 'Trust me, nobody fancies a girl with cheesecake crumbs down her front.'

'Gross!'

Beth grinned as they sidled towards the buffet. She made to slip her arm through Owen's, then, 'Damn,' she said ruefully.

His wicked eyes sent an inappropriate thrill through her. 'Dear me, Mrs T, whatever were you thinking of?'

'Never you mind. I'll make do with quiche instead.'

Owen scooped up champagne cocktails for them.

'I'm driving.'

Natalie looked back. 'By the time you've talked to Dad you'll be sober again. Talking of whom...'

'Nats! Rob! I might have known you'd be by the food!' Alan turned with no diminution of hospitality to Beth. 'You're looking well.'

No thanks to the Sugar Plum Fairy. 'You too. Happy birthday, Alan.'

'Yeah. Happy birthday, Dad.'

'Thanks.' Alan's eyes went briefly to the drink in her hand and then lifted with the hint of a question to Owen.

'You remember Owen Pendragon? One of our regular B&B visitors.'

'Oh yes. An actor.'

'Many happy returns. Ms Hennessy very kindly included me in the invitation when she heard I was staying.'

Alan's smile didn't reach his eyes. 'She thinks of everything. Even a disco for the kids, I understand. You'll have to give me a dance, Natalie.' Natalie, her mouth full of pastry, made a horrified noise he took for assent. 'Oh, and I've got you a job in the sales office for the summer.'

She swallowed hastily. 'No way! I'm

touring with *FOOTLIGHTS.*'

Beth's sustaining gulp of champagne went down completely the wrong way. She choked in the sudden, dead silence.

'*What?*' roared Alan.

'Tremendous opportunity, isn't it?' said Owen conversationally.

'This is your fault!' yelled Alan, turning on Beth. 'Filling their heads with nonsense. Encouraging them. Giving houseroom to losers and dead-beats.'

Owen's hands stilled. Out of the corner of her eye, Beth saw Doone moving towards them in a ripple of spangly tulle-sheathed steel. 'It's only for the summer. Between GCSEs and the start of her A-levels. Don't make such a fuss, Alan.'

'I'll forbid it. I won't give my consent.'

'I'm sixteen, Dad. You can't stop me.'

'Can't I? We'll see about that! I'll–'

'Natalie, honey, you look divine. I just knew that silver top would suit you! No shortage of partners for *you* once the disco starts!'

'That job I lined up – it seems she's going to be too busy prancing about on stage to take advantage of it.'

'I'm singing Lucy in a professional production of *The Lion, The Witch and The Wardrobe!*'

Doone looked amused. 'My word, the things you do when you're young! I remember I once spent a whole summer demonstrating twenty-three ways to wear a silk scarf. In Liberty's that was, for a friend of mine who was just starting up in business for herself.' She sighed and turned to Alan. 'Felice Grant – we had dinner with them – she's worth a mint now.'

'But – the office!'

Doone tucked her arm in his. 'Poor baby,' she said archly. 'He was really looking forward to those increased sales. Never mind, there'll be other summers. You have a lovely time, Nats, I'm sure the theatre people will be really glad of that pretty voice of yours. Alan, honey, have you said hello to the Glovers? They put that big order in, remember? We'll catch up with you guys later.' They moved off in an inexorable billow of 'let her get it out of her system, darling'.

'There's masses of food,' observed Robin. 'I think we ought to eat it before they come back and make us feel ill again.'

'Good idea,' said Owen, filling a taco.

'I hate him,' said Natalie in a low, passionate voice. 'How dare he say such foul things about Seb?'

'And I assumed he was referring to me.'

'Of course he was,' Beth snapped. 'He doesn't know about Seb unless Nats has told him, which seems unlikely as she can't generally bring herself to utter two words in his company. Really, sweetheart, why you

should choose *now* to break with tradition...'
She finished her drink. 'Damn, I need another one. You're right, I'd forgotten the effect Dad has on my sobriety.'

Owen winked. 'There's a tray still on the bar.'

Her eyes followed him, lingering on his fluid, toughness-held-in-check motion. She could *murder* Doone for having arranged this tonight.

'Make the most of it,' he said when he got back. 'There's a paying bar as soon as the champagne runs out. Three pounds fifty for a glass of wine.'

It was the last straw. Beth looked at him, outraged. 'Good God, I could buy a *bottle* for less than that!' She stormed across the room to grab another two glasses.

Jumping lights and a blare of sound announced the start of the disco. 'Mum! What are you doing?' screamed Natalie. 'It's going to take you ages to get back under the limit! I want to go home *now!*'

'Well, we can't! You and Rob have got to add sparkle to their disco and I've got to circulate and not bear grudges. I *hate* needing Dad's money this much.'

'I'm not dancing with that Gordon nerd.'

Owen flexed his muscles. 'No need, sparrow. You can dance with me. Not that anyone will be watching us once Rob gets his feet into gear.'

Natalie shuddered. 'Thank God for that.'

Beth met his eyes, startled. He gave the ghost of a shrug. 'You'll do better without me, mistress. Besides, much as I want to, I don't dare dance with *you* if you want to avoid a custody order slapped on you over Rob.'

She looked at him despairingly. 'This isn't how I wanted to spend our last evening.'

'Money talks.'

She gave a short laugh. 'Alan's doesn't, it swears.'

Owen grinned. 'Cheat. You pinched that from Dylan.'

Natalie's eyes widened. 'Dylan Thomas said that? Wicked. Which poem?'

Warmth coursed through Beth, interlaced with champagne cocktail bubbles and aching longing. '*Bob* Dylan.' *Oh God, Owen, I'm going to miss you.*

His eyes were spiced with wicked understanding. 'Cheer up, beloved. I shouldn't wonder if I don't need a shower after cavorting in a disco all night. And as for this being our last evening – it wasn't *that* bad last time, driving down to London at six o'clock Monday morning.'

CHAPTER 16

Beth was just back from collecting Rob from tap when Owen rang. 'Hi, lover,' she said. It had felt so *weird* going into the bedroom earlier and not seeing any of his stuff there. Weird and joltingly empty. 'How are you?'

'I'm not. It's bad news. I won't be able to come up during rehearsals.'

Beth's world trembled. 'Damn. After I got in extra shower gel too.'

'There's something in the wind. The rehearsal sheet has to be seen to be believed, ostensibly because it's the lottery tour and we might be inspected, but Cate thinks there's more to it and she's acting like a nuclear bomb waiting to go off because they won't tell her what it is.'

'How's everyone else?'

'Griping about the schedule. Jockeying for sleeping partners.'

Beth gripped the phone more tightly. He sounded so casual about it. 'Who have you got your eye on, then?'

'Even if I wanted to, mistress, I wouldn't have the time or energy. We don't even get Sundays off.'

There was a small pause. Beth cast around

for something to lighten the conversation. 'Talking of Sundays, Yob interpreted the assembly on Looking After the Environment as an invitation to spray-paint the school dustbins this weekend. He was most aggrieved to get detention because of it.'

Owen gave a faraway chuckle. 'They'll award that lad the Turner prize yet. Seb sends his love. His schedule is even worse than mine because he's got understudy rehearsals on top of everything else.'

'So, he won't be coming up to see Natalie?'

'Not unless he's discovered a way to clone himself.'

Beth was conscious of a guilty wobble of relief. 'It's an ill wind. Although it is horrible seeing her unhappy.'

'*He's* not exactly on top of the world, but a lot of that is Annis mouthing off. It's shaping up to be a god-awful tour. I miss you, Beth.'

He'd said it first. Thank God, oh thank God. 'I miss you too. I found myself saving you a bowl of stew tonight. I never did that when Alan left.'

'I'd better go, I need to crash after this morning's early start.'

She'd had an early start too. Plus a full day's work, tomorrow's lessons to be prepared and a pile of poems lurking in her box waiting to be read. And he hadn't asked how *she* was at all. 'OK, lover,' she said. 'Speak to you tomorrow.'

Upstairs, Natalie's CD player belted out *The Calling*. In the lounge, Rob had turned on the television. Beth put the kettle on, feeling quite horribly alone.

'They're not happy,' said Cate.

Ned looked up from the notes spread over his desk. 'They'd be even less happy if we laid half of them off because we couldn't afford to pay them.'

'I'm not happy either.'

'Cate, just because you are the smartest ASM we've ever had, it doesn't mean you can get lippy with me.'

'I wouldn't need to get lippy if I knew what was going on.'

Ned threw down his pen. 'OK, you've asked for it. You're not being put fully in the picture because you don't yet have the emotional restraint to handle it.'

'*What?*' Incredulous fury coursed through her.

Ned returned stare for unblinking stare. 'I'm thinking specifically of the way you blacked Luke's eye. You and he obviously have some sort of history and before you hit me as well, it's not my business and I don't want to know the details. What *is* my business is that a supposedly responsible member of this company lashed out without giving any thought to the consequences. What if you'd broken his nose? What if you'd put him in hospital? Where would we have been for the rest of the run?'

Cate gaped. 'I–'

'In brutally honest terms, Cate, you need to grow up. And until you do, you, like everyone else, will operate on a strictly need-to-know basis.'

Tuesday. Beth heard the phone while she was still fitting the key in the door. Owen, she thought, and wrestled frantically with the lock. She dropped her bag and the box of books on the step, stumbled over them and sent the base unit of the phone crashing to the floor as she tried to get to the receiver before Owen gave up and rang off.

'Good, you *are* in. I want to talk to you!'

Alan! Beth could have wept with disappointment. She slumped against the wall, cursing silently.

'Beth? Are you listening to me?'

'Sorry, we've only just got back. I haven't even had a cup of tea yet.' She mouthed a thank you to Robin who was bringing her stuff in from outside.

Rob grinned. 'How are the rehearsals going?'

She shook her head and mouthed 'Dad'.

Rob put his hands to his throat, making choking noises as he staggered into the kitchen to put the kettle on.

Beth chuckled, even though Alan was saying, 'You drink too much tea,' in a disapproving tone.

'It's the only vice I can still afford. What did you want to talk to me about?' As if she couldn't guess.

'This ridiculous job of Natalie's. I'm putting my foot down.'

Beth took a grip on her temper. 'She's sixteen; all she's signed is a limited, eleven week contract. And before you ask, I *did* check through to make sure it was reasonable.' She'd been going to add 'and that she wasn't signing her soul away to the devil' but reflected that Alan's sense of humour probably wasn't up to it.

He was breathing heavily. 'So, in addition to having unsuitable people in the house you're happy to let your daughter wreck her life, are you?'

'They aren't unsuitable, Alan, and it won't wreck Natalie's life. It will teach her exactly how hard that sort of job can be *before* she makes any irrevocable career decisions.'

'*Career decisions? What do you mean, career decisions?*' Even Robin, coming into the hall with a mug of tea heard the bellow of rage emanating from the phone. 'That does it. You're not fit to be her mother! Let me speak to her at once!'

'She's at a singing lesson. And when she

gets back she is going to be deep in revision for her Maths mock-GCSE tomorrow. If you want to talk to her, you'll have to leave it until the middle of next week.'

'What's she doing at a singing lesson? I told you I wasn't paying for them any more.'

'You're not paying, Alan. I am. That's why I'm providing bed, breakfast and evening meals to anyone who can afford my rates, as well as holding down an extremely demanding full-time job *plus* taking time out to argue with you over things you can't change anyway. Anything else? No? Good.' She slammed the phone back into the holder which Robin had rescued. 'God, he makes me so mad,' she said. She looked wryly at Rob. 'Sorry, I shouldn't sound off about him to you.'

Rob made a face. 'He's going to go mental when he hears I've applied for a dance scholarship.'

Beth took a grateful gulp of tea. 'Rob, love, we don't *have* to tell him.'

She gave Owen a condensed version of the call later. 'Pillock,' he said. 'Ignore him. We've started blocking already. Ned claims it's so the understudies have time to learn our moves as well as their own. I think it's so we're all too knackered to put up a fight when he calls a snap rehearsal. At this rate we'll be dead on our feet by the opening night.'

No they wouldn't, thought Beth as she replaced the receiver. They might do the dress rehearsal in their sleep, but come the first night they'd all be a hundred per cent on-top-of-the-world professional. Because that's what they were. Professional. Which was why Owen was becoming more and more wrapped up in the show and only vaguely aware that the rest of the world existed. Like her. And how she was. And whether she was missing him.

On Wednesday she got home from a parents' evening to the intelligence that Owen had rung to say he had a late rehearsal, Ned was a slave driver and this was the worst way in the world to make a living. 'Oh, and he said he was sorry he missed you,' added Rob.

Beth left a message with his answering service to say that she was sorry she missed him too and he could ring her later if he wanted.

He didn't. She felt cold and lonely by the time she went to bed. His Aztec For Men jumped treacherously out of the bathroom cabinet when she opened the door. She sniffed it, remembering all the times it had swirled headily in her nostrils, and sprinkled some on the pillow to try and recapture his taut grace and wicked smile. The fragrance only intensified her sense of loss.

On Thursday, Owen didn't ring at all.

Neither the message she left on his home machine nor the one on his mobile elicited any reply. Beth sat by the mute receiver all evening remembering how he'd kissed her cheek before he'd left. 'Back to the treadmill,' he'd said cheerfully. And she'd known it was his life and had said 'Happy blisters,' with a smile just to prove how unstressed and undemanding she was. And she was. Really. She simply hadn't expected him to temporarily forget her existence quite so soon.

Owen's Thursday had started innocuously enough, as far as any day could which didn't include waking up next to Beth. The afternoon was when a fight broke out between Seb and Annis.

'It's *true*, Ned!' yelled Cate. 'While you and Red were concentrating on that half of the room, Mr Annis made a hand sign to Mr Matthews and Mr Perry here, and they all three skipped a step to make it look as though Seb was lagging behind. I was almost sure the last time it happened. This time I'm convinced.'

Annis shrugged. 'I was just doing the routine.'

'Bastard!' spat Seb.

'It doesn't matter to me which of you is mis-timing,' thundered Ned. 'We will *all* reconvene for an extra hour tonight to get it right!'

'That won't bloody stop him,' said Cate, exploding past Owen to spin the temperature control knobs on the tea and coffee urns. 'Suppose they pull the same bloody stunt on stage? It won't be just Seb he discredits, the whole company will look crap!'

Owen glanced at the smug expression on Annis's face. Sod it, he thought.

'I'm impressed, sweeting, I've never seen him this wrecked.'

Unable to dissuade Seb from alcohol, his friends had perforce accompanied him to the Jolly Bargee. They were now on guard in the Snug, two stout widths of mahogany separating them from the Public where Annis and his cronies were carousing.

'I've seen him this wrecked,' said Cate. 'But I've never known him refuse food before.'

From the Public came boisterous calls for more beer. Owen was aware of a sharp impatience. Christ, he must be getting old. 'Time to go,' he said. 'We'll get a cab.'

Cate pulled on her coat. 'No point. Seb's place isn't far. If you and I take an arm each we should make it before he throws up. Night, everyone.'

Which was why Owen roused next morning to find every vertebrae in acute pain and the hammers of hell thumping at the inside of his head. Cate's spiky, upside-down face stabbed at his eyeballs. 'Tea in the kitchen. Rehearsal call at ten. I'm going in. I've had an idea.'

'Jesus! You can think? After last night?'

'That's me. Fully operative in the face of extensive alcohol consumption. One of my more valuable qualities if only my bloody family realised it. See you later.'

Owen closed his eyes, stifling a groan. Was he really lying on a blow-up mattress on Seb's floor? Memories of dissuading Seb from slashing Annis's tyres, listening to him far into the night over phenomenal amounts of his flatmate's Courvoisier and Cate bagging the sofa came to him. He rolled cautiously to his feet, viewed Seb's supine body with loathing, and moved with infinite care to the kitchen where he found a pot of tea and a box of paracetamol. Somebody, he vowed, was going to suffer.

During rehearsal, every over-loud note seemed hell-bent on lingering in his skull as long as possible. He could feel them ricocheting around inside his head.

'What's the matter with you all?' yelled Adrian. 'No one's even staying on the note, let alone in time! Take five and have some tea.'

'Which bloody note?' mumbled Seb. 'I've got dozens, all fighting each other. What *happened* yesterday?'

'Whatever it was, it's put me off brandy for life.'

'Psst! You two.' Cate pulled them into the kitchen and handed them bacon sandwiches from the microwave.

'Cate! Oh God, I love you,' said Seb indistinctly, his mouth already full.

Owen took a bite and felt his hangover immediately sound a retreat. After the first moment of purely physical bliss, reality surfaced. 'What do you want?'

Defiance flickered in Cate's face. 'For you to sing better than Annis for a start. Also your help in setting up the video camera later.'

Seb licked his fingers. 'You can do that with one hand tied behind your back.'

The microwave beeped. Cate produced a second sandwich each. 'I talked to Stella. Unlike my uncle, she *hasn't* forgotten certain incidents last tour, but she needs hard evidence. I can set the camera on auto to record, but it has to be focused where Annis is likely to cause trouble and for that I need bodies.'

'OK,' said Seb. 'Except I've got an understudy rehearsal tonight.'

Owen saw his precious free evening slipping away. He tried ringing Beth, only to discover that he must have left his phone on yesterday and it had run down. With an extremely bad grace he spent the evening loitering on various marks in Studios One and Two. By the time he got back to his flat, plugged the mobile into the charger and listened to all his messages, he was in no mood to be conciliatory. 'Hi,' he said shortly when Beth answered.

She gave a quick, sighing breath. 'Hi, how are you?'

'Bloody awful. You don't want to know about the last two days.'

A split-second pause. 'Of course I do.'

His sense of ill-usage ebbed. Her voice, soft and soothing, plugged all the right gaps as he recapitulated the previous forty-eight hours. 'I don't even know why I'm doing all this!' he complained.

'Because you care about Seb and don't want Annis to mess him up. Because you care about Cate and want her to prove herself to her family.'

'It was a bloody sight more comfortable before I discovered morals.'

'Ah, but were you a fully rounded person?'

'Shallowness I can cope with. Living up to ideals is sodding tiring on top of a stressful week. Thanks for listening, Beth. Christ, I'm knackered. Goodnight.'

The line must be playing up. He thought she paused again. 'Goodnight, minstrel. Sleep well.'

Worse was to follow. Next morning he looked up to see Cate, an evil smirk on her face, ushering Davy into the studio. 'What are you doing here?' he said, irritation, astonishment and uneasy alarm churning inside him.

The thin face shuttered defensively. 'You told me to! You said come along one Saturday!'

A faint memory of having indeed advised his son to find out how much bloody work went into a musical before criticising what he did for a living forced Owen to adopt a smile. 'Is it Saturday already? They're working us so hard I forgot.'

'What's next?' said Owen after lunch. He ached in every muscle. With Davy watching, he'd put as much effort into the rehearsal as he would a performance.

Seb ran a finger down the schedule. 'Act One dialogue and moves while Adrian beats seven bells out of the orchestra next door.'

'Followed by a repeat performance for the understudies,' said Luke. 'Joy.'

'I forgot to ask – is this focused enough for you?' said Owen to Seb.

Seb grinned. 'Close.'

Davy drank it all in with great hungry eyes.

Thank God, thought Owen when they finally broke. A quick Chinese, home and *sleep*. He spared barely a thought for whether Seb and Annis would kill each other at the under-study rehearsal. It seemed unlikely. Ned would almost certainly be working them too hard.

'That was good,' said Davy, coming out of his corner.

Jesus wept! Owen tried not to let the fact he'd forgotten his own son show in his face.

'You were right,' Davy continued as if he was conferring a favour. 'I shouldn't have knocked what you do. But there was lots I didn't understand. And I'd like to watch the understudies to see how different they are.'

'Another time,' said Owen. 'It's getting late and I'm shattered.'

Davy's face fell into resentful lines. 'It's only an hour-and-a-half home on the tube and I had to really nag to come this time. You'll be on tour by the time Mum and Dad let me do it again. If Natalie or Robin had wanted to stay you'd have let them.'

'And the worst of it is he was right,' admitted Owen into his mobile to Beth.

'Mmm, kids are born knowing how to make adults feel guilty.'

'Tell me about it. I'd best go. He's promised his mother I'll see him on to a Colindale train no later than nine o'clock. Christ, Beth, I don't need this. I'm not a responsibility person.'

It would be OK, thought Beth. She could cope. She had the memory of those six lovely loving weeks to sustain her, even if all she seemed to be now was an outlet for Owen's grouches. The relationship had moved on, that was all. He no longer felt the need to woo her. Which was nice. If only she could lose the gut-wrenching fear that he'd got her out of his system.

On Monday Cate rang for another rant about how Ned was behaving. 'I can see his point,' she said fairly, 'because I was so mad at Luke that I really *didn't* think. But, honestly, if I thump anyone this tour, it's going to be Annis, and he won't be a loss at all. He's being *horrible* to Seb. I can't believe Ned is turning a blind eye.'

'Maybe he thinks everyone will be too tired to make trouble.'

'Owen's told you about the killer schedule, then?'

'Just once or twice – every call.'

'Everybody's livid about it. But – it's weird, the aggro actually seems to be making Seb *more* determined to do the best he can. It's as if he's finally thought, stuff this, I'm not going to knuckle down this time.'

'Good for him. Dare I ask how Luke is?'

There was a pause. 'The same. But I'm not being taken in any more. I knew it was over at Christmas.'

'I'm sorry.'

'So am I. Sorry I made such a prat of myself.'

'At least you didn't *marry* him just for the sex.'

Nice as it was to talk to Cate, the call left Beth more unsettled than ever. They really were all immersed in *FOOTLIGHTS*. It was a different world, one she didn't belong to. What hope could there realistically be that Owen would settle for a lifelong partnership with someone outside it? He hadn't even summoned up any interest in the fact that one of the kids at school had gouged a wide scrape along the side of her car.

'Charge it to the insurance,' he'd said.

'I can't,' she'd replied. 'Bloody Alan put the excess up on the sly. By the time I can afford a respray, the damn door will have rusted through.'

'Bastard,' he'd said, and had gone on to tell her how Ellery and Monty's dispute for centre stage was spreading through the company.

The next day, something happened to disturb her even further. She was shooing a class into the library when she saw Natalie at the far end. Richard Manning was next to her, sitting very close and evidently explaining something. His arm brushed hers. Natalie didn't move away. Beth saw her face tip towards his.

She hastily moved behind the shelves. She would hate Nats to think she was spying. But she was uneasy all the same. Not about

Richard, he was a nice lad and she hadn't expected Nats to do a Marianne Dashwood for ever; she'd known being apart for weeks on end at her age after such a short romance with Seb would sever the ties. It just was the *speed* with which it had happened. Everyone was breaking up: Cate and Luke, Nats and Seb... Suppose it was contagious?

'There's a party on Friday to celebrate the end of the Mocks,' said Natalie that evening. 'If you or Sue can take us, Richard says his dad will bring us all back.'

'Fine.' Beth cleared her throat. 'You'll have to warn Seb not to ring that night.'

Natalie flushed. 'It's only a party. He went to the end of panto one without me. And anyway, all he talks about these days is the show and how busy he is.'

'Tell me about it,' muttered Beth. She didn't take Owen's locket off that night. She awoke with her hand clenched around it, almost as if her subconscious had decided it was symbolic and that Fate might find him someone else if the chain was off her neck. And once the horrible thought had entered her head, she couldn't shift it. Invigilating her last exam was a nightmare. Three solid hours with nothing to do except invent humiliating ways for Owen to leave her. She thought later no English papers could ever have been marked quite so thoroughly before: only by drowning herself in them could she ram her terrors far enough into the background not to turn her into a quivering mass of insecurity.

With breakfast came a phone call from Alan. He'd wanted to be sure of catching her in, he said, and what were the exact dates of Natalie's summer tour? Because it didn't seem reasonable that he should pay upkeep when she wouldn't be at home. Oh, and he'd be over tomorrow night and wasn't currently eating anything with gluten. Just a short-term thing, but Doone and he were really feeling the benefit of it.

That afternoon Beth had to exercise extreme self-control when Felicity told her she was looking tired – probably that was the reason she was snapping at them for not doing their homework.

'Yeah, an' I couldn't, could I?' said Yob. ''Cos I was in detention.'

Star pointed out the only time Yob *did* do homework was in Det.

'Yeah, but it was me English book I was fighting wiv. It still 'ad Martin Shaw's blood on.'

'Miss, Miss, they were fighting about Felicity, Miss!'

Beth blinked in disbelief. *'Felicity?'*

A chorus of assent rose from the class.

'I didn't ask them to,' said Felicity with an offended toss of her beribboned bunches.

'Martin Shaw said she was a pain, see, 'cos

she told 'im not to chuck 'is crisp packet down in the corridor.'

'But she's *our* pain, i'n't she?'

'And we're a team, aren't we, Mrs T? That's what you said.'

'Yeah. So I 'it 'im. An' 'e never gave me no crisps.'

'It was well good!'

Beth belatedly grasped the conversational reins, told her class it was *not* well good and suggested they think of better ways of resolving conflict by the next PSE lesson. She also reminded them that it was their parents' consultation tonight. Which meant another evening when she wouldn't be able to have a decent talk with Owen.

'Thank you, Mrs Goodchild.' Beth stood up and held out her hand. 'I'm glad you're happy with the way Felicity–' She broke off as an unshaven skinhead barged past the queue of parents, towing a gelled, multiply-pierced, fearsomely eye-shadowed girlfriend behind him.

'You Mrs T?' he demanded, towering over her.

'Um, yes.' Out of the corner of her eye she saw Ian Baxter at the next table shift to face the opposite way. Coward.

'Well, really!' said Ursula Goodchild, whisking away, a little pink in the cheeks.

'Our Yob says Martin Shaw nicked a chisel

and ran it along yer car.'

'We don't actually *know* that it was Mar–'

'Know the Crowther Street garage?'

Beth averted her eyes from his girlfriend's quite remarkable metalware. 'Ye-es.'

'Take yer car there Saturday afternoon and my mate Dave'll fix it for a tenner. Only it has to be Saturday, see, 'cos his boss skives off at two, so he won't know.'

'That's, um, incredibly kind of you, but I wouldn't want–'

'Our Yob says yer all right. Says yer can get him a GCSE.'

Beth's eyes widened in alarm. She didn't remember ever having been quite that definite. 'Only if he keeps coming to lessons.'

'Be the first one in the family, that will.'

'Do you like his hair?' said the girlfriend suddenly. 'I do it for him. I won a prize with him last year.'

'It brightens my day,' said Beth truthfully.

'See yer, then.' As an afterthought Yob's brother tossed a couple of two-pound coins on the table. 'For that book.'

Beth watched them go, stunned.

'My goodness,' said Star's mother, settling herself comfortably at the desk. 'Talk about Mohammed and mountains. That's the first time Yob's family have turned up to anything. Should raise your stock in the staff-room no end. I'd ask for a pay increment if I were you.'

Beth didn't think she'd go quite that far,

but the comment had given her an idea. The next day she suggested to Owen that if he didn't have time to drive to Cambridge to see her, maybe she could come to see him in London on Saturday since she didn't have any B&Bs booked. 'It's only an hour on the train. I could visit the Globe if you're rehearsing in the afternoon. I've wanted to do that for ages. Then stay overnight and come back here Sunday.'

There was a pause. She sensed the reservation in his voice even before he spoke. 'I don't think it would work. I've got late calls tonight and Saturday. I'll be shattered.'

Beth felt her heart hunch in on itself. 'No problem. It was only a thought.'

'I'll see you Sunday week, OK? On my way to Leicester.'

'Yes. Sure. See you then.' She put down the phone, trying very hard not to feel rejected.

Owen was in a savage mood as they came out of the studio on Sunday evening. Why had he been so bloody *stupid* as to put Beth off this weekend? Yes, he was tied up with rehearsals. Yes, he was so exhausted that all he wanted to do at night was sink a large whisky and roll into bed, but if this lousy fortnight had shown him anything, it was that he desperately needed the safety valve of Beth's presence in his life.

If he *hadn't* dissuaded her, if he *hadn't* had the insane thought that she'd be embarrassed by his flat's thick carpets, deep chairs and air of hedonistic comfort, if he *hadn't* imagined she'd be revolted by its tidiness and lack of character, he could have woken up with her this morning. If he hadn't decided, in a moment of moronic aberration, that he wanted to keep her whole and untainted and separate from his working life, he could have spent last night reacquainting himself with the lovely curves of her body. He could have felt her hair drifting against his skin, he could have traced her smile in the dark with his fingertips. Stupid, he thought. Stupid, stupid, stupid. The first thing he was going to do when he got home was ring her up and apologise.

Beside him, Luke ran lightly down the steps and draped his arms around Cate and the youngest dancer. 'Golden Dragon? Or Tandoori Nights?'

Cate slid out from under and moved between himself and Seb. 'Either, so long as bloody Annis is somewhere else.' She dropped her voice. 'He tried that skip-step trick again this afternoon. Did you spot it, Seb?'

'Mmm. Just as you scalded yourself on the tea urn.'

'Worked though. It concentrated Ned's attention on your half of the room.'

'I suppose it's no use telling you *not* to keep looking out for me?'

'None at all. This is my production too, don't forget.'

'How could we?' said Owen. 'Your glowering expression is going to be one of the abiding memories of this run.' That and the aggravation and the bone-tiredness and the ache of not going home to Beth every night. *It's your own fault*, pointed out his demon. *Lots of people commute between London and Cambridge perfectly successfully.*

The rest drew ahead, still debating Chinese versus Indian. 'Maybe I'll just go home,' said Seb, kicking a loose stone out of the way.

'And pass out because you haven't eaten?'

'Jesus, Cate, you're turning into my mother.'

'Your mother would *give* you the last spare rib, not fight you for it.'

'OK, it's easier than arguing. Coming, Owen?'

'No, I'm so knackered I'll fall asleep with my face in the rice.'

'See you tomorrow, then.' Seb and Cate hurried after the others.

Owen stood for a moment breathing in the faintly acrid Docklands air and savouring the silence as the noisy group disappeared down the road. One more week and he would see Beth again. One more week and he could—

'Hello, Owen,' said a throbbing voice.

He turned. A woman stood a little way along the street. She wore a long coat with a scarf wrapped around her throat and thrown carelessly back over her shoulders. He knew he ought to recognise her.

'I had to see you,' she said in a dramatic accent.

Recognition came, appallingly. 'Christ Almighty! Michelle!'

'I swear, Beth, if I'd been able to move, I'd have been back inside before you could say Rottweiler.'

Beth chuckled down the phone line, rather unfeelingly he thought. 'For shame, minstrel! When she'd travelled the length of London to find you?'

'Too bloody right! Christ, you'd think after sixteen years and however many kids she's got she'd have outgrown histrionics. She accused me of seducing her first-born away from the True Theatre. Said it obviously wasn't enough that I'd corrupted my own immortal soul for the sake of Mammon. I was clearly jealous of Davy's Natural Aptitude and was trying to ruin his chances in the business to ease my own resentment.'

'Do we gather from this that Davy has changed his views on musicals?'

'Much I care!'

'Come off it, you hated it when he criticised you!'

'Because he didn't know what he was talking about!'

'Not because he was your son?'

'At this moment I would be ecstatic never to see him again. Or his mother. Or his step-father who is no doubt just waiting for my next free evening in order to discuss the way I've been encouraging Davy to waste his time.'

'Give him Alan's number. They'd have a lot in common. Owen, however much Michelle has irritated you tonight, I honestly don't think you can blame Davy for wanting to get to know you. You're his father.'

'He should hate me! I abandoned him! All I've ever done is send him guilt-money!'

'And maybe bequeathed him some of your talent. And forced him to address his prejudices...'

'So?'

'So it's flattering that he's taken enough of what you said on board to consider broad-ening his outlook.'

'No it isn't. He's rebelling. I'm a handy scapegoat.'

'Owen, that's unreasonable. Adolescence is foul.'

'I remember. Nobody bloody helped me!'

'I really think you're being too hard on him.'

'Jesus wept! I'm going to bed!'

Tears trickled down Beth's cheeks as she put the phone down. Men were all the same. As soon as they'd got what they wanted, it was self, self, self. Not once in the last fortnight had Owen asked how *she* was. She was someone to sound off to. Out of sight, out of mind. He hadn't apologised for not ringing, hadn't asked whether Alan was following up his threat of non-payment of maintenance, hadn't asked how Natalie's Mocks had gone, hadn't even remembered Rob was applying for a scholarship at his dance school this week. Ian Baxter had. He'd been angling for a dinner invite for some time. Well, if bloody Owen didn't make up for things this coming weekend, she might just extend one!

It was pure chance that Cate was in the video gallery when Annis, Matthews and Perry lounged into Studio One on Friday morning. She was resetting the focus and putting in a new tape to record the run-through when voices made her peer through the narrow window.

'First ones here. Shall we dance?'

Her hand snapped across to the record button without conscious thought as they swung into the Mikado routine.

'And *now...*' Annis's voice said as they

skip-stepped at the exact same point they had at rehearsal. Got them! Bloody got them!

Ned stared at his niece as if she'd taken leave of her senses. 'We open at Leicester in four days' time and you want me to sack two understudies and a third Ensemble player?'

'Just Annis would do. You saw the tape! Also he's belligerent, he's a stirrer and he gets ugly-drunk all too often. What more do you want?'

'I want it to be the next tour! I'm sorry, Cate, but there are reasons.'

'Reasons?' Anger ran through her in a magnesium flare. 'He's been bullying and baiting another company member for months and you say there are *reasons* why you can't sack him? I'd like to bloody hear them!'

'Listen, he's not going to let anything affect his stage performance, is he? He's got too much at stake himself. I promise if events proceed beyond petty, he's out.'

'How much beyond *petty*? Visible bruising? A nervous breakdown?'

'Have some discipline, please.'

'God Almighty, Ned! This is *my* bloody company too! In case you'd forgotten, backstage is *my* responsibility! I refuse to turn the other bloody cheek when someone's chucking gauntlets at me left, right and centre!'

'You're too close to these incidents to see them dispassionately.'

'Dispassionate?' Cate could hardly contain her rage. 'Dispassionate about my job? Dispassionate about deliberate sabotage? Dear God, I'd rather die!' She stormed out of the office and slammed the door, her brain already running through counter-measures. Stage surveillance at all tour stops, spare props...

Owen had lost count of the number of late rehearsals they'd had this week. He ached in body and soul, he couldn't remember when he'd last spoken to Beth and the morale in the company had reached rock bottom. Cate's revelation, delivered in a furious undertone, had been the last straw. He stormed up to the office.

'Owen, you've been in the business long enough to know that you get shows now and again where nothing seems to go well,' said Stella.

'But never one where the management hasn't made at least a token effort to put things right. You tell the Guvnor from me that he needs to look very hard at his priorities. This is the worst profession in the world for keeping secrets. What Ned should be thinking about is who is going to get the blame when the balloon goes up.'

By Saturday night the whole company was edgy and full of tension. 'That's it,' were Ned's parting words at ten pm. 'Enjoy your day off. Full cast call in Leicester at midday on Monday.'

It was raining and the traffic was awful. Stop-start all the way. It was midnight before Owen got back to his flat. Fulham had seldom looked more depressing. He was past caring. Tomorrow he would wrap himself in Beth and relax. He found his key and inserted it in the lock. Across the road, a car door slammed.

'I've been waiting for you,' said Davy's adoptive father.

Despite the lack of phone calls this past week, despite the brevity and unsatisfactory nature of the conversations they had had, it had never occurred to Beth that Owen might not actually arrive. She vacuumed the visible bits of carpet on Saturday, had a shower, let the last visitors in at midnight and stayed up ironing to the late film.

By the time Sunday afternoon had come and gone, the duster was in shock, there were no books left to mark and an incredulous alarm had set in. She'd checked that the phone was still connected. She'd phoned the AA for accident news. She'd re-run all the messages for the last week. Pride wouldn't let her dial his mobile. That night she lay in bed in appalled, dry-eyed, icy-gutted terror.

Owen hadn't come. It was over.

CHAPTER 17

Monday morning. Beth got stiffly out of bed and made her way downstairs. She wrapped her hands around her mug and stared out at the dispirited garden. It was a damn good thing it was half-term. She couldn't possibly have taught feeling like this. It was so much worse than when Alan had left. She felt open, raw, bleeding. *No fool like an old fool*, ran a trace of thought in her head.

Why hadn't Owen come? Why had he not even rung? For the same reason she didn't dare phone him, perhaps. Because he was with someone else.

Round and round, back and forth went the arguments in her mind. He *couldn't* have someone else because he hadn't the time and he wasn't like that. Except a quickie didn't necessarily take either time or commitment and he was an actor, for God's sake. Everyone knew they came with a completely other set of morals, just look at Luke.

But suppose there had been an accident? Beth's heart faltered. Suppose his car was even now in a rain-filled ditch with him inside unconscious, trapped by the seat belt, unable to get out? Suppose there had been a smash and he was in hospital? They wouldn't know to ring her. She'd just be an entry on his phone menu.

Outside, the sky grew lighter. Beth could stand it no longer. One way or another she had to know. She dialled his mobile. 'Owen, it's Beth,' she said to the message. She heard the wobble in her voice. 'Ring me?'

The good luck card on the dresser mocked her. It was all sealed up, ready to give him. With shaking fingers she wrote 'c/o Haymarket Theatre, Leicester' after his name and stuck a first class stamp with infinite precision to the corner of the envelope.

The first Dress was a disaster. The heating had broken down so the Haymarket was freezing. A wiring box blew up, delaying the sound checks. The orchestra pit was damp, a box of light filters had gone missing and when, on top of all that, Annis unguardedly skipped a couple of steps right in front of Ned's eyes, Cate thought her uncle would break the sound barrier. 'This company is a *team!*' he roared. 'Teams do not let grudges get in the way of professionalism! Mr Annis, I am warning you, one more stunt like that and you'll be out of *FOOTLIGHTS* with the imprint of my boot on your Levis!'

All of which gave Cate a grim satisfaction. Although it was unfortunate that a reporter from *The Stage* had chosen that particular moment to arrive.

The flash of the message light was the first thing Beth saw when she got back from shopping. She dropped the carrier bags and hesitated a long moment before pressing the button.

Owen's recorded voice sounded distracted. 'Sorry about yesterday. I won't be able to phone tonight, either. Rehearsals until Christ alone knows when.'

A thousand thoughts careered through her brain. *He was all right. He rang. He was all right. He didn't sound guilty. He was all right.* Slowly, she tapped out his number. 'Thanks for phoning,' she said to his answer service. Tears stood in her eyes. 'Break a leg, minstrel.' *I love you.*

At his lodgings, Owen listened to Beth's message and a prickle of fire warmed him for an all too brief moment. She was his detachment, a slender thread of sanity in this close-confined world. Come hell or high water he had to get to Cambridge after Saturday night's show. He carried the plate of neat, clingfilmed sandwiches and thermos of tea that his landlady had left up to his warmed room. It wasn't enough any more. He longed for Beth's cluttered kitchen, for the sight of her smooth hair swinging back over her shoulder as she turned from burning the toast to laugh with him. He reached for his phone, then caught sight of the time. Too late tonight. He'd ring after school tomorrow.

Thursday.

'Bye,' called Beth as the visitors got into their car. 'Come again.' She closed the front door on the latest cloudburst and massaged the fixed-smile ache from her cheeks. 'I wish the weather would clear. I feel so guilty pushing people out into the rain.'

'Decent tip,' commented Robin, pocketing a two-pound coin.

'Snap,' said Natalie, clearing a trayload of breakfast crockery from the dining room. 'They'd probably have left it even if it wasn't half-term.'

'I wonder if Dad has any idea how mercenary he's made you both?'

'You mean he thinks about us unprompted? He'd reckon he'd done us a favour by toughening us up for life. Is it OK if I go over to Lisa's once we're done? Sue's going into town and she said she'd give us a lift.'

'Of course. The next visitors don't arrive until tomorrow evening. I hope you won't get too wet. Any tea left in that pot, Rob? Where did you put *The Stage?*'

'Mum?' said Natalie slowly.

Beth sipped her tea and riffled through to the reviews page. 'Mmm?'

'What should I do about Seb?'

'You have to tell him how you feel, sweetheart.'

Natalie clattered bowls and soap suds. 'The thing is, he's like two hundred and ten per cent involved in *FOOTLIGHTS* and I'm not. Not yet, anyway. And Richard's here, isn't he, and... It's just not sensible, is it, when we're apart for so long?'

Beth found the reviews and smoothed out a picture of Owen as Lord High Everything Else gesticulating grandly to the Ensemble. Just the way he stood, the energy of him even on the printed page made her stomach clench in lust and loss. 'I suppose not, love,' she said. 'Look, there's a photo.'

Natalie peered over her shoulder. 'Do you think he'll be all right about it?'

'I'm sure he will,' said Beth, hardly hearing. A headline had leapt to her eyes. *'TROUBLED TROUPE LOPPED BY LOTTERY.'* Her heart stuttered.

'What is it?' said Natalie, her voice sharpening. 'You've gone white. What's the matter, Mum?'

Beth pointed.

Natalie dripped water on the page as she read the paragraph aloud. 'Dogged by uncertainty over their future, the *FOOTLIGHTS Musical Theatre Company* nevertheless overcame their problems to open the tour with a faultless production of *Hot Mikado...*'

'See page 3 for further reports.' Beth scrabbled frantically backwards through the pages. 'Here it is. *FOOTLIGHTS*, the only musical touring rep in Britain, have been rehearsing day and night in a desperate bid to regain lost funding...' Fear assailed her, frost-sharp and twice as unexpected. 'Oh God, Owen said there were some undercurrents this run. How will he manage if *FOOTLIGHTS* finishes? It's his whole world.'

'What about the summer tour?'

Beth scanned the rest of the column, almost too agitated to read. 'Jinxes', 'Favouritism' and 'Desperate Measures' assaulted her eyes in rapid succession. She looked up, head whirling. Her hand went to the phone. *No!* Damn being passive and civilised and sensible! The only place that got you was out of your mind with worry. 'I have to see Owen,' she said. 'I have to *be* there.' And given the paucity of his calls this week, if he had got someone else she'd surprise it out of him.

'Mum, you *hate* driving through thunderstorms! And they're in Leicester, for God's sake!'

'I know. Get Rob to fire up that route planner thing on the PC, will you?'

Owen came out of the stage door into yet more rain. His head was pounding and he was coldly furious. *Three times* they'd had to halt the matinée because of camera flashes from the audience! Three bloody times! Annis, Matthews and Perry weren't saying a word so smugly that the entire company knew it was them who'd talked to the *Stage* reporter. As the rain struck maliciously through his jeans, Owen had never felt closer to chucking it all in. Sure when he was on stage sweating his bollocks off the adrenalin rush was better than sex, but when the gantry was shut down...?

He became aware that he was being watched. He turned up his collar and glanced around. And felt his jaw drop and his heart fall away. 'Beth?' he said in disbelief. 'Beth?' His headache vanished, his bad temper atomised. Lightning flash-danced through his soul, reconnecting frayed veins. *'Beth!'*

She was ghost pale, rivulets of rain ran down her coat, her knuckles gripping the umbrella were white. Owen crossed the alley in a single heartbeat and crushed her to him, kissing her until her icy cheeks warmed and her frozen lips started to thaw. 'Christ Almighty, woman, don't *do* that! I thought I was hallucinating! You're drenched. And beautiful. What are you doing here?'

He barely heard her whispered words. 'In *The Stage* ... knew you'd ... didn't phone ... missed you so...'

The umbrella slipped. A flash bulb went off and a raucous voice shouted, 'Who's the lady, Mr Pendragon?'

He turned his head to the leering newsman. 'None of your effing business.'

'Give us a break. It's bleeding perishing out here!'

'Serves you right for believing everything you hear in bars!' He steered Beth towards the stage door. 'You need tea, beloved. And to get out of those wet things.'

'But you were leaving...'

'Not any more.' God, she could hardly move, she was so cold. He hauled her inside, peeled her coat off and hugged her again. 'You're mad,' he said, settling her next to the radiator in his dressing room. 'Completely barking.' But he was grinning as he said it and as he sprinted up the corridor to get two teas from the machine and steal Cate's private supply of ginger biscuits, there was such a glorious warmth coursing through him that he felt like a blast furnace in full production. She was here. She'd come to see him. Life was wonderful. 'Get yourself round these. Jesus, Beth, your hair's soaked.' He pulled his towel off the hook and rubbed the dark, silky strands. 'What the hell couldn't wait until Saturday?'

She choked indignantly, colour coming back into her blanched cheeks. 'For God's sake, Owen! What reason did I have to think you'd be coming?'

He stared. 'Of course I'm bloody coming!'

'Yes? You didn't damn well come last weekend!'

'Beth! That's unfair. I told you about–' He stopped, a hideous uncertainty taking root in his brain. 'Didn't I?'

She eyed him over the rim of her cup. 'Your phone calls, minstrel, have been brief to the point of non-existent. You could have dumped me and I'd never have known. That's the other reason I came.'

'*What?* Beth, that's crazy!'

'Crazy. Desperate. What's the difference? I don't know a single bloody thing about the way you are when you're not with me.'

There were tears mingling with the rain on her face now. Owen kissed them away, appalled. 'Christ, Beth, the only thing that's kept me going this run has been your voice on the phone.'

'You might have told me.'

'I must have done. I *must* have done!'

She shook her head. 'I'd have remembered.'

'And I never told you about– Oh, God!' He pulled her onto his lap and kissed her remorsefully. Christ, he'd missed this. The kiss became less remorseful. Much less remorseful. She felt so *good* under his hands. A stray thought gatecrashed his libido. 'Shouldn't you be at school?'

'Owen!' She attempted to wriggle free, but he wasn't about to let her go, not after this long without her. 'See what I mean?' she said. 'If you'd been listening to me at all you'd know it was half-term this week.'

Oh yes. Maybe he did vaguely remember. He frowned. 'Are you telling me I'm self-centred?'

'Just a little.'

It gave him an unpleasant jolt. His hold on her loosened. 'Jesus, mistress. Really?'

She fanned his hair gently between her fingers to take the sting out of her words. 'One hundred per cent cad, lover. And if you don't believe me, tell me how I've been these last few weeks.'

'Shit.' He stared at her, horror crawling over his skin.

She gave a wry shrug. 'Something like that.'

Her mouth was inches from his. In her eyes was an expression he didn't recognise. The nearest he could get was please-don't-hurt-me-but-if-you-do-I'll-make-a-joke-and-pretend-it-doesn't-matter. To hell with that. He took a deep breath. 'I didn't come up last Sunday because Michelle's husband was waiting for me at the flat. It was sodding dawn before I managed to persuade him I wasn't after either his wife or his eldest son – he really does think of Davy like that. I lay down, intending to kip for an hour before driving up – and the next thing I knew, it was five in the afternoon, I felt as if I'd been pegged out in the desert for a hundred years, Davy was on the phone saying everyone including me had betrayed him and he was coming to live with me anyway, Michelle was screeching down the extension that everyone had betrayed *her* and she was taking Davy and the girls to an experimental commune in Wales, the other kids were wailing in the background and Barry was swearing a blue streak and threatening to knock heads together if someone didn't give him his tea in the next half-hour.'

A smile trembled on Beth's mouth.

Thank God for that, thought Owen. He traced her lips with his finger. 'I am so sorry.' Her hand crept inside the front of his Aran jumper. Relief sheeted over him. *Nothing* had ever felt so good. He pulled her closer. 'Believe me, I have never been more pleased in my life not to have any legal ties.'

Her fingers faltered.

'Don't stop,' he breathed. 'Bloody remind me next time I take you for granted, will you?'

'Minstrel, only you could make out that you neglecting me is *my* fault!'

He grinned into her eyes, saw her try to hide a flicker of lust. Arousal stirred in every pore. He saw her feel it. 'Are you staying? Shall we get a hotel room?'

'What with? Next week's food budget? No, I'll go home. As long as I know you really are coming Saturday night, I can cope.'

'That makes one of us.' He nuzzled her neck through her hair, heard the tiny gasp she made. His need for her grew. 'How about it, mistress?' he said huskily. 'Ever made love on a dressing room floor?'

He felt a ripple run through her body. 'Won't there be cleaners coming in?'

'You evidently haven't. Prepare for initiation, beloved.'

'Owen, we can't!'

He slid his hand under her tee shirt. 'Want to bet?'

Her fingers tiptoed down to the waistband of his jeans. Her voice was muffled. 'I suppose you did say I ought to get out of these wet clothes...'

She stayed for the second house, went backstage after the show and joined them all for supper. Owen walked her back to the car. 'I thought some sod had gouged a scratch along this?'

'One day,' she replied, 'if you're very, very good, I'll tell you about parents' evening and Yob's brother's mate's garage.'

'I don't deserve you,' he said and held her close, his head bowed to hers.

'And *FOOTLIGHTS* really isn't folding?' she said after a while.

'No, that was Annis being bloody-minded. I'd have thought a teacher would know better than to leap to conclusions with only half the facts.'

She stroked his cheek, feeling the slight roughness of stubble under her fingers, loving the way his arms were holding her as if she was precious and amazing and undeniably his. 'Whose fault is it I didn't have them?'

His smile looked strained in the utilitarian light of the car park. 'I've been stupider this past month than in my whole life before. But I'm not sorry you came. See you Saturday, beloved. Wait up for me.'

So that was that. And as if to emphasis that God was in his heaven, the storm had blown itself out. Beth checked Robin's printout and drove off down roads that still gleamed wet. The shiny tarmac now seemed exciting and sexy rather than industrial and depressing. *There wasn't anyone else.* Owen's reaction had proved that. Lowering as the thought might be, the simple fact that the first thing he had wanted was to make love to her had bolstered her confidence more than any of his belated explanations. It would be degrading if that was all he *ever* wanted but right now, with only forty-eight hours until she saw him again, it felt pretty damn good.

It felt pretty damn good on Saturday night, too. As soon as he arrived, they tumbled headlong into bed and made glorious, wonderful, wildly satisfying love. The sort that covered half the bedroom and only just managed not to spill out onto the landing and the stairs. Beth hoped her B&B visitors (two American couples 'doing' Cambridge in a weekend and wanting to stay in a typical English home while they did it) were too exhausted by viewing all thirty-one Colleges to notice the excess activity.

She slipped out of bed in the morning blushing hotly at the state of the room and even more hotly at the thought of what might be to come. With any luck she could feed and dispatch the Americans before Owen surfaced. Robin was going swimming with Jack, and Natalie had already said she'd be at Lisa's most of the day (though that was almost certainly more to avoid Owen mentioning Seb than filial delicacy). But it meant they'd be free to have a lovely lazy shower together and then he could distract her as much as he liked from the tidying up.

The Americans were cooperating beautifully by not lingering over breakfast when Owen appeared in the kitchen, took her waist in a snug hold and kissed the back of her neck. Dear God, he was in his midnight-blue bathrobe. And her with four lots of toast and marmalade to get through yet. 'Please tell me the visitors didn't see you like that?' she said, twisting around to kiss him.

'The door might have been open a crack, but it's OK – I'm wearing boxers underneath.' He nibbled her ear. 'Want to check?'

'No! Well, not until after they've gone. There are such things as hygiene regs, you know. Sit down, for goodness sake. I'll do you some bacon.'

'Uh-uh. Apologies before pleasure. I wanted to tell you I was wrong.'

She stiffened. 'Wrong? When?'

He took a firmer hold of her and tipped up her chin so he could look into her eyes. 'When I said it wouldn't work, you coming down to London for the night.'

Beth bit her lip, remembering the pain of that rebuff. 'Doesn't matter. Forget it.'

'It does matter. I spent the whole weekend kicking myself for being such a prat. Partly I wanted to keep you separate, but mostly I was ashamed of my flat.'

Beth stared at him, incredulous. 'When my home looks like this on a *good* day?' She gestured to the teetering piles of paper on the crowded dresser.

Owen folded her to his chest. 'My flat, mistress, is tidily, sinfully, minimalistically luxurious.'

Beth laughed softly into his bathrobe. 'Oh, minstrel. What an admission.'

There was a tap on the door. 'Mrs Trower, I wonder if – oh my, I'm sorry.'

It was one of the visitors. Beth whirled

around, her cheeks flaming. 'Not at all. Can I get you something?'

'We wondered if we might have some more of this excellent coffee?'

Beth took the proffered coffee pot. Out of the corner of her eye she saw Owen strategically shaking open the Sunday paper. 'I'll bring it as soon as it's ready.'

'No hurry.' The visitor eyed Owen with frank admiration as she closed the door.

'You,' said Beth, 'are a shocking distraction.'

'So are you. It's the first time I've had erotic notions about someone in an Oxo apron. When are they going?'

'As soon as I've made their toast. Stop it, Owen, the more you do that, the longer it will take. And that's Robin's bike I can hear. Sit down and behave. I'll do a nice fry-up to take your mind off things.'

'Spoilsport.' But he grinned and filled the kettle for her, contenting himself with squeezing her hip as a token of the delights to come.

Beth eyed him. 'It said in one of Sue's magazines that men think about sex every six minutes. Is that true?'

Owen's eyes gleamed wickedly as he slid onto a kitchen chair. 'I suppose it *might* be that long...'

'Have a nice day at school, beloved,' said

Owen next morning. 'I promise I'll turn everything off and lock everything up before I leave.'

'Safe journey, minstrel. And I hope Canterbury goes better than Leicester.'

'It'll have to pull out all the stops to be worse. I'll ring you tonight. And if I don't ask how you are, bloody remind me, all right?'

'OK. See you in three weeks.'

He kissed her. 'Or sooner, if we happen to collide in any dreams.'

'Are your dreams safe places to be?'

He grinned. 'You'll never know until you've tried.'

Nice words, but Beth was betting they'd be back to normal by tonight. Owen would be immersed in the show twenty-four hours a day and she would be waiting for his phone calls. At least he'd stilled her worst fears. A secret grin wound through her body at the thought of the way he'd amply demonstrated his love over the past thirty hours. Except – in startled disbelief she fumbled the gear change and stalled half-way across a junction. As car horns blared on all sides, she ran back over those hours. Maybe it was an oversight, but so far as she could recall, not once had Owen actually said he loved her...

Cate and Seb ate Mrs Harris's excellent

breakfast in a companionable silence. She wondered if his haircut had always been that sexy and his eyes so unprintably blue? 'I'll leave you the rest of the toast. Fit-up awaits.'

'Need any help?'

To cut up her peace even more? There hadn't been a flicker of anything stronger than friendship for six weeks now. She supposed it was her own fault for making herself one of the boys so bloody success- fully. 'You'd be in the way.'

'No, I wouldn't. It would be interesting to watch. And I could bag the decent bit of mirror in the Ensemble room before the others get there.'

She narrowed her eyes. 'Spit it out. Why don't you want to be here when Owen arrives?'

He swallowed hastily. 'Damn you, Cate! I don't want him to tell me how miserable Nats is, OK? Or worse, that she's perfectly happy and living for my next phone call. Go on, crow.'

She stared at him. 'You mean you're not—' He reddened. An absurd glow spread through her. 'Hasn't it occurred to you to ring her yourself?'

'I do. I tell her about the show. She tells me about school. Things are nice and friendly, and I'd like them to stay that way. I don't want to hurt her.'

Cate licked crumbs off her fingers, telling

her sex drive to get down and stay down. 'Friendly with your ex. There's an interesting concept.'

'I don't even know if she is an ex yet. So say it. Get it over with.'

'Say what?'

'*I told you so.* Hurry up, Cate, suspense is really bad for my digestion.'

She drained her cup and stood up. '*I should lecture you?* I couldn't pick a decent bloke if his CV came with a gold border and had little hearts stamped in the corners. And if you repeat that to *anyone* you won't need to worry about Annis making your life a misery any more.'

'Surely – at Christmas – I thought you and Luke–'

So he had been paying some attention. A quick flicker of gratification ran through her. 'Better hurry if you want a lift in. I'm leaving in ten minutes.'

It was after warm-up that Stella announced the news. 'Company,' she said formally, 'it is with regret that I have to inform you of Mr Valentine's intention to sever his connection with *FOOTLIGHTS* at the end of next week prior to joining the new tour of *Joseph And His Amazing Technicolour Dreamcoat* in the title role. Whilst we are sorry to lose him, the management know you will join them in wishing him all the best in this prestigious part.'

Cate caught sight of Seb. He looked sick at heart, exactly the way he'd been at college when a part he'd been trying for had gone to someone else. As everyone offered insincere congratulations to Ellery, she crossed the stage. 'Give me a hand with the tea urn, Seb?'

'Er, sure. Cate–?'

She shoved him out of earshot of the stage. 'Don't say it. Not until you know you want to.' He blinked at her. She glared at him fiercely and tugged a Mars bar out of her cargo pocket. 'Here. Eat that until your brain comes back off holiday!'

'Smart move, sweeting,' said Owen. 'I would stay to chat, but I rather think I'd best catch Ned before he makes any ill-considered decisions...'

'From March 11th the role of Nanki-Poo will be taken by Luke Bartholomew (Owen Pendragon to cover), and that of Pish-Tush by Sebastian Merchant. Jeremy Rider will play Gentleman of Japan #2 and cover Pish-Tush.'

Cate admired Owen's mirror-smooth countenance as he came past the notice board the next day. 'Going to take a miracle of make-up if you have to go on,' she said under her breath.

His mouth quirked. 'Think I can't? Sweeting, you didn't see a certain person's face.'

Luke drifted over wearing the same dreamy smile he'd had on since Ellery's announcement. Cate viewed him with exasperation. 'You must be the only person in the company who is genuinely pleased for the Voice.'

'I wish it had been me more.'

'You wouldn't have given yourself the trouble of auditioning. Would *you* have walked? If you'd been offered *Joseph?*'

'I wouldn't have started on this tour,' said Luke. 'But if you're asking whether I'd have left *FOOTLIGHTS* to play Joseph or any of the brothers... Cate, it's a Bill Kenwright No 1 tour! A guy would be crazy not to!'

She was startled by the passion in his voice. 'But you know what they say – works you to death, zero time off. Would you really want that?'

'It's a passport to the West End! Broadway, even! Can you imagine it? Broadway? You bet I'd want it!'

'But you'll be playing leading roles here once the Voice has gone. Making magic for hundreds of ordinary people six nights out of seven.'

His smile was brilliant, amoral, seductive. 'Cate, the West End is what we all dream of.'

Cate felt a burst of pride as the Swindon first night audience cheered the company to the rafters. Both Luke and Seb had been magnificent, Luke more carefree and ingenuous in the leading role than the Voice had ever managed, and Seb really *becoming* the deeply cool Pish-Tush. Watching him take his second bow, Cate knew that for sheer acting ability he was second only to Owen. As he returned to his place, he stumbled. Owen clapped an arm round his shoulders and continued to wave. The company was still waving as the curtain fell.

'Ice,' said Owen fiercely in her ear as, still with that casual hold on Seb, he turned them both towards his dressing room.

Cate shot a startled look at Seb's bloodless face and the way he was limping and pelted for the office. She didn't even hear her aunt's question as she evicted the celebratory champagne. Detouring at lightning speed to the fridge in the kitchen, Cate realised she was praying.

'I saw the bastard do it!' Owen grimly cut the laces from Seb's shoe and plunged his rapidly swelling foot into the ice bucket. 'Deliberate kick with the side of his tap.'

Adrenalin sang in Cate's veins. The VHS! She dashed back the way she'd come. Please let it still have been recording – she'd never ask for anything again!

By the time she returned, Stella was on her knees beside Seb. 'Badly swollen. Cate, I promise if Mr Annis doesn't get dumped this time, I'll give him to you to play with.

How is it, pet?'

'You tell me,' said Seb with a faint smile. 'I can't feel anything below the knee. What did you do, Cate? Mug the all-night fishmonger?'

Cate didn't answer. He was so *pale*. She pushed towards him, fumbling with her pocket.

'Leave it in the ice as long as you can bear it,' Stella was saying, 'then I'll strap it up. You should be able to go on tomorrow if you don't do *anything* in the meantime.' Go on? Was her aunt insane? Hadn't she *seen* Seb's ankle? 'Do you feel sick at all?' continued Stella.

'Hungry,' said Seb. Cate brusquely passed him a Twix and a Bounty.

'Stella?' came Ned's voice. 'Why is the chocolate machine in the middle of the corridor with the back wrenched off?'

There was no time to assemble anything like a defence. As Seb's startled eyes flew to hers, Cate felt the blood pound into her face. 'I'll fix it,' she mumbled, dashing out before anyone could ask questions. When she squeezed back in, Stella was brandishing the video tape at Ned.

'You'd better have this too.' Seb got his fan out. It had a thick slug of glue along one edge. 'I used the spare Cate bullied me into carrying.' He looked up and mistook her expression. 'It wasn't your fault for not spotting him, Cate. It was in *my* pocket and I didn't notice.'

Cate was aware of Graham making a muttered exclamation and leaving the room. 'Moron,' she said shakily. 'Don't you realise if you'd put your hand on it before it had set, the bloody fan would be grafted to your skin by now? Ned, if you don't do something really terminal you're going to be advertising for a new ASM tomorrow, family or no family.'

'Not a problem,' said her uncle cheerfully. 'Not now we know no one else is emulating Mr Valentine.'

Hers weren't the only eyes which snapped to his face. '*What?*'

Graham came back in with a tray of hot drinks. She grabbed a cup gratefully. 'Would you care to repeat that?' asked Owen, a dangerous edge to his voice.

'Timing,' said Ned as if this explained everything. 'We couldn't afford to kick Annis out until we knew how many of the Ensemble might be defecting to *Joseph*. Not with the Lottery Board making their decision any day. Can you imagine it? A solitary Gentleman of Japan capering about trying to look like a crowd?'

'You knew about *Joseph?* You *knew* Ellery was leaving?' Cate's voice came out in an outraged squeak.

'We knew they were casting a new show.

387

And we knew they'd been sniffing around *FOOTLIGHTS*. Those scouts in Cambridge, remember?'

And neither he nor Dad had said anything to her! *Nobody* had said anything to her! She felt like bloody resigning anyway. *'When did you know?'* she said through gritted teeth.

'One of your father's contacts got a strong whisper during the rest period. Don't look at me like that, Cate. We didn't know who they were after and, given a certain episode at Christmas, we decided you were potentially too involved.'

'You didn't trust me.' Dad and Ned had thought her affair would compromise her loyalty if it turned out to be Luke the *Joseph* people were interested in. How *could* they? She turned away, humiliated beyond belief.

Seb's hand shot up to grip her arm. 'God, I can't believe how stupid I've been. I thought it was just a personal thing.'

Cate scrubbed a sleeve across her face. 'What are you talking about?'

His fingers on her arm were white. His eyes looked anguished. 'Remember that time I came to the office? I'd just been offered Benjamin plus Joseph's cover. I didn't tell you because I didn't want it to sound like boasting. God, egotistical or what! It never *occurred* to me to put two and two together, not even when we were being kept in understudy rehearsals until midnight. I would have told you if I'd realised, Cate. I would.'

Through her misery and shame, she saw his gaze burning compellingly clear. His words slowly sorted themselves into a sensible order. She stared. 'You were offered Benjamin? And you didn't take it?'

Seb flushed. 'I remembered what Owen said about his stint on the show. And besides – I quite like it here.'

Owen clapped a hand over his mouth. 'Not in front of the management! You'll lose all your bargaining power for the next pay rise.'

Stella chuckled and left with the tape and the fan. Ned followed. Cate looked at the door, then bit her lip.

'For what it's worth,' said Owen, 'I'd be pissed off with your bloody family too if they'd done that to me. But you'll probably punish them more by mentioning principles once or twice a day for ever than by leaving.'

Graham coughed meaningfully. 'Cate dear, Michael is getting a tad uncomplimentary about tidying the stage on his lonesome.'

As she left, Owen nudged her. 'Give. I'll see he gets them.'

His expression was impossible to read. She felt her cheeks flame again as she handed over two Dairy Milks and a Lion bar.

His mouth quirked. 'Fear not, sweeting,

your secret is safe with me.'

'It had bloody better be,' she muttered. 'Because I know about certain panto scripts.'

His eyes crinkled appreciatively. 'And you haven't used it yet? I'm impressed.' He flicked her cheek. 'Stop worrying. I'm sticking to the lad like our unlamented friend's choice of hemp noose for the foreseeable future.'

CHAPTER 18

'They got here then?'

Beth looked up from turning Robin's sausages. 'Half-past midnight. They're still in bed.' Her heart twanged at Natalie's overly-casual air. 'Seb's ankle doesn't seem too bad, but he's under orders to rest it. Stella's driving his car across.'

'He's dancing, though?'

Beth broke an egg into the pan where it promptly amalgamated with the bacon rashers. She made a face at the resultant mess. 'Yes. Apparently it's a the-show-must-go-on-even-if-you're-strapped-up-and-on-triple-strength-painkillers thing. Rob! Breakfast!'

Natalie made some toast and drifted upstairs to do homework with the help of *Robbie Williams* at his most raucous. Beth hoped fervently she wouldn't be back to *Westlife* and a box of tissues after a heart-to-heart with Seb. She herself had achieved a measure of peace due to Owen's rigorous phoning of her every day and talking about *her* life as well as his own, but the fact remained they inhabited different worlds. When they were together it didn't matter.

His presence was enough to move both of them to a separate plane where anything was possible. It was during his absences that all those damning phrases wove shrouds in her head.

'I was never more pleased in my life not to have any legal ties.'

'Christ, I'm fed up with this. I'm not a responsibility person.'

And, most terrifying of all, *'I swear, Beth, I came alive. I was free. Free, free, free. There was colour in the world again, snatches of song on the wind.'*

Owen was a free spirit. A wandering player. A troubadour. And yet he had acted last night as if he'd been living only for the moment when he was back in her arms. He hadn't let Seb's presence behind him on the path detract one iota from that first rib-crushing, breath-stopping embrace as she'd opened the door to them. She simply didn't know what to think any more.

Robin clattered his plate into the sink, hugged her and returned to the lounge to save the world in the company of a second-hand Joanna Dark and a truck-load of sound effects. Beth heard the slither of exercise books hitting the floor as he threw himself on the sofa. She glanced at the clock; Cate had said she'd be here at ten. Would she have eaten? The doorbell chimed. Beth went to let her in.

'Good morning, Beth,' said Alan, and before she had time to do more than gape in amazement, he had stepped over the threshold with Doone, immaculately coiffured and perfumed, just a pace behind him.

'We were on our way to the Golf Club,' Doone confided expansively, 'when we thought – hey, haven't seen you people for a while – let's drop in for coffee!'

Oh God, what did they want *now?* And why today of all days? Beth gathered her wits together and tucked Owen into a safety-valve corner of her mind. *Minstrel, if you have any feelings for me at all, don't choose the next half-hour to come downstairs wearing nothing but Aztec For Men and your midnight blue towelling bathrobe.*

'Lovely,' she said mendaciously. 'It's only instant.' Dirt cheap Supasava instant at that, which should ensure they didn't stay too long.

Alan peered into the dining room. 'No B&B guests?'

'They're still asleep,' said Beth. 'And another due this morning.'

'Not before you clear up, I trust.'

Owen never criticised, she realised suddenly. In spite of his luxurious, tidy flat he never commented on her heaps of exercise books or sketchy dusting skills or pile-it-all-on-one-plate cookery. He accepted her the way she was. Peace settled on Beth like a mantle as her unwanted visitors perched on kitchen chairs and squinted sideways at 7.1's posters illustrating *The Little Shop of Horrors*. What did it matter whether this thing with Owen went on for weeks or months or – daring thought – years? Just having him in her life at all was enough.

'Realistic, aren't they?' she said cheerfully, nodding at the posters. 'I think Yob actually used his own blood on that top one.' Or possibly someone else's.

Doone shuddered. 'I expect you have to be dedicated to appreciate it.' She glanced around, her eyes missing nothing. 'I wonder you've never had this room extended. Friends of ours have made the *sweetest* breakfast room by building a conservatory on to their kitchen. It *so* blurs the boundary between house and garden.'

Beth carefully didn't look at Alan. 'Sounds delightful. Robin used to do his own blurring of outlines between the kitchen and the garden when he was younger. Especially on football days.'

Alan cleared his throat. 'This summer job of Natalie's – I won't stand in her way if it's what she wants to do.'

You mean you've checked and found that after the last Friday in June she's officially past school leaving age and you can't do anything about it anyway. But, 'Thanks, she'll be so pleased,' she said diplomatically.

'It wouldn't be my choice, but as Doone says, young people have to make their own mistakes if they're to learn.' Doone managed to look saintly and omnipotent and sweetly forbearing all at once.

Beth thought it was a wonder they couldn't hear her teeth grinding. 'Absolutely. What about her allowance?'

Alan waved his hand. 'Might as well continue it if she's definitely returning to do A-levels.'

At this, the penny dropped. Alan wanted something *badly*. It had better not be the bloody house. 'Of course she is. We've told you often enough.'

His generous behaviour seemed to have unnerved him. He rose. 'Mind if I avail myself of the facilities?'

'You know where they are.' *Oh God! Owen was still in her bed!* 'Use the family bathroom. The en-suite loo is playing up. And remember I've got paying guests. Don't go looking through any doors.'

'Really, Beth!' said Alan huffily.

Doone took off her coat. 'Beth, dear,' she said with a steel-masquerading-as-lambs-wool smile, 'while we're on our own there's something I've been meaning to network with you about...'

You amaze me, thought Beth, and mentally rolled her sleeves up as she rearranged her face into polite inquiry.

'It's Alan. I hate to see him unhappy.'

'I didn't realise he was.'

'He's getting *so* concerned about not being able to regularise our relationship.'

Beth's jaw dropped. 'He wants a divorce?' She couldn't believe her luck! Of all the things she might have imagined to be on Alan's agenda, she would never in her wildest dreams have thought of that! It *had* to be Doone's doing.

Possibly her incredulous tone was misleading. Doone gave the pseudo-sympathetic smile of the victor. 'Ah, he was right. He said it would hit you badly. And I have to admit it hadn't escaped my notice that Mr Pendragon does look just the teensiest bit like him.'

'Pardon?' said Beth, bewildered.

'Temporary transference of subliminal emotion to a physical likeness. It's a well-documented phenomenon. Now, Beth, don't resent this. I'm sure we can come to an arrangement to ease the denial you're going through.'

My God, they think I want him back! They think I'm going to make difficulties! That must be why Doone had always been so defensive around her. Because she'd spent all those years building up her own business and then looked in the mirror and realised she wasn't getting any younger. Maybe she thought Alan was her last hope and was determined to make sure of him while she could. Beth passed a shaking hand across her forehead to shield her face until she could get her expression under control. 'It's just – well, it's the house really... When he left, Alan promised I'd be able to buy his half off him once the mortgage comes to term. I suppose I thought, since he's never made any mention of formalising it...'

'He'll talk to the solicitor first thing tomorrow. A legal break is often the first step towards accepting the inevitability of independence. Anything else?'

'The car,' said Beth in a faltering voice. 'I realised when the insurance renewal came through that it's still in his name...'

'An oversight, that's all it will be. Alan will get it transferred. Naturally you need transport to get to your job and for all the kids' activities.'

'Thanks.' Beth dropped her eyes and swallowed, wondering if she was overdoing things. 'I suppose this is all for the best, really.'

'Believe it, honey.' Doone's voice took on the smallest, smoothest touch of industrial grade titanium. 'Incidentally, my friends were *very* appreciative of the way you took care of them a couple of weeks back. It gave them a real feel for English village life. I said I'd be sure to pass on their thanks.'

Her friends? Oh, damn and sodding blast,

the zealous Americans! Beth bade farewell to any lingering hope that Doone was unaware of her precise relationship with Owen and shelved the idea of asking for a new shed for the bikes.

'*DAD!*' Natalie's horrified shout from upstairs made them both jump. 'Do you, er, want to talk about my tour?'

'No need, darling, I've told your mother it's OK. She said the toilet was playing up. I thought I'd–'

'No point,' Natalie broke in breathlessly. 'Lisa's dad's coming to sort it out later. Is Doone downstairs? I want to ask for the name of those disco people for our GCSE party at school.'

Across the table, Beth met Doone's eyes. 'Doone,' she said without having to inject any false sincerity into her voice. 'I won't deny that when Alan left me last year, I thought my world had fallen apart. But life goes on, and whatever our differences, I have to accept the fact that you seem to make him happier than I ever managed. I wish you both joy.'

For the first time in their relationship, she had the satisfaction of seeing the other woman nonplussed. 'Why thank you, Beth. I just know we're going to get on *so* well now we've cleared the air between us.'

From a distance, thought Beth. Please God, from a distance.

After Doone and Alan had refused a second cup of coffee with only the most infinitesimal of shudders, Beth and Natalie looked at each other in shell-shocked silence.

'Nats, you were *wonderful!* I can't even *begin* to imagine the fall-out if Dad had found Owen in my bed!'

'*I* can't believe they thought they had to bribe you into divorcing him.'

They heard footsteps on the stairs. 'Er– Hi,' said Seb, coming into the kitchen.

'Oh. Hi,' said Natalie awkwardly.

For the second time that morning, Beth had to fight to keep a straight face. 'Do you two want to be alone? Or would you like breakfast first?'

Natalie shrugged. 'Said it all on the phone, really.'

Seb reddened. 'Breakfast would be...'

'I'll make a fresh pot of tea,' said Natalie. 'Mum needs it. Rob's playing *Perfect Dark*. I'll bring it in.'

Out of the corner of her eye, Beth saw Seb catch her daughter's hand. 'We do need to talk,' he murmured.

'OK.' The doorbell sounded. 'That's probably Cate. She'll want tea too.'

'As you were,' called Owen from the stairs.

Natalie looked at Beth. 'What if it's Dad back?'

But it wasn't. 'Jesus, Pendragon, at least in

Canterbury you have the decency to get dressed before I see you in the morning!' There was the sound of a case thudding to the floor, then Cate appeared in the kitchen. 'Yum, is that bacon sandwiches I can smell?'

Beth grinned. 'Could easily be. Nats, look after the frying pan for a sec, will you?' She slid into the hall to find Owen. 'You decided to get up then?'

His eyes danced wickedly as he pulled her into his arms. 'Come here, you. What do you mean by leaving me to wake up alone after three weeks on the road?'

Her heart lifted. The future could take care of itself. With her new-found serenity she returned his embrace as fully occupied by the now as he was. 'You damn near weren't alone,' she said, burying her nose in the triangle of chest at the top of his bathrobe.

He chuckled and stroked her hair and kissed the top of her head. 'So I realised when an eldritch shriek penetrated my slumber. What did he want?'

She kissed him, exploring his chest with her lips, heady with his glorious scent. 'What he's always wanted. To be king of his own particular castle. And this time Doone is hell-bent on being its chatelaine.'

'God, what a terrifying thought.'

'Mmm, but I can't honestly find it in my heart to get too wound up about it.'

After Cate had left for the joys of get-in, and Rob was banished to homework, Natalie brought two mugs of tea into the lounge. Crunch time, thought Seb, and patted the settee next to him.

'How's the ankle?' she asked, sitting down warily.

'Not too bad. Ned worked me out some different moves.' He handed her a script. 'He thought you might like to read *The Lion, The Witch and The Wardrobe* before the summer.'

To his surprise, her face clouded. 'Seb – is it going to be awkward for you with me on the tour?'

His heart twisted. She had *so* no idea about actors. 'Nats, practically everyone in the company has slept with everybody else so many times, I don't think they'd know embarrassment if it danced naked in front of them!'

'Including you?'

He flushed. 'Well, no, not me.'

'Oh. Seb, I'm sorry if I–'

He took her hand. 'No, *I'm* sorry. I didn't mean to hurt you.'

She bent her head. 'You didn't. I did most of it myself. You were great.'

He lifted away her curtain of hair and took her hand. 'Natalie, *you* were great. You did something no one's ever done before. You fell in love with me simply because I was *me.*

Not because you wanted anything from me. Not because you had an axe to grind. Do you have any idea how spectacular that made me feel?'

'Were you really in love with me?'

The reluctant words were a dagger twist. 'Yes,' he said, holding her eyes so she'd know it was true. 'For a while I honestly thought– I care about you still, Nats, I always will, but not–'

'Not like a proper boyfriend-and-girl-friend thing. I know. I feel the same.' She let go of his hand. 'It makes it easier really. It's not like breaking up. We can be friends, like we were before, like you are with Rob. I'm glad we didn't–' She met his eyes again and looked away hastily. 'Never mind.'

Seb felt his cheeks reddening. 'It's just one of those things. It wasn't that I didn't want to exactly, but–'

'Yeah, I know. It would have spoilt it. Seb – is there anyone else?'

'No-o...' But Cate scowled in his mind: irascible, efficient and just recently, curiously gruff with him. 'That is ... I don't know. I think there might be. I wanted to sort things out with us first. And if it turns out there is, well, you might not like it very much and I hope it doesn't make you feel awkward but I promise it isn't the reason for us unbreaking up.'

She smiled. 'Nice phrase.' She cleared her

throat. 'Actually I, er, might have someone else too.' She turned her head aside, blushing.

Seb felt a wave of relief wash over him. Thank God. It was more than he deserved. 'That's good. I wish you well.' He nodded at the book in her hand. 'Do you want to go through the script?'

'What, now? Cool.' She turned to the first page. 'Where do I come in?'

When Cate arrived later, she was instantly aware of the change in atmosphere.

'Shit,' said Natalie in the act of piling pudding plates. 'I've still got a history essay to finish for tomorrow.'

'That's what comes of singing songs from musicals all afternoon,' said Beth. 'What about you, Rob? Did you finish everything?'

'Pretty much,' said Robin airily.

Beth tutted. 'Upstairs the pair of you. If there's one thing I can't stand it's the sorrowful looks I get from the other staff whenever either of you skip homework.'

Cate grinned and followed Seb into the lounge with the remains of her drink.

Seb was carrying the half-empty wine bottle as well as his glass. 'I told Nats,' he said, easing himself on to the settee and stretching his injured leg carefully in front of him. 'She was OK about it, but I felt like a real shit.'

That was the difference. Cate felt a swirly wriggle of delight both for the fact that he'd done it and that he'd told her he'd done it. 'Good,' she said. 'You deserve to.'

'I know. I feel better for clearing it up properly, even though things had already petered out.' He glanced across. 'Freer.'

She went over to the CD rack to give herself time to think. 'He thought I was cute,' she said abruptly.

There was a small pause. 'Who did?' said Seb.

She felt a surge of irritation. 'Luke, of course! Who do you think?'

'He needs his head examining. You're not cute. You're Medusa without the snake-locks.'

A smile started inside her. 'I'll have you know it was very nice being cute and irresistible for a while.'

'It was nice being adored too, but you can't live like it. Every time you slip you feel guilty.'

'Luke didn't mind. He liked me being bossy and taking charge. He'd have let me organise him right up until the moment he slid out of my life telling me he was just going round the corner for a paper.'

Seb chuckled and sipped his wine. 'Sorry. It's difficult not to like him.'

'Tell me about it. But it doesn't blind me to how lazy and spoilt he is. He counts on his charm to get by. I was furious with him most of the time we were together.'

There was another pause. 'I didn't realise you *were* together,' said Seb ruefully. 'Not for any length of time.'

She met his eyes. 'You weren't supposed to. No one was. That was part of the problem.'

He filled their glasses. 'Did you sleep with him?' He looked away, as if her answer didn't matter.

She flushed. 'Jesus, Seb! He's drop-dead bloody gorgeous! Of course I slept with him! How could I not have done?' And what would have been the point otherwise?

He grinned. 'Cate, you're unbelievable. How can anyone so spiky be such a sucker? That's just like Stuart Melville at college. And probably the guy you told me about in Swansea too. Don't you ever learn?'

She abandoned the CD rack and strode crossly back to the settee for her wine-glass. 'It was *nothing* like Stuart Melville! *He* was a Class One arsehole and I *have* learnt and you weren't supposed to remember Swansea.' She took a large swig and glanced at him. 'Were you really terrified of me at college?'

He laughed and flicked back his fringe. 'Absolutely and completely. We all were.'

She sat down. 'Did you sleep with Natalie?'

He looked at her for a moment with an expression so transparent it made her ashamed to have asked. 'How could I? I was her first grown-up love. No way could I have spoiled that.'

She felt a perverse gratification. 'I told Beth you were too much of a gentleman to take advantage.'

He put his glass down and took hers from strangely nerveless fingers. 'Not *that* much of a gentleman,' he said, and kissed her.

A deep bubble of joy fizzed and frothed inside her as her lips met his. 'So, how come you're not scared of me now?' she asked when she was able to speak.

He ruffled her hair, keeping the other arm around her. And *this* arm, unlike Luke's, showed no inclination to cop out if the going got tough. 'I know you better now. I know how much you care. You're a perfectionist. You can't bear seeing things done badly.'

'You can talk! You couldn't give a poor performance if you tried! I've seen you rehearsing when you think no one's looking.'

He grinned and dropped his hand to trace her jawline. 'You see everything. It might have taken a while to get through to me, but I did eventually realise that if it hadn't been for you I wouldn't have lasted two minutes once Annis decided I was surplus to requirements.'

She narrowed her eyes. 'If you just kissed me out of gratitude for looking out for you the same way you kissed Nats out of gratitude for falling in love with you, I'll bloody kill you!'

He tipped her chin up. 'Did it feel like gratitude? I kissed you because I wanted to. Because you're bloody-minded and partisan and loud and energetic and I can't imagine my life without you striding about in it. That's the real reason I turned down Benjamin, though I'm not sure I knew it at the time.'

'Bloody hell!' Cate was elated and appalled all at once. 'Sebastian Merchant, you are not fit to be out of the asylum!'

'I think I might love you, Cate.'

This time her heart really did stop. She freed her hand and held his hair away from his eyes. 'Really?'

He twisted to kiss her wrist. 'Really. And don't tell me you don't feel the same way because I won't believe you. People don't vandalise chocolate machines and utter death threats and threaten to resign from life-blood jobs out of pure, disinterested friendship.'

Something odd had happened to her circulation. 'They might.'

His eyes were blue and laughing and loving. 'Darling Cate. Not you.'

Darling! Her heart thumped erratically.

'Supposing, just for the sake of argument, that I do feel–' she blushed 'like that too? What do we do about it?'

'Let it happen, of course.' He bent his head. As their lips met for the second time she thought she might erupt with joy. 'We're not going to keep this quiet, are we?' he murmured. 'Because quite apart from wanting to shout that I love you from the rooftops, I want you to wear that red dress and dance with me all night long. Someone is bound to notice.'

He hadn't forgotten! 'Your wish is my command,' she said demurely.

'That'll be the day.' There was a moment of silence so accomplished that Cate ran through the female complement of the company in startled calculation. 'I can't believe you're this soft and yielding,' he said.

That snapped her out of it. 'I'm not, you caught me by surprise. I can't believe you're this decisive. Why didn't you say anything before?'

'Because I hadn't finished with Natalie. And because you were just being normal, prickly, grudgingly-friendly Cate Edmonds.'

'Shit. And because you didn't, I thought the party thing was simply a nice, plastered grope. So I kept quiet. Couldn't face making a tit of myself again.'

'Also,' he said, very cautiously indeed, 'I wasn't too keen on having any bones broken.'

She looked down, ashamed. 'Hell, Seb, you'd think after the length of time we've known each other, you'd realise I'd never do anything like that to you.'

'I nearly knew it.'

'Am I going to have to learn how to be nice?'

He laughed joyously. 'I don't think the world's quite ready for that.' He slipped a hand inside her sweatshirt and made her whole body quiver. 'But I could take lessons in being bad...'

Owen sat on the table to open another bottle of wine while Beth plunged into the washing up.

'That's a bit profligate,' she said. 'There's plenty in the one Seb's taken into the lounge.'

'If I don't miss my guess, he's going to need every drop. I think he and Cate will be having a revelatory conversation about the nature of their relationship any moment now.'

'Lord, what it is to be an actor. All those long words and you didn't stumble once. Hold on a sec,' she stared at him in surprise. 'Seb and Cate? Really?'

'He's been like a cat on a hot tin roof this week, waiting until he could get things sorted out with Nats.'

'We're going to be back to *Westlife* for the week. I can hear it now.'

'You told me she went to a party with someone else.'

'Owen! You listened to me! You remembered!' She was so gratified she let him feed her a mouthful of wine.

'I thought it was time I redeemed myself.'

Beth blew him a kiss. 'Still, even if Nats is going out with Richard, it's going to feel horribly as if she's been dumped the first time she sees Seb and Cate together.'

'Trust the lad to sort it.' He took a drink himself. 'This is better,' he said.

'It's special for tonight. We're back on the Bulgarian tomorrow.'

He looked at her over the ruby red rim of his glass. 'Being here for a whole week is better. Better than being on the road, wondering what you're doing. Better than niggardly, one-day stopovers when I almost can't bear to go to sleep for fear of missing a few hours of you. Much better than Leicester, watching you drive away.'

Beth rinsed the plates slowly and stood them in the rack to dry. 'Do you think I don't miss you, minstrel? Do you think I haven't thought about what might be going on your end as soon as you switch the phone off? I know how actors behave.'

'Not me, beloved.'

'You said that before. But I'm not totally stupid. You didn't get all that stuff in the shower out of books.'

His eyes danced. He fed her some more wine and then rotated the glass until he could drink from the same spot that her lips had touched. It was an astonishingly erotic action. 'Not me any more,' he said softly. 'Not now I've met you.' He refilled both glasses, perfectly at ease, genuinely unbothered by her alarms.

She swept the cutlery into the sink. By turning her head sideways she could see his lean, dancer's body relax against the table as he sipped from his glass. She could see the way his just-the-right-length-hair framed his face as he riffled through her form's posters. Her heart reached out to him.

'Now this one's got style,' he said approvingly, picking up Yob's blood-stained offering. 'We'll have to get him on set design if we ever revive *Sweeny Todd*.'

Beth chuckled and sipped her own drink.

Owen continued to turn the posters over. He picked up another and studied it. 'I have to admit it makes *my* blood run cold, but what exactly is it about this which makes it a *Little Shop of Horrors* poster?'

She emptied the sink and dried her hands. 'Felicity's,' she said, tucking her hand in his arm, feeling his muscles rearrange themselves to acknowledge her proximity. 'If you look really carefully, you'll see none of the flowers have been watered and all the bows round the plant pots have frayed and tattered edges.'

His eyes met hers, brilliant with love. 'And you've given it a B-plus, the same as your gore-minded friend. Marry me, Beth?'

Her mouth dropped open in shock. 'P-pardon?'

'Marry me?'

'Because I gave Felicity a good mark for getting as close to horror as she could without being physically ill?'

He took her in his arms. 'Because you care. Because you are a 3D person in a 2D world. Because I love you very, very much.'

There was an immense lump in Beth's throat. She had to squeeze the words past it. 'You haven't said that for ages. I thought maybe you didn't any more. And so I didn't dare say it because I didn't want you to think–'

He blocked the words with such a deeply loving kiss that it made her head swim. 'I'm not letting you go until you say yes. It's an actor thing, beloved. I need the reassurance. I'm not asking you to come on the road with me because I know it wouldn't work.'

'It wouldn't work with you staying here all the time, either. You'd never find enough to do in Cambridge.'

'That's not what I'm suggesting. We both need our work and some of the time I could commute. But I desperately need to make a commitment to you, Beth. I need you to make one to me. That way, even when we're apart, we'll still be together.'

Beth felt her eyes fill. 'Owen, I want that more than anything in the world. I never want to go through a weekend again like the one when you didn't turn up. It was the only time in my life *including* when Alan left me that I truly wished I was dead. Because if I was dead, minstrel, I wouldn't have the pain of losing you.'

His hazel eyes were so openly loving she could hardly look at them. 'For me it was Leicester. The sight of you in the alley when I thought you were miles away. The realisation that I might have lost you through being so stupid. And then that bloody photographer. I could see the caption in the paper, "Owen Pendragon with his long-time mistress", and I knew it wasn't enough.'

Their lips met. Beth felt tears on his face and didn't know if they were hers or his. She clung to him, burying her face in his hair.

'Please, Beth, I need an answer.'

His low, passionate voice wreathed around her head and turned her bones to water. She felt her mouth curve into a smile. 'Fool man, of course I'll marry you. I can't believe you don't know it already. I promise, Owen. Just as soon as the Decree Absolute arrives.'

'I have every faith in Doone's ability to speed up the divorce courts as they have never been sped before. All I want is for you to be mine. And for me to be yours.'

She pulled away just far enough to look into those wickedly sexy eyes. 'Always and forever, minstrel?'

His arms hardened around her, familiar, comforting and deeply exciting. 'Always and forever, mistress.'

The publishers hope that this book has given you enjoyable reading. Large Print Books are especially designed to be as easy to see and hold as possible. If you wish a complete list of our books please ask at your local library or write directly to:

Magna Large Print Books
Magna House, Long Preston,
Skipton, North Yorkshire.
BD23 4ND

This Large Print Book, for people
who cannot read normal print,
is published under the auspices of

THE ULVERSCROFT FOUNDATION